Jewels

of the

Bahamas

A Novel by

W.L. (Stan) Martin

To my friend Andrea! Thanks

JEWELS OF THE BAHAMAS

[signature]

Nov 15/2002 .

Capricornus

JEWELS OF THE BAHAMAS.

Edited by:-   *Dr. Dannabang Kuwabong.*

Readers: *Ann-Marie Spooner & Errol Williams.*

Cover Designed by:- *Stan Martin*
Photograph by:- *George Walters, New York.*

Canadian Cataloguing in Publication Data.

Martin, Stan, 1942.
    Jewels of the Bahamas
        Sequel to: Murder in Jamaica.
ISBN 0-9682646-5-4

    I. Title.
PS8576.A786J49 2000   C813'.54   C00-900000-3
PR9199.3.M388J49 2000

First Edition Published July 2000
Published and Distributed By:-
Capricornus Enterprises Inc.
Hamilton, On. Canada.
Phone: (905) 574-0043   Fax: (905) 574-2404
            Toll Free: 1-800-616-6760
Email: martinwl@netinc.ca *WWW.Capricornus.com*

Printed in Canada/ Fabrique au Canada

About the Author

W.L.(Stan) Martin, born in Jamaica January 6th.1942, has been a citizen of Canada since leaving England in 1967. He resided in Saskatoon, Saskatchewan for three years before making Hamilton, Ontario his home.

Dear Zachariah,
   You, being a proud Jamaican of Maroon descent, can also be proud of your offsprings for attaining the things you educated them to be.
   Thanks Dad.

Acknowledgements

Respect to the people most responsible for these writings.

Ethlyn Veronica and Cornelius Zachariah Martin	1942
Pamela Martin	1955
Anne S. M. Golding	1957
Patrick M. O'Reilley	1960
Amnah B.E.Small	1991
Vince O.Hall Snr.	1991

Thanks to all the readers and admirers of my first books
"LOYALTY and INTEGRITY," and "MURDER IN JAMAICA,"
for their patronage, phone calls, letters, Fax and Email.

Christine Hawn and Mark Newman- Brabrant news. Gerald Paul-Caribbean Camera. Eddie Grant, Colin Rickards and Lionel Gayle - The Jamaican Gleaner. Margaret Cannon - Globe & Mail.

Disclaimer Note:-

"See that flag," said ackeeface to the baby, *"it might not seem as much to some, but every time I look at the black and green with the yellow X, I get a shiver down my spine to think of their meaning. Anywhere in this world you go and mention the name Jamaica, they know who we are and realize that we are a proud people who are determined to succeed at anything we set our mind to."*

Preface

Jewels of the Bahamas, is another adventures of Christiana and the Dreadlocks Cop. The thrill they experienced a year ago in Jamaica, lingered in their souls, and a thirst for more.

After their marriage and the birth of their first child, Christiana, being home on maternity leave, accidentally stumbled upon a newspaper article about the murder of four students in Toronto, and another in Hamilton. The connotation of these killings raised her curiosity and she connected them to those in Jamaica. They requested, and Commissioner Dillon granted them the privilege of conducting an investigation into these mysterious murders, and gave them specific information, obtained through his informant, about a Toronto - Caribbean crime syndicate.

Their lead took them to the beautiful Caribbean islands of The Bahamas, Jamaica, Trinidad, Barbados and St.Lucia; also to the country of Guyana, to find the killers. In the process, they discovered the other business of the people they sought.

Piracy in the Caribbean Sea, is an historical fact. The thoughts of encountering those modern-day Pirates, the necessary deceptions required to infiltrate and decipher the plot, intrigued Christiana and Dready. And at all time, in danger of being killed for the same reason as the people before them; especially when they weren't sure who and where is the Octopus.

"An Octopus has one head and eight tentacles," said Christiana. "How the hell do they make love? or can they?"

Contents

Chapter One   *On the Job.*

Chapter Two   *The Godfather.*

Chapter Three   *Liars and Thieves.*

Chapter Four   *Carmichael Cook Shop.*

Chapter Five   *House on Abaco Island.*

Chapter Six   *Christmas in Jamaica.*

Chapter Seven   *The Blackjack Dealer.*

Chapter Eight   *So they live, so they die.*

Chapter Nine   *The Pork knocker's Story.*

Chapter Ten   *The GT Party.*

Chapter Eleven   *Agents, Dealers & Couriers.*

Chapter Twelve   *The Octopus.*

Chapter one

On the Job.

$\mathcal{C}$hristiana, dressed in track suit, sat at the kitchen table with her feet upon a chair having a well deserved coffee break. She had completed her daily exercises, which her aerobics teacher had given her for home use, and was now able to take a break. She was in a hurry to get her figure back into shape; and since she had gotten a six months maternity leave and couldn't use the police gym, she resorted to other alternatives.

She was delighted for this solitude. She had just fed and put young Venrece -Thomas, her first child, to bed. Since giving birth on October 13th, she had spent all that time at home with him and had been enjoying it, while eagerly looking forward to fulfilling her promise of having three more.

"I must do this to keep my husband's interest," she had told her aerobics instructor, "I don't want him looking at other women."

She was happy to do her exercise routine at home, and was delighted that they were now preparing a vacation to Jamaica for the purpose of introducing her son to the rest of the family, also just to get away from the winter chills of Toronto.

She leisurely leafed through the morning's newspaper as though uninterested in the news or in search of something specific; reading only bits and pieces of the items therein. Finally, something caught her eyes. The article was about a young Bahamian student

1

named Colin McKenzie, who was found dead in his apartment in Toronto and was ruled a suicide by the police.

"He killed himself to save face," said the investigating officer, "under the pretext that the undergraduate curriculum was too hard for him."

The author stated that it was the fifth of it's kind in the last few months, with one of the incident happening in Hamilton. She observed that three of the others were girls.

"Why would they commit suicide? What could be so bad that they had to kill themselves? These things aren't natural in these days and age," she pondered.

She read the article four more times to assure her mind of its contents, as the suspicion began to build within her. She grabbed the telephone and dialled the number.

"Hello! Commissioner Dillon here," he answered.

"Hello sir," she said, "this is Christiana Fel....I mean Perkins sir."

"Well! Hello Christiana!" said Dillon, "how's the baby?"

"He's doing excellently sir," she answered. "Matter of fact, we'll be taking him to Jamaica in a few weeks time for his first Christmas."

"Good," said Dillon, "they're going to love him to death. Now what can I do for you Christiana?"

"Sir, I know that this might sound bizarre to you, but I was reading in the papers about five Bahamian students who committed suicide, and wondered if there were any investigations done. Is there?" she asked.

Her question seemed to shock Dillon somewhat, because there was a long pause before he replied.

"I really don't know Christiana," he said. "That problem is with the Ontario forces and I'm sure they would leave it up to the regional people to solve."

"I see," she said, "but could you please find out what has been

2

done about it sir? I'm very interested."

"Why the interest?" asked Dillon.

"One of the names mentioned, sounds familiar to me, and I'm curious," she replied.

"Oh! Right-o then, I will make some enquires and call you back, okay?" he said.

"Thank you sir, goodbye," she replied and hung up the phone.

She decided to call Winston at work; something she has been doing since the baby was born. She dialled the number and waited for the operator to connect her to his extension. All she knew was that he was a civilian writer attached to the RCMP office in Toronto.

"Hello Christiana," he said into the receiver. "What's the problem now?"

"Nothing serious darling," she replied, "only that I was here reading the newspaper and saw an article about a Bahamian student named Colin McKenzie, who has committed suicide, and wondered if he was connected to Peter and Tanya MacKenzie of our case in Jamaica."

"Maybe he is," replied Winston, "we could check it out."

"Yes we should, I'd love to do it because there are four others who've done the same thing in the last few months. I find that too coincidental to be normal," she said.

There was a long period of silence as he gave thoughts to what his wife just told him. It made sense because he had just recently returned from a week's assignment in Nassau.

"What date are we leaving for Jamaica?" he asked.

"The fourteenth darling. Why?" she answered.

"I could call Bernard Graves and ask him if Colin McKenzie was related to Peter and Tanya."

"That would be excellent darling," she replied, "and while you're at it, could you ask him to be godfather to Venrece-Thomas also?"

"Yes I will," he said, "but as the new Commissioner of police, I don't think he'll have time to........"

"Yes, he will, I won't let him forget his promise," she interjected. "Also I've requested Commissioner Dillon to check out the who, what, and why of those students from our end."

"Good," said Winston, "we'll know something soon then."

"Thank you darling, I know it doesn't look like much, but my curiosity is aroused."

"Not a problem, darling," Winston said. His curiosity was also aroused.

Christiana was satisfied with her morning's achievement. She lay on the chesterfield to watch the soap operas, but fell asleep instead. It was the ringing of the phone that woke her up.

"Hello," she answered.

"Hi Christiana, it's me, Commissioner Dillon. That case is in the hands of the Metro Toronto police. I spoke to Chief Mathews and he said it was closed, since there wasn't any real evidence of foul-play, and to waste any more time on it would be criminal."

"Could I talk to the detective on the case?" Christiana asked.

"You sure can," said Dillon, "here's the number to call him, he might have something more concrete to tell you."

"Thank you sir, goodbye," she said.

Christiana hung up the phone and sat contemplating the reason she felt something was wrong with the incidents. She decided in her mind to speak with Winston about it when he got home. The baby woke up and she ran upstairs to attend to him.

An hour later she was on the phone again; this time to Chief Avery Mathews.

"Hello Chief, I'm Christiana Perkins, RCMP. I'm calling to find out about that apparent suicide of the McKenzie boy. You know the Bahamian boy who was......"

"Yes, yes I know," Mathews interrupted her. "Commissioner Dillon called me earlier and told me of your interest," said Mathews. "We couldn't find any witness or anyone who could attest to the boy's character. We think it's his drug habit that drove him to suicide It's a case of plain old depressive suicide."

"How did he do it?" she asked.

"According to the report, with a knife. One stab wound to the upper mid section of his chest," answered Mathews.

"Could anyone else have done it?" she asked.

"Yes, but no. It was his prints alone on the knife," said Mathews.

After a long pause Christiana said,

"I would like to see his apartment and speak to the detective if I could."

"You sure could, I'll give you his number. As for seeing his apartment, you'll have to arrange that with the superintendent of the building where he lived," he said. "But remember, they might have already thrown out his belongings."

"I realize that sir," she said, "but I only want to see his nest. It might not amount to anything."

"Here's the super's name and number," he said and read it to her. "And here is detective Jack Colley's's number."

Christiana took the numbers and within minutes she was on the line to Mrs. Maggy Walker, the superintendent.

"Ma'am," she said, "I'm a friend of Colin McKenzie's family and would like to see his belongings."

"You sure can," said Maggy, "but you'll have to dig through a lot of rubble in the basement for the purpose. It will be going out with the other garbage next Tuesday evening, so you'll better do it soon."

"Was there anything unusual in his possession?" Christiana asked.

"No, nothing that I could see any way," replied Maggy. "He had lots of books and maps. He seemed to have a lot of girlfriends also."

"Why do you think so?" Christiana asked.

"Because I found a lot of used condoms in his garbage bin," said Maggy.

"Did you show them to the police?" asked Christiana.

"Yes, but they didn't take them," replied Maggy.

"Please don't throw them out, I would like to examine them," Christiana told her.

"I really can't see why, but if that's how you get your kicks .....Cest la vie," replied Maggy laughing.

"Okay," said Christiana, "I'll be there tomorrow afternoon; bye for now."

Christiana realized that she was embarking on a mission, strictly on a hunch, which was not sanctioned by Winston or her boss. She hurriedly retrieved a note book from the cupboard, cut out the article and pasted it on the first page. She made a diagram of the locations where the bodies of the other four students were found, and began to make notes of her conversations and the possibility of connections to the dead boy. She gave thoughts to the case in Jamaica and realized that it could be an after thought act.

"What if he was Peter's son? What if somebody who wanted revenge on Peter, decided to kill this boy instead?" she thought. "Could Colin McKenzie be involved in something unscrupulous, as did his father?"

The phone rang and it was Commissioner Dillon again.

"Yes sir?" she said into the phone.

"Christiana my dear, I think you might have stumbled onto something," he said.

"And why so sir?" she asked.

"I just had a conversation with Avery Mathews, and he said something about the case that disturbed my thoughts. I felt their investigation wasn't completed, yet they refused to reopen it. I would like for you to get involved and follow your thoughts, even if it doesn't lead to anything. I will get Winston to write a story about the entire investigation. You should have a conversation with Jack Colly as soon as possible so as to get a feeling of what has already been done."

"Good sir," she happily replied. "Winston and I work well together."

They talked for almost an hour about her suspicions and about his feelings.

"Okay sir," she said. "I will talk to Winston this evening and get back to you tomorrow."

The hardest part for her, was the wait for Winston to reach home. She approached him as soon as he entered the room and hurriedly got him to the table, served his dinner and began to show him what she had done.

"Look at this darling," she said, "I've drawn a diagram of the places, dates and where the bodies were found. This is where Colin McKenzie was living. Celia Bachstrum was living here on Sheppard Avenue in Scarborough. Salina Mason and Zena Hendicott lived on Ellesmere."

"Okay," said Winston, "what's their common denominator? What's the connections between them?"

"They all came from Nassau and attend school here in Toronto," she replied.

"What about the boy in Hamilton? What do you know about him?" he asked.

"Not much," she said. "I know he lived on King Street West in that city and attended McMaster University. His name was Robert (Coolie-man) Reynolds. We'll have to find out more about his so-called accident also."

"Why don't you call detective Jack Colley and see if you can get the reports?" Dready suggested.

"I will, as soon as we finish supper," she told him..

Dready sat quietly listening to her describe the scenario of the case until she felt it was time to call Colley.

The call to detective Jack Colley was made.

"Hello Colley, this is officer Fels...I mean Perkins, I'm calling for the......."

"Oh yes, I was expecting your call," he said interrupting her introduction, "Chief Avery Mathews told me you wanted the reports of those students. But I will tell you right now that you won't find anything substantial."

"That's alright; do you have them?" she asked.

"Yes, right here on my desk. You can pick them up whenever you like," he replied.

"I'll be there in about twenty minutes," she answered and hung up the phone. That call meant a lot to Christiana's mind.

Quickly she called her friend, who lived a few houses away, and asked for her daughter to babysit for her. In a few minutes Brenda was their. Christian and Dready raced down to fifty one division to get the reports from detective Colley. She promised to up date him later, and left in the same hurry.

While Dready sped to the apartment building of Colin McKenzie, Christiana tried to read as much as possible about the victims. They were there in a few minuted. Christiana knocked on the door and waited. In a couple of minutes it was opened by the superintendent.

Maggy Walker was a short stocky woman in her mid to late fifties with a ring on every finger. Her obvious unkept hair protruded from her baseball cap as her steely grey eyes pierced through you. She wore a set of very small tights that divided her arse into east and west, and her breasts seems to be extricating themselves from her tank top. The vermillion red lipstick she wore seemed to jump from her, beginning to wrinkle, rose-pink face to yours.

"Hello Maggy I'm Christi......."

"That's fine deary, come in. Hi handsome!" she said to Dready. "Are you married?"

"Yes," reply Dready. "and this is my wife."

"Pity," she teased and took them to the empty apartment. "Are you a police officer also?"

"No, I'm a journalist," he replied.

"I thought you were a police man who wouldn't mind a little....." she said smiling, "never mind."

They looked around the empty one bedroom apartment and decided to see the things in the basement instead. They searched through everything that was Colin McKenzie's possession, but nothing of significance was found amongst his clothes and the many books and maps he left behind.

Turning to face Maggy, Christiana asked, "Did he have many friends?"

"Not many male friends, only a few girls who sometimes come here to see him," answered Maggy. "They seemed to do a lot of.....you know, screwing."

"Ahhh! Why do you think so?" asked Christiana.

"There is always used condoms in the garbage bags," said Maggy.

"I see," replied Christiana. "Anybody else?"

"No, but about two weeks prior to his......." Maggy paused, waved her hands in the air, "....you know? His death; a man came," answered Maggy.

"Can you remember what he looked like?" asked Christiana.

"Mmmmm," mumbled Maggy rubbing her chin with her hand. "He was a tall, well dressed coloured man; you know, half white, that's all. Nice looking but not sexy."

"What about his eyes? His hair and......"

"Hey! That's funny," she exclaimed interrupting Christiana. "He had a streak of grey hair right down the middle of his head. Nothing on the sides, only in the middle. He reminded me of a skunk, but he never came back."

"What about his eyes?" asked Dready.

"Dark brown," she answered. "They were dark brown, nearly like black."

Both Dready and Christiana paused to look at each other.

"Can I take some of Colin's books with me?" Christiana

9

asked.

"If you want, you can take them all," Maggy suggested. "It would save me the energy of throwing them out."

Quickly she assisted Winston to put the things in the trunk of their car, wished Maggy a good life and left for home.

After the books and clothes were put into the garage and the baby was cleaned, fed and put to sleep, she settled herself in the living room to read the reports. Dready walked the babysitter to her home, two blocks away and returned.

"What did you find?" he asked on entering the house.

"Nothing concrete darling," she replied, "but look at this, Colin had a list of names in this book, and some are those who have committed suicide."

She read the list of names and compared them to those in the reports.

"I think a search of the other victims's apartment should be done," she told Winston.

"I agree," he replied, "it could prove something was going on between those students."

"But what," she stated.

"That we will have to find out," he said as they got into bed.

The next morning, after seeing Winston off to work and attending to Venrece-Thomas, she made phone calls to the owners of the places where the other victims lived. In each case, she was told that she would have to do the search herself.

Firstly, she got dressed, called Winston to advise him of her intent, then got the babysitter and instructed her on the necessary care of her son. She drove to the address where Salina Mason and Zena Hendicott lived. She took a quick glance at the letters in the mail box and realized that the house was owned by a Frazier Hendicott.

"Maybe he was her father," she thought as she knocked on the door.

10

The man who opened the door to her was a tall gangly man of about six feet, with dark brown eyes and low chopped salt and pepper hair.

"Can I help you?" he asked.

"Are you Zena Hendicott's father?" she asked as she flashed her identification in his face.

"No," he replied, "she is my niece. Zena came to stay at our place while she was attending university."

"Oh, I see," said Christiana. "And what is your name?"

"Frazier; Frazier Hendicott," he answered.

"What do you do for a living Mr Hendicott?" she asked.

"I'm an out of work actor, but I sell insurance part time," he answered.

"Where did Zena stay?" asked Christiana.

"Downstairs, in the basement apartment," said Frazier.

"I would like to see it please," Christiana requested.

"Why?" asked Frazier.

"Because I'm the new investigating officer on the case," she said, digging out her badge again to show him.

Frazier didn't hesitate in directing her to the side of the house.

"Good," he said, "I didn't think they did a good job the last time. Hope you can."

"I hope so too," she replied.

"The house has two entrances," said Frazier, "and they had their own keys. I never saw much of them and had no idea of their movements. I like to allow young people the latitude to do their own thing."

"Who found her body?" she asked.

"I did," said Frazier.

"How did you happen to come around this side?" Christiana asked.

"Well," said Frazier, "she left a note asking me to replace some bulbs in her apartment, but when I came and knocked there was

11

no answer, so I went back into my house and called her on the phone and still there was no answer. I got the spare keys and returned to open the door, and there she was."

"Where was she laying?" she asked.

"Across the bed that way," he said indicating the direction.

"Was she dressed?" she asked.

"Partially," he answered. "She was only in a short tee shirt and panties."

"Could you see the wound?" she asked.

"Yes," he quickly replied. "It was in her chest about here," he indicated to a point on her body.

"Was the knife still in or out of her chest?" she asked.

"It was out and lying over there on the floor," answered Frazier.

Christiana made a rough diagram of the position of the bed, the body and the knife.

"She lived here with Salina; didn't she?" asked Christiana.

"Yes, but Salina was not always here at nights," replied Frazier, "she sometimes went to Celia's place."

"Did you ever meet any of their friends?" asked Christiana.

"No, only one boy from Hamilton. I think his name is Robert something," he replied.

"What about her girlfriends?" Christiana asked. "Did any of them come to visit her regularly?"

"Yes, there were a couple, but I don't know their names," answered Frazier.

"Would your wife know them?" she asked.

"I don't think so," said Frazier.

"Why not? Christiana pressed.

"Because we both worked permanent afternoon shift, and didn't get to see her or Salina in the evenings," he firmly replied.

"Where's your wife now?" asked Christiana.

"She's in Nassau on holidays, I couldn't get the time off to go, so she went alone."

"Could I come back to talk with her sometime?" Christiana requested.

"You sure can," said Frazier. "She'll be back next Thursday night."

"What's her name?" asked Christiana.

"Sasha," he replied.

Christiana took as much of the girls belongings as she was allowed, thanked Frazier for his time and left for the address of Celia Bachstrum on Sheppard Avenue.

Mr Cecil Wright was a tall, skinny clean-shaved man in his late forties, and spoke with a Caribbean accent, which Christiana believed was Trinidadian. He was happy that she came and even happier to tell her about his tenant's activities.

"I watched them like a hawk," he said. "I kept a close eye on them. I never give any tenant the opportunity to break up my place or do anything illegal in it."

"How often did she go to the Bahamas?" asked Christiana.

"It's a strange thing," he began. "I often wondered why she would take time off from school to travel back to the Bahamas; sometimes three times in a month; and more."

"Where do you think she was getting the money to do this?" asked Christiana.

"I couldn't tell for sure, but judging from the weird looking boys and her lesbian girlfriends that came here, I think she was selling drugs or the pussy. There were always condoms in the garbage."

"How did you know that they were lesbians?" Christiana asked. "Unless you peeked."

"Yes, I did on a couple of occasions, and saw them......you know, doing it."

"Did you see anybody else?" asked Christiana.

"Yes ma'am, one time a man about my age came and they, eh ....you know, got involved." said Cecil.

"You were peeking again!" said Christiana.

"Yes," replied Cecil. "Maybe he was the one paying for her trips to Nassau."

"Why? She could've gotten it from her parents, couldn't she?" Christiana asked.

Cecil flashes a grin.

"I don't think so," he said, "there were always quarrels between them. Once I overheard her father telling her not to bother coming home and she telling him that she didn't have to, because she has her own money to live by."

"How did you hear this?" Christiana asked.

"I'd rigged a wire from their phone line to the upstairs, and add a phone to it so as to listen in whenever I felt like it."

"What does your wife think of your activities and your interest in the girls?"

" I don't have a wife and I don't want one either," he replied. "They are all a pain in the arse."

Christiana decided to asked the important question,

"Did you find the body?" she asked.

"Yes I did," replied Cecil. "She was lying there across the bed with blood all over her body."

"Do you know Salina Mason and Zena Hendicott?"

"Yes," said Cecil. "They're the lesbian friends I was talking about; and sometimes the fellow from Hamilton would come for the weekend."

"Did you ever try to seduce any of them?" she asked.

"Not really, but once when I was down there repairing a pipe, I didn't know Salina was asleep in the bedroom. She came out in the nude and saw me, I think she was on some kind of drug, because she forced....I mean begged me to fu....I mean screw her right there. She even supplied the condom."

"Was that the last time?" Christiana asked.

"No, she came back a couple of times after, when Celia was

at school, and we did it in my apartment," said Cecil.

"Did you ever have to pay her?" she asked.

"No, never," said Cecil. "Although once I had to lie for her, telling Celia she was with me when she wasn't."

"Any reason why she wanted an alibi?" she asked.

"No reason at all, although I'm not sure. She never came back to see me after that. I was shocked the morning when I peeked into the room, and saw her laying there beside Celia in the pool of blood. Why did she do it? She was such a pretty girl too," said Cecil.

Christiana could see he was becoming emotional as the trickle of tears began running down his face, and realized that he missed his little young thing.

"Well Mr. Wright," she said. "I think I should look at Celia Backstrum's room and her things now."

"You can look as long as you want, they're in the same place the police left them," he said.

Christiana looked around to see the girls clothes were approximately where they were supposed to be, her clean panties put away and the dirty ones still in the laundry basket along with some blouse and shorts. Her shoes were neatly stacked in a rack. Christiana took out each draw from the chest and emptied them on the bed and began going through each item. She refolded them and put them back where they belonged.

It wasn't until she emptied the last draw that she saw the envelope taped under the bottom. Quickly, she hid it from Cecil Wright's eyes and waited until he went into the kitchen before stuffing it into her waste band under her shirt.

"Well, Mr Wright," she said, "there's nothing unusual here. Maybe I will have to come back to cut through the walls to see if she hid anything behind them."

"I don't think she hid anything in the walls," he said. "I would've seen where it was cut when I came down to do the repairs."

"Well, if you do see anything abnormal, please call me at this number," she handed him a slip of paper with her name and number. "And please don't throw out her clothes until I get to see them again."

"No I won't," he replied. "This apartment is not for rent in a hurry."

Christiana realized that Wright was in love with Salina, and wondered if he might be the one who killed her for rejecting him or because she preferred to screw with women.

"Where was the knife? Still in her chest or on the floor?" she asked.

"Right over there where the chalk mark is," he pointed to the corner.

Christiana made another diagram.

"Remember you mentioned a man who came to see her?" she asked.

"Yes, the guy she screwed with," replied Cecil.

"Same one," said Christiana. "What does he look like? Can you describe him"

"Medium height, black, in his forties and ugly," replied Cecil.

"Any distinguishing marks or features?" she asked.

"Ugly dark brown eyes, a bushy moustache and a white streak in the middle of his hair," he said and began laughing.

"What so funny?" asked Christiana.

"The man looks like one of those Canadian animals," he replied. "You know, like a......."

".......like a skunk?" she asked.

"Yeah! And smells like one too," he answered.

Christiana thanked him with a hand shake, and left.

That evening, Dready came home to see Brenda feeding his new born son, and wondered why the babysitter was doing it.

"Where's Mrs. Perkins?" he asked.

"She's in the garage sir," replied Brenda, "she has been searching through some old clothes and books all evening."

"Leaving my child alone?" he said, and angrily stormed out the door leading to the garage.

"What the hell are you doing woman?" he said in a course tone. "You have left Venrece-Thomas in the hands of Brenda, an amateur, and is out here searching through this rubble?"

"Yes my darling," she calmly said. "I apologize for doing so, but look at these things, they're from those student's homes and I've found something to connect them."

She pulled out the large envelope and emptied the contents on a table.

"Diamonds darling," she said grinning. "I found these in Celia Backstrum's place, and this letter from somebody named TB in Nassau. What do you think?"

The anger left Dready instantly and he began looking at the things Christiana had on the table. He looked at the maps, recalling a time in Jamaica where they did the exact same thing in search of evidence to her mother's death.

"These maps are of the Bahamas, Jamaica, Florida, Chicago, Toronto and....." he said.

"......and they were found in Colin's possession," she said. "I think they are of locations for their business."

Dready looked at them and noticed the faint pencil dots marking Kingston, Nassau, Tellahassee, Chicago and New York city.

"Mmmmm," he mumbled, "this could be the locations for something or someone."

"What about the girl?" she asked.

"Aaaah," he said, "That girl was mixed up in smuggling diamonds from Nassau, I wonder who is TB and how many more are mixed up in this."

"Quite rightly so my love, the very reason for the condoms in the garbage. But there aren't any diamond mines in the Bahamas or Jamaica, so it has to come from somewhere else," she said looking directly into his eyes.

"Guyana?" he asked and continued, "but by whom and to

where and who?"

"That I don't know as yet, but we certainly know a TB in Nassau," she said.

"Maybe we should run this by Commissioner Dillon to see if he heard anything about that business," said Dready.

"We certainly can, but I would like to see what was in Robert Reynolds place in Hamilton first, to see if it's the same as at Colin McKenzie's. Then I want to check the names on the list to see if they are students here."

"Good," said Dready. "Use your computer to get access to the computers linking the universities across Canada, you could find the people much quicker that way."

"Great idea!" she said. "I'll get started tonight."

Dready was delighted with the way in which she went about her business that evening, meticulously searching the Internet for universities, and at the same time fussing over the baby and himself. In the mean time, he sneaked off into the bedroom to make a call to Commissioner Dillon and talked about the case for sometime, then he made another call to Bernard Graves in Jamaica, all without her knowledge.

In bed, he laid there watching her reading and sifting through the notes she had made, and wondered. He realized how thorough a person she was, and was certain she would find clues somehow. He also observed that Christiana seemed happy to be involved in something interesting after the long layoff from the Jamaica case.

"Find anything?" he asked.

"Not yet," she answered, "but I can feel something is in the making. Tell me; when you were in Nassau on that last story, did you ever hear of any diamond smuggling business there?" she asked.

"No, but I heard of some dreadlocks who were dealing ganja from there and were arrested," he replied.

"Maybe you should have spoken to the chief of police to know what else was going on in that country," she said.

Dready smiled to realise that she seemed to have forgotten what he does for a living.

"Maybe I will," he said, "because he told me to get in touch with him if I needed more information for the article."

"Good," she said as she flopped herself into the bed beside him.

"Are you tired tonight?" she asked.

"Not really," he replied. "Why?"

"I would like to get started on the next child right away," she said.

"Are you crazy woman!?" he asked.

She didn't reply, just smiled that familiar smile as she took her night dress off.

The morning's drive down the QEW to Hamilton seemed romantic to Christiana. She was delighted to be alone with her husband on a mission to that lovely city, where she had been many times with Ludwig to visit his friends. This time they were going to search Robert Reynolds apartment for any clue to the list of names and the dots on the many maps in Colin McKenzie's apartment.

She smiled as a memory came to her mind and told Dready a story of the last time her father took them to Hamilton to visit his friends. They laughed.

"....but we never came back here; I don't know why," she concluded.

"Are any of Ludwig's friends still alive?" he asked.

"Don't know," she replied. "Never saw them again."

Dready pulled in front of the address and parked.

The search proved nothing and took less time to do than the drive to that city. The landlady had already cleaned out and rented the apartment. His things were all packed in boxes and stored in the basement.

"He owed me fifty dollars that he borrowed a week before killing himself," said Emma Griswold, the landlady.

19

"Why would he......?" Christiana began to question, then changed her mind.

She quickly paid Emma the fifty dollars Robert apparently owed her so as to get what was left of his belongings and hurriedly stuffed the boxes in the trunk of the car.

"You know she was lying about the money," said Christiana.

"Ha, ha," laughed Dready. "I do realize that."

They drove back to Toronto discussing the integrity of Emma Griswold.

He parked the car in front of the garage and unloaded the boxes. They immediately began a thorough search through the things. Dready was going through an old winter coat when he felt something hard in the lining; something that felt like a marble. He quickly got out his knife and cut through the lining to get it out, and as he thought, it was a diamond; a very large one at that.

"Now!" said Dready holding up the stone. "Where the hell could this guy get a diamond this size? This damn thing is probably worth ten thousand dollars in any market."

"Maybe he bought it for his lover," she offer back jokingly.

"I doubt it," said Dready. "You told me his parents couldn't afford to pay all his tuition and he had to work part-time to pay his bills. Then his landlady said he borrowed fifty dollars from her."

"That's right," said Christiana.

"So it's quite evident that he was involved in something illegal. Either as a currier or as a thief," offered Dready.

"The girls were carrying the diamonds into Canada, then he and whoever else were distributing them to somebody," she replied.

"Maybe," said Dready, "but that's also doubtful. According to the report, he didn't have a car, never even rented one; and it seemed all his personal friends were here in T.O."

The duo sat in bed discussing the findings. Their conversation about these young people activities lasted a long time and had no logical explanation. It was recognized that there was a definite diamond smuggling ring in force, but the people they knew, were either dead or in prison. And the only thing they had, was a list of names for people who could be anywhere in the world. The realization that Colin McKenzie could very well be the son of imprisoned Peter, and the possibility of a connection of old ideology still maintained, bothered their minds.

The morning sun shone brightly through the window as they sat having their breakfast. Christiana was so excited about going to the Commissioner's office, she couldn't eat. Winston on the other hand devoured his bacon, eggs and toast, drank three mugs of coffee and had a banana.

"Come along darling," he said, "we mustn't be late; you know how ticklish Dillon is about tardiness."

"Look who is talking," she said as she grabbed her bag, stopping just long enough to kiss her son and to give Brenda some last minute instructions on taking care of Venrece-Thomas. "A while ago you were stuffing your mouth and weren't in a hurry, and now you're hurrying me."

He laughed, kissed her and got into the car.

Dready didn't spare the gas getting to RCMP headquarters. He parked and they both ran up the stairs to the office.

"Hello Commissioner," she said as they entered the room.

"Hello Christiana," said Dillon, kissing her on the cheek, "you look lovely."

"Thank you sir, it must be the baby," she said, "and another might be on the way."

"So soon!?" asked Dillon.

"Well, yes sir, I'm supposed to have four and I might as well have them quickly to satisfy my husband's request," she stated.

Dillon looked at Dready and he shook his shoulders in a wondrous gesture and began their conversation. Dillon explained to her what he suspected was going on in Nassau and some of the names which he had acquired from an agent stationed there.

"Now officer Perkins," said Dillon, "would you kindly tell us

21

what you have in mind?"

Christiana took out her book and diagrams and began her show. She explained the things she found at the students residence, where and the position they were in and the location.

"Some of these things were among the clothes and in their books," she stated, "I think sir that these people were murdered."

"What's your theory?" asked Dillon.

"The murder weapons were all thrown on the floor or in a corner after executing the deed," she said, "and anyone preforming Hari Kari wouldn't pull out the knife and throw it into a corner. They would have left the weapon in the wound."

"The report said Robert Reynolds weapon was still in his chest," said Dillon.

"Maybe so sir," she said, "but the report also said there was a struggle. Which indicated to me that they were all killed by the same person, and it had to be someone they knew and trusted."

"Good point," said Dillon, "but what if Robert Reynolds did them in then took his own life?"

"I doubt that very much sir," she replied.

"Why?" asked Dillon.

"If he did kill them, there wouldn't be a reason to kill himself," she replied. "There would not be any fear of him being caught. No, it had to be someone who didn't want to leave any witnesses to their operation."

"Where is the answer?" asked Dillon.

"In The Bahamas sir," she answered. "The answer is somewhere in the Bahamas and somebody knows all about it."

Dillon looked at Dready and back to Christiana.

"Maybe you will have to go there to find it," he said.

"I think we will have to sir," said Christiana.

Dillon gave thoughts to the proposition, and decided that since he had already sanctioned their research into the murders he would allow them the latitude for a trip into The Bahamas. He realises that Dready was already in possession of some information and that his informant had not supplied any for a few weeks and really wanted to know why. He began by telling them about this person in Nassau and some of his functions for gathering information on some Canadians living there.

For Christiana, this theory was an exciting adventure, and the fact that she would be involved in solving these mysterious deaths, titillated her soul. She sat quietly listening to the Commissioner as he gave them both a proper talking to, with specific instructions on their conduct, strictly for their safety whilst in Nassau. He told them of the RCMP's interest in a couple of people there, who might very well be involved with the suicide of these young students in Canada. He told them that the department has been watching and has a person already on the inside, and for them to make contact with him on reaching there.

"Christiana," he said, "I would like you to go to Nassau, using the name Felscher, to be a mule in a shipment. You'll be carrying an amount of diamonds with you from Nassau, we don't know who, when or where they will make contact, but we're hoping that some-one will. Your job is to behave as a naive person and follow their instructions to the letter. Remember that Winston will be near at all times and our other people will be there also. But still, don't take any unnecessary chances."

"I won't sir," she replied smiling. "I have a husband and a child to take care of, and I want to live long enough to have three more; children that is."

"Good," said Dillon, "I want you back here in one whole piece."

Dready seemed concerned as he asked,

"Tell me sir, will Commissioner Graves be involved in the case?"

"Yes, and so is Captain Maraj in Guyana. I'm sure they have some ideas about the people. I want you to make as much connections as possible of these students and the other suspects," he instructed.

"Why use Ludwig's name, and how are we going to justify our association with him?" asked Christiana.

"Ah, ah," said Dillon, "they already know that he's dead, and is quite aware of the others long term prison sentences. There is nobody with whom they could check to verify your identity, and they will be too concerned about the loss of business to care. We must take advantage of their vulnerability at this time and strike quickly. Furthermore, the students are dead, somebody killed them and we must find out who and why."

To her, his instructions were valid and she understood quite well the dangers she could face among those criminals.

"...and furthermore," said Dready, "you will have to leave for Jamaica as soon as your part of the deal is completed, because I don't want you in the line of any possible fire, understand?"

"Okay sir, loud and clear," she said saluting him. "But if I'm needed all you have to do is phone Jamaica and I will be on the next flight to Nassau."

"That's a deal," said Dready.

They got up and were leaving when she asked,

"Commissioner, how about spending cash?"

"Through the usual channels my dear," he replied. "It will get to you."

Christiana didn't really understand, but nodded her head in acknowledgement.

As the days passed, Christiana was kept busy studying the reports from detective Jack Colley and the other police investigations in Hamilton. She checked every piece of the students belongings, trying to evaluate then for any oddity or similarities that could tie the victims together. She was well aware that it would take a forensic scientist to do what she wanted, but Commissioner Dillon wouldn't allow it. Matter of fact he couldn't justify reopening the case without causing a rebellious eruption within the metro police. Somehow, she wasn't able to get beyond her deep suspicions to prove that there was something sinister within the reports. But what she knew was that somebody had made their deaths happen and for a reason.

She made many calls to all the landlords where the students resided and contacted many of the people with simular names on the list she found in Celia Backstrum's room, through Email. Although she was enjoying being on the Internet doing her search, she felt a little disappointed not finding anything concrete.

"It's strange," she said to Dready as they sat eating supper, "all these names on this list and none of them showed up in any of the universities students lists."

"Maybe they're not students," replied Dready. "What if they are residents of Canada but are illegal? You wouldn't find their names anywhere."

"Maybe so, unless they went to a hospital with an illness or were arrested," she said, "and even then they could use a false name and address."

"Absolutely," he replied, "but what if they were in need of money, where would they go for help?"

"To the welfare office?" she answered.

"Right, or to a community centre," Dready suggested.

With that, she got up, washed the dishes and they adjourned to the livingroom to watch some television. Dready got busy playing with the baby while Christiana flipped through the channels. Finally the news came on and the announcer showed a photograph of a young man being arrested in a night club stabbing incident in Scarborough.

"Look!" she hollered, "they said that fellow's name is TB Lewis, I wonder if he is the TB in the note?"

"Maybe," said Dready as he reached for the phone, "I will make a call to 51 division to find out if he has any connection to any of the people on the list."

After the phone call, Dready told her that he was going down town to talk to the young man and would be back shortly.

As he left the house, Christiana sat looking at the television.

"He is a cop," she whispered to herself, "but both him and the damn Commissioner have evaded telling me. Why?"

She made a couple of calls to her brothers Creag and Alwin, and chatted for a while with Sandra and Paulette. She gave thought to many things relating to Dready and couldn't get past her suspicions of him. Finally, she fell asleep.

Christiana got up early to attend the smallest but loudest man of the house. Last night she was too tired for anything and didn't hear a sound when Dready returned from his trip downtown and into bed beside her. She put on the coffee to perk while making Winston's breakfast after feeding Venrece-Thomas. She could hear him singing in the bedroom.

"What happened last night?" she asked him as he entered the kitchen.

"Well I ravished you and I......"

"No, not that!" she shouted, "I mean downtown and the young stabber."

"Nothing," replied Dready, "his real name is Tyrone Boyd Lewis and never been to Nassau."

"Oh well," she said, "it was just a thought; and furthermore if you did ravish me last night I would have known."

"No you wouldn't," said Dready laughing, "you were sound asleep."

"Then why didn't you awaken me?" she asked, "I wanted to have some too."

"You did?" asked Dready surprisingly, "and here I thought you were tired."

They both laughed at the misadventure. He kissed her and rushed off to work.

Chapter Two

The Godfather.

$\mathcal{T}$hey exited the Sangster airport to see Carlton standing at the door waiting for them, just like he was last year.

"Hey Ackeeface! How are you old boy?" Christiana shouted in the Jamaican patois.

"Girl, I'm here just the same way," replied Carlton, as they greeted each other with hugs and kisses.

"Give me the baby," said Ackeeface, 'it's a long time since I held one this small."

"Hold him good," said Dready, "he's only two months old."

"Come here boy, give uncle Carlton a kiss," said Ackeeface taking the child from his mother. "Welcome home bad boy," he said and hoisted the child in the air. "See that flag flying on the roof over there?" he said to the baby, "it might not seem as much to some people, but every time I look at the black and green with the yellow X, I get a shiver down my spine; to think of their meaning and to know that it belongs to me. Anywhere in this world you go and mention the name Jamaica, they know it and realize that we are a people who are determined to succeed at anything we set our minds to. This is your land and when you grow up I man is going to teach you our language, personally."

He returned the child to his mother and hurriedly got them across the street to the parking lot. He loaded their baggage into his new van and began their exit to the road. The conversation was about anything and everything.

"We'll have to get him to his grandmother fast," said Carlton, "because she is excited about you all coming for Christmas."

"Where is Evelyn?" Dready asked.

"She's at your mother's house waiting for us to get there," replied Carlton.

Dready and Carlton kept a running conversation about their lives since they last saw each other, as Carlton sped along the road. Christiana held the baby to the car's window, showing him the towns as they travelled towards Savanna-La-Mar.

"This is your country," she told the baby, "look at it and love it. And we will go to visit your grandmother's grave also."

The two men were too busy talking to care about what she was doing in the rear seat with her baby. It wasn't long before they were in the drive-way of his parents house. Elsa was the first to reach them. She took the baby, kissed both Winston and Christiana and hurried to the door of the house with the youngest of her grandchildren.

"You did well," said Elsa excitedly, "both of you did well. He is such a beautiful child."

She began fussing over him, removing his clothing to make him comfortable in the warm heat.

"Get Thomas!" She shouted to the gardener. "Tell him his grandson is here; and hurry."

While Christiana, Elsa, Evelyn and Pamela chatted, Dready went to make a phone call to his good friend Bernard Graves.

"Hello Bernie, we're here," said Dready, "come to meet your Godson."

"I'll be there this evening about six thirty," said Graves, "and I have the information you asked for."

"Okay my friend, see you," said Dready

Their conversation was short, and Dready resumed his chat with Carlton. They talked about Carlton's new house in Runaway Bay, which was almost completed, although they had already moved in, and about the new van.

"I man have another boy driving the car, and he is doing alright," said Carlton. "I pay him very good, so he's working hard to maintain his job."

"Good," replied Dready, "just remember to treat him right."

"I man will never forget what you did for I," Carlton stated, "and will treat him nice."

Dready found that although he was happy to be home showing off his family to his parents, there was something nagging at his mind. Commissioner Dillon had told him about his suspicions of the students deaths in Toronto and Hamilton, and the possibility of a cartel working out of Nassau. He told him to follow his leads to wherever, to resolve the problem..

He gave him a contact in Nassau, a man named Chrittendon, who was a paid informant for the Mounties, but who had not been seen for almost a year. He sat in his father's lazy-boy chair watching the family gawk over his son.

"Venrece-Thomas Perkins," he whispered in thoughts. "I sincerely hope nothing will happen to either your mother or I, but if it happens you'll always have a home here."

Something flashes across his mind.

"Christiana," he said, "remember to call your father, he might want to come over to see his grandson also."

Quickly she got the phone and called him.

"Hello father," she said into the phone, "we're here now at the Perkins home in Savanna-La-Mar and......"

There was a pause.

"Okay then, I'll see you in a while."

"He'll be right over," she said to Dready, "he's on the road here. I got him on the cellular."

"Good, I would like to ask him some questions also," said Dready.

He smiled at the knowledge that Venrece had done only six months of his two years sentence for his involvement with the old gang, and was happy for him to be out on parole. Any lesser person might have been devastated and ashamed of his down fall, but Venny seems to be bouncing back from his. He was anxious to see his father-in-law and to see Venny's reaction to his grandson.

Just then Graves car entered and parked in the driveway behind Carlton's.

"Hello Bernard, what's up?" Dready greeted his friend as he entered the verandah.

"Not very much. The water is rough although the sea is calm," answered Graves, "but I will have to wade through it, won't I?"

"Congratulations Bernard on the new position, you're the best man for the job," said Dready.

"Yeah, after you refused it," said Graves.

He walked over to the women, took the baby, kissed him and held him aloft high above his head.

"Boy, as long as I live you'll always have a father. But we'll meet in church on Sunday to make it official," said Graves.

"Don't squeeze him too hard," shouted Elsa, "remember he is only two months old."

"I've held babies before," said Graves as he hurriedly handed him over to his grandmother.

Graves looked at Dready and the two men quietly left the house to talk outside.

"Here's the information about Colin McKenzie," said Graves as they sat on the bench, "he's the oldest son of Peter and Tanya McKenzie. We found out that after Peter and Tanya split up, she took the children to Nassau before going to Miami. He was left in the care of a middle income farming family named Hodgkins, who live in Bimini. He used to visit his Miami based mother frequently in the past, by hitching a ride on boats to enter the US illegally; but after she was shot, he moved to Nassau and obtained a visa to travel to Miami freely to see her. He was already attending the University of Toronto when things were happening here last year. We still don't have any concrete evidence of him being involved in anything illegal."

"Thank you," said Dready. "Now tell me what's happening in the diamond business these days."

"Dready my boy! Since the case was over, there's been a lull in the trafficking business. I've noticed a lull in all activities at our airports, although I've heard that some others have already began another cartel. We were only able to catch a couple of petty ones but I have a good idea where the big fishes are. When I spoke to Captain Maraj in Guyana last time, he told me that nothing was moving in the usual way there, although they suspected another group was in operation there also."

"Good," said Dready. "They will have to keep an eye out for anything that looks suspicious."

"Is there something happening in the diamond market of Canada?" asked Graves.

"I don't really know as yet," said Dready, "but as I told you about the dead students in Toronto, we found an un-cut diamond in the possession of one of them and a bag of sixteen smaller ones in another. I'm concerned that the old Burkowitz/Bass gang is still operating, although Burkowitz is still doing his twenty-five years in a Guyanese prison and Bass is dead. I have a feeling that they're using the young ones now to carry the stuff around the globe."

"But how are they getting it out?" Graves asked.

"The same way as always. Girls carrying it in condoms in their pussy, and the boys acting as their escorts," said Dready.

"Maybe Captain Maraj might have some ideas," said Graves. "We might have to shake down a couple of them to make the point felt or to make some kind of arrests. I'll call him. Dready my boy, there are more crooks operating in the Caribbean now than ever before, and there are many in Jamaica."

31

"I know," said Dready, "some of them posing as business men and tourists; and the leader for this one is in Nassau. But we can't just shake down everybody, we'll just have to get a lead on who, then associate them."

"Right!" replied Graves. "We just don't want the flunkies, we want the big boys. The ones with the status."

"What about Arthur Collins?" asked Dready. "Is he allowed to make any phone calls or to see anyone?"

"Yes," said Graves, "but all his calls are taped and screened, and all his visitors are searched going in and coming out. It would be hard for anyone to bring things to him and to take it out."

"I'm sure Bernard," said Dready, "but we can't read minds, can we?"

The two policemen sat on the bench under the mango tree, and talked for most of an hour until Christiana came out to join them. Graves told her of his positive identification of the boy in Toronto.

"Well Chrisy, it seems you've stumbled upon another one of those age old mysteries again," said Graves.

"It seems like it," she replied. "I thought it looked weird that the son of Peter McKenzie would commit suicide in Toronto at a time when he had nothing to worry about; unless he was involved with someone or something that had some form of repercussion. I noticed the autopsy report on each one of them said they were stabbed in the upper chest. Colly told me that although it looked suspicious, the coroner believed it was self-inflicted because of the position of the wound and their finger prints on the weapons."

"Good," said Graves, "but is there any evidence to show a common relationship to each victim?"

"Yes, they were all university students and all came from the Bahamas," she replied.

"Did you not say some were from other Caribbean countries?" asked Graves.

"Yes, they were," she said, "but for some odd reason, they all

32

resides in The Bahamas. The reason I would like to know if there is any connection with parents and whether the parents knew each other and where they met."

She told Graves all that Commissioner Dillon told her about the contacts they will be meeting in Nassau, and where they should be at any given time.

Dready waited until Christiana went back into the house before removing the papers from his pocket and handed them to Graves.

"This is a list Christiana found in one of the student's books. We traced some of the people on it to universities across Canada and the United States. Many of them are Caribbean born, while others are Americans, Dutch, Scottish and Canadian born. I would like to know why he had them on a list. I already have Commissioner Dillon checking on those in Canada, for their frequency of travel to Guyana, and to make any connections to those from The Bahamas."

"...and you want me to check for any Jamaicans on the list, right?" asked Graves.

"Sure, I would like to know who, what and where," replied Dready.

Should I fax it to Captain Maraj also?" asked Graves.

"No, you'll never know who's looking on those machines. We'll have to do it personally."

"It looks like you'll have to go there to find a connection," said Graves.

"Yes my friend, so it seems," replied Dready.

Graves sat quietly for a moment.

"Who do you suspect is the leader now? Knowing that Bass is dead, and Collins....I mean Lyle Alexander is in prison? " asked Graves.

"Don't know as yet, but when we get to Nassau, I certainly will find out," he replied.

The sound of the car entering the yard caught their attention.

It was Venrece Alexander. He hurriedly exited his car and rushed over towards them. It was the first time Dready was seeing him since they left Jamaica almost a year ago, and for Graves it's been two weeks since he last spoke to Venny.

Christiana saw Venny drove in and rushed from the verandah to greet him. They hugged and kissed and talked about their feelings as they walked over to the others.

"Hello father," she said, "I'm glad you're in good health after all the problems you've faced."

"Well, thank you for being there for me darling," he said. "Your letters were my comfort and the pillar of hope for my future; but you didn't have to write every day."

"I wanted to," she replied, "and furthermore I had to keep you up to date on my pregnancy. I didn't want Venrece-Thomas to think his grandfather wasn't interested in him."

"Well, thank you," said Venrece as he kissed his daughter again. "How's your leg?"

"It's not too bad, just a scar where the doctors repaired the bullet hole," she answered.

"Hello Winston," said Venrece, greeting Dready with a hug. "It's so nice to see you again. Hi Bernard."

"You look good Venny," said Dready.

"Yes I do," replied Venrece, "for a man who just done a prison term. Winston, I'm delighted to be relieved of those long ago secrets, it was killing me inside. I did the term knowing that I would be coming out to see my daughter, my grandson and you. Where is he?"

"In the house," said Christiana as she hustled him off. "I have to tell you about Creag and Alwin, and about their families."

"Good," replied Venrece, "I definitely want to hear how they accepted the news about their father. I mean Ludwig.

Both Venny and Christiana hurried into the house to see the baby.

34

"Do you realize Christiana loves that man?" observed Graves.

"Yes, I know that," said Dready. "She has enough love to share with everyone of us, and I don't know where she finds the energy. She had it pent up for years, and now she has a reason to let it out. She wrote to him every day telling him everything about us in Canada and every intricate detail of her pregnancy. You should see her fuss with the baby. She very seldom allow anyone to have him for any length of time, even the sitter."

"Typical mothers," said Graves. "Mine does the same to me, even at this age; now she does it through the grandchildren. What are you going to do with the baby when you have to go to Nassau?"

"We'll be leaving him here with mother," replied Dready.

"What about Christiana, how will she feel?" asked Graves.

"I don't know as yet," said Dready, "I haven't got a clue. I intend to make her a proposition later. I will propose that after she makes contact with the people we want to, she can return to Jamaica and I will complete the assignment there."

"Good luck," Graves said smiling, "If I know her the way I do think, she would not want to leave you there alone."

"Well, if it comes to choosing between Venrece-Thomas and me, it will be him," said Dready, "and I'm counting on that."

The two old friends shook hands in agreement and headed for the house.

They got inside to see Venny feeding the baby. They could see the sparkle of happiness in Venrece's eyes, and felt the thoughts of a man who was denied that privilege many years ago.

"When was the last time you've done this Venny?" Graves asked.

"Never," replied Venrece, "but there is always a first time, right?. This seems like a good place to start because I heard that there are three more to come."

"I guess you're right, and I will have to practice my diaper changing techniques again," said Thomas. "But as they say, once you've done it you never forget it."

The two grandfathers were fussing and enjoying their new offspring so well, nobody else was allowed to get close to the boy.

"He'll have to see the farm tomorrow," said Thomas.

"What!?" shouted Venrece, "and let mosquitos eat the boy alive? No way."

"It's alright father," said Christiana, "he'll have to get used to it, because he'll be spending some times here too."

"I don't say nay," replied Venrece, "but in a cleaner, more comfortable environment without pests."

Everybody laughed.

This argument reverberated throughout the evening with everybody demanding for the child to be with them. Christiana began to write out the allotted time for each of them on a piece of paper. Winston, realizing that his opinion didn't amount to anything, stayed mum. Graves stated that although they were grandfathers, he will be the boys godfather and he will have to get his time also.

Graves left with a promise to see him in church on Sunday. Venny also got up to leave but Elsa told him to stay for the night so as to visit the farm the next day to protect his grandchild.

Everybody was up early the next morning. Elsa, Christiana, Pamela and the maids were busy in the kitchen preparing breakfast and the picnic baskets for their visit to the farm. Dready, Thomas and Venny spent the time reading the newspaper and talking about things. It wasn't until Dready mentioned the dead students in Canada that Venrece began to recall some of the things that happened during their days in the bridge club.

"You know something Winston? We had some vicious people in that club back then," he said. "There were people there who didn't give a damn about anyone or anything. Their whole interest was focussed on the well-being of themselves and their friends, and screw the rest."

"That I realize," said Dready.

"Take Karlheinz Bass for instance," continued Venrece, "he wanted to be head of everything just to be able to control those around him. Then he had Peter and Walter behaving in the same way as himself; ruthless murders."

"Not anymore," said Dready.

Venrece told him about some of the diamond people of past and their deeds.

"Have you ever heard about a girl name Celia Bachstrum?" asked Dready.

Venrece's eyes popped open on hearing the name.

"There was a man named Zenon Bachstrum, who was a close friend of Karlheinz Bass and later with Ivan Burkowitz. He came to Jamaica during the early fifties and stayed at the bridge club, then disappeared a couple of years later. She could be his daughter."

"Have you ever seen her?" asked Dready.

"No, but on one of my trips into Nassau, I accidentally ran into Zenon's wife Amanda, who owns a gift shop on Market street in Nassau, she told me that Zenon died in a boating accident. It sank off the course of Florida a few years earlier."

"Did you believe her?" asked Dready.

"No, I think he was given a new face by Karlheinz Bass for a reason and is in hiding or living somewhere else."

"Do you think he's alive now?" asked Dready.

"I'm not too sure," replied Venny, "but I can give you a friend's address in Nassau. His name is Lincoln Grey. He could tell you if Zenon is really dead or alive, and he also could take you to Amanda's store."

"Was Zenon involved in the diamond cartel also?"

"He sure was, only he had other people working for him. He was never up front like Karl and Ivan," said Venny. "I have a picture of him in my safe at home."

"Good, I might want to see it. Do you think your brother Lyle might know him?" asked Dready.

"I don't know," answered Venny, "but if Lyle, when he was Arthur Collins was going to parties at Karlheinz house, they would've met."

Dready thought about the connection Venrece had just given him.

"Do you think Lyle could still be getting information to his colleagues from prison?" he asked.

"I don't know how, but I was told that it could happen," replied Venny. "Look," he continued, "when Patricia Green had her nervous breakdown at the trial and was put into the hospital, I asked Barbara Smith what was in store for her. Barbara told me that there was plans for an appeal, but if that fails there was another alternative. How could anybody know Patricia was planning a suicide?"

"How did she do it?" asked Dready.

"Somehow she got hold of some narcotics," replied Venny. "I am still wondering where she got it."

Dready gave thoughts to that answer but remained silent.

"Did you ever speak to Barbs after that?" asked Dready.

"No, remember we were sentenced and imprisoned," said Venny, "and since I got out I haven't checked on her."

"She got twenty-five years, didn't she?" asked Dready.

"Yes," replied Venrece.

"Where's her son now?" asked Dready.

"I don't rightly know," said Venny, "but he does have a lot of money at his disposal; inheritance from his grandfather."

Dready and Venrece discussed all the names mentioned by Venrece, for a long time. Dready realized that a real possibility of a Jamaican connection was eminent. And the more he thought about it, the more Lyle Alexander aka Arthur Collins kept coming to mind. He also recognised that some of the people that Karlheinz had given new identities, were still alive and active in the diamond smuggling business.

"Celia Bachstrum's father, Zenon, was a very close friend of

Burkowitz," he thought. "He mysteriously disappeared in The Bahamas some years ago and apparently died in a boat that sank off Florida, why?"

"Tell me Venrece," he said aloud, "have you ever heard of a man named Charles Chrittendon?"

"Chrittendon, Chrittendon," Venrece pondered the name. "Yes, the name sounds familiar. If I'm right, he was at a meeting with Peter McKenzie, Harvey Ambross, Zenon and Rosita in New York. I think he is a Canadian."

"How would you know that?" said Dready. "You told us last year that you only went there once, to make a delivery."

"No I didn't," said Venrece. " I told you it was on my first visit that I found the body of Malcolm Richards, then I went to Nassau for a few weeks. Sure I did make other trips and it was on the last one that I saw the three of them in a serious conversation."

Dready gave thoughts to the statement and realized that Venny was right.

"So you'd met Mr. Bachstrum and Mr Chrittendon. What did you talk about?" asked Dready.

"We didn't," said Venrece. "They did all the talking and I listened. He was trying to get Peter to sell him some diamonds that Rosita had promised, and Peter was reluctant to do the deal."

"Did it materialize?" asked Dready.

"I believe so, because Amanda came to Jamaica about a week later to pickup the merchandise from Peter. The next time I saw him was in Nassau, when I attended a party at his house. He seemed to be living quite good in a big posh house near the South Ocean Beach area, and I heard that he had another one on the far-out islands."

"Did you speak to him then?"

"I sure did, but the conversation was about women and horses. All that night Amanda kept throwing herself at me," replied Venny.

"Did you take it?" asked Dready.

Venny broke into a smile.

"No, I was too late," he said smiling. "By the time I decided to take her offer, she and a young fellow named Tullis something or another, went off somewhere."

Venrece began laughing again.

"What's so funny?" asked Dready.

"The whole damn thing. Chrittendon had an eighteen year old girlfriend at the party, and the word was that the girl was the daughter of Peter Bass's estranged wife Althea; whose maiden name is Wakefield. As the story goes, she divorced Peter and ran off with an Englishman named Smithers to St Lucia and bore the child, after that. Peter Bass blamed his brother Karlheinz, who was a friend of Mr. Smithers, for his involvement in the incident. Peter began having an affair with Karlheinz wife Olivia, and you know what happened to them."

"Yes I know," said Dready. "They were poisoned and their bodies shipped back to Germany........."

".......with the diamonds inside them," completed Venrece. "Look my boy, most of those people are in the diary I gave to Bernard for use in the case. Get it from the courts and you might be able to make connections with those people."

"I will," said Dready, "Graves will get it. What was the girl's name?"

"What girl?" asked Venny.

"The girl with Chrittendon," said Dready.

"Don't know," replied Venny. "I never got around to talking to her."

Just then Christiana, Elsa, Pamela and Thomas emerged from the house, ready for their trip to the farm. They got loaded into the van and Winston drove out the gates towards their farm. When they arrived, everybody took the things from the van to get setup for the picnic.

"Where's the donkey?" shouted Christiana. "He has to learn how to ride the donkey."

The helper came running from behind the cattle building.

40

"I will get him ma'am," said the helper and disappeared into the bushes.

"You're not going to put that boy on the donkey's back, are you?" Venrece asked Christiana.

"Yes father, he will have to experience everything I didn't at his age," she replied.

The helper returned with the animal and installed an hamper and saddle. They insulated a blanket and sheet in the hamper.

"You could put the baby into the hamper and he wouldn't fall out," said the helper.

Christiana mounted the donkey for her ride, with Thomas at her side. While Christiana was busy carrying on with her child's familiarization of the farm, Pamela and Elsa were busy preparing the picnic table.

"Since you all wanted the child to be in this smelly place, we might as well present it well," said Ella.

They ate and did everything Christiana wanted her son to see, touch, taste and smell. She even convinced Winston to take him to the river for a dip. Thomas, who was also excited to have the baby there, did things to clean up the area. Venrece, who didn't want the baby there in the first place, had to admit that he was enjoying himself, and having the conversations with Dready was delightful.

Finally they left the farm, as the night began to swallow the day, and headed home to a more hospitable atmosphere.

At the house, Thomas and Venrece took turns telling stories about their boyhood days and their times in college, to the laughter of the family present.

"You know something?" Christiana whispered into Dready's ear. "I think this is the best thing that ever happened to Venrece for a long time. Having me and his grandson here seems to make him happy. Did you see how excited he was last night when I told him about having another one?"

"You're so right," replied Dready. "We've had such a nice

conversation about some of the past people in his life. I hope we can talk more, because some of them are still active in the old case."

"I would like for him and I and the baby to spend a day alone together at his house," Christiana suggested.

"That's fine by me," said Dready. "You two can decide on the time."

"Yeah," said Christiana, "but it will have to wait until I return from Nassau. Remember, I have a job to do there?"

"I know, but we could complete it and you could return here to do that with him," said Dready. "I might have to stay there to wrap up my part of the story."

"That might be a very good idea," she said smiling. "Only one thing, don't get involved with any of the women there."

He laughed.

"Getting worried already?" he asked.

"No, just a warning," she replied. "I still wear a gun and I do have three more children to go."

The church was packed to the rafters. There were many people there to have their newly born children baptised. Luckily the preacher wasn't about to waste time and the proceedings progressed smoothly and quickly. Finally it was their turn.

"Aaah, the Perkins child. Where are the godparents?" asked Reverend Johnson, taking the baby from Christiana.

Bernard Graves got up and so did Mrs. Evelyn Stewart. The preacher questioned them on their responsibility to the child and they acknowledged their understanding of it.

".....and remember; if anything should ever happen to Winston and Christiana you two are responsible to see that he is raised right," said reverend Johnson. "In the church!"

"Yes sir," replied Graves, "we are aware of our obligation and will certainly live up to it."

Just then Venny put up his hand. The reverend saw him and quickly head off his question.

"Mr Alexander, you will get your turn; grandparents will have their share of responsibilities also."

Everybody laughed.

"In the name of the father, son and the holy spirit, I Baptise you Venrece-Thomas Oswald Perkins," said reverend Johnson as he splashed the baby with the water.

When the ceremony was over, everybody left the church.

Back at the house the party began. Everybody came to meet the newest member of the Perkins family with gifts and other well wishes. Those who came for the Christmas festivities from England, America and other parts of the island were still there milling around and all seemed to be talking at once. Everybody was happy to see each other again.

"We have to go to Nassau, mother," said Dready, "would you mind taking care of Venrece-Thomas for a few days?"

"Not at all son," said Elsa. "we'll have a lot of fun together. And Venrece," she said looking at him, "you could stay here to be with your grandson if you want to."

"Thanks for the offer Elsa," said Venrece, "but I have some business to look into, you know, trying to put my life back together, but I will be here as often as I can."

The talking went on until late, it seemed nobody wanted to go to bed. Finally Thomas got up.

"Sorry people," he said, "I have to be up early in the morning to feed some pregnant cows; so goodnight."

That seemed to do the trick, because everybody who had to, decided to leave for their abode, and those who lived there, went to their rooms.

Dready laid beside his wife with his son between them.

"Don't roll over too hard," he told Christiana, "you might crush him."

She laughed.

"For nine months I carried him," she said, "and I didn't crush him. Stop worrying about me doing that to him now."

"Okay," he said and cuddled the baby in his arms, "and no sex tonight either."

"Okay," she replied, "but maybe tomorrow morning?"

"Maybe," he replied.

Dready stood at the window watching the morning sun rising over the Cock pit Mountain. He lit a cigarette and sipped his Blue Mountain Coffee as he enjoyed the scene. He had been up for twenty minutes assisting Christiana to change and feed young Venrece-Thomas, who had alarmed the household thirty minutes earlier of his desire for an early breakfast.

"It's going to be a nice day," he whispered.

"What did you say?" asked Christiana.

"I said it's going to be a nice day," he repeated. "Any time the sun comes up looking shiny like that, you can tell it's going to be a nice day."

Christiana stopped doing what she was, and gave thoughts to his logic; then when she seemed to grasp his meaning, she said,

"Absolutely, It's going to be a great day."

They sat at the kitchen table chatting until the young gentleman decided to go back to sleep. Within minutes, Thomas was up and began collecting his tools and other things to leave for the field.

"Can I come with you Dad?" asked Dready.

"Certainly, get your clothes and meet me in the truck," replied Thomas.

The task of getting appropriately dressed took a few minutes, and as quickly they were on the road to the farm.

"Winston," said Thomas, "why are you in Jamaica this time? Are you on another case?"

"Yes Dad," replied Dready, "and this time I have to go into Guyana and Bahamas to do most of it, because some of the people I'm interested in are there."

"What about Christiana," asked Thomas, "is she going with

you?"

"No; I will be going there alone," he replied. "I cannot afford to have her with me because she has to be here to take care of the boy. Although she has to go to the Bahamas with me to initiate a contact, I will send her home as soon as that is done."

"That's fine," said Thomas, "we will take good care of them here."

"Thanks Pop," said Dready. "You'll have to keep her near and not allow her to go into town alone."

"Why?" asked Thomas.

"Remember she was shot in the leg last time? I don't want her rushing off downtown where somebody might recognize her," he said, "and I don't want her wanting to be with me after she completed her assignment in Nassau either."

Thomas paused in thoughts, then when he believed he had the solution he said,

"Then get Graves to keep her busy with some police work; that might keep her mind occupied."

"Good idea," said Dready, elated for his father's suggestion. "Maybe Graves could give her a job checking the list of names."

The two men talked as they got stuck in to the work of feeding the animals and chickens.

By noon they had completed the chores and were on their way back home for lunch.

"Where have you been?" shouted Christiana as they entered the Verandah. "Why didn't you tell me where you were going?"

Dready stopped and stared at her menacingly.

"I don't have to tell you everything," he softly said, "but if you really want to know, I went to see a horse," he told her.

"Horse? What horse?" she asked and quickly realized that it was pointless to continue the senseless conversation.

"Horse my arse," she whispered and followed them into the house for lunch.

45

At the table, Dready told his mother of his plan to leave the baby with them and that Christiana would return from the Bahamas, after her assignment.

"How long will we be gone?" Christiana asked.

"Don't rightly know," he replied, "but I hope it will only be a week."

"Good," she said, "this fellow likes his breast milk better than the powdered stuff, so I will have to be back quickly."

"He could have the cow's own?" suggested Thomas. "We could have it scalded and he would never know the difference."

Christiana thought about it for a moment.

"Yes, but he might like it too much and not want mine when I return," she said.

Everybody laughed, and quickly the conversation became focussed on her fears of losing her son to a cow.

That evening Graves came with a lot of papers, and the three police officers sat at the dinner table for hours reading and discussing the possibility of who they thought were involved in the smuggling business.

"Have you told Peter McKenzie of his son's murder?" Dready ask Graves.

"No, not yet," replied Graves. "I wanted to tell him when we can make other connections linking him to the diamond business; he might be willing to talk then."

"Good," said Dready, "because telling him now might cause him to become suspicious and send a message to alarm the others."

"How could he do that?" asked Christiana. "He is in prison, isn't he?"

"He sure is," said Graves, "but those people can bribe guards to carry out a message to somebody for them."

There was a long pause.

"I think we should investigate the people that Karlheinz Bass had given new faces to," suggested Christiana, "maybe we could find some of them are involved and still carrying out the business with others."

"That might be a good job for you Christiana, after you come back from Nassau," said Dready. "Maybe you will have the answers of connections that would help me there."

"Yes," said Graves, "you could be his eyes from here."

"Good!" she said jovially, "then I would still be on the case."

"You sure would be," said Dready, "and still be close to Venrece-Thomas."

"Agreed," she said and shook hands with them.

When it was time, Dready escorted Graves out to the gates.

"Could you get Venrece Alexander's diary from the courts?" asked Dready.

"Sure can," said Graves. "Why?"

"It could have some names that might be pertinent to this investigation," said Dready, "and furthermore it could keep Christiana busy while I'm away."

"Yes, she could do some research on the people and inform you," answered Graves.

"Thanks Bernard," he said, "keep her busy and I will not have any concerns for her safety."

"That's alright friend," said Graves, "just remember to apply the same safety for yourself there. Those boys are just as dangerous as ours here and you could easily run into some of them."

"I will definitely do that my friend," said Dready, "and I will be on the blower to you at every opportunity, so listen for me, okay?"

The two friends parted company and Dready took his time getting back to the house. He sat on the Verandah in the dark contemplating all the possibilities. He gave thoughts to Arthur Collins being involved and wondered where his investigations will lead.

"I must get in touch with Earl as soon as I get there," he thought, "and find out if he got the information I asked of him."

Dready was so engrossed in his thoughts that he didn't hear her until she was standing in the doorway.

"Coming to bed?" Christiana asked.
"Yes dear," he replied and got up.

Chapter Three

Liars and Thieves.

$\mathcal{T}$he customs officer's name tag said Tullis Burke.

Christiana stood looking at him, wondering if he was the TB in the note found in Celia Bachstrum's apartment in Toronto. He looked at her passport and immediately closed his port.

"Welcome Miss Felscher, will you come this way with me?" he said leading her to an office and directed her to a chair, "please sit."

"Thank you," she said cautiously, "but what do I owe for this personal hospitality?" she asked.

"My name is Tullis Burke," he said stretching out his hand to her, "I'm a customs officer but also a friend."

"Pleased to meet you," she replied taking his hand. "I guess a friend will be a welcoming feeling to have in the Bahamas?"

He nodded his head and said,

"Yes it is, I've heard that you're related to a man named Ludwig Felscher, are you?" he asked.

"Yes, he was my father," she replied.

"I heard he died last year," said Burke.

"Yes," she said, "he had a heart attack when the police came to arrest him."

"Too bad," said Burke. "There are some people here who wanted to talk to him, but since you're here, maybe the matter could be rectified."

"That's what I'm here for," she said, "where can I find this person?" she asked.

"Don't worry about it, someone will contact you in due time. You're staying at the Crystal Palace, aren't you?" he asked.

"Yes," she replied.

"Good, then someone will come to see you there," Burke said smiling as he led her out of the office and through to the outside.

Christiana preceded through the gate without looking back. It's the first time in her life she was going to do something illegal. But the commissioner had told her about the diamond smuggling ring operating out of Nassau, remnants of the old Burkowitz people and some new ones, and doing it was in the line of her new duties.

Dready was already sitting in the car waiting for her. He had flown in a couple of days earlier from Jamaica and rented a car.

"So what happened?" he asked as he placed the transmission into forward and drove out of the airport.

"I've met the TB in the letter to Celia Backstrum," she said in a whisper. "He's the customs officer, and his real name is Tullis Burke. The cover sent by commissioner Dillon seemed to work."

"Good," replied Dready. "They are now aware of you and somehow will feel confident of your loyalty through your father."

"Maybe so," she said, "but I will never trust anybody. Look what a simple phone call can produce; I was able to make contact and walked freely through the customs, unchecked."

"Good, it means that we're getting closer and probably will get to meet the people at the top soon," said Dready smiling.

"This fellow, Tullis Burke, told me that someone will come to the hotel to see me at the appropriate time," she said.

"When?" he asked.

"He didn't say, only that someone will come," she explained.

"Okay," said Dready, "we'll have to hang tight at the hotel until then. Are you afraid?"

"Yes I am," she answered, "but I am capable and still want to find out who is using and killing those students."

There was a long pause.

"That's good," he said, "but be very careful not to get overly excited. Just be calm and observant," he instructed.

Dready manoeuvred his car along the JFK Drive to Blake Road and onto the dual carriage-way towards cable beach. He handed her the key to the room, quickly kissed and dropped her off in front of the Crystal Palace Hotel. He aimed the rented car in the direction of Gladstone Road to get to Carmichael Road, an area that tourists are warned to stay away from; but seeing that he didn't consider himself a tourist and the fact that he was going to see his friend Earl, he wasn't afraid. He was comfortable going into the Carmichael village area because a lot of Jamaican Rastifarians also lived there, amongst the local ones.

He gave thought to Earl, whom he met on his last visit to Nassau while assisting Bernard Graves and the Nassau police in investigating a case of Jamaican ganja growers in the Bahamas, and struck up a friendship with him. He had hired Earl as a permanent taxi driver for doing his travels around the islands, land and sea.

He had asked Earl to set up an introduction with a man named Chrittendon, whom Commissioner Dillon told him was the RCMP's Nassau connection, and who he believed was involved in the business, for a ganja sale between Chrittendon and a man named Wakefield. He wanted that information in a hurry, and anxiously wanted to know how well that went and if Earl had carried out another function he had requested.

Dillon told him that no one had seen Chrittendon for some time now, although his code is still being used to transmit to Canada, and it was his belief that Chrittendon might be dead and someone else is using his password. It was Dready's duty to find out if that is true and if so, find out who, why and for what reason. Well now that the question of diamond smuggling came into the picture he was more anxious to know than ever.

"There must be someone else at the top. Nobody has seen Chrittendon for awhile now, and I must find out wh,," he reasoned.

He drove down the dirt road until he was near the beach, parked the car on the side of the road like the Bahamians do, and entered the little restaurant. There he saw Earl at a table and approach him.

"Hey brother Earl!" he said as he sat. "What's up?"

"Hey Dready!" said Earl. "When did you get into town? I thought you'd have called me first?"

"I tried to, but your woman said you don't live there anymore," said Dready. "Problems at home?"

"Yeah man, lots," said Earl. "I man is in hiding because the damn police is looking for me, man, and I'll either be shot or be going to prison if they find me."

"So tell me why?" Dready prodded.

"Well, I went to make the sale to Mr. Wakefield at a house on Coral Harbour road near the beach as planned, but some boys from Andros burst in on us, and I man had to run. I jumped into the sea and swam under the pier to hide."

"What did they want?" asked Dready.

"The stuff and money," said Earl.

"What about Wakefield?" asked Dready.

"Oh man!" said Earl, "he tried to run also, but fell and hit his head on the concrete floor. When the boys left, I came up to check him and he was dead."

Earl removed a newspaper from his pocket and showed him a picture of himself on the front page.

"Somebody saw me going into the fucking house and gave my description to the police, they looked up my records and think I did it, and here I am wanted for a murder I didn't commit."

"Oh shit!" said Dready. "Then you didn't get the ID?"

"Yes I did, I have it right here," said Earl, handing over the document. "But what can you do for me? I'm a wanted man now."

"Don't worry my friend," said Dready, "I will speak to the Chief and they will get it sorted out."

"Please do," said Earl, "because I cannot go to my woman's house for a fuck. They are watching her house like hawks, looking for me."

Dready opened the wallet and took out the papers.

"What's happening here?" said Dready. "This man had two ID's. One is for a Bartholomew Wakefield and the other is for a Smithers; a Austin J. Smithers. I'll have to find out why and which one he was using to deal with Chrittendon."

"I don't know that and I don't care," said Earl. "My arse is in a sling and all I want is to be off the hook with the fucking police."

There was a long pause.

"Maybe he was an imposter like Burkowitz was. With false face and papers. I wonder who might know for sure?" said Dready, totally ignoring Earl's concerns.

"I don't know and I don't give a shit either!" said Earl abrasively, "but I could show you the man he was with that night."

"Hey Earl!" said Dready. "Do you think it was a Mr. Charles Chrittendon?"

"Maybe, but no, I don't rightly know," said Earl, "I don't know anybody named Charles Chrittendon. I will show him to you and you can decide."

"Okay," said Dready, "pick me up tomorrow about mid-day and take me to him."

"No I won't," said Earl.

"Why not?" asked Dready.

"Because he only comes out at night to gamble at the Casino on Paradise Island and I'm not going there in the day light, I might get arrested," answered Earl.

Dready looked at Earl and saw that he was serious.

"Fine," said Dready, "I'll straighten out things with the Chief tomorrow morning and we'll go there in the evening and you can identify him then."

"Sure can," replied Earl. "If you get them pricks off my back, I'll show you anything you want to see."

As Dready was about to leave, a thought flashed across his mind so he stopped and sat back down.

"Have you ever done business with a woman named Amanda Bachstrum?" asked Dready. "She has a gift shop on Market street,"

"No, never done business with her, but I know her daughters," said Earl.

"She has daughters? How many and what's their names?" asked Dready excitedly.

"Yes, she has three daughters," said Earl, looking into space. "Bernice, Rosita and Tanya. The one named Tanya got married to a Jamaican man named McKenzie; but when they divorced she moved to Miami and was living there when she was shot. She moved back to Nassau after leaving the hospital and is now a blackjack dealer on Paradise Island."

"Where are the others?" asked Dready.

"Bernice married to a man whose name I don't know and lives somewhere in Toronto, Canada. Rosita married a mad fellow named Harvey Ambross and lives in New York. Amanda also has two sons, Hubert and Ralph; but the one named Ralph disappeared some years ago, and the other one lives here," Earl replied.

"Disappeared? When and where?" Dready asked and at the same time wondered if Earl knew about Celia Bachstrum in Toronto.

"I don't know, but some say he died in the boat that sank near Florida with his father Zenon and a couple of shady people, and others say he was in South America," said Earl.

"What kind of shady people are you talking about?" asked Dready.

"You know the kind," said Earl. "The ones that do my kind of business but on a larger scale. The big boys from State Side and

South America."

"Oh, I see," replied Dready, "them boys. What about the other son?"

"He is still here, and the word on the street is that he has taken over from his father Zenon," said Earl. "His name is Hubert and he is a ruthless individual to deal with."

"I see," said Dready, "he kills people then?"

"You bet," said Earl.

"Okay," said Dready, "see you tomorrow."

This time when Dready got up from the table, he quickly exited the place.

Dready left Earl and sped back to the hotel. He parked his rented car in the back parking lot, away from the others. He entered the hotel through a side door and hung around the casino for a little while, then when he felt he wasn't being watched he rushed off to the elevator and to his room. Christiana was laying in bed watching television when he got there.

"What's up Doc?" she greeted him. "Did you find your friend?"

"Yes, and things aren't copasetic as I believed it would," he replied. removing his clothes. "The man I was to make contact with was accidentally killed and the friend I went to see is being sought for murder. My problem is even more complicated because the dead man had two identifications and I don't know which one he was using to do business, and my friend is afraid to show his face in public."

"That's easily checked darling," she said throwing her arms around his neck. "We could call Graves in Jamaica, who will call the Chief here and explain everything. He will give us the information we need tomorrow."

"Very good dear, I will call him in the morning," said Dready.

"Better yet, call him at home right now and you'll get it by morning," she added.

Dready made the call to Graves home in Jamaica.

"Hello Bernard, Winston here," said Dready into the phone, "I have two problems."

"Name them," said Graves.

"I have a man that is vital to the operation here," said Dready, "who is wanted for a murder which he didn't commit. It was an accident and I want him free to take me places."

"Done," said Graves, "give me his name; and what's the next one?"

"His name is Earl Monroe; and could you call the Chief of police here to get me some information on a man named Wakefield or Smithers."

"Sure can," said Graves. "Donald Daniels and I go back a ways. What room are you in? I'll have him call you right away."

Dready gave him the room number and hang up the phone.

The half hour wait seemed long to Dready but he waited. He sprang out of bed to answer the phone as it rang.

"Hello!" he anxiously said into the receiver.

"This is Chief Daniels, are you Winston Perkins the reporter?"

"Yes sir, that's me," answered Dready.

"Commissioner Graves in Jamaica called and asked me to assist you in any way I could. Why do you want information on Mr. Wakefield?"

"Well sir, his name came up in a investigative report I'm doing for a magazine article, and I wanted to check it out before I go to press."

Chief Daniels told Dready all about Mr Wakefield.

"He came to the Bahamas some years ago from St Lucia with his wife and a daughter, and stayed," said Daniels. "He was a businessman and travelled regularly throughout the Caribbean and since he was never in trouble with the law here or anywhere else, we allowed him to stay. He died recently, in what appeared as a botched up burglary."

"What happened to his wife?" asked Dready.

"The last I heard she went back to Germany after their

divorce," said Daniels, "and the daughter is living in the States some-where. He married an English girl half his age and they lived on the far-out island of Great Inagua, in a town named Mathews town."

"How did he die?" asked Dready.

"He was hit on the head after he was poisoned," said Daniels, "and we think it was murder."

"Which one killed him?" asked Dready.

"The poison," said Daniels. "According to the autopsy report, the clunk on the head wasn't strong enough to kill him, but the poison cut his stomach all to hell while he was asleep."

"Why would anyone want to knock an almost dead man over the head?" asked Dready, "unless they weren't the one to administrate the substance."

"I don't know that, but they wanted him dead for some odd reason," said Daniels.

"Do you think you have the killer?" asked Dready.

"Not yet," said Daniels, "but I thought we had a local hustler named Earl Monroe, until Mr Graves call from Jamaica to say he was working for you. He will be taken off the wanted list tomorrow."

"Thank you Chief Daniels," said Dready, "Earl and I will definitely come in to see you tomorrow."

After a pause Dready thought about something and asked,

"One other thing Chief, what name did Mr Wakefield use coming into Nassau?"

"Wakefield of course," replied Daniels, "well that's what was on his ticket and in his passport."

"What about a Mr Smithers? Can you tell me anything about him?" Dready asked.

"Not much," said Daniels, "he's a very mysterious English businessman; comes and goes frequently and flies his own plane. But I could get you that information in the morning."

"Thank you Chief, I'll come in to see you tomorrow about the other matter," said Dready, "good night."

Dready realized that Donald Daniels wasn't cognisant that he was the cover Graves used in their last investigation of the ganja deal in Nassau, and didn't make him any the wiser.

He told Christiana the entire conversation before they made love and went to sleep.

They were up early in the morning. He went to the beach for a quick dip before breakfast. Then he went to the desk, made a phone call to order food from room-service then later joined her in the room.

"I'll have to leave you alone today love," he said. "I have some business to conduct and we can't be seen together, because that could blow the entire investigation."

"That's fine, I have to wait here for my contact anyway," she replied, "see you later."

They kissed as he prepared to leave the room.

"Hey!" said Christiana, "It's been two days and nobody came. Do you think they smell our sting?"

"I don't think so love," answered Dready, "they're checking to make sure you're not the police or being followed by the police."

"What are we going to do today?" Christiana asked.

"Well, firstly I have to meet with Chief Daniels to straighten out Earl's little problem, then we'll be going to one of the far-out islands. I think the man I'm looking for lives there," said Dready, "and we'll have to check for another on Paradise Island after supper."

They kissed again and he sneaked out of the door.

The short bus ride down town took twenty minutes; somebody had run over a dog and the traffic snarled. He sat patiently until the bus reached the corner of East Street where he got off. A short walk up the road brought him in front of the station, where he entered the police headquarters.

"Chief Daniels please," he said to the desk clerk.

The clerk looked at him scornfully then picked-up the phone.

"Excuse me sir," said the clerk, "there's a Rasta man here to see you."

In a short minute Daniels was standing at the doorway.

"Come in Dready," said Daniels stretching out his hand for a shake, "Graves told me all about you."

They entered the office and Daniels closed the door behind them.

"Now, we have to talk about your friend Earl Monroe, right?" said Daniels.

"Right sir," replied Dready, "he is innocent of......"

"That's all taken care of," said Daniels interrupting him, "he's off the wanted list. But what about this Wakefield fellow?"

"Well, as I told you, his name came up in an investigation I am doing for my magazine and I wanted to know if he was related to a Wakefield I'd met in St Lucia."

Daniels shook his head negatively.

"I don't really know. Ever since he came to Nassau, he has been clean and never got mixed up in anything going on here, so we let him stay.

"Well, I could be wrong," said Dready, "but I get curious whenever a person of his status gets poisoned and banged over the head for no apparent reason. It looks like murder to me."

"And to us also," said Daniels. "I think he must have been mixed-up with some of those shady people from South America who have been coming in here of late. The pirates of the Caribbean. The only problem is, we don't have enough police to monitor them. Just like Mr Smithers, the fellow you asked about last night. Now, there's a shady one for you. He flies in and out like Santa Claus in the middle of the night and very seldom seen in the crowds."

"Have you a picture of him?" asked Dready.

"No, we are never lucky to have a camera at hand whenever he is around," said Daniels. "If you get lucky and find one, please share it with us, will you?"

Dready assured him that he would and left the office.

The short walk to the Bahamas Yacht club took ten minutes. Dready took a seat at the counter and recognized that he had time to have a coffee before signalling Earl that he was there. When he did, Earl pretended as though he was picking up fares as normal and approached Dready. They talked a little, then Dready accompanied him to the boat and got in along with the six other people. Earl steered his boat out to sea and aimed the bow towards the far-out islands. The other passengers sat in their seats while Dready sat beside Earl as he drove.

"You'll never guess what happened last night," said Earl. "A man chartered my boat to take himself and five others to Alice town in Biminis and then to Eleuthra. We got there and they spent about an hour talking to some people, they seemed to be arguing about something I don't know what. They angrily left and we headed towards Eleuthra. Not even a mile out, another boat pulled along side and a fellow started shooting at us."

"Did anybody got hurt?" asked Dready.

"No, it seemed the shooter didn't really know what he was doing, he fired at the wrong target and missed. But It scared the living shit out of the people in the boat."

"Could you recognize the gunman if you see him again?" asked Dready.

"Sure could; he's a friend of my brother Garth, and I'm gonna kick his fucking arse when I see him. But that will be later."

Dready thought about it for a moment.

"Why would your brother's friend be shooting at you?" asked Dready.

"He wasn't shooting at me," said Earl, "he was shooting at somebody on my boat. You see he works for one of the men we went to see on Bimini and I'm sure he was sent to kill the man who had the argument with him."

"Did you report it to the police?" asked Dready.

"No!" shouted Earl.

"What about your passengers?" asked Dready.

"No, they didn't want it reported either; they didn't want the police involved so things were left untold."

After Earl let the passengers off on Crooked Island, the rest of the ride to Long Island seemed long to Dready, he was very anxious to reach there because he was petrified of the seas, even though he had a life preserver on. He doesn't mind flying, but something about being on the water bothered him. He laid on one of the bench seats and gave thoughts to what he wanted to see and the questions he wanted to ask Mr Smithers.

"If he really was Smithers, and there is a definite connections between himself, Wakefield, Karlheinz Bass, Ivan Burkowitz and maybe even Arthur Collins, then the case of diamond smuggling is really from the old days and they are utilising the young people to carry it to Canada," he thought.

To distract his mind, he got up to look at the basket of fish Earl had gotten from a friend on the last island stop.

"Hey Earl!" he shouted. "Why did you buy all those fish from that fellow? you can't eat them all?"

"No I don't," said Earl, "I buy them for two reasons; first to help out the people there with some money, and secondly for my disabled mother."

"What kind are they?" he asked.

"I will show them to you when we get back to Nassau," said Earl.

Dready was intrigued with the colours of the fish and couldn't wait to get back to Nassau. He got up from the seat and began searching through the basket. Earl told him the names of every fish, as he held them up.

"That one is an octopus," said Earl, "imagine it has one brain and eight legs and can use each one independently, yet a human has two brains and some people cannot move one arm without moving the other."

Dready smiled at Earl's analogy and laid back on the bench to

61

resume his thoughts and of the ride to the far out islands.

"Mmmm, Octopus," he thought. "One brain and independent arms eh?"

Christiana sat alone at the breakfast table wondering what was happening to Winston. She was feeling a little anxious being alone and frustrated that the contact person hadn't come. She wanted to make a phone call to Jamaica to enquire of her son's health, but that would be risky because someone might overhear her conversation and blow her cover. She began to eat only to feel a shadow standing over her. She looked up to see Tullis Burke and another man standing there.

"Good morning Miss Felscher," said Burke, "I sincerely hope you've been having a wonderful time in Nassau. May we sit down?"

"Certainly, by all means," she replied indicating to the chairs.

"Christiana, meet Mr Hubert Bachstrum, the son of Zenon Bachstrum who was a very dear friend of your father," said Burke.

"Pleased to meet you sir," she said extending her hand for a neglected shake. "Are you the father of Celia Bachstrum?"

"Yes," said Hubert, "she's a wonderful girl, do you know her well?"

"Not really, I met her once at a party in Toronto through a mutual friend, but I haven't seen her since," she answered.

Christiana scrutinized Bachstrum's demeanour carefully to see his reaction, but there wasn't any. Hubert was a well dressed, medium height, clean shaven, slightly balding man in his late forties or early fifties. His perfectly even teeth seem to glitter whenever he smiled although his penetrating steely grey, tan-brown eyes, which seemed like laser beams, never seemed to waver from the object they was trained on.

"Nice to meet you," he said. "So you're the daughter of dear old Ludwig Felscher, eh? How's the old fart doing these days?"

"He's dead sir," she replied. "He died last February from a

heart attack in Canada. I presume it happened because of the news about his friend Karlheinz Bass and the others in Jamaica."

"Who told you about the death of Karlheinz?" Hubert asked.

"My father did," she replied. "You see I was at home when the police came to arrest him and......."

"Okay," he said. "you can do the business for me. All that is required is for you to take the package to Toronto, and someone will contact you. They will then give you what is coming to you at that time, and if we will require your service in the future that same person will contact you."

"What if I get caught at the airport? Whom shall I contact?" she asked.

"You'll take the rap and do the time in prison without any mention of anybody here. We will make sure that your family is taken care of financially."

"Do you know where I live," she asked to be certain.

"Yes we do, Bowmansville; and we have a key to the house also. Your father gave us one many years ago and if the locks are changed, we'll find a way in," said Hubert.

Christiana realized that he was talking about her dead father's house and not hers. It seemed that Hubert was not aware that it was she who arranged Ludwig's arrest.

"Okay," she said smiling, "I hope nothing will go wrong."

"Good; Tullis here will come to see you some time on Friday with the package and he will give you specific instructions at that time. I want you to follow them precisely and behave as normal as can be."

"Will someone be escorting me on the trip?" she asked.

"Maybe," said Hubert as he quickly got up and left her alone to eat. She waited until they were totally out of sight before leaving for her room.

"Well," she thought, "I've met Mr. Bachstrum and Tullis Burke, and is certain of their rolls in this diamond smuggling thing.

I will have to tell Winston and have him call Dillon in Toronto to prepare for my arrival at the airport."

She sat by the window quietly thinking about the fact that Mr. Bachstrum does believe she still lived in her father's house in Bowmanville. She reflected on Ludwig's reaction when she brought her brothers to witness the things she had intended to confront him with, and his denials and feeble excuses for lying to them about their mother's death. She smiled to remember the look on his face when they opened the trunk which was kept locked and stored in the basement for all those years. This time she laughed aloud.

"Poor old Ludwig didn't realize that the diamonds from Lyle Alexander's coffin, which he thought was safely stored in his trunk, was gone."

She wondered where they were taken and by whom. She raked her mind trying to recall who visited their home and when, but to no avail. She knew that it had to be someone of his friends who had visited their home, but couldn't decipher who. She finally gave up and fell asleep watching some ignorant love story on television, waiting for Winston to come back.

Earl, being an expert boat's man, knew just where to park his carriage.

"Here's a good place to dock," he said, "nobody will ever think of looking for intruders here."

"Why not?" asked Dready.

"It's remote and rocky and a good walk to the house from here," Earl said smiling at Dready, "and if you can't make it up the hill, I will find you a donkey."

Dready smiled. He was in good shape and didn't mind the walk up the hill to the house. When they got close to the house, Earl signalled for him to get down on the ground. They surveyed the house and when it was assumed that nobody was home they curiously approached it. Dready tried the glass door and it easily slid open, he peeked in and softly entered and tiptoed around looking into every room, then he went upstairs closely followed by Earl. He came upon a partially opened door, and could hear someone moaning inside, he slowly pushed it open to see a naked woman laying on the bed masturbating. He waved to Earl and pointed for him to also see. They both watched until she had completed her orgasm, then knocked on the door.

"Who the hell are you?" she shouted in a nervous English accent, anxiously grabbing for her dressing gown. "What the fuck are you doing in my house?" she asked angrily.

"Are you Mrs Wakefield?" asked Dready.

"Yes," she replied and asked; "who the hell are you? I'll call the police."

"We are friends of Mr. Wakefield and would like to see him," said Dready.

"Well, he's not here, he's......." she began but stopped. She quickly put on her gown and brushed her hair.

"When do you expect him back?" asked Dready.

"I don't know where he is," she nervously answered, "and if I did know when he was coming home I wouldn't be doing this alone now, would I?"

"I don't know that and I don't care," said Dready, "all I want is to see Mr. Wakefield. Has he been gone long?"

"I haven't seen him for a few days now," she answered, "but he does this sort of thing so many times, I really don't have a clue as to his whereabouts. Will you be staying here long?"

"No," replied Dready, "I will have to be back in Nassau this evening."

"Shit," she said, "and I needed a screw."

"Not from me," said Dready, "I'm married, but Earl here might help you out if you ask him nicely."

She smiled and began walking towards Earl, Dready waited until she kissed Earl before he exit the room, closing the door behind him.

He realized that she didn't know Wakefield was dead; and cared less, now that she was about to have a sex with Earl. For that reason he knew that he had the freedom to roam the entire house. He searched many shelves and cupboard draws looking for anything incriminating. Finally he came upon a wall safe behind a picture and began trying to open it, but without success. He sat at the baby grand piano with the intent on waiting for the woman to complete her interlude with Earl to get the combination.

He began to play the piano, only to find that it was badly out of tune with a few notes that didn't make any sound at all, and closed it. He was about to leave the room when something struck his mind and he returned to the piano, opened the lid and looked inside to see a large book lying on the strings. He picked it up and began leafing through it, when he noticed one of the pages were bent at the edge and turned to that page. It was an article on composer Bach. The author spoke about the place, date of birth and death of the great musician. He observed that someone had circled the page number 76. He found some paper and a pen in a desk drawer and began playing around with the numbers of the musician's date of birth and death, also the page number. He wrote a series of combinations, then something struck his mind.

"Ah, the safe combination, he whispered."

Quickly, he went to the safe to try out his theory, somehow he hit the right combination on the forth try and the door opened. There wasn't much inside except a stack of money and a small box with some jewellery. He examined them and was about to put them back when he saw a piece of paper with some names on it. He was about to look at it when suddenly he heard the woman and Earl laughing and giggling coming in his direction. Quickly he closed the safe door and put the paper in his pocket.

"That was good," she said hanging on to Earl's arm, "do you have to leave this evening? Please stay, please say you will."

Earl, who seemed satisfied with his performance looked at Dready.

"No, we can't stay," said Dready looking at the woman. "We have things to do in Nassau; but if Earl wants to come back tomorrow, he's free to do so."

"Ohhh," she said turning to Earl, "then I will see you tomorrow?"

"What about your husband?" asked Earl.

"Don't worry about him," she said waving her hand in the air, "I can't depend on him anymore. He leaves me alone in this God dammed house so many times, I'm beginning to think that he has another woman in town somewhere."

"How often does he do that," asked Dready.

"Almost every week," she said.

"Where does he go; do you know?" enquired Dready.

"Not really," she replied, "but every time that Trinidadian comes into town, he leave me for business. I think they are lovers."

"Is he a Homo?" asked Dready.

"Homosexual? I don't think so, but I would never put anything past that man, he's capable of anything."

She paused for a breath, then offered and they accepted her invitation for a cup of tea.

"If we are going to talk as friends, allow me to introduce myself," she said, stretching out her hand to Dready, "I am Judith Wakefield the lonely woman of this castle, in which my husband keeps me locked, but my friends call me Judy."

"I'm Dready Winston," he responded and saw the questioning look in her eyes, "just Dready, you know, for my locks."

"No last name?" she asked.

"Yes, but it might be trouble for you to know it," he said.

Oh, I see, the underworld eh?" she stated, "well it's nice to meet you."

"Were you his first wife?" asked Dready.

"No, he was once married to a German woman named Althea, who had divorced her husband for him. He treated her badly and

67

when she got the opportunity to, she took off to America with her daughter and got divorced."

"Did you ever speak to her before you married him?" asked Dready.

"Yes, we met before for teas and things," she replied, "but I didn't care what he was. He had the money and I wanted a place to live."

Dready realized that Judith, like some European women, who comes to the Caribbean to meet men that would support them, was willing to do anything with anybody to make that a reality.

"So when do you expect him home?" Dready asked, repeating a previous question.

"I don't know!"she barked. "As I told you, he is a very com -plex man and goes when, where and with whom he feels like. I don't know his business and I don't ask. All I know is, he has some gambling friends with whom he is acquainted at the Paradise Island Casino, and if you want to find him you will have to go there."

"I'm sure you've seen many of his friends when they come here to this house, and I'm sure you have entertained many of them in the past," said Dready.

"I did," she replied, "but their names I cannot recall."

Dready gave a little chuckle as he said,

"My people want their money for their cocaine and I'm sent here to collect it," he said. "I really don't care who pays, but some-body will have to, one way or another. All this time you've been telling me lies that you don't know where he is and I'm getting pissed off. I am ready to hang you upside down in the sea and watch as the sharks eat you in little bites at a time."

"No! No! No!" she shouted in a nervous tone, "I really don't know where he is and what's his business."

"Then you'd better come up, and quickly, with some names and description of his friends, otherwise you'll be shark's dinner."

Judith was becoming very nervous so Dready signalled Earl to come closer.

"Tie her up good," he instructed, "and stuff a rag into her mouth so that nobody can hear her scream when we throw her into the water."

"Wait a minute!" said Judith nervously. There was a trickle of tears in her eyes. "He has a book locked in the bedroom safe, maybe if you could open it you could get some names from it."

Dready felt sorry for her but he had to behave in that way to be convincing. He followed her to the bedroom to the safe which was located behind a vanity.

"Where is the combination Judith?" he asked in a demanding tone of voice.

"I don't know, he never let me near it," she said crying.

Quickly, Dready got the paper from his pocket on which he had worked out the combination for the first safe, and sure enough the two used the same numbers. He opened it and saw bundles of money and the book. He looked through the book and found some names with notes, dates and the transactions performed for them.

"This will do," said Dready, "but we will still have to feed you to the sharks because you will warn him as soon as we leave you alone."

"No I won't," she said, begging for her life, "I promise not to tell him or anybody else of your presence in this house. Take the money, take anything you want, just let me live."

Dready looked at Earl and he quickly grabbed the parcels of money and stuffed them into a plastic duffel bag.

"Consider this as a partial deposit on the payment he was supposed to make," said Dready, "I will be back to collect the rest later. Furthermore, I will be cutting your phone line so that you cannot alert them."

"That's fine by me," she said, "but it would be better if Earl stayed with me. Could you Earl?"

"He could come back if he wants to," said Dready, winking at

Earl.

Earl quickly walked over to her and placed a kiss on Judith lips.

"I will be back later," he said, "just keep the door open and the pussy worm."

They got to the boat and sped off in the direction of Nassau.

"Did you get what you wanted?" asked Earl.

"Don't know as yet," replied Dready, "I'm going to check this out first. You go back to the house to keep an eye on her."

"What about the money?" asked Earl.

"I'll decide later," answered Dready.

As they sped towards Nassau, Dready noticed a few ships and speed boats malingering in the waters.

"What are those ships doing out there?" he asked.

"Could be anything," answered Earl.

"Pirates of the Caribbean?" asked Dready.

Suddenly Earl cut the speed of his craft, set the auto pilot to cruise and turned to Dready.

"Where the hell did you hear of such people?" he asked.

"From Chief Daniels," said Dready. "Are there many in these waters?"

"Literally thousands," replied Earl. "My friend, these new breed of pirates have hijacked ships with their speed boats and killed many for the goods they carry. They are people from many walks of life and colour, and they are ruthless in their dealings."

"Just like those friends of your brother?" asked Dready.

"Yes," said Earl, "and they would kill anybody for a dollar."

"Are you one of them?" asked Dready.

"No man!" said Earl. "I am a man of integrity. My business is to transport tourists to good fishing spots and to show them romantic out of the way places. But some times I do odd jobs for some shady people."

"Like what?" asked Dready.

"Like picking up things from other islands and taking people to meet people in some very secluded parts of my country," said Earl.

"Did it ever occur to you that you were doing something illegal?" asked Dready.

"Yes man," said Earl. "But I never killed anyone doing it."

"Then why are you doing it?" asked Dready.

"Strictly for the money," said Earl. "Look brother Dready; I am a survivor and is wise enough to know when it spells trouble, and to get my arse away from those who are trouble. In all the years as a sailor, I never hijacked anyone but seen many and know many of the pirates, like my brother's friends. There are white ones from Europe, Chinese and Indian from Asia. The Caribbean ones now want a piece of the action and will stop at nothing to get it."

"What are they dealing in?" asked Dready.

"Drugs, guns, diamonds, gold, women and American dollar bills," he replied.

Dready realized that Earl knew much more and wondered why he didn't tell it to Chief Daniels.

"Have you told this to the police?" asked Dready.

Earl laughed.

"My friend," he said, "there is a lot for you to learn. The Caribbean has become a new world, with young and old people of yesterday, today and tomorrow creating history with their modern instruments; you can either join them or live within their sphere without involvement."

"You said that you know many of the pirates personally, right?" said Dready.

"Right," replied Earl.

"You haven't spoken to the police about them, right?"

"Right," said Earl. "And I'm not going to either."

"Why not?"

"Because I need to stay alive, and the police cannot protect me," said Earl.

Dready gave thoughts to Earl's words.

"Maybe you could introduce me to some," said Dready. "I would really like to meet them."

"Mmmm, Maybe," replied Earl as he returned to his driving.

It was almost night when Earl dropped him off at the docks, gave him the bag of money and quickly turned the boat back in the direction they came from. Dready smiled as he watched the craft slowly drift from his view knowing that Earl's intention was to keep Judith occupied while he checked out the names in the book.

"A dedicated citizen," whispered Dready.

By the time he got to the hotel, he had read all the contents of the book and realized that Mr. Wakefield was a different person from Mr Smithers and that Smithers was alive and well somewhere.

He got to the hotel and quickly rushed to the room to check for Christiana.

"Hello darling," she shouted from the bathroom, "did you have any luck?"

"Yes I did," he shouted back, "and you?"

"Yes, I was contacted this morning by Tullis Burke and a man named Hubert Bachstrum," she said as she came out to greet him.

Dready recognized the name as one in the Wakefield book.

"What does he want?" asked Dready.

"He wants me to carry a shipment to Toronto on the Tuesday afternoon Air Canada flight, only he won't tell me who my contact will be until I get on the plane."

"That's okay love," he said, "I will be at the airport to see the person, then I will alert commander Dillon of the flight and he will take it from there. Then when that is over, you can catch the flight back to Jamaica."

"That's a great idea," she said. "And what about you, what did you find?"

Dready gave her the book and she began reading some of the

entries.

"Oh my God!" she exclaimed. "Look at some of the names here. Peter McKenzie, Arthur Collins, Barbara Smith, Patricia and Lilly Green, Ivan Burkowitz\Mitchell, Zenon Bachstrum, Hubert Bachstrum, the son of a bitch who came to see me, Austin Smithers, Harvey Ambross, Karlheinz Bass and Venrece Alexander. What is this a roster?"

"You might call it that," replied Dready, "and if you notice there is a tick mark beside all those names."

"Yes," she said, "they are all dead or in prison, except Dad. Venrece Alexander, my father. Do you think he is still mixed up in this smuggling thing?"

"I'm not sure at this time, but if he is and have been telling us lies......" said Dready, as he was interrupted by Christiana.

"......I would be very upset with him and would lock his arse up for it," she said angrily.

"Good, but don't jump to conclusion as yet," said Dready removing the rest of his clothes, "he might have been on that list for what he did for them in the past. Now turn to page 37 and tell me what you see."

Christiana turned to the suggested page and read,

"Ralph Bachstrum, Geologist died in jungle of Venezuela or Guyana, wife Sandra marry a man in New York. Frazier Hendicott, the son of Albert Hendicott, married Sasha and lives in Toronto. His niece Zena lived with them until she was killed. Hubert Bachstrum, the man in the Caribbean. He found out that his wife Elta was having it off with Zenon. They both died when the boat sank killing Zenon Harry Mason and Austin Smithers. His daughter Celia was killed in Toronto so was Mason's daughter Salina. Tanya McKenzie-Bass, divorced from Peter, shot in Miami and is now a dealer at the casino. Amanda Bachstrum still owns the gift shop on Market street and does quite a business for Hubert. Althea Bass the ex wife of Peter Bass and ex wife of Bartholomew Wakefield, returned from Germany to marry Rupert Reynolds the orange farmer, but found him already married to someone else. He still works for them."

There was a long pause.

"What do you think?" Dready asked with a broad smile on his face.

"I think this person was keeping a diary for the purpose of self preservation," she said, "and is hoping to get to the top eventually, by blackmail or any means necessary."

"Maybe so," said Dready, "or maybe they were working for the law and got discovered."

"You mean Chrittendon?" she asked.

"Yes," replied Dready, "I think he was using those dead people's identification to keep within the group and was found out, and killed."

"Then he was passing off as Wakefield and Smithers?" she said. "It must have been hard for him to be the three people at the same time."

"Probably was, but now we'll never know," said Dready, "although there's someone who is the head, still not mentioned. It has to be someone who knows the RCMP's codes to keep them from finding out about Chrittendon's murder and someone who understand police work."

"Arthur Collins?" she asked. "But he's in prison, is he not?"

"Maybe so," said Dready, "but somehow we'll find out."

"Imagine, Althea returned to marry Rupert Reynolds," she said. "I wonder if he is Robert Reynolds father?"

"Maybe," said Dready, "I can always ask Earl."

"Do that," she said, "it might lead to somewhere."

Dready made the call to commander Dillon explaining his find and the connections that were made.

"Excellent," said Dillon, "you should be able to wrap this up soon."

"I am not sure about that as yet sir," he said, "but I do have the feeling that your man Chrittendon was murdered a few days ago."

"What! Are you sure?" shouted Dillon. "It cannot be my man

74

Chrittendon, we got a confirmed coded communication from him only yesterday."

"Could you fax it to me at the hotel sir? I would like to see it personally."

"I will do that tonight at about ten thirty," said Dillon, "go to the office to receive it. Make sure it was him and not someone else using our codes."

"Yes sir, and thank you for the information," said Dready, "I will be at the office waiting for it after I speak to Captain Morrow on the details of Christiana's arrival in Toronto."

"Goodbye Winston," said Dillon in an anxious tone, "keep me posted."

He lay for a few seconds then he made the call to Captain Morrow giving him the details of Christiana's arrival in Toronto.

"I will call you as soon as her flight leaves here," he told Morrow, "then you can have your people check the other passenger for any connections and by then she will have a location to take the stuff."

"Maybe we should bug the house just in case they choose to meet her there instead of at the airport," replied Morrow.

'Good idea," said Dready, "but be sure that she is covered at all times, I don't want her to be alone with anyone at anytime."

"We will do just that," said Morrow, "goodnight."

Both Dready and Christiana laid on the bed discussing the ramifications of their task and realized that there are some degree of danger in it.

"Darling," said Christiana, "I hope nothing goes wrong, because you wouldn't be there to assist me. Anyway I am sure I could take care of it."

Dready was worried about the unknown but felt confident that she was capable of defending herself, if it came to that.

It was ten-twenty. He got out of bed and hurried off to the office to get the fax.

"There's a fax coming in from Canada for me can I come in to get it?" Dready asked the attendant.

"Certainly sir," she replied, "come through the side door over there."

He rushed into the office and within a minute the document came through the machine. He took the papers from the attendant and read them. Quickly he thanked her and rushed back to the room to show them to Christiana.

"Look at this," he said pointing a pencil to a line of coded message, "if there is an imposter using police information this line would tell you."

"Why is that so?" she asked.

"Because the word changes every eight hours and they can tell if the person sending the message was under duress or just don't know the changes," replied Dready.

Christiana sat on the bed in disbelief, just looking at Dready.

"How did you know that?" she asked. "You're a reporter, and reporters are not privy to detailed police codes."

"Ahhhh!" replied Dready, "only if that reporter is working directly with the police. Furthermore, I am doing them a favour being here doing this shit," he said trying to alleviate her thoughts

Although Christiana was still curious of his knowledge of the secret police codes, she had no intention of prolonging her inquisition.

"Maybe we should call Chief Daniels for Wakefield's autopsy report," she said, "we could match it to any other that is available. Maybe the British police have something on him and could help us to know more."

Dready, who was in deep thoughts, replied with a nod of his head. She realized that he wasn't about to talk anymore and might fall asleep when she was ready to make love. She quickly jumped into bed, cuddled up into his arms and began fondling him.

"Want another baby already, I see," he said turning to face her.

"Not right now, but it wouldn't hurt to keep in shape," she answered as she threw her leg across his body.

The next morning they were up early because Tullis Burke had told her that he would be coming at 8:30 with the stuff. They both got into the shower together.

"Was there any improvement in our sex last night?" she asked.

"Not really," he replied, "I can see we'll just have to keep practising and probably we'll perfect it before the second child comes along."

Christiana laughed as she began soaping his body.

"I know what you're doing," she said, "you just want to screw in the shower and is telling me that our sex needs improving just for the purpose."

"Maybe," he said grinning.

It didn't take long for them to perform the act under the stimulating sprays of the shower. She felt elated that they both had the same sexual zest as their first time in Jamaica, and proud to have him as her husband.

"I love him," she thought, "although he is a horse trader who never tells me everything."

By the time they concluded their sexual interlude, the phone rang. It was Tullis Burke.

"Hello Miss Felscher," he said, "you were supposed to meet me at my hotel at 8:30 this morning, remember?"

She realized that TB was also a liar, but since she wanted to get the job done there weren't any reason to argue with him. She looked at the clock and realized that she would be late to meet him, and so the hurry to get dressed, began.

"Goodbye darling," she said as she grabbed her overnight bag, kissed Dready knowing that she would not be able to do so at the airport and dashed for the door. She ran across the street to the taxi.

"The Colonial please," she said and got in, "and make it fast."

The driver didn't spare the gas and in a few minutes she got out in front of the hotel door. Quickly she paid the driver and ran to the front desk.

"Mr Burke please," she said in a puff.

"Room 512," said the clerk.

She got off the elevator and looked to see the room was obliquely across from where she was standing. She knocked and he opened it almost instantly. He was wearing a Chinese Ninja dressing gown with a large red dragon on the back. She could see his muscular legs occasionally protruding from the opening and realized that Mr Burke was an attractive man who kept his body in shape.

Behind him, on the sofa, sat a middle aged woman with greying hair rolled up in a bun. Her clothes, looked expensive but didn't fit her properly. Her make up, which seemed to have been applied by a mason or a carpenter, tried desperately to hide the wrinkles and age spots, but without success. Christiana noticed that although the woman was probably in her late sixties, she was sure that she must have been an attractive woman in her younger days.

"Aaaah Christiana," said Burke, welcoming her. He seemed happy to see that she made the effort to be prompt and finally got there. "Come on in and sit, this is Mrs. Althea Ba........., never mind, she is a friend and will show you how to stow the goods, follow her instructions and everything will go perfectly."

Christiana noticed that the woman, who didn't acknowledged her gesture of hello, kept a constant stare on her.

"Did you have breakfast?" asked Tullis taking her bag.

"No, not yet," she answered.

"Well, we will," he said and called the room service.

"Go with Althea and do what she says," said Burke waving his hand.

Althea got up and Christiana followed the silent woman into the bathroom, as suggested by Tullis Burke.

"Take your clothes off ," said Althea, "use the washroom and lay on that table over there."

The woman's husky voice surprised Christiana somewhat, but she obeyed the command and watched as she reached into a cupboard for some rubber gloves and a tube of vaginal cream.

"Take off your panty," said Althea, "and open your legs."

Christiana followed orders and the woman began to lubricate her body parts. She noticed that Althea began to get flushed just preforming what she was doing, which nearly brought her to an orgasm and realized that the woman was an old lesbian. Within a minute, the woman inserted the tube containing the diamonds.

"This might feel uncomfortable for a while," said Althea, "but when you get on the plane you could take it out and reinstall it before getting to Toronto."

"That's fine," said Christiana, "I'm familiar with the procedure. Do you always do this sort of thing?"

"Most of the time, dearie," replied Althea, "maybe you could come to see me when you return to Nassau, I could make life very interesting for you."

No thank you," replied Christiana, "I still do enjoy a man's attention."

Christiana smiled as she put her clothes back and returned to the room.

"Will there be anyone to escort me to Toronto?" she asked.

"Yes," said Burke, who was already dressed and waiting, "the person will meet us at the airport and there I will introduce you both."

They sat to have breakfast while Althea hurriedly left the room.

"Aren't there any special instructions?" asked Christiana.

Burke paused for a long moment contemplating her question.

No," he replied, "but the person on the plane will tell you where to deliver the goods."

She thought about asking some other questions but changed her mind so as not to look suspicious and mess up the operation.

"Let's go," said Burke, "the flight is an hour from now."

He took her bag and they left the room and were out side in a flash.

"Where to Mr Burke?" the taxi driver greeted Burke as they exited the hotel door.

"The airport Samuel," said Burke as they settled into the rear seat.

It was a silent trip to their destination. She watched as Tullis handed the man a wad of money without counting it. They entered the lounge. Tullis walked directly to the ticket counter and spoke to the clerk and within two minutes he returned with a folder and handed it to her. Burke waved and a tall slimly built young man approached them.

"Christiana," said Tullis, "meet Paul Mason; he will be on the flight to Toronto with you."

"Pleased to meet you Paul," said Christiana as she shook hands with the handsome young man, "I hope you have a gun to protect me from any hijacker."

Neither Burke nor Mason found her humour funny although he cracked a faint smile.

"I don't think we will be hijacked," said Mason, "the airlines usually check everyone carefully, they are very particular these days you know."

"So I understand," she said, "but it was only a joke."

Tullis whispered something to Mason and quickly left the airport without saying a word to her.

When the flight was announced, she picked up her bag and began walking towards the gates. Mason quickly joined her and took her arm into his, maybe as a precaution against her running off with the diamonds or as a gesture of friendship. There was only silence as they walked with the crowd to the plane. They found their seats, stored their carry-on bags and got settled for the three hour flight to Canada.

The plane's engines roared and within minutes they were airborne. She sat thinking of the time, a year ago in December, when she was on her flight to Jamaica and met Dready, only this time she wasn't as angry; and sitting beside another black man didn't pose a problem for her now; although she knew that he would be arrested when he got to Toronto.

During all this, Dready, who had to keep his distance from Christiana, had positioned himself at the airport to observe the actions there. He checked all the passengers for possible suspects and saw when Tullis Burke introduced Christiana to a tall, very handsome young black man. He took particular care in observing the man's description, like any good police officer would. When he was sure that they had boarded the plane and watched it take off, he rushed to a pay phone to make the call to captain Morrow in Toronto giving him the full details of the young man.

During the flight, Christiana noticed that Paul Mason seemed relaxed, and realized that he was a regular flyer, and since this was her fifth time on an aeroplane, she thought she should strike up a conversation with Paul to relax herself.

"So tell me Paul," she said trying to open some kind of dialogue with him, "what do you do beside escorting beautiful ladies to Canada?"

Mason, at first, seemed reluctant to talk but maybe the thought of going through this long flight without talking, changed his mind.

"I am an accountant," he said, "my father owns a company in Nassau and I work for him."

"And how often do you travel to Canada?" she asked.

He hesitated in thoughts and when he felt he had an answer for her, he said, "You're a nosey bitch aren't you?" he said, "I think we should just carry-out the requested assignment without these friendly discussions, don't you think?"

Although Christiana felt insulted, she knew that somehow she had to get him to talk to her.

"Well," she said, "I will just have to tell Hubert that I won't be working with you in the future because you refuse to talk to me. It doesn't look natural for two people who are supposed to be friends, not to talk in public."

After a long pause, Paul took a glance at the empty seat beside him and said in a whisper,

"I don't like this business anymore, I want out, but I'm sure they wouldn't allow me to withdraw peacefully."

"Why do you want out?" she prompted him. "There's a lot of money in it for you and the glorification of meeting all those beautiful girls."

He signalled for her to keep her voice down.

"On the surface it might appear to be nice," he said, "but some of my friends are already dead because they wanted out."

"What?" she said, acting surprised to hear, "who got killed? When?"

"There was a boy named Colin McKenzie, we lived near each other and went to the same school together, he was killed in Toronto, then there is Collie-man Reynolds who was killed in Hamilton and it was reported as a suicide. Then there was Celia, Salina and Zena, they also died mysteriously and I don't like it."

"Where did this happen?" Christiana asked.

"In Toronto," replied Paul.

"Oh shit, I'd better be careful then," she said looking at him sidelong. "Who could I turn to for some protection, just in case they have plans to dispose of me also?"

Mason hesitated and contemplated his response carefully.

"There's a man living in Markum, who told me to contact him if things got too rough for me, he is a very good friend of my father, but I am reluctant to do so because he was also involved in the old days with some of the people and now he is playing some kind of a game."

Christiana really wanted Paul to tell her where to find this man, but had to play coy for him to do so.

"You could be right," she said, "but if I'm in trouble he might be the best person to get me out, and maybe you should reconsider, seeing that you're not comfortable with what's happening at this time and wanted out."

"Yes," whispered Paul, "maybe I should."

Christiana realized that she had him convinced so she played another card.

"Do you think he could help me also?" she asked.

"I don't know," Paul replied, "seeing that you're a stranger to him and......"

Christiana quickly glanced around to ensure she wasn't being heard and leaned closer to his ear to say,

"Let me tell you about my father and his friends who were dealing the same business out of Jamaica. My name is Christiana Felscher and my father was Ludwig Felscher," she began and told him a fabricated story about her young life under her father and his gang. By the time the pilot announced their landing in Toronto, she had already got an address in Markum from Paul and the names of the people he knew in Nassau.

When they got to the custom check-out counter, Christiana hung on to Paul's arm like a lover would. She plunked her passport on the counter and even had their bags checked together.

"Are you bringing anything into the country?" asked the officer.

"No," replied Christiana, "only a disease, and that's personal."

"I see," said the officer looking at her passport, "are you being facetious Miss Felscher?"

"Not really," said Christiana, "but you people always give citizens who are lucky to have a good racial relationship, the hassle."

The officer seemed to get agitated by her remark and quickly wrote on her form and signalled for an officer to take them to be searched.

"See what I mean," she said to Paul. "Whenever a white woman is in the company of a handsome young black man as you, it brings out the racism in those bastards like her. Don't worry about it, I will handle them."

Paul was dumfounded because things were happening too fast for him to comprehend, and didn't speak throughout all of this. He couldn't believe it was happening to him.

"Wait here," said the RCMP officer to Paul. "We will search her first then you."

He knew that he was clean, but was afraid for Christiana. About forty minutes went by then the officer called him in and told him to strip; they searched every crevice of his body. He was told to get dress again and was lead to another room where he saw Christiana sitting on a chair in a corner crying. He wanted to talk to her but the officer guided him into another office.

"I am captain Morrow RCMP, and I would like to ask you some questions. "Do you know that woman?" asked the officer, pointing at Christiana.

"No," he began, "I mean yes, we met on the flight here."

"Never met her before?" asked Morrow.

"No," Paul replied.

"She told us that you were introduced at the airport by a mutual friend, is that correct?" asked Morrow.

"Yes, we were; but I never knew her before today. What has happened?"

"She was found to be illegally carrying diamonds into the country for the purpose of distribution, do you know about that?" asked Morrow.

"No," replied Paul, "I don't. I only met her at the airport when Tullis introduced us. I don't know anything about diamonds or anything else, can I make a phone call?"

"Why? You're not under arrest at this time," said Morrow.

"I don't care, I just want out of this bullshit and fast," replied Paul.

"Good," said Morrow, "you are under arrest until we can

check your story with the Bahamian police. Take him to the jail in Toronto, and no phone calls for seventy two hours."

Christiana was handcuffed also and advised of her rights in front of Paul. She was pleased to know that he was a professional at his game, all the crap he told her on the plane about wanting out, amounted to nothing.

"You'll be staying in jail until a judge can hear your plea," said Morrow as he led her away.

They made sure that Paul could see them putting her into a car, but by the time the officers drove off with him, she was released and brought back inside for some more talk with Morrow.

"We have to call Dready to let him know that Paul Mason was arrested and you have obtained the address in Markum; also the names of the people there in Nassau," said Morrow. "Let's send some people over there to arrest whoever is in that house."

"No sir," said Christiana, "why don't I deliver the stuff and then you would have them with the evidence in their hands?"

Morrow thought about her suggestion.

"Maybe we could persuade Paul to cooperate with us to make the sting work, then we could arrest him as assessory to the fact," said Morrow.

"No," said Christiana. "Hold him on the murder of Celia Bachstrum, Reynolds and McKenzie. Tell him that you have evidence of him being in Canada when they died and that you have a witness to testify to him going into their homes. I'm sure he would talk. You could then suggest for him to cooperate in the sting for a lesser charge."

"You're right," said Morrow, "let's do it."

While Morrow left to implement the plot against Paul Mason, she spoke to Commissioner Dillon and requested from him to allow her to accompany the officers to the house because she wanted to see the people there.

"That's fine by me," said Dillon, "but be careful, I don't want your cover blown for any stupid reason."

"Okay sir, I'll stay in the background," she promised.

About an hour later she was taken from the cell to Morrow's office. When she walked in, there was Paul Mason, properly dressed, sitting at ease in a chair next to the desk.

"Oh Paul," she cried, rushing towards him, "thank you for coming back to get me. I was worried that you might have forgotten me."

"I'm not here for you bitch," he replied, "there are other things on my mind and you are not one of them."

She stopped in her tracks in a state of shock.

"Aren't you taking me with you?" she asked. "I thought you and I worked for the same people and you would........"

"Shut-up," he shouted, "I'm here to save my arse and you cannot do it for me."

Christiana felt satisfied in her mind to know that Paul was about to rat on his friends.

"What will Hubert think when he hears of this?" she said tearfully. "What will he think happened to me?"

"Absolutely nothing," said Paul. "By the time you get out of prison, I would have explained everything to him, and I'm sure he will believe me."

Morrow signalled the officer and he escorted her out into another office where she could watch the proceedings on a television screen. She saw them placed the wires on him and heard Paul make the phone call.

"Hi Roger," said Paul, "sorry I'm late getting to you, but I had a little problem with the girl who carried the stuff," he paused, "no she wanted more money and a screw, so we spent a couple of hours in a hotel room," this time he snickered and said, "and I left her there for the police to find her. I'll be bringing the product over this evening, can you have everybody present so as not to waste time?" pause again, "I would like to rush back to Nassau tonight," pause again, "no my friend, unfinished business in Guyana," pause again, "see you," he hung up the phone.

She was happy that Paul had taken the bait, and watched as another officer handed over the package she had carried all the way from Nassau in her pussy, to him. In a few minutes they were out the door and on their way to the appointed sting.

She sat in the car watching the people who were brought out, she didn't recognize anyone. One of them was a rather large burley man of about sixty plus years, except for the little hair around his ears and the back of his head, he was totally bald. His features were nothing to the description given by Maggy Walker about the man with a white streak in the middle of his hair.

Although she was aware that criminals could look like decent citizen, none of these looked like hardened criminals to her. When it was all over, she asked the driver to take her to the Constellation Hotel on Dixon Road because she didn't want to alert her neighbours of her presence in Toronto by going to her house. She had already requested that the commissioner book her in a hotel for the night, with the intent on catching the first Air Canada flight to Jamaica in the morning. She felt excited because she really wanted to have Christmas dinner with her new son and the Perkins family.

Chapter Four

The Cook-shop.

D ready stood on the balcony of the airport watching his wife being escorted by a strange, but handsome young man, and wondered about her fate and safety. He absorbed as much of his demeanor so as to give a precise description of him to the police in Toronto. He watched as they walked to the plane, and waited to see it take off. Only then he left his post to make the call to Commissioner Dillon in Toronto.

He was happy to have found Captain Morrow in the office of Commissioner Dillon also. It was like killing two birds with the same stone. Dillon put the call on the speaker so that they all could talk. Dready wasted little time giving them the description of Paul Mason.

"Well sir," he said in a whispered tone, "she will be arriving on the Air Canada flight from Nassau, please make sure that the young man witnessed her arrest. We want it to be very authentic and convincing. ”

"That will be done," said Dillon.

"Will you be at the hotel this evening?" asked Morrow.

"Yes," he replied, " call me there but code it; remember that people could be listening in on the phones there."

"Right," said Morrow, "talk to you later."

He felt a slight nervousness within his soul to know that the life of his wife could be in danger, and that he wouldn't be there to assist her, if need be. He gave thoughts to the plot and the possibility of having her recognized by someone who would take revenge for getting their people arrested.

He left the airport and drove mindlessly along the coastal highway for a few minutes, just clearing his mind and absorbing the fresh sea breeze while admiring the lovely homes along the way. Then it dawned on him that he had to see Earl. He quickly spun the car around and headed towards the little restaurant in Carmichael Village. He wanted to speak to his friend Earl, badly, because he had not done so all day and was interested to find out what has been happening.

As he drove, he began to reflect on the many times he had been to Nassau, either for pleasure or on official police business, and wondered if he could really live there. Outside of Jamaica, Nassau would be the ideal place for him, but his station was in Canada and there is no way they would station him here.

He recalled the very first incident when he was sent to investigate some Jamaicans, who were growing ganja and shipping it to Miami from that same area in Bahamas. He smiled to remember how Earl saved his life by throwing him off a cliff into the water when some gun-men cornered them and almost killed him. He laughed to himself remembering how Earl had to jump in after and drag him to the boat. It was the first time he had met Earl, whom he had chartered to take him to the far out island for the purpose. Later that evening, Earl took him to the Carmichael restaurant for dinner and some talk. That was how they became friends.

He entered the restaurant and asked for Earl.

"He's 'round back," said the waitress.

He found him in back of the restaurant on the beach sitting on a log. He somehow realized that Earl was concerned about something and decided to assure his friend of his assistance in whatever was the problem.

"What's going on bro?" said Dready as he plopped himself beside Earl on the log. "Seems there is a problem on your mind."

"Nothing friend," replied Earl. "Except for the fact that I'm free of suspicion for the murder of Wakefield, is able to move around and not hiding from the police; not a damn thing."

"That's strange for you," said Dready, "you're always making things happen, why not now?" asked Dready.

"Well, the bitch I lived with threw me out saying that I was a wanted criminal and refused to give me a screw this morning, and the other one wouldn't let me into the house this afternoon," Earl replied.

"That's a damn shame," offered Dready.

"But I'll be going out to see Wakefield's sex starved wife later this evening," he said, "and that might be fun."

"Good for you," said Dready, "Judith seemed to be starving for a man's attention; and she living alone in that big house, doesn't comfort her. I'm almost sure that Mr. Wakefield did not satisfy her passion , so it's my belief that she is hungry for love. All I'm asking is for you to pay attention to what she says; maybe she will mention something that might be of interest to us."

Earl was quiet in thoughts and Dready realized that there was more in store; but what, he couldn't say. Then he remembered something that was said during the Jamaica incident by Peter McKenzie about his wife making it with a sea pilot friend in Nassau. He decided to play on a thought he had for some time now.

"You're still in love with Tanya McKenzie aren't you?" asked Dready.

The question caught Earl by surprise, because he suddenly swung his head to face Dready with his eyes wide open. There was total silence as he sat looking at his friend in a unbelieving, dumbfounded way.

"How did you...." he began but changed his mind. "Yes I am; we grew up together and went to the same school, but seeing that I was a poor boy her parents wouldn't let me near her. Then she married that aristocrat businessman from Jamaica, and that was the beginning of the end of our friendship."

Dready began a little chuckle.

"That is pure bullshit," said Dready abrasively, "you both had been lovers for years, even after she got married. When her husband Peter found out and divorced her, you thought you had the chance to have her but instead she dumped you."

"No man," said Earl in a sombre tone, "you've got it wrong."

"Oh yeah?" said Dready. "Then tell me how it was then and is now."

Earl, realising that he was cornered, decided to tell his friend the truth.

"You see," said Earl, "Tanya and I met at school about age twelve, but she being a Bachstrum was totally out of my league; so I stayed far away from her. Man that girl was nice, she was the loveliest thing I had ever seen, and fell in love with her instantly."

"Was she in love with you also?" asked Dready.

"Yes man, she loved me too," said Earl, "but like I said, she was from a rich family and mine was poor, so we only made eyes at each other from across the room."

"Then what happened," insisted Dready.

"One evening after school, I got the chance to talk to her," said Earl remembering the incident fondly. "It was pouring rain and we both ran into a shop for shelter. We stood beside each other and I was happy just to be beside her and to smile at her. When the rain subsided and we left the shop for home, she came beside me and spoke for the first time. I was shocked when she offered me shelter under her umbrella to walk home. Which we did and talked about many things that day. She asked me to meet her at a beach out near Lyford key on that Saturday afternoon. I did and we enjoyed the nicest day of my life on the beach; swimming, talking and even kissed. Man she was the sweetest thing I had ever touched."

"Did you make love to her?" asked Dready.

"No man, we were only twelve and thirteen years old," said Earl.

"Ah! ah!" said Dready, "keep telling."

"Well, she and I kept meeting there almost every Saturday afternoon for about two years. Then one day we were caught by her brother Ralph who followed her there."

"And what happened?" prodded Dready.

"Well, the brother told the family. Me and my parents were called to their house and unjustly ridiculed for my action with their little girl. I was promptly told never to be seen talking to her or I would be put in jail."

"You could have eloped and...." began Dready.

"We were too young!" said Earl angrily, "and furthermore her parents hated me because mine didn't have any money; and the truth is I was scared and didn't pursue her beyond that."

"Okay," said Dready, "go on."

"Just after her fifteenth birthday, her parents sent her to a school in the States. We never meet again for five years, and when we did she told me that she was getting married to this, this Jamaican man."

"Were you upset?" asked Dready.

Upset? I was raging mad," said Earl, "I was furious because I was in love with that girl and so was she with me, and they were forcing her to do something she really didn't want to. I cursed her parents and the man for taking her away from me, but that only drove her further away."

"So, were you invited to the wedding?" asked Dready.

"No man, I watched it from the fence of their home like many did," said Earl. "She had a big wedding, and although I was vex, I was happy for her. Then about a year later I met her again. It was when she brought some American tourist friends on board the boat I was working on, and we talked secretly. She told me that she was unhappy with her never-home husband, so I suggested and she accepted my invitation to a picnic on Abaco. On that lovely day we both got reacquainted and even made love on the beach; that's when it got started."

"So maybe her children could be yours, then?"

Maybe, they could be," said Earl, "but she never told me that."

Dready paused in thought, recalling the conversations he had with Peter McKenzie in the Jamaican affair about his estranged wife and a man in Nassau. He realized that although Earl knew the family, he wasn't aware that Tanya was Karlheinz Bass' daughter and not a Bachstrum. He also felt assured that Earl wasn't mixed up in their smuggling business, although he could have done favours for Tanya and not know what it was for.

"So you've been bopping her all these years then?" he asked.

"Yes, until she got mixed up with that South American guy," said Earl. "I was the one who was there for her when she got shot in Miami, and even risked my neck to get her back home before they could finish the job."

"When did you get her from the Miami hospital after the shooting?" asked Dready.

"About three weeks after," answered Earl. "But it wasn't easy. I had to pay off a nurse; one thousand dollars it cost to let me hide in the hospital for the night, then when the coast was clear she put on the clothes I brought and we slipped out virtually un-noticed. Then I called her brother and he came with his boat the next morning and took us back to Nassau."

"You risked your life for her," said Dready. "Would she have done the same for you?"

"Maybe," said Earl, "but then again I wouldn't ask her to."

"She bought your boat for you, didn't she?" asked Dready.

"Yes she did, but nobody else knows about that," said Earl, "and please don't ever mention it to anyone else."

"I won't my friend," said Dready, "not unless I'm under oath. Did the family ever thank you for getting her out of the hospital?" asked Dready.

"Her brother gave me back my thousand dollars and that's all," he replied. "And at the same time warned me to stay away from her, or else."

"And now she thinks you hate her and won't talk to you," said Dready.

"That's right," replied Earl.

"Life is a bastard, isn't it?" stated Dready.

"It sure is my friend," said Earl.

The two men sat on the log for a long time talking, until the cook-shop owner came to advise them that the soup was getting low and would be finished if they didn't come to get theirs immediately.

They occupied their usual corner seat, near the opening where a window should be, and began a conversation about the tourists that flocked the little out of the way restaurant. Dready sat watching the patrons coming into the small restaurant and realized that the food must be good for them to come all the way from the posh Cable Beach Hotels restaurants, to this one.

"I'll have the stewed Kingfish with rice and peas," he told the waitress, "and keep the beers coming until I say stop."

She gave a little chuckle and turned her attention to Earl.

".......and the same for you sweet buns?" she asked looking at Earl with an alluring eye.

"Yes, but first bring me a turtle punch," he instructed, "I man will need all the strength I can get for this evening."

"Ah! Ah!" said the waitress, "have something fresh tonight, eh?"

"Damn right," he said grinning, "and I man must preform good, even though I haven't practised all week."

"Crap!" she said. "I was here and available all week, so you didn't want it."

He slapped her on the bum and she rushed off to place their order. When she was out of ear shot Earl said,

"That girl has been offering herself to me for the last three years. She does not know we are cousins."

"So why don't you tell her?" asked Dready.

"What! And stop the great treatment I get from her?" replied Earl.

They both laughed at the thought.

"Is this Wakefield man very important?" asked Earl.

"Maybe," said Dready. "I think he was involved in some kind of smuggling and somebody didn't appreciate the way he does business, thus the reason he was killed."

"Well, it wasn't me," said Earl, "but I know the boys who hit him."

Dready realized that Earl didn't know that Wakefield was poisoned and that he was a friend of Smithers and Bachstrum.

"Now remember," he said, "while you're making it with Mrs. Judith Wakefield tonight, ask her questions about his South American friends. I want names and features, anything that we could use to identify them."

"I will try my friend," he replied. "Imagine, I'll be making love to a woman for information and not pleasure."

"Bullshit," said Dready, "you won't remember your own name when you're with her muchless mine. Have a good time tonight anyway."

"Thank you," he said, "and I will tell you all about it tomorrow."

The waitress brought the food and the two men got stuck-in. In the meantime three English looking tourists came in and sat at the table next to theirs.

There was this slightly balding-well dressed-middle aged man of about six feet tall, with two nice looking younger women as escorts. One was a tall skinny flat-chested blond of about twenty-five, who wore a tight black one-piece shorts-like-jumper with nothing underneath. Although she had a nice smile, Dready concluded that she had false teeth and spoke very loudly as though she had an hearing problem. Dready noticed that she was the one carrying most of the conversation while the other, who was a dark haired slightly large, buxom woman of maybe forty-five, listened. He also noticed that the dark haired one had too much make-up on, because under the tropical heat, her perspiration was causing it to run down her face. He surmised that she might be the man's wife and the girl was a friend rather than their daughter.

Earl, being the businessman he was, overheard them talking about going fishing and quickly handed the man his card.

"If you ever want to go out on the high seas for a day of fun, call me and I would be pleased to show you the best place to catch a nice fish," he said.

"Have you a boat?" asked the man in his mid England accent.

"Certainly sir," said Earl, "and as my witness you could ask this gentleman here. I took him out today and he caught a very large Marlin, which is being stuffed for his trophy room in Jamaica."

The man looked at Dready scornfully at first, then nodded his head.

"Pleased to meet you," said the man. "Do you like fishing?"

"On occasions," replied Dready, hating the idea of Earl putting him on the spot, because he hated the sea, and the only time he likes a fish is when it's cooked and on his plate, "but today was exceptional."

"Good," said the man to Earl, "then come to get me at the hotel tomorrow morning for a day on the high seas."

"Not tomorrow morning sir," said Earl, "I already have a client. Make that Wednesday morning at seven-thirty sharp."

"That's a deal," said the man happily, as the waitress brought their dinner.

For the rest of the time they sat there, the conversation ran from his first holiday in the Bahamas to his business in England. Sometimes the flat chested blonde would begin a story and the man would finish it. The quiet dark hair woman seemed uninterested and wanted not to be there, although when asked, she would add something colourful to his stories. After dinner the three tourists got up to walk on the beach, leaving Dready and Earl alone.

They sat in silence for a long time, finally Dready got up from the table.

"See you tomorrow Earl," he said, "and next time don't tell anyone that I love fishing, even if it's just to plug your business."

Earl laughed a loud roar and said,

"Thanks friend, I knew I could count on you. Will you pay this bill?"

"Yes, I will," said Dready.

"Hey! What about the money we took from Wakefield's house? What are you going to do with it?"

"I will tell you tomorrow; see you," said Dready as he dropped five twenties on the table. "Give the waitress a good tip and buy some gasoline for your boat, I don't want you running out of gas in the middle of the ocean. Be early in the morning; bye."

He got as far as the door when the dark haired woman, who was coming back inside from the beach, met him. He noticed that the darkish frock she wore was really green, which almost matched her eyes.

"Leaving so soon?" she asked.

"Yes," he replied, "I have some reading to do and......"

"I was hoping that we could talk a little more," she said. "What hotel are you staying?"

"The Palace," he replied.

"Good; so am I. Maybe I will see you in the casino later this evening then?" she asked. "Do you like blackjack? I do."

"Weeeel," he reluctantly replied, "yeah, that might be a very good idea. See you there about ten thirty."

He left Carmichael for the hotel to look over the book he had retrieved from Wakefield's safe, but when he got into the hotel the telephone operator saw him entering the door and beckoned for him to come to her.

"Mr. Winston," she said, "there was a Canadian call for you sir and I left a message in the room; but if you want I could try the number for you while you go to your room.

"Thank you miss eh," he replied peering to see her name tag.

"Cynthia, sir," she said extending her chest so that he could see the badge, "Cynthia Mason."

"Thank you Cynthia Mason, call me in the room," he said and dashed off to the elevator. He got into the elevator wondering if something had gone wrong and Christiana was hurt. He laid on the bed waiting for the call. The twenty minutes wait seemed long, but finally the phone rang and Cynthia came on the line.

"Hello Mr. Winston, your call is ready sir," she said, "go ahead."

"Hello," he said into the mouth piece.

"Hello darling," said Christiana, "how are things with you in Nassau? Are you enjoying your vacation?"

"Good," he replied, "I'm having a wonderful time fishing and doing the party thing I'm supposed to do. Did everything go well for you?"

"Yes my darling, everything went well," she replied, "and the shoes fit."

"Excellent," he said, "I will be going to Jamaica tomorrow afternoon, maybe you would care to join me there?"

"I definitely would, as long as my jealous husband doesn't get suspicious and follow me there," she said. "At this very moment he believes I am having an affair with a young man named Paul Mason, who incidentally was having it on with a girl named Celia Bachstrum in Toronto. As long as he believe that, we can have our affair without any danger of him finding out about us."

"Excellent idea my love, see you in Jamaica tomorrow," he said and hang up the phone.

He smiled at the phone to know that someone in the hotel office was listening in on his calls.

He had a quick shower, changed his clothes and literally ran down to the casino to meet the green-eyed woman he had met earlier at the Carmichael Restaurant. He sat at the bar and ordered a scotch. Within twenty minutes he saw her coming in.

"Hello," he said approaching her, "did you have a good time tonight at the restaurant?"

"No, but I met you and is very anxious to get to know more about you," she said smiling. "Could we have a drink before we begin to gamble?"

"We sure could," he said and steered her towards one of the alcove near the bar, and sat.

"My name is Rona Samuels," she said stretching out her hand to him, "and yours?"

"Winston," he said. "Dready Winston."

".....and what is your business Mr.Winston, if I may ask?" she said.

Just then the waitress came to take their order.

"Scotch on the rocks," said Dready, "and the lady will have a......"

"Harvey wallbanger," said Rona. "I just feel like a stiff one tonight."

They both laughed at her little pun.

"Very well," said the waitress and disappeared.

"You were about to tell me what your business was, Mr. Winston," said Rona, to reopen the conversation.

Dready thought about her question and responded after looking around for prying ears and eyes.

"I'm a diamond dealer," he whispered.

"Fascinating," said Rona. "Is there much diamond business in these islands of The Bahamas?"

"Yes," he replied, "but it could be dangerous if anyone knows that I'm......."

He stopped as the waitress brought the drinks and took his

money.

"It could be dangerous if anyone knows that you're what?" she said restarting his statement.

"Oh yes," he said, "It could be dangerous if some people know I'm here to do business, so I have to be careful who I speak to and......."

"What kind of danger are you talking about?" she interrupted.

"You know, kidnappers, gangsters, that kind of danger," he said.

Rona thought about his words then smiled and said,

"I know that you're only pulling my leg, but don't worry about those kinds of people, you and I will be together from here on; and if anybody tries anything, they would have to deal with me also."

"Thank you my dear," said Dready, "I might need your protection after all."

They had two drinks then she went to the cashier to purchase a thousand dollars worth of chips.

"Let's go lover," she said, literally dragging him towards the blackjack table, "we are going to gamble now."

Dready saw that the more Rona played the more she drank, and the more she drank the more she wanted to play. Finally he detached himself from the table to visit the bathroom. As he left the boys room he ran smack into Cynthia leaving work for the evening.

"Through for the night?" he asked.

"Yes," she replied, "it's almost mid-night, care to take me home?"

"I would love to my dear, but my wife is at the blackjack table and......"

'Is your wife here also?" Cynthia asked in a surprised tone interrupting his statement. "I thought she was....never mind, good night."

"Wait a minute," said Dready hustling after her, "she's drunk at the table and once she goes to sleep I could meet you outside."

Cynthia thought about his request, nodded her head and

walked back to the front desk.

"I'll be waiting here for you," she said.

Dready returned to the blackjack table and quickly got the intoxicated Rona to cash in what was left of her chips, and took her to his room. He deliberately walked pass the desk drawing Cynthia's attention to his deed. He dumped Rona into his bed and quickly returned to the anxious girl waiting for him.

"Sorry to keep you waiting," he said on reaching her.

"That's fine," said Cynthia. "Where is your car?"

"In the parking lot," he answered, "come this way."

They got into the car and he drove away.

"Where to?" he asked.

"To my house," she said. "Make a right turn here."

Except for the few directions, they drove to her home in virtually silence and parked outside her gate.

"Can I come in for a night cap?" he asked.

"I've been thinking about that," she replied. "You're some kind of a man. Is that a normal thing for you to do?"

Dready thought about it for a moment.

"Just awhile ago you were ready to have sex with me," he said, "now all of a sudden you get a spasm and get rigid on me. What happened?"

Cynthia smiled.

"Imagine, you can put your drunken wife to bed and just like that you want to jump on another woman," she said angrily, yet not making any move to leave.

"Don't worry about that, she won't even miss me," he said. "Furthermore she doesn't care who I spend the night with."

Cynthia sat quietly for a long time.

"Don't worry about it," he insisted, "many people have affairs to satisfy a need you know, and as you can see my wife is a lush and we wouldn't have any fun tonight anyway."

"I can see that," she replied, "and you seem to have many affairs, don't you?"

"Not me," he said smiling, "I don't usually do those sort of things, well not often anyway."

"Then what about the woman in Toronto who will be meeting you in Jamaica tomorrow?" she said angrily. "Both of you are cheating on your spouses and here you are trying to get me into bed."

"You listened to my phone call?" he asked in a surprised tone, while deep inside he was snickering to the thought that she did.

"Well yes," she said, "I accidentally switched your lines and heard the conversation. Then I saw you with your wife at the elevator and wondered."

"But you still waited for me," he pointed out, "which means you're still interested."

"Yes, I waited," she said, "because I was curious to see what kind of a man you were. You're despicable, and so is the woman in Toronto; she seducing that young boy as a diversion to her husband."

"What's the matter with that, is he related to you or is he a friend?" he asked.

"He's my cousin and I don't like the games your lover is playing with him," she said.

Dready was happy that Cynthia got upset and was angrily letting off her steam. This way he could find out what he wanted without much commitment. He sat looking at her as though he, himself, was upset.

"Well, it seems you have found out my deep dark secret," said Dready, "and it appears that it's your intention to use it to blackmail me. I happen to know that it's illegal for hotel operators to listen in on private phone calls, and since you won't allow me into your bed, I will simply have to tell your boss about your act of listening to my call. I'm sure they won't take it lightly and you could easily lose your job."

"Oh shit!" she said realizing her mistake, "I'm sorry, but it was an accident and I......."

"To hell with the accident excuse," he said, "you have ruined

103

my little thing in Toronto and now you don't want to...."

"I beg you not to tell on me," she said, "please forgive me, let me make it up to you. Come in and we could make love all night. I would do anything for you."

"No sweetheart, it's too late now," he said applying the pressure to her, "I couldn't trust you for any reason after this."

"No, please come with me," she pleaded, "I will make it up to you and I wouldn't tell anyone else about your aff......"

She paused for a moment just watching Dready's reaction, hoping that he would accept her invitation to have sex. But Dready was deep in thought, seeking an angle to present his next question.

"I want to know about your cousin Paul," he said, "because if her husband ever find out about us, I want to be able to defend myself. Your cousin might have to be the fall guy in our affair or a divorce."

"But why?" she asked.

"Look," he said, "I'm a poor dreadlocks Rasta from Jamaica. My wife is a very wealthy woman and I want to be close to her money, but she is a lush, always gets drunk and fall asleep, so our sex life is almost dead. That woman in Toronto is also a poor girl married to my wife's rich brother, and she is also sexually deprived. So we decided to satisfy each other's needs whenever we get the chance. She being a sister-in-law, makes it easy for us to do what we want without interference or suspicions; but her husband who is in the diamond business thinks she is screwing with Paul and we want to keep it that way."

Cynthia sat in silence giving thoughts to Dready's little tale. He realized that he had her undivided attention.

"Ever wonder why Paul goes up to Toronto often?" he asked her.

"Yes, I often wondered his reason, but he assured me that it wasn't anything illegal," said Cynthia.

"Ever heard of the diamond smuggling thing in Nassau? Ever

thought he might be involved in that thing coming out of here?" he insisted.

"That might be a possibility," she said, "but he never indicates his interest in any such thing and...." she paused, "and furthermore, he is an accountant and works for his father's company. He has never been in trouble with the law....., except the time he was arrested in Trinidad along with some friends who were carrying coke."

"Did he go to prison?" he asked.

"No," she responded, "his father and Hubert Bachstrum got him off on some kind of technicality."

"When did that happen?" he asked.

"About a year ago and again in Tor...." she paused. "Holy shit! That boy is a devil, and here I am defending the little bastard."

Dready was happy that he was able to get Cynthia to talk about her cousin, Paul Mason.

"Tell me about the Bachstrum family," said Dready.

"Well," said Cynthia, "they are a very wealthy family in this country. They have ships, planes, hotels and stores. They travel abroad like I go into town. I don't know where they came from, but they sure do a lot of business from here."

"How did you know that?" asked Dready.

"My older sister, Paul's mother, use to work for them as a helper before she married to Mr. Mason, who was a friend of that family; she told me," said Cynthia proudly.

"Do you know a man named Tullis Burke?" asked Dready.

"Yes," she said, "Tullis and I used to be school mates, but since he got the job as custom officer and was married to that young girl who died in Toronto, we seldom talk."

"And why not?" asked Dready.

"I don't know, he's a big-shot now, and since his wife died he is more big, and I'm still a telephone operator," she replied.

"How did his wife die?" asked Dready.

"I really don't know, but rumours had it that he killed her for having another man," said Cynthia.

105

"Did he go to Toronto often?" asked Dready.

"I really don't know," she responded, "I only know of two times. You see she was a student there and he occasionally went see her there, or she would come down here for a few days and so on. Paul could tell you better."

Dready stopped the questioning and sat quietly in thought. He realized that Cynthia Mason was really the aunt of Paul Mason and not her cousin as she first indicated. Yet she lied. Now it slipped out that he was her sister's child which makes him her nephew. He also suspected that Cynthia was madly in love with Tullis Burke, by the tone of her voice when talking about him. She might even be giving him information on occupants of the hotel.

When she thought he might be falling asleep, she prodded him in the rib.

"It's three o clock in the morning," she said, "come inside so we can make love, will you?" she offered.

"No my darling," he replied, "it's too late now and I'm not in the mood after hearing that you listened to my phone calls."

"I'm sorry," she said, "it won't happen again. What can I do to make up?"

"You will have to listen to other phone calls and then tell me about them, when I return from Jamaica. And don't tell anything to my wife or you will surly lose your job."

"I won't, I promise," she said. "Anyone in particular you want me to bug?"

"Yes, I'm trying to locate a man named Smithers and I'm sure that he stays at that hotel occasionally," he said while watching her from the corner of his eyes.

"Smithers? I know him!" she said. "Well to say, I know of him. He usually stays in the penthouse whenever he is there."

"Good," said Dready. "Listen for him and have something to tell me when I return. I would like to meet him face to face."

Cynthia nodded her head.

"Ever heard of a man named Chrittendon?" he asked.

106

"Yes, he stays at the Bahamian Hotel just down the road," she replied, "and he sometimes comes to the Palace for a drink or two. Bug his calls also?"

"Yes," said Dready, "him too."

She kissed him on the cheek and begged him not to tell on her.

"I'll think about it," he told her.

"Thank you," she said, then she exited the car and ran into the house.

It was about three forty-five in the morning when he left Cynthia with a lot of information, and the assurance that she would inform him of calls from any of these people's phone.

"She is lying," he said to himself as he entered the elevator.

He returned to the room to find Rona still asleep in his bed. He quietly changed his clothes and slept on the couch.

The next morning he got her up early for breakfast.

"Come on lover, it's time to leave," he said, "your husband will be curious about where you stayed last night."

"He's not my husband," she shouted, "and he wouldn't give a damn where I spent the night," she replied in a distinct assured tone.

They showered separately and went into the restaurant for breakfast. Dready kept a sharp lookout, although Rona told him that she wasn't married, hoping that the man didn't see them together. They ordered the food and began to eat.

"Dready whatever.....," she said smiling.

"What's so funny about my name?" he asked.

Rona paused her eating.

"I know that you're a smuggler," she said starring intently into his eyes from across the table.

"How did you guess that I am?" he asked, pretending to be surprised. "Are you familiar with those kind of people?" he asked in a whisper as he looked around to assure that nobody heard her.

Rona stuck some food into her mouth and snickered as though

she had made a humungous discovery, or had a fish on her hook.

"Well firstly," she said after swallowing her bite, "last night you told me that you were here to make a diamond deal but didn't want anyone to know of your presence, then you talked about the danger of gangsters kidnapping or killing you. Then I remembered your friend saying that you were a Jamaican and wondered why a Jamaican Rasta man would come to Nassau to fish, when there are many such charters in your own country. And yes, I'm familiar with those kind of people."

"You got me there," he replied. "Are you the police?"

"Hell no!" she said grinning." "I'm just like you. I'm here to make a deal also, but the man I was supposed to contact, is dead."

"That's a damn shame," said Dready. "Coincidentally, so is my contact."

"Shit!" she exclaimed. "Is his name Wakefield by chance?"

"The same," replied Dready, and to assure her of his connection, said, "he was poisoned."

"By whom?" asked Rona.

"I really don't know," answered Dready, "but I presume it's by someone who doesn't want him to deal with me."

"Mmmmm, also me," said Rona, as she lapsed into a silence. Which seemed to last a long time.

Dready, realizing that Rona had a lot to offer him about the Nassau operation, kept quiet for a while and when he believed she had collected her thoughts and was ready to talk again he said,

"My people in Canada are depending on me to get the stuff; at least some. I would hate to leave without getting the deal I came for. I've heard about a man named Smithers but haven't got a clue what he looks like or where to find him, if he does exist."

Rona remained quiet for awhile, so Dready played another card.

"Well, I'd better leave you alone to finish your breakfast," he said, "I don't want your man to see us together and cause me some trouble."

"No, don't leave," she said, "I would like to ask you a few more questions."

"If it's about my smuggling thing, you can forget it friend," he replied, "I'm not about to reveal more than you already know."

"No! No! No!" she said, "I wanted to know why you didn't screw me last night when I was drunk."

"It would have been a wasted effort my dear," he answered smiling. "I would like to make love to you when you're sober and conscious of the fact."

"Oh, I see!" she said, "a gentleman Rastafarian. I have never met one before."

"Well now you have," he replied with a grin.

Just then a shadow crossed their table. It was that of a man and woman. Dready recognized them from the Carmichael restaurant.

"Good morning Mrs. Samuels," said the man in that mid England accent, "you left so suddenly last night we didn't get the opportunity to say goodnight."

"Good morning Mr. Smithers, Miss. Heron," replied Rona. "It was a sudden decision, and furthermore, I wanted to do some gambling in the company of a good man. Dready, meet Austin J. Smithers and Cindy Heron; and to inform you Mr. Smithers, we spent a wonderful night together "

Dready was surprised to have met the man he sought, and so easily.

"Pleased to meet you again sir," he said extending his hand to Smithers, "we have so much in common to talk about."

"Yes we do," said Smithers. "Would you like to join me on our fishing trip tomorrow morning? Maybe you could show me some techniques."

"Thanks for the invitation," said Dready, relieved to know that he wouldn't be able to, "but I will be leaving for Jamaica in the morning. Maybe another time."

"Fine," said Smithers, "maybe you'll return here for that excursion some other time and we could share a drink or two."

"Maybe," said Dready, "but I have some urgent business to conduct before leaving for Jamaica. I was about to leave for Abaco to see a man about some diamonds, but since you're here I would prefer to do business with you."

Smithers thought about Dready's statement and flashed an eye towards Rona and back to those of Dready.

"Sorry to disillusion you sir, but I'm not the person to do business with," said Smithers. "Furthermore, what made you think I am in the diamond business?"

Dready softly laughed as he said,

"Because sir, your name is big in some circles in Jamaica."

"Name the circle," said Smithers, leaning across the table to further stare into his eyes.

"Well, the people who hired me are connected to a man named Peter McKenzie, who is in prison along with Arthur Collins, Ivan Berkowitz, Harvey Ambross and......"

"Okay, okay," said Smithers, "they were then, I want to know who now."

"Well," said Dready, "I really don't know. You see, my dealings were always with a woman named Rosita Ambross in New York city, but since the Jamaican problem I am now taking orders from the daughter of Ludwig Felscher, and all of our conversations are by tele phone. But once I met with a man named Frazier Hendicott when he wanted someone to take care of a couple of problem people and I......."

"Okay, okay," said Smithers again interrupting him. "What and who was the problem?"

"Well," said Dready, hoping to convince Smithers, "there was a girl named Salina Mason and a boy named Robert coolie-man Reynolds, but somebody else took care of it and my service wasn't required."

"Do you know a man named Tullis Burke?" asked Smithers.

"No," replied Dready after some thoughts, "the name doesn't ring a bell."

"What about Hubert Bachstrum?" asked Smithers.

"Not him either," said Dready, "but I've heard about a Zenon Bach...."

"Okay," said Smithers in a relieved tone, "maybe we could do some limited business after you return from Jamaica; and may the dogs eat your supper if you are found lying to me."

Dready got up from the table, stretched out his hand to the man and said,

"Thank you sir, but for this time I will have to purchase from the people in Abaco as agreed. Our Canadian money is as good as anyone else's, you know."

"Goodbye for now Mr Dready," said Smithers. "Let's hope that will be so."

Dready left then and began walking towards the doors with a big smile on his face.

Rona chased after him.

"May I see you tonight?" she asked as she caught up to him.

"Maybe," he replied, "and thanks for introducing me to Mr. Smithers; dealing with him might cut the time overlay and cost."

"It certainly will," she said, "just remember to meet me in the casino this evening, I'm dying to sample your wares."

"Maybe you will," he said, "it all depends on what happens on my trip to Abaco, if a deal can be reached or not."

She kissed him a good wet one and waved as she rushed back to the table. He turned to see the girls at the front desk watching him, including Cynthia Mason.

He quickly left and drove down to Carmichael Road to find Earl. He found him in the same corner he was the evening before, having a beer.

"Okay," he said as he sat, "tell me about last night."

Earl waved for the waitress to bring a beer for Dready.

"It was good," said Earl. "That woman was in dire need of a sexual encounter and wanted to screw all night."

"Yeah, yeah," said Dready, waving his hand. "that's good, but I want to hear what she talked about during the intermissions."

"She told me about the many friends of Mr Wakefield, who came to their house whenever they are in town. They are from many parts of the world, but mainly from South America," said Earl, " but she was never in their meetings to hear their conversations. She told me about two men, one named Chrittendon from Canada and the other named Smithers who is from England. She said Chrittendon usually comes there to talk with Wakefield about land ownership and money. A week ago they both got into a heated argument about some land in Abaco, that Wakefield sold to an Arab and didn't pay Chrittendon his share."

"When did she last see Chrittendon?" asked Dready.

"That evening," said Earl. "That evening he disappeared along with Wakefield and she hasn't seen any of them since."

"Maybe, like Wakefield, he's dead," said Dready.

"Maybe," said Earl. "Maybe the Arabs had them killed. What if they had stuck it to the Arabs and they had them killed? It could happen you know."

"Yes, I know it could happen," said Dready, "but the Arabs would have their own people do it, not strangers. They wouldn't hire local boys to commit a murder for them; well not in just a shady deal. If it was against Allah's will, then they might."

"You could be right," answered Earl, "but here in our back-yard our boys want to be hired."

"What else did she say?" asked Dready.

"Well, she talked about the Bachstrum family and how she think they are part of a gang working with Wakefield and Smithers," said Earl.

"What does Smithers look like?" asked Dready.

"He is a tall six foot plus white man, with dark brown eyes, black hair, beard and a moustache. He has a scar above his right eye, maybe from a fight."

"Yeah sure," said Dready, "that could be anybody in Nassau. I want distinguishing features, something that makes him different from others."

"That's what she gave me," said Earl.

"And what else," asked Dready.

"The only other thing she said was, Mr Smithers has a white streak down the middle of his head, you know, like a skunk."

Dready sat quietly for a long moment thinking. That was the third time he had heard of a man with a white streak in his hair. Maggy Walker, the landlady in Toronto had told them that a coloured man with bark eyes and a white streak in his hair had visited the girls. Then Cecil Wright said he was a black man with dark eyes. Now Judith described him as white with those same features.

"How did he get from Coloured to Black to White?" he asked himself, knowing that the Smithers he met in the Carmichael restaurant, and again this morning, although white, has no scar or streak in his hair.

He sat in thought for a long time, without any disruption from Earl. He was certain that Wakefield was dead, poisoned by an unknown person, Chrittendon is missing and presumed dead and the man posing as Smithers might be an impostor with a disguise.

"Somebody, who knows what Chrittendon was about, killed him and is using his identity. It has to be someone who also understands RCMP codes," he thought.

"I have to see Chief Daniels right away," said Dready getting up from the table, "want to come with me?"

"No sir," said Earl. "I don't like or trust that man. And I don't like going into police stations either, they always want to lock me up."

"Okay then, meet me at the Bahamas yacht club in about two hours time," he said and hurriedly left the restaurant.

Dready parked the car in the visitors spot and dashed up the steps and without warning to the front desk Sergeant, knocked on Daniels office door.

"Come in," shouted Daniels from inside the office.

"Good morning Chief," said Dready as he reached out over the desk, which was piled high with papers, to shake the policeman's hand, "sorry to barge in on you this early in the morning, but there are some questions I would like answers to and it couldn't wait."

"That's fine," said Daniels, "I'm used to it from you news writers. Sit and tell me what has been happening."

"Well, I've met an English man called Austin J. Smithers who told me that he was a diamond dealer and is in Nassau to do some purchases. Have you any knowledge of him?" asked Dready.

"Sure," said Daniels, "he's a regular on the island. He comes here for a month at a time, does his legal business and leaves."

"Where and from whom does he purchase his stuff?" asked Dready.

"From a licensed dealer named Amanda Bachstrum on Market street," answered Daniels.

"Is Hubert Bachstrum a licensed dealer also?"

"Mmmmm, let me see," said Daniels as he switched on his computer and made some clicks on the keyboard. "No he is not a licensed dealer, but he manages his father's business who hires licensed personnel. Zenon Bachstrum was his father you know."

"What do you know about a man called Chrittendon?"

"Nothing at all," replied Daniels.

"Whose body did you find on the South Ocean beach then? Was it Chrittendon or was it Smithers?" asked Dready.

"How would you know about that?" asked Daniels.

"A little bird told me," said Dready. "Ever heard about a man named Karlheinz Bass?"

Daniels stopped searching the computer. He paused to look at Dready's face. Finally he said,

"This information is classified and can only be given to the proper qualified personnel," replied Daniels.

"That's okay," said Dready, "I wrote about him last year, but if you feel...."

"Not that it's a secret, but I would have to dig up the info," said Daniels.

"Okay sir," he said as he rose from the chair, "see you later."

Dready dashed out of Daniels office and hurried down the road towards the Yacht club to find Earl. He paused to scrutinize the many yachts, cruisers and speed boats parked in the harbour. He wondered which of them belonged to pirates.

"Let's go to Abaco, I want to see the man who sent the boys to kill your friends on the boat," he said to Earl. "I'm sure it was Hubert Bachstrum and he's someone I might want to talk to. Which of these are pirate vessels?" Dready asked as they walked along the dock towards Earl's boat.

Earl smiled as he answered.

"Almost half of them," said Earl "You realize that you're taking a chance getting tangled with that man? Hubert Bachstrum could be dangerous you know."

"Certainly," said Dready. "But that is the business. Taking chances, that's how I get my stories to make the kind of money I do."

Earl remained silent as he started and drove the boat out of the dock.

"Ever heard about a young man named Robert Reynolds?" asked Dready.

"Yes," said Earl. "Well, not him but I know his mother."

"You do? Where can I find her?" asked Dready.

"Right near where we are going now," he said.

"Could we go to see her first?" asked Dready.

"Certainly," said Earl. "She just loves visitors."

"Why?" asked Dready.

"Because she makes those special Johnnie cakes for special people," said Earl. "You know, the ones with the stuff in the middle."

"You mean ganja cake?" asked Dready.

"Yes," said Earl, "the ones you could eat all day and never put on weight.

Dready sat back as Earl manoeuvred the craft towards the larger of the Abaco islands and within minutes he was docking at a secluded spot.

"Are you sure this is a good place to stay?" Dready asked.

"It sure is," said Earl, "nobody would be looking for us here."

Chapter Five

House on Abaco Island.

$\mathcal{T}$he walk was long. The hill was steep and the path was winding. But it was an easy walk for them. They went all the way up to Edith Muir's modest four room house. Dready waited until Earl completed the introduction before asking the woman any question.

"Why do you live in such a remote part of the island?" he asked. "Do you know that there are good places in the larger towns?"

"Yes I do know," she answered, "but it wouldn't look right to see a highly respectable Voodoo priestess as I, leaving bars and night clubs intoxicated. Now what can I do for you?"

"I would like to pick your brains a little," he said, "and I don't want any ganja cakes either."

Edith giggled a little.

"Some people come especially for them, you know," she replied.

"Is Robert Reynolds your son?" asked Dready.

"He sure is," she answered. "I gave birth to him."

"I heard that he died in Canada last year and would like to know what happened," said Dready.

"Yes, he was killed in Hamilton, Canada. They told me that

117

it was suicide," she angrily replied, "but I know that some-somebody deliberately killed him. It was murder."

"Why do you believe that is so?" asked Dready.

"Because I can see," she said. "I'm psychic and can see many things. I know my son very well and I don't think he would've killed himself, no matter what the circumstances were."

"Did you know any of his friends?" he asked.

"No," she answered. "The only two I ever met were a boy named Paul something or another, and a girl named Celia Bachstrum. She was a little bitch."

"What made you think so?" he asked.

"She was always after Coolie man," she said. "Ever since secondary school she has been pursuing him, and even came into my house to.....to seduce him."

"Where is his father now?" asked Dready.

"He's an orange farmer on one of the far-out island," she said. "He got married and acquired some cheep land there, but I think he's farming something else."

"Like what?" he asked.

"Drugs," she responded. "I think he's farming drugs with his wife, because all of his children are driving new expensive cars in Freeport, Nassau and in San Andros. Believe me my boy, I know because I can see things which aren't clear to others."

"If you're such a good psychic why didn't you put a spell on your son's killer?" asked Dready.

"I did," said Edith, "but it takes time to work. My work is only for healing people not for evil things. But if you should kill them, I would fix it so you won't get caught."

"Okay," said Dready, "then tell me what do they look like."

Edith closed her eyes, turned to face away from him and began mumbling.

"One is black and the other is white," she said. "They both have covers on their faces and resemble each other."

"How can they have different pigmentation and resemble each

other?" he asked.

"Don't know," replied Edith, "but that's what I see."

Dready thought about Edith's words and thanked her for the time.

"Thanks for the information," he said, "and if I get the chance to capture the killers I will certainly come back to tell you. See you."

He signalled Earl for them to leave.

"Bye Edith," said Earl, "mother is doing better since you gave her that medicine."

"I try my best son," she replied as the two men began walking away from her.

"Can we get to where we are going from here?" asked Dready of Earl.

"No, we'll have to dock in another part of the island to get there," said Earl.

"Fine by me," replied Dready, smiling pleasantly to know that he had met Edith the mother of Robert Reynolds. He stopped.

"Maybe we'll meet again," he said as he shook her hand. "Have a good life; goodbye."

Edith Muir waited until Earl walked away from them.

"You're a cop," she whispered to Dready, "and a very good one at that."

"Thank you," he replied.

They back tracked down the hilly pathway to the boat. At a glance he could see Edith Muir still standing watching them. Dready smiled to think the woman was really a good obeah woman.

"Earl, how long would it take to the far-out islands?"

"Depending on which island," he answered. "Any where from half hour to two hours. Want to go there?"

"Yes, I would like to see a house on Long island," he said.

"Then we could go there tomorrow," suggested Earl.

Earl directed the boat away from Edith Muir's house. Within twenty-five minutes, they, docked at a remote side of the same

119

island. They walked up a hill towards the intended house. They got to within a hundred yards of the house when Earl indicated with a hand wave to lie flat on the ground. Earl whispered that it would be best if they crawled the rest of the way up the little hill to the house.

They looked around for a while then tried a door. With his skill of lock picking, Earl opened it and they cautiously entered the livingroom. They realized that nobody was in the house, but caution and silence was still necessary just in case there were alarms and other security devices around. While Dready attempted to seek-out a hidden safe and papers for evidence, Earl got busy looking for other things. Their search took almost an hour.

"Nothing here," said Dready, sounding disappointed.

"Hey!" said Earl, "let's look in the basement."

"I thought houses in the tropics don't have basements?" stated Dready.

"Not normally, but this house has one. If I were building a house to conceal illegal things, I would build one into my place for that purpose," suggested Earl.

They searched around and certainly there were a basement. They found the stairs hidden in a clothes closet off the master bedroom. Quickly Dready felt around and found a light switch and they descended the stairs to a large cellar. To their surprise, the place was like that of a warehouse with boxes, bags and many suitcases everywhere with a door leading towards the beach. It didn't take long for them to find what they were looking for. The boxes contained the cocaine and guns, while the suitcases had the money.

"Looks like a pirate's hide-out," said Dready.

"Yes, it is. We'd better get the hell out of here," said Earl. "Those boys wouldn't like to know that we found their stash. Man, this place stinks. I think they have a dead body somewhere in here."

Dready acknowledged Earl's statement.

"I will call the police," he said.

"No man!" said Earl nervously, "they might pin it on me like last time. Let's get the fuck out of here, then you can call them from

120

the main land."

Dready contemplated Earl's suggestion, but although he was curious as to the occupants and the business conducted from that house, he agreed to do so, even though he would have liked to take some for evidence. They left the house almost as they found it and walked back down the hill towards the place where Earl had neatly parked the boat. But as they were getting into the boat another craft approached.

They hid behind some rocks and trees to watch in silence as four men and three women alighted from the boat and walked briskly up the incline towards the house.

"Do you know any of those people?" asked Dready.

"Yes," replied Earl, "they are the same people who were on my boat when that idiot shot at us. You know the ones I took to the far-out island to pickup the fish."

"Pickup what fish? Why?" asked the curious Dready.

"Well," said Earl, "the next day after the shooting, I took them to the far-out islands where they picked up some crates of large fish. Grouper, Snappers and octopus..........Hey! do you think they were bringing in the drugs in the fish?"

"Possibility," said Dready. "You might have a point there."

They watched until all the people entered the house before leaving.

"What are their names?" asked Dready.

"Don't know," replied Earl. "The two Indians sounds like Trinidadian, the two white men are English, the bald headed one does not speak at all. The short one with the moustache does all the talking while the women sound like Americans."

"All white?" asked Dready.

"Yeah, all white," said Earl.

All the way back to Nassau Earl described to Dready his observation of the people's action. Then he smiled.

"Okay," said Dready, "what's so funny?"

"See that tall red haired woman? The one in the tight white shorts?" asked Earl.

"Yes," said Dready.

"Well, all that day she rode at the wheel beside me and kept feeling my dick at every opportunity," stated Earl. "I couldn't believe she wanted me while her husband was in the room down below with their friends. I told her not to, but it seemed she was hell bent on doing it in public."

Earl stopped and there was a lengthy silence.

"So?" asked Dready, anxious to hear the rest of the story.

"Nothing happened on the boat," said Earl, "but when we got back to Nassau she invited herself back aboard after they left. Well, seeing that it was night, we screwed right here on deck."

"What's her name?" asked Dready.

"I don't know," said Earl angrily, "she told me but I cannot remember. Darlene, Daniel, DeLeon.....something like that, I don't remember."

"Did you ever have sex with her again?" asked Dready.

"No man, this is the first time I've seen her since we got back to Nassau," Earl answered.

"Why don't you.........?" began Dready.

"No! No! No!" objected Earl. "I'm not doing that again. I'm not going to seduce any more woman to get information for you. I'll introduce you to her and you can bang her to get what you want."

"Chicken," dared Dready. "Remember now; you are the one who told me that you could seduce any woman and get whatever you want from them, and....."

"Yes, I did say so; but with her, I'm not about to take the chance and have her husband shoot me, or to walk the plank." Earl protested. "Look brother Winston," he continued, "those people are mad and I'm not going to be a sacrifice for anybody. I will introduce you to her and you can take it from there, okay?"

"Okay," said Dready realizing that he really couldn't convince Earl to test his expertise to get the information he needed. "What about the two Indian men, who are they?"

"I really don't know," said Earl. "That night was the first time I ever saw them."

The two friends argued the issue of Earl seducing the red haired woman to get some information, all the way into the yacht club dock. Dready decided to do it himself.

"When can you introduce me?" asked Dready as they exit the boat.

"I don't know," said Earl. "First of all, I would have to make contact with her, then arrange it for a place where her husband or his friends cannot see us talking, then I could...."

"Okay then," said Dready, "make it for after I return from Jamaica."

"Good," replied Earl, "that would give me enough time to set it up properly."

Dready sat with Earl in the club restaurant long enough to have a small conch soup and a scotch on the rocks.

"Tell me Earl, have you ever met or spoken to Rosita after she married Ambross?" asked Dready.

Earl searched his memory for a long moment.

"No, never spoken to her since the marriage," he replied. "But I knew her as Rosita Bachstrum in school."

"How many of Tanya's friends do you know?" he asked.

"Not many, just some of her family," answered Earl.

Dready paused to think of what Earl just told him, before excusing himself to see Chief Daniels.

"Come to get me about nine-thirty in the morning for the airport," said Dready.

"I will, I will," said Earl as he turned his attention to the very attractive bartender in the short dress.

The short walk to the police headquarters took about fifteen minutes. Dready thought about what and how he wanted to present his findings to Daniels without implicating Earl, and attract the policeman's attention to his investigation into other things, other than what he had told him he was doing for his magazine.

"Hi Chief," said Dready, flashing a wide grin on entering the office, "nice day isn't it?"

"Absolutely," said Daniels. "What's up?"

"Well," said Dready as he sat across the desk to look into the policeman's eyes, "I almost got killed this morning by a jealous husband and I think he's still upset and might come back to finish the job."

Daniels smiled as he put down his pen, folded his arms across his chest and leaned back into the chair to hear the story.

"You see," began Dready, "last night I was at the Carmichael Restaurant when the most damnedest thing happened to me. I met this tourist woman name Rona Samuels and we returned to the casino, had a few drinks, gambled until it was late and ended up in bed. Well, this morning at breakfast, her husband saw us leaving my room and accused her of being unfaithful, and me for enticing her.

He created a small scene in the restaurant at the hotel and threatened to kill me. As I was driving out towards South Ocean Beach, a car pulled alongside me where a man with a gun, hijacked and forced me to abandon my car. He took me on a boat to a house on Abaco where, for almost an hour, he terrorized me. At first, I thought he was going to torture me before killing me, but instead he showed me the basement of his house where he had boxes of cocaine, guns and cash money. The place had a pungent aroma like a corpse was down there, although I didn't see one."

Dready paused waiting for a response from Daniels, but nothing happened so he continued.

"Well, to my surprise, some other people arrived and began drinking, not caring for my presence. They all sat around talking while this un-named man explained that I was to take the rap for the death of another man which they killed some time ago."

"Where's this place?" asked Daniels.

"I don't know the name of it," said Dready, "but I could show it to you."

"How did you escape?" asked Daniels.

Dready snickered before answering.

"You see," said Dready, "there's this horny red haired woman who was a part of their gang, she seemed to like black men and wanted me badly. She excused herself and requested that I follow her. We left the others in the livingroom and went into a bedroom where she literally raped me. For some reason she dozed off leaving me awake, so I got out through a window and ran to the beach. I saw a passing fisher-man and waved for him to stop and he brought me here to Nassau. Now, I'm not sure if the man will come after me again."

Daniels starred at Dready for a long moment. Dready felt he had seen through his lies, then as though something hit his mind, he picked up the phone and called in another officer.

"Rupert Abbot, meet Dready Winston," he said and watched the two men shook hands. "Rupert, I want you to get six men, some guns and meet me at the police dock for a trip to Abaco island; in fifteen minutes. I don't want any screw-ups on this one, but be ready to meet some criminals, and bring along the forensic doctor also, we might need him."

Dready was happy that Daniels didn't question him any further and was about to act instantly. They walked in silence to the dock and got on board one of the police launches. He gave the driver the general direction and sat back for the ride. He was surprised that he was able to remember the area and pointed out the dock in which to park. The policemen wasted little time getting to and surrounding the house. It was empty so they entered and began the search. Dready guided Daniels to the closet and showed him the entrance door to the basement. They, along with three of the other police officers, entered.

"Good God!" exclaimed Daniels. "What the hell is in this place?"

"This is some sort of a warehouse for their coke, guns and money," said Dready, "and this is where they took me. I presume to leave evidence; finger prints etcetera, to be found by the police later."

"Holy shit!" said Rupert Abbot, "they must have been using this as a slaughter house also."

"Get started on the gathering of evidence," ordered Daniels, as he got on his police phone to headquarters. "Let me speak to Irene Balsam please," he said to whoever was on the other end, "hello Irene," he continued, "send a chopper and the T.V. crew out here, I want everyone to see this and to know that we are doing something to curb the operations of the criminals in this country."

He bade the person goodbye and turned to Dready.

"How did you stumble onto this?" he asked.

"I told you the story," said Dready, "and it's going to be an intricate part of my magazine story also."

"Okay," said Daniels, "but please keep out of the way when the T.V. people get's here. I don't want you muddling up the picture."

"Who owns this house?" asked Dready.

"Some Arabs recently bought it from the dead Mr Wakefield, who acquired it from the daughter of a man name Sanderson," replied Daniels.

"Did Sanderson build this house?" asked Dready.

"Yes, but he died a short time ago," said Daniels.

"How?" enquired Dready.

"He fell over board his yacht when a fish he caught pulled him in," said Daniels. "It seemed that his harness accidentally broke when the driver of the boat suddenly sped off. Now, that was a mystery, because that man was a great swimmer and a professional deep sea diver, and there were many other crafts in the area at the time also and none went to his rescue."

"Did he have any alcohol in his blood at the time?" asked Dready.

"None what ever," answered Daniels. "My instinct tells me it was murder but the coroner ruled it as mis-adventure so that his daughter could collect the insurance and this house."

"Where is she now?" asked Dready.

126

"She moved back to Tellahassee Florida about two years ago, to her ex-husband and two children and never return here," said Daniels, "then Wakefield sold it to the Arabs and then this."

"Where are the Arabs now?" asked Dready.

"Don't know," said Daniels, "but I will find them. They are material witnesses and I have a few questions for them. Did you say that the people who brought you here were whites?"

"Yes," replied Dready, "and wealthy looking."

"Including the red haired woman?" asked Daniels.

"Yes," replied Dready. "Do you think they were some of the pirates you told me about?"

"Definitely," said Daniels. "I would really like to see that red haired woman also."

"I will point her out to you after I return from Jamaica," said Dready. "Going home for Christmas dinner."

"Okay good," said Daniels, "but if you run into Bernard Graves, please say hello for me, he's a good man."

When the TV camera crew and police photographers came, Dready left the house for the cleaner air outside. He sat on a bench thinking of the development since they landed in Nassau. Some of which has tied into his previous case when he was there to neutralize the Jamaican ganja boys and a lot seemed to be connected to the Jamaican affair of last year.

The words of Earl Monroe keep ringing in his ears.

"We went to an island to pick-up fish; crates of large fishes. Snapper, Grouper and Octopus," Earl had said.

Dready gave thoughts to this; and the more he did the more he was convinced that the cargo of fish was laden with diamonds from Guyana or cocaine from somewhere else. Then he thought about the phony Mr Austin J. Smithers, the man with the white streak in his hair like a skunk. He gave thought to Hubert Bachstrum, Paul Mason and Tullis Burke. He gave thoughts to Cynthia and her lies about her relationship to Paul, whom she described as her nephew and sometimes, cousin.

"Maybe, he could even be her son," said Dready.

He gave thoughts to Paul Mason's connection to the dead students in Toronto and his attempt to disenfranchise himself from the last arrest with Christiana.

"Aaah Rona," he thought, "she's up to her arse in this and trying to sucker me into doing something for her and the phoney Smithers, and the missing RCMP Chrittendon."

He sat thinking for a long time until Rupert Abbot came to talk to him. He noticed that although Rupert was a long serving officer, he didn't appeared to be a bright chap, and concluded that he was a protected specie on the force.

"Hey Dready!" said Abbot. "Couldn't take the stench down there eh?"

"No sir," replied Dready, "I had to get some fresh air. What was it?"

"My friend, they found three cadavers and a crate of overdue fish down there," said Rupert.

"Did they identify the bodies?" asked Dready.

"No," said Abbot, "but two of them are women, one black and one white. The doctor said the man has been dead for a long time."

"Any name attached to him?" asked Dready.

"Not yet, but you can bet assured that Daniels will come up with a name before long."

"How long have you been on the police force Rupert?" asked Dready.

"Almost eighteen years," replied Abbot, "and I've seen many things, even some very questionable ones."

"I presume you've worked for Daniels all those years?" asked Dready.

"Yes sir, and he's a fine officer," replied Abbot.

"He told me that there are pirates operating in the Bahamas, true?"

"Thousands of them," replied Abbot. "But Daniels has his

eyes on them."

"Do you know any of them?" asked Dready.

"Not personally, but know of them," said Abbot. "Many ships have been hijacked in these waters, and their cargo disappear, but always out of our jurisdiction."

"Tell me Rupert, have you ever heard of a man name Charles Chrittendon?"

"Yes," answered Abbot, "we found his body on the South Ocean beach about three weeks ago, but Daniels wanted it kept quiet from the media. How did you know about him?"

"A little bird told me and I'm wondering where he came from and how he fits into my story," said Dready.

"Well, the most I can tell you is, he came from Canada and was working for the police to find out about the smugglers, but it seemed something went wrong and he was killed. Nobody is saying by whom, but nevertheless he's dead."

"I see," said Dready. "If Karlheinz Bass was alive or if Arthur Collins wasn't in prison, I would certainly suspect them. That's something they would do."

"Who are they?" asked Abbot.

"Just a couple of criminals who are not in circulation at this time," answered Dready. "One is fertilizing the grass and the other is getting his arse reamed in prison."

"Oh," said Abbot, "are they related to Chrittendon?"

"Not to my knowledge," said Dready. "Ever heard of a woman named Rosita Ambross?"

"No, but Daniels might," answered Abbot.

"I must remember to ask him," said Dready.

"Daniels came to the door and hollered for Abbot; so Dready resumed his thoughts about the people in this case. He must have sat for an hour before Daniels came to him.

"We'll be leaving in a few minutes, so if you want to talk to the reporters do so now, because when I close the case it will be closed to everyone."

"That's okay by me," said Dready, "I really don't want to know who they are at this time. Furthermore, if I need to add them to my story I could always come to see you, right?"

"Right," said Daniels, "you can always come to see me,"

It didn't take long for them to parcel up everything in the house and stow them onto a boat. Dready watched with interest as Daniels directed the crew in every phase of the packaging and moving. He got into the police launch as directed and in silence they rode back to Nassau.

"Thank you for the tip," said Chief Daniels, "I will remember your good deed."

"Mmmmm," said Dready as they shook hands. "Just keep the red haired woman's husband away from me."

They parted company.

"He never mention anything about a suspect," reflected Dready and headed towards Bay Street.

Dready walked in the direction of the straw market and the British Colonial Hotel. He wanted to go there for a drink and a little chat with the barman he had met on his last visit to the city and whom had been mentioned by Venrece Alexander.

Lincoln Grey was a short stocky man in his mid forties, but looked late twenties. He had assisted Dready the last time and was proud of it.

"Hey Linc," said Dready as he sat at the bar. "How the hell are you, the wife and children?"

"They are all doing fine, except me," said Linc as he stretched his hand for a shake. "Nice to see you again Dready boy, when did you come into Nassau?"

"Only a few days ago," replied Dready, "but have been busy."

"Glad to see you man," said Linc as he placed the beer in front of Dready. "What can I help you with this time?"

"Well," said Dready as he sipped his beer, "I'm trying to find a man named Charles Chrittendon and....."

"Dead," replied Linc, without waiting for the completion of the question.

"How about Austin J. Smithers?" asked Dready.

"Dead," said Linc.

How about Bartholomew Wakefield?"

"Dead," said Linc. "Why don't you ask me about people who are alive? I might be able to help you."

"Okay, do you know Hubert Bachstrum?" asked Dready.

"Know the entire family of criminals," said Linc in a whisper. "They are the Dons of the Bahamas and do make people disappear."

"How would you know that?" asked Dready.

"As a barman," said Linc snickering, "I hear a lot of things after people have had a few, and I use that knowledge to keep my job in this establishment."

"Then tell me about them," said Dready, "and don't bullshit me."

Linc went over to serve a couple of men at the other end of the counter then returned.

"Those people are ruthless people, from the father, the sons and the wives," said Linc. "Rumours have it that Hubert killed his father to get control of the drugs and diamond business, he even dumped his brother Ralph and his niece Celia. His aunt Althea's husband was also fixed by him. He likes to do things personally, because he gets a kick from it. Dready my boy, take this advice from a friend, don't get tangled up with him."

"Has he ever been convicted of anything?" asked Dready.

"Not to my knowledge," replied Linc. "I think he has some police in his pocket and they are making sure that nothing points to him."

"Thanks for the advice," said Dready. "Have you ever seen Judith Wakefield the wife of Bartholomew Wakefield?"

"Sure, she used to come in here for a few drinks every night," answered Linc, "then she disappeared. I will bet you one hundred

131

American that she's dead."

Dready thought about it and almost took the bet, then he realized that the woman he met in Wakefield's house could also be an imposter.

"Why would she be killed?" asked Dready.

"She wasn't afraid to talk," said Linc.

"What does she look like?" he asked instead.

"Short, fat, dark hair, grey eyes and wears raggy clothes," said Linc. "Have you seen her?"

"No, but I will keep an eye out for her," replied Dready.

Linc went to replenish the fellows drinks and to serve a couple others, then quickly returned to Dready.

"Man, as a bartender, I see and hear a lot. But I'm smart, I don't get involved with their business," said Linc proudly, "but every time I think of how much it cost to send the children to school, I wish I had joined them."

"How much do you know about Tullis Burke?" asked Dready.

Linc's mouth fell open as though Dready had kicked him in the arse.

"What's the matter," asked Dready, "did I touched a button?"

"Yes you did," replied Linc looking around for listening ears, "I would like to tell you about him some other time but not in here."

"Does his name scare you?" asked Dready.

"Certainly does," said Linc. "If you meet me on my day off tomorrow, I will tell you all I know about that boy."

"Okay," said Dready, "and I would like to hear of his relationship with Cynthia, Salina and Paul Mason."

"That's easy," said Linc, "Paul is the son of Cynthia. Cynthia and Fran are sisters from the same mother and father, while Salina and another girl is the father's daughters. Tullis is their half brother from the same mother and another man, but I cannot tell you the entire story here. Meet me on my day off and I will set you straight."

"Okay then, I want to know about Zenon's daughter Tanya

also," said Dready.

"Tanya is not Bachstrum's daughter," said Linc. "She's the daughter of Zenon's brother Karlheinz in Jamaica."

"Do you mean Karlheinz Bass?" asked Dready.

"The same," replied Linc.

"But Karlheinz is Bass and he is Bach......" said Dready.

"Bachstrum change his name before coming to Nassau," added Linc.

"Ah! ah!" said Dready. "So little old Tanya is not a Bachstrum. When did she come to the Bahamas?"

"She and her sister Rosita came to live with the Bachstrum's after her mother and uncle was killed in Kingston; poisoned."

"How old was she when she came to Nassau?" asked Dready.

"About five years old," said Linc. "Anyway, I will tell you about it later."

Dready got up from the bar and dropped a couple of American twenties on the counter.

"How come you know so much about these people?" asked Dready.

"I spent sixteen years on the police force, you know," said Lincoln.

"You did? What happened?" asked Dready.

"I was forcefully removed for improper conduct," said Linc, "but I will tell you the entire story tomorrow."

"Thanks Linc," said Dready as he slid off the bar stool, "and please pay for my beer."

He decided to have a solo dinner at the restaurant across the street when he had a mind flash. He grabbed the phone near the hotel door and dialled the Palace number.

"May I speak to Mrs. Rona Samuels please," he said into the phone.

A few clicks later, she answered.

"Hello, Rona Samuels here," said the voice.

"It's me, Dready; what are you doing for dinner?" he asked.

"Well, hello Mr. Dready Winston," she replied in a pleased tone. "I've been looking for you all afternoon, where have you been?"

"As I told you this morning, I had to go to Abaco to make a deal, well I'm finished now and am back in town," he said. "Would you like to meet me down town for dinner?"

"Certainly, where?" she asked.

"At present I'm at the Colonial, but you could meet me at the Pirate on Shirley street near Highland," he suggested.

"Good," she answered, "I'll take a taxi and be there in a few minutes."

They hung up the phones and he trekked back along Bay Street to Mackay to Shirley and the restaurant, only to get there a couple of minutes before she arrived.

"Hi Dready," she said approaching him, "been waiting long?"

"Yes, I was about to leave, because I thought you had changed your mind," he said lying.

"Sorry, but I had to go up to change my clothes," she said in an apologetic tone. "I grabbed a taxi to get here as quickly as he could drive."

"Fine," he said, "let's go have something to eat, I'm starving."

They descended to the lower restaurant and found a corner table that was out of the main traffic. He pulled the chair for her and she sat. Within a minute the waitress came and took their order.

"Didn't those bastards feed you today?" she asked.

"Yes, but I didn't want their food," he said smiling, "I was afraid they might poison me like they did to poor old Wakefield."

"Oh shit!" she said in a whisper, "it must have been Hubert or Clinton who did it."

"Who the hell is Hubert? Is it Bachstrum?" he asked as though he was hearing the name for the first time.

"Yes, the same one," Rona answered.

"And Clinton?" he asked.

"That's Reeves," she answered. "Clinton Reeves is a fellow we met on our last visit here. He's an American from New Jersey who came to Nassau as a dealer at the Casino over there," she pointed. "He jumped to the enforcement business and is now working exclusively for Hubert. He is a freak who loves to beat up or kill people for pleasure."

The waitress returned with the drinks.

"Here's to us tonight," said Rona. "There will be a tonight for us, won't there?"

"Sure," said Dready, "tonight is for us."

They chinked glasses and resumed the conversation.

Dready was surprised that Rona wasn't afraid to tell him about her friends and associates, who committed crimes and had not been penalized for it.

"Do you know a Charles Chrittendon?" he asked her.

"Yes, I met him on my last trip also," she replied. "He was some kind of a dealer with connections somewhere in South America. All I know is, he only hang out with Hubert, Althea and two other men from Trinidad."

"Ever heard about Karlheinz Bass?" asked Dready.

"Yes, I met him at a party in Jamaica a long time ago, along with Arthur Collins and Peter McKenzie. I heard he's now dead," said Rona.

"Party in Jamaica, eh?" Dready stated.

"Yes sir," said Rona smiling. "My father was a good friend of Karlheinz and Captain Smith, so I was required to escort him to these functions there at their exclusive bridge club in Kingston, all the way from England. Don't let my present looks deceive you. During the fifties I was once a very pretty girl and many men wanted me, but I choose and got married to Colonel Ellary Samuels and moved to Germany where he was stationed."

"I see, so what happened to Colonel Ellary Samuels?" he asked.

"He was killed in a single car accident on our holidays back in England about a year later," she said.

"Intoxicated?" asked Dready.

"Yes, blind drunk," she answered.

"I guess life was rough for you there after," Dready stated.

"Not really," said Rona smiling, "actually his friends were very attentive to me and saw to all my needs."

"So, how did you get into the smuggling business?" asked Dready.

Rona smiled as she recollected her thoughts,

"One day I got a visit from Captain Smith, who was on holidays in England, he asked me to come to Jamaica for a rest. I did, and had a wonderful time. Then when I was leaving he asked me to carry a shipment up to England for him. It was then I discovered the word snatchel."

"What the hell is snatchel?" asked Dready.

"That's when the women carry the stuff in their pussy," she replied.

Dready laughed out loud as though he was hearing the terminology for the first time.

"What's so funny?" she asked.

"It's your accent, when you say snatchel," he replied.

"I'm a scouse; you know, from Liverpool," she said, "maybe that's the reason it sounded funny."

"Maybe," said Dready. "Why didn't you just say pussy?"

"That's in reference to a cat," she said, "anyway that's what Smith called it in Jamaica, and since then everybody always used that terminology to describe the procedure."

"So, I presume you have met many friends at the bridge club then?" he asked.

"Certainly; I got acquainted with Barbara Smith, Lilly and Patricia Green," replied Rona. "Then there were people like Peter McKenzie, Arthur Collins and many others."

Dready didn't comment, only acted surprised.

136

"Ever met Venrece Alexander?" he asked.

"No, not that I can recall," she answered. "Was he a member of the club?"

"Yes, he was a tennis star," said Dready.

Rona shook her head negatively. Dready changed the subject.

They completed the dinner and had desert. Rona suggested they go to the casino to gamble for awhile before going to bed for that intercourse she expected.

They left the restaurant and took a taxi to the Palace.

"Meet you in the casino in half hour," said Rona as she dashed off to the elevator.

He visited the men's room, then went into the bar and had a quiet beer. The phone rang and the barman brought it to him.

"For you sir," he said to Dready.

"Hello," he said into the mouth piece hoping that it would be Christiana calling to see how he was. But it was Cynthia Mason.

"Hi handsome," she said, "where have you been? I've been looking for you all afternoon. Can you meet me outside tonight at eleven thirty? I have something for you."

"Your pussy?" he asked sarcastically.

"Yes, that too," she replied, "but I have some information you asked for."

"Okay," he said, "outside at eleven thirty."

He gave the phone to the barman, finished his beer and headed for his room. There he checked on the money he stashed in the ceiling of the clothes closet, had a shower and laid on the bed for almost an hour thinking about the case. Finally he got up. It was almost eleven o'clock, so he put on some clothes and slowly walked down to the casino.

He found a happy Rona at her favourite blackjack table. She wore a short baggy pale-orange dress that seemed to hang around her body, rather than fit. Her large breasts appeared as though they wanted to extricate themselves from her braless, low-cut neckline while her footwear was her bedroom slippers. He noticed that she had nice shapely legs for a fifty plus woman.

"Hello Mrs. Samuels," he said approaching her, "winning I see."

"A stroke of good luck darling," she replied. "Come sit beside me for awhile, I will need your assistance to carry this money home."

He sat beside her. He realized that she had a couple of stiff drinks before he got there from the empty glasses sitting on the counter. Rona drank as the dealer slide the cards on the table, game after game. Finally she took his hand and placed it between her legs under her dress. He casually looked around to assure himself that nobody could see his hand under her dress in the dark. She slowly placed her hand on his and directed it to her crotch, and felt that she didn't have any panty on.

"Keep it there honey," she instructed. "That feels great," she whispered in his ear.

"For you maybe," he said.

He got up from the stool and kissed her on the cheek.

"Are you leaving me alone again?" she asked.

"I'll be back," he said as he walked off.

"Crazy woman," he said in thoughts.

He got to the front door, after first going to the washroom, to see Cynthia standing across the road waiting for him. He crossed to face her.

"What have you got?" he asked.

"Not here," she said, "my place. We didn't do it last night so we can tonight in style and comfort."

"Look Cynthia," he snapped pretending to be annoyed from the quarrel they had the night before, "I'm leaving for Jamaica in the morning to meet that woman and have to pack and get some sleep, so keep the thing warm until I return, okay? You can wait can't you?. Now tell me what you've got."

Cynthia got angry instantly.

"Why the hell did you asked me to wait if you didn't want to have sex?" she whispered angrily.

"Because you told me that you have some information," he shouted in a whisper back at her. "Now, either you give it to me or get lost."

Cynthia contemplated his suggestion and decided to tell him.

"Hubert Bachstrum will be coming to the hotel to meet a woman name Rona Samuels tonight," she said. "I heard her telling him that she have a petty smuggler that could be used to transact the South American deal, only that he might need persuading."

"What room will the meeting be held?" he asked.

"Room 937 at mid-night," answered Cynthia.

"Good, I will see if I can get an invitation to that meeting," he said. "Do you know what Rona Samuels looks like?"

"No, never seen her," said Cynthia.

Dready felt pleased that Cynthia did not connect the woman with him and the name.

"Thank you," he said as he moved in closer to kiss her, "and please keep it warm until I return. I might be really in need if things don't work out right in Jamaica."

He stuffed Cynthia into a taxi cab and handed the driver a twenty and waved goodbye as the cab pulled away. Within minutes he was back in the casino beside the, now drunk, Rona again. He looked at the stock of chips piled high in front of her and quickly signalled the floor man to come to cash her in.

When all was done and he collected the six thousand and change from the cashier, he guided Rona to the elevator. He found room 937 and fumbled in her purse for the key to open the door.

"Come on darling, it's time for bed," he said.

She began taking off her clothes but couldn't, so he helped her. He laid her on the bed and covered her with the top sheet and went into the livingroom to wait.

He didn't have to wait long because the knock on the door alerted him. He looked at the clock and it was five minutes to twelve. He opened the door, and there stood in front of him was the man he saw escorting Christiana in the airport; and since he knew she was meeting Tullis Burke, he knew this was him in person.

The other man was about six foot tall with a large slightly balding head and was dressed in shorts and a floral shirt. He looked more like a European tourist than a resident of the Bahamas.

"Who are you?" the balding man asked as he pushed pass Dready.

"My name is Dready Winston," he answered.

"What are you doing here?" the balding man asked.

"Well, I met Rona in the casino and had a few drinks together, we gambled a little then she invited me to her room. We were here making love, but she fell asleep so I was on my way out. I was about to leave when you knocked. I thought it was room service because she wanted something to eat and might have called them when I was in the bathroom. I hope she's not your wife."

The man sized him up as Burke mixed them a drink.

"No, she's not my wife," said the man, "and I don't give a shit who she lays."

"Well," said Dready, "I didn't know Rona was expecting visitors this late, but evidently I was wrong. She's asleep in there so I might as well leave you here with her."

He was bluffing, hoping the man would stop him from departing. He got to the door before the man spoke again.

"Sit down Mr. Dready Winston," said the man, "my name is Hubert Bachstrum and I really came up to see you. Rona told me that you might be here with her tonight so you're in good company. She also told me that you are in the diamond business and was seeking an agent in Nassau."

"Right," said Dready, "I came to Nassau to meet a man named Bartholomew Wakefield, but I heard he's dead and I was grasping at anything. I went to Abaco to see another man named Chrittendon but

140

he is also dead, so I'm leaving tomorrow for Jamaica to see a friend of mine who might know somebody there. I really cannot go back to Canada empty handed."

"Well you're in luck," said Hubert Bachstrum, "I might be able to assist you in your dealings."

"Great!" said Dready as he hustled across the room to shake hands with the man.

"No hand shake please," said Hubert, "I don't know where your hands have been. All I want to hear is how much diamonds and where is the money."

"I was thinking about $300,000 dollars worth," said Dready, "and if they are good quality, I would recommend the next purchase to be $2.5 million," he said.

He could see the light went on in Bachstrum's eyes on hearing the class of money he would be dealing with.

"You would have to pay extra for the couriers," said Bachstrum, "and the pick up would be at my designation."

"Whatever you say," replied Dready. "Our money is real."

"And no monkey business," said Hubert, "although we will have our people there to assure there isn't any rip off."

"I can assure you Hubert," said Dready, "our money is good clean and in a safe place in the Grand Caymans."

"Good," said Hubert, getting out of the chair, "just tell Rona whenever you're ready to do the deal. She knows where to find me."

He signalled Tullis Burke and they quickly left the room. Dready closed the door behind them, checked to see Rona was still asleep and laid on the sofa for about an hour before leaving for his room.

Chapter Six

Christmas in Jamaica.

*H*e stood in the middle of the crowd outside the Sangster Airport anxiously awaiting his wife's emergence. He had arrived three hours earlier, on the American airlines flight from Nassau and had gone to have lunch with Carlton at their favourite Whitehouse restaurant, and returned just in time for her Air Canada flight. In his mind, there were much to talk over with her about the case, but for now he was mostly interested in the season and the happiness that it brings; also the fact that they would be together with the family.

"Look! There she is!" shouted Ackeeface. "Get ready to grab her bag before any of the other taxi drivers can get to her."

Dready smiled to see his woman in one piece. All the time that she was away in Canada, he was worried knowing that the arrest would have taken place and she could be identified by the fellow's cronies, as the woman who got caught to break up their ring.

"Hello darling," she said kissing him, "how was your flight from Nassau?"

"Very well, thank you," he replied, "how was your adventure

into Toronto?"

"Excellent," she answered happily, "Morrow and his boys did a fine job to keep me above suspicion. Mason and his colleagues will think for a long time that I was arrested and imprisoned for the diamonds. They also will think that it was he who squealed on them. Hello Ackeeface," she said, pausing to greet her old friend who taught her to speak patois on her first visit to Jamaica, "how are you doing?"

"Just fine," Ackeeface replied. "Except for the new van, and the work on the house, everything is fine."

"Great stuff," she said, "you'll have to take me there to see the house. I want to spend a day in it with Evelyn and the children."

"That I can do," replied Ackeeface.

Quickly her mind shifted from Carlton to her own child.

"How is Venrece-Thomas? Is he okay?" she asked.

"I don't know," said Dready, "I haven't reached home as yet, but I assume mother has her hands full with him."

"Well let's go, I want to see my son now," she said.

The long drive to Savanna-La-Mar was relaxing as usual. Christiana sat comfortably in the back seat recalling the events of the previous year and comparing it to the Nassau incident. She realized that there were thing in this one, that are simular as last year.

"Carlton," she said, "I must come home more often because the longer I stay away the more patois I will have to learn."

"That's true," said Ackeeface, "it's a language that you must practice."

"So right," she replied. "Carlton, please stop at our favourite coconut man, I would like a nice cool jelly."

"Yes darling," replied Ackeeface, "that was the exact thing on my mind."

Dready sat quietly listening to the two old friends chat about the events of their lives of the past year. Although he wanted to be involved, his thoughts of the Bahamian operation stuck in his mind and was too busy chewing over some of the things he had encountered, privately.

"I must talk to Bernard and Commissioner Dillon tomorrow," he said in thoughts, "and I must get Graves to keep Christiana busy after I leave."

He was so engrossed in his thoughts, he didn't realize where he was until Carlton pulled alongside the coconut man's cart.

"One each," said Ackeeface.

"....and I want mine with a whole lot of meat, sir," said Christiana.

"What about you sir?" said the coconut man to Dready.

"Just jelly," replied Dready, "soft one."

They all had the cool fruit drink and got into the car again. All the rest of the way there he listened to Carlton and Christian talk about life.

"Ackeeface," said Dready, "what's happening for Christmas? Any parties?"

"Man!" said Carlton, "those boys have a big dance lined up for the Grand Lido that same night, with five well known bands. Men will be coming from Trinidad and Antigua, but you have to buy the tickets early."

"How soon?" asked Dready.

"Don't worry about it," said Ackeeface, "I will go get them tomorrow, I have a friend name Larry Chung down there and he will look after me."

"Fine," said Dready, "I will leave that in your capable hands."

"Chung?" asked Christiana, "is he related to Orville Chung that got killed?"

"Yes," replied Ackeeface, "he is the younger brother, who was in England when Orville get killed, but he came home to live a month after."

"Where does he live?" asked Christiana.

"In Lucie," said Ackeeface. "I know where he lives, why?"

"I would like to talk with him," she said.

"When?" responded Ackeeface.

"Next week some time," she said.

"Alright, I will tell him, and take it from there," he said.

They pulled into the Perkins driveway. Christiana didn't waste any time getting out of the car and into the house.

"Hello, I'm home," she shouted as she entered the verandah. "Anybody home?"

"Elsa must have seen them coming because she was at the door with the baby to meet them. Christiana took the baby from her arms, kissed her mother-in-law on the cheeks and her baby.

"Hello big boy," she said cuddling him to her breasts, "were you a good boy for granny?"

As if the baby understood, he began to gurgle a laugh. Dready and Carlton stood back watching her performance, waiting for their turn to rub their face in his stomach.

"Oh, I missed you so much," she said.

"And what about me?" asked Dready.

"I missed you too darling," she answered and kissed him lightly and just as quick, resumed her cuddling of her baby.

This went on for a long time with Christiana telling them about going into the Bahamas and her fast trip back to Toronto before coming there.

"I didn't get a chance to see anything," she said.

"Maybe after it's over, you two could spend a few days alone there," suggested Elsa.

"Absolutely right mother; what's for dinner?" she asked.

"We have Gungu soup, fried fish, rice and peas, fried plantins and..." said Elsa.

"That sounds great," she said, interrupting Elsa. "When can we eat?"

"Right now," said her mother-in-law.

Christiana handed over the baby to Dready and rushed off to

the kitchen. Everybody followed her and quickly got seated. While Elsa was busy dishing out the food, Christiana got busy setting the table.

"How about a beer?" asked Dready, "any in the fridge?"

"Yes," said Elsa, "father put some in there just for you and Ackeeface."

He got up to fetch the beers for himself and Carlton.

"Where's father?" asked Dready.

"You don't have to ask," said Elsa, glancing at the clock on the wall, "he's still at the farm but will be home in a few minutes."

They ate and chatted about many things until Thomas came home.

"Hello father," Christiana greeted him with a kiss, "hiding from me, eh?"

"Not at all, my dear," said Thomas, "I had to spend some time with one of my cows who decided to have her calf this evening."

"And did she?" Christiana asked.

"Yes, and it was easy," said Thomas. "It's her second one."

Christiana gave thoughts to the cow's plight and in a smiling tone said,

"Will my second be just as easy?"

"Maybe," replied her father-in-law, "I think it will be."

They wrapped arms and strolled into the diningroom to announce the cow's achievement.

Suddenly, an air of excitement overtake the gathering. Everybody wanted to rush to the barn to see the new calf, but they had to wait for Thomas to eat his dinner. The trip to the farm was quick and the time spent was exciting for Christiana, because she was able to touch the new born calf.

"What is it?" she asked Thomas.

"It's a bull," he answered, "and I can get big money for him in a year's time."

"Why? Do you really have to sell him? He is so cute," she said rubbing her hand over the animal's face.

"Because," replied Thomas, "that's how the business goes my dear, it's not right to interbreed the herd."

She made so much fuss about a woman giving birth and compared it to her own experience, that Elsa had to remind her of the six she bore.

"It's getting late," said Thomas, "let's go home now."

They got back to the house to find the other brothers and sisters there, and the excitement began all over again. For Christiana, it was nice to see Dorothy and Barrington again and to talk with Ezrah and his wife Jean, who came all the way from England for the Christmas. Johnnie was now a qualified doctor after his graduation from Illinois State University in Chicago. Sister Monica Thom and her husband Anthony, from Port Antonio, seemed comfortable to be away from their very demanding clothing and grocery business.

This year, Pamela came home early from Kingston to assist her mother with the preparation for Christmas. The conversations ranged from their trip to Nassau and hers into Toronto to the expected preparation for the Christmas dinner, which was only two days away.

As expected, the boys left the house and went into town for a few drinks while the women discussed the procedure for the festive season. The pool table was empty, so Ackeeface and Dready began a game, which turned into a sort of tournament. Some of the other men in the bar came over to join them and the laughs went on until late. Nobody cared to know the time, and it was nearly midnight when they left for home again.

"Now, that was fun," said brother Ezrah as they got outside. "Winston, do you realize that you and I had not enjoy any time together for almost five years?"

"That is so," said Dready, "maybe we should make this a point to do in the future."

"Maybe we should get a table for the house when I move

back, and meet there for a tournament every year," said Ezrah

"Agreed," said Dready. "Are you really moving back home? When?"

"Right now," replied Ezrah. "Jean and I decided to come home and start an import business here and leave the cold country to younger people."

"Good," said Dready, "you two can surely make a living from that."

"Sure can," said Ezrah.

"Where are you going to live?" he asked.

"I was thinking of buying a piece of land near here but......." said Ezrah.

"Last year we bought some near Ocho Rios," said Dready excitedly interrupting his brother. "Ask Carlton and Christiana to take you there to see it. Maybe you could purchase and build near us."

"Maybe I will," said Ezrah.

They shook hands.

"So what about this assignment in the Bahamas?" asked Ezrah. "Is it as involved as the one in Jamaica last year?"

"Definitely is," answered Dready, "I'm finding out that some of the children of the people involved in the last case are deeply involved in this case. It seemed that the tentacles of the octopus are spread out far and wide, and some of the children who were being groomed at that time for this very same kind of action, have taken over. Can you imagine? They have a never-ending stream of criminals at their disposal with the young people doing the things the older ones had done at another time. Which makes it hard for us."

"How long are you staying in Jamaica?" Ezrah asked. "Maybe we both could......."

"No we couldn't," said Dready, interrupting him. "I have to be back in Nassau in a week's time."

Ezrah gave thought to his brother's answer, then said,

"Then what about Christiana, where will she be?"

"She will be staying here in Jamaica," said Dready.

"Why?" asked the concerned brother. "The Bahamas could be a nice holiday for her you know?"

"I know that, but I don't want her there when the shooting starts, and secondly I don't want her to know that I am a cop as yet. As far as she knows I am an investigative crime reporter, and she must be kept in the dark for now."

"Why do you want her to still think you're a reporter when she is assisting you to solve the cases? When will you tell her?" asked Ezrah.

"Someday soon," said Dready. "All I want from you is your word not to tell her anything and to make sure that she is protected whenever she goes into town."

"Okay, I won't tell her, but if she ask me, I won't lie," his brother answered. "I still think it's wrong to deceive your wife like that."

"Dear brother," said Dready in a stern tone of voice, "it's absolutely necessary to prevent anyone taking reprisal on her because of me. Remember she was shot in the leg last time? I don't want that happening again."

"Well," said Ezrah, "she'll be in good company with Bernard, Venrece, Dad and myself."

The two brothers hugged and joined the others for the trip back to the house. On reaching, they found the entire family was still up talking, waiting for their return. They joined in, until Thomas announced his departure for bed.

On the morning of Christmas eve Dready was up early to assist in the feeding of Venrece-Thomas. He wondered why this little person could wake an entire household with just one little sound. Christiana fed and change the baby and in a few minutes he was asleep again. Dready couldn't fall back to sleep, so he got up and went outside, sat under his favourite mango tree for some fresh air, solitude and a smoke. He was delighted that the entire family was able to be together for the last three days without a quarrel or disagreement. He was able to enjoy as always his usual debate with Barrington on the finer points of laws that separated the criminal's defence. He felt happy to know that Christiana didn't get upset when Barrington informed her that these people had rights to a defence.

He sat there in deep thought and didn't move until Pamela announced breakfast. Only then he get up and go to the bathroom for his daily constitution and take a shower.

At the table he sat quietly listening to the conversations of his family and realized that they really cared for each other, and although he felt the same for them, he had a most demanding problem on his mind. He knew that he had to get Christiana away for a chat, but to find the right time to do it, seemed impossible.

"What are you doing today Winston?" asked Christiana.

"Well, firstly I have to get down to the beach for a dip, then I have to see someone in Black River and......" he said, "want to come along?"

"Certainly," she said, "maybe we could take...."

"No," he said, "we have to leave the baby at home."

"Okay then," she said, "let's go."

Within minutes Christiana was ready and they got into the car. He steered the car towards Black River. Christiana was delighted at the scenery and noted almost all the small towns they passed.

"Ferris Cross, Bluefields, New Hope," she said. "Where did you say the beach was?" she asked wondering why he chose to travel such a long way.

"Ever heard of Treasure Beach?" he asked.

"No, never heard of it," she replied.

"Well, you're going to love it," he said. "It's a beach that most Kingstonians like to come to."

Christiana could see that familiar grin on his face. That, 'something must be talked about,' grin, which she knew so well, but didn't question.

"This is Black River," she shouted. "You're passing the place we were supposed to be going."

"No," he replied. "I said we are going to Treasure Beach, remember?"

Christiana, although curious, remained silent. Even after Dready got off the main to the secondary road.

"Here we are," he said as he parked the car on the deserted beach.

She looked around at the perfectly laid-out, white sand beach, and didn't see a moving body anywhere and wondered why he took her to this beach. In less than a minute he took his clothes off and splashed naked into the calm warm water.

"Come on in," he shouted, "the water is lovely."

Without hesitation, she followed suit and dove in. They swam and splashed around for a while then back to shore. They both sat on a rock facing the water.

"Okay," she said, drying off their bodies with the towel she brought, "I know that you brought me here to talk, so talk."

Dready paused for a long moment.

"Isn't this pretty?" he asked.

"It sure is," she replied putting on her bathing suit, "but I know that this is not the objective."

"Darling," he said also installing his bathing trunks, "there are pirates everywhere in the Caribbean sea, and there seemed to be no stopping them."

"Okay, so there are pirates, what has that have to do with anything?" she asked.

"Do you remember last year I told you about the pirates of Port Royal.....?" he said.

She nodded her head.

"......well, they are still active in these waters today."

"Now, how the hell did you arrive at that?" she asked.

"You see," he began, "the pirates of yester years used to sail the Caribbean sea, bringing slaves from Africa. Some of them decided, while travelling throughout the Caribbean and to South

America, to begin hijacking and sometimes sinking each other's ships to get the treasures they bore. 'Let's dock in Tortuga,' the captain would say. At times, the bloody fights would last for days on end, even on land; with each country supplying new bodies and vessels for the purpose. That led to many wars between the Spanish and English in these waters, strictly for territorial rights. In those days, the weapons were cannon balls and powder on the ships, and the sailors carried knives and machetes. Today, the new improved modern pirate are much more sophisticated than their predecessors; with high technology radios, radars and telephones. The weapons have also improved to M16s, AK 47s, Uzies, Glacks, Berettas and in some cases, larger calibre weapons; and believe me, these sailors aren't afraid to use them. The treasures then were gold, diamonds, food and water. Today it is gold, diamonds, cocaine, money, marijuana and guns."

"Why are they doing it?" she asked.

"Territorial rights and the almighty dollar," said Dready.

"Do you think the people we are investigating now are some of these pirates?" she asked.

"Absolutely," he replied. "But I am looking for the big ones; the big fish; the ones in charge."

He told her everything about the Nassau investigation. His meeting with Cynthia Mason, her listening in to his their telephone conversation, her lies about her relationship to Paul and her lies also about all the dead students. He told her about meeting Rona Samuels, and what she told him about Clinton Reeves, Tullis Burke and Hubert Bachstrum. He added what Lincoln, the barman, told him about the Bachstrum's family and the murders of Ralph, Zenon and Celia Bachstrum, Salina Mason, Robert Reynolds and the others. He talked about Tanya McKenzie who was a Bachstrum, and how Earl is still in love with her after so many years. He ended by concluding that some of the wares was transported in by boats, and how that caused the piracy.

153

Christiana waited until he had exhaust all this thoughts.

"Do you think Earl could be working for the family?" she asked.

"I really don't know, although I'm confident that he is not lying to me," said Dready.

"Just be careful in your dealings with him," she advised.

He told her about going to Abaco and how he had to get the police to go there to recover the money, drugs and the dead bodies.

"We found three bodies in that house in Abaco, but we don't know who they are as yet," he said, "although I'm sure that Chief Daniels will come up with names for them soon. I suspect he is either involved or being paid off by the family to hide evidence."

"That's another thing," she said. "Why do you suspect him of being paid off by the Bachstrum family and of diverting any enquires into their affairs?" she asked.

"Well, he seemed to be a feared man in that country and has kept the death of Chrittendon secret until I asked. He seemed to be in control of the men under his command. Then there is still the problem of the RCMP codes."

"What about the RCMP codes?" she asked.

"It's still being used by someone although Chrittendon is dead," he answered.

"By whom?" asked Christiana.

"Don't know as yet, but somebody is using them to cover their mules going into Toronto."

"And you think it's Chief Daniels?" asked Christiana.

"Don't know as yet," he replied, "but he certainly appears suspicious."

"Why don't you talk to Bernard about him?" said Christiana.

"I probably will," replied Dready.

They talked for a long time about his findings and the pirates.

"Pirates in deed," said Christiana.

Dready smiled at her.

"Don't believe me eh?" he said. "Look; if you leave this spot on Jamaica and go in that direction, you will get to Venezuela and Columbia. In that direction one could reach Costa Rico, Nicaragua or Panama."

"So, are we going there?" she asked.

"No, but ships do," he answered. "See that one parked out there?" he said pointing to one standing about a mile out. "I bet it is waiting to do some illegal business."

Christiana looked and was surprised that she had not noticed the ship before.

"What the hell are they doing there?" she asked.

"Don't know," he replied and quickly dialled a number on his cell phone.

"Hello, Graves here," the voice said.

"Bernard, there is a ship anchored off the coast and I think they are awaiting some other boats to come to them."

"Where are you?" asked Graves.

"I'm at Treasure Beach looking out," answered Dready.

"Good," said Graves. "Stay right there. I'm going to call the coastal boys and will call you back, okay?"

Christiana and Dready had another couple of dips in the water and kept a watchful eye on the ship.

The cell phone rang and Dready answered.

"Yes Bernard," he answered.

"The boys will be in your location in a few minutes," said Graves. "They have been watching that ship also and Johnnie Baker is near to you."

"Good," said Dready, "I would like to meet him."

They hung up and waited. About an hour passed before the Landrover drove up and four men alighted.

"I am Johnnie Baker," said the officer in charge. "We have been expecting something to happen; and thank you for spotting them."

"I'm Dready Winston, the journalist," he said. "Can I stay to get the story?"

"You sure can, my friend," said Baker.

Within minutes Baker got on the phone and began instructing others on what he wanted done. Dready and Christiana sat quietly to watch the action. Two hours later they saw four speed boats leave land near Black River, heading out towards the ship.

"Wait!" shouted Baker in his phone.

The wait continued for what seemed like another hour.

"Now!" he shouted. "Hit them hard!!"

Within minutes there were an eruption of noises. Helicopters and boats came to life, speeding towards the ship. Minutes later there was gun fire as the police boats chased the other boats. A minute later one of the pirates boats literally exploded. Two planes looking like American fighter jets passed over-head towards the ship. It was all over in twenty minutes with the remaining three pirate boats in custody and two police launches beside the anchored ship.

Dready waited until Baker was satisfied before approaching him.

"Who are they?" he asked.

"Colombian bad boys," said Baker, "but we'll have to wait for the search before knowing what the cargo is."

"That's fine," said Dready. "I can always get the report from Graves."

"Okay," said Baker. "We'll talk later."

Immediately Christiana and Dready splashed into the water, swam around a little before having a shower to wash off the salt then they were on their way home.

"Where are we going now?" she asked.

"To visit an old friend," he replied.

"Where?"

"In Black River," he answered.

It didn't take long to reach the town. There were already talks in town about the boat that exploded. He carefully drove to the house and parked. Christiana recognized it and asked,

"Isn't this Jeremiah Bailey's house?"

"It certainly is," he responded.

He got out of the car and knocked on the wrought iron gate. In a minute the ex-police officer came to the verandah. He didn't look raggy as the first time they met him last year.

"What the hell do you want....oh it's you Dready. Come on in. Hello Christiana, how has life been for you?"

"Great," she answered. "We got married and have one child and is expecting another........"

Her statement was cut short by the jab from Dready's elbow. Jeremiah smiled.

"Want some sour-sap juice?" he asked. "I quit drinking last year. No more alcohol for me. Just real Jamaican fruit juices from now on."

"Yes, please," said Christiana.

Jeremiah went inside and returned with the glasses, ice and the delicious juice.

"Okay Dready, what brought you to my humble home? It's not often I see the big boys as you. Although Graves do come by to talk occasionally, and even more regularly now since his promotion. But then again, you do not live in Jamaica."

"Right," said Dready. "Jerry, I am having a little problem with a case I'm working on in The Bahamas, and believe that some of the people are connected to those in the Arlene Felscher murder here. I know you did an in dept investigation of the Bridge Club people and thought maybe you could identify some of these for me."

"Ha, ha, ha," giggled Jeremiah. "I could try. Just tell me who those persons are and I will look into my brain for them."

"Last year Graves shot a fellow named Denrick Miller. He was identified as the son of Barbara Smith. Was he her only child?"

"No, he was not. He was the second son of Barbara Smith. The older one disappeared and is not in any of the Jamaican records," replied Jeremiah.

"How come?" Christiana asked.

157

Jeremiah smiled and began telling them of his investigation into the lives of those Bridge Club members. He told them about his findings and his suspicions of the different people there. He talked about everything he found which he wrote in his report.

"Those reports were taken by Captain Smith and I don't know where they are or what was removed from them," said Jerry.

They questioned, and Jeremiah was delighted to tell all he knew and who he believed went where to do what. After an hour they thanked him and prepared to resumed their journey home.

"Christiana and Bernard will definitely come to visit with you again," said Dready as they shook hands.

"Okay," he responded. "Oh Christiana, Graves told me about last year's case. Were you satisfied with the results?"

"Yes I was," said Christiana. "But we'll talk later."

As they drove towards Savanna-la-Mar, Dready noticed that Christiana had a broad smile on her face and wondered what was on her mind.

"Spill it," he said demandingly.

"Spill what?" she asked as though she was unaware of her grin.

"Whatever that's going on in here," he said pointing to her head.

"It's nothing," she replied, "absolutely nothing."

"Then why the grin?" he asked.

"I was just thinking that we could have had sex on the beach this morning without interference, before that action,," she said. "Do you realize that we were the only ones there?"

"Yes," he replied smiling to know that she had not lost her lust for him, "we could have done it but I thought you........."

"Bullshit," she said, "you were so engrossed in telling me about those people in Nassau that you didn't feel my touches."

"I see, you were only interested in my dick not the case," he stated sarcastically.

"That's right sir," she answered, "so find a place where we can do it before we get home; because when we reach there, we will not get the chance again."

Quickly, Dready found a little cluster of woods and drove in.

"This will have to do," he said, "and if anybody sees us, then we'll have to explain that we are married."

Christiana laughed.

"As if they would care," she said as she hurriedly removed the necessary clothing and began their love making.

They were again on the road to home when he asked,

"So what happened with you and Tullis Burke?"

"That was an experience," she said. " I discovered that Althea is a lesbian."

"How did you come to that conclusion?" he asked.

Christiana told him everything that happened in the hotel room that morning, describing every little detail of her meeting with Althea.

"How was her demeanor?" asked Dready.

"Well," said Christiana, "she seemed discontented, as if she really didn't want to do it. The impression I had of her is that she was being forced to do it or wasn't satisfied with the wages. She invited me to spend an evening with her in Nassau. Imagine, that woman is in her sixties and still have a sex drive."

"I guess it's the same for older men," he said.

"I presume so," she answered as he turned the car into the driveway.

"Maybe we should talk to Althea to find out where her mind stands with the gang, and what she knows about the diamonds," said Dready. "Maybe she would be willing to tell on her friends."

"Maybe," agreed Christiana. "If I could come to Nassau, I might be able to tempt her into talking without the sex."

"Do you want to take that chance?" asked Dready.

"I'm not sure," she answered, "those people could get vicious if they are deceived and...."

"I'll check it out when I return there," he said, "and if I see it's warranted, I will call and you could come for a day."

For the rest of the evening he hung around the home area with his brothers drinking beers, talking about their younger days and doing absolutely nothing. It was very relaxing for him. At one time he went into the house and found Christiana alone in the kitchen. He began kissing her and massaging her buttocks when Dorothy walked in.

"Aaah," said Dorothy, "getting horny, eh? Do you want to have another baby right now?"

Dready smiled and replied,

"Not yet, but after this afternoon, I'm not too sure."

Dorothy laughed aloud.

"So that's what you both went away to do," she said, "a little something on the beach eh? I wished Barrington would be that spontaneous with me."

"Maybe you should take the initiative to instigate it my dear," said Christiana. "Sometimes it could be fun."

Dready realized that his sister could take some lessons from Christiana, so he left the kitchen giving them the space to talk.

The entire family attended the Christmas eve party, which was held at Graves house in Mandeville. Dready, Christiana and the baby rode with Ackeeface and Evelyn in their car, while everybody else teamed up with others. Carlton, being the taxi driver he was, parked in a spot where he could get out in a hurry if need be.

Except for Dready, almost everybody had to be introduced to Graves wife. She was a low profile person and wasn't publicly known. Thomas and Elsa, who had met her before, didn't recognize her instantly.

Clara Graves was a tall soft spoken, light complexion woman of about thirty years old, with long black hair and a most exquisite

160

smile. She was a disciplined well educated woman from a rather well-to-do background. She showed no signs of a woman who had borne four children. She showed the grace of a perfect hostess who had done this kind of entertaining many time in the past and was very proud to be the wife of the new Commissioner of Police.

"Welcome to our home," said Clara. "Please make yourselves comfortable, and help yourselves to the bar. Dinner will be served in fifteen minutes, so please excuse me for a few minutes."

Clara disappeared into the kitchen end of the huge house leaving her husband with the crowd of more than thirty-five people to entertain themselves.

Dready wandered over to the bar to converse with Bernard and Venrece Alexander. He wanted to bring them up to date with what was happening in Nassau, plus he wanted to find out what had happened to Venrece's notebook.

Bernard told him about the names on the list that he sent from Canada and that he would get the book from the courts in order to cross reference them with those in Venrece's book.

"Am sure that the children of some of those past Bridge Club people are involved with the diamond business at present," said Dready.

"Damned right," Venrece whispered, "and many of them have new faces and names to go with their locations."

"Like whom?" asked Dready.

"Like Garfield Smith," answered Venrece. "You know, the son of Barbara Smith; fathered by Lord Brimley."

"Where is he now?" asked Dready.

"I heard he lives in England, but returns here many times to do business. I really don't know where he resides now, but Graves could check," said Venny. "Better yet, we should search through Karlheinz stuff to find a picture of him."

"Well," said Dready, "pick out the ones who might have had new faces and those you met at the bridge club, and anyone who appeared like a candidate. I want them."

"Okay," said Venny, happy to be of service.

"Graves," said Dready turning to his friend, "please get Christiana and Venny involve in the checking of the faces and anything they can find in the junk at Karlheinz's house," Dready instructed.

"Will do," answered Graves. "We will read the books, talk to anyone Venrece recommend we interview and compare the people on the list."

"Good," said Dready. "But take every bit of precaution not to let her be alone anywhere."

"Don't worry about that," said Venny, "I will be near at all times. Nobody will get close to my daughter to hurt her again, unless they kill me first."

Dready was about to tell Venrece that his name was in a book found in Mr Wakefield's safe, when they were interrupted.

"Dinner is served," announced Clara.

Quickly the three men shook hands and got in line for the buffet style layout.

"Any information you can gather," said Dready to Venrece, "please don't hesitate to give it to Graves or Christiana."

"That I will do," said Venrece.

Dready didn't want Venny to know that the fellow, Denrick Miller, who was shot at his house was also Barbara's son.

When dinner and the clean up was over at about ten thirty, the dancing began. But for most, the conversations were the high-lights of the evening, and the star of that show was a local comic named Allan Allen. He told many stories about the country living of his family, himself as a boy, and of his friends. He kept the crowd in stitches for almost three hours, before leaving the party. At that point, many others also left for their homes, including Ezrah, Jean, Elsa and Thomas Perkins.

"Should we take the baby home?" asked Elsa of Christiana.

"No mother, we want to take him to the Christmas market in

Mobay in the morning so we are going to the hotel tonight."

Elsa was about to argue the issue but realized that both Christiana and Winston had agreed on the matter.

"Right," said Elsa, "we shall see you in the morning then."

They left the party at about five-thirty. Carlton drove at high speed and they were in Montego Bay in an hour. Carlton and Evelyn collected their children from his mother's house and went into town. Christiana was proud to be showing her son the spectacular event that many young Jamaicans look forward to at this time of year.

She repeated every word Dready told her on her first experience of the event to her son. After the two hour trek through the crowded streets, they had breakfast at Smoky Joe's then they spent most of the day with Mrs. Stewart, Carlton's mother, talking and playing games with the children. They made a couple of short visits to other friends in the city. Finally everybody went to the Perkins home for the long awaited Christmas dinner.

Christiana was as excited as her first time there, to see the lavish setting and different types of foods that was to be consumed.

After dinner, Christiana took Winston out into the yard. They sat under the mango tree, which provided such solitude, to talk.

"Darling,"she said while kissing him, "I want you to be very careful in Nassau, because those people don't appreciate under-cover police in their midst."

Dready was shocked at her sudden statement.

"You knew that I'm a police officer?" he asked.

"Yes," she answered.

"When did you know?" he asked.

"I suspected that you were since last year," she answered, "but didn't pressure you for an answer. Then I got suspicious in Nassau when you received the codes from Dillon and knew how to use them, but I was sure yesterday when you mentioned that someone was still using them."

He laughed.

"And here I am thinking that you didn't have a clue, and was asking my brother not to tell you," he said in a relieved tone.

"That's fine sweetheart," she said, "but be very careful there. I want you back in one piece to help me raise these two children."

"What two children?" he asked. "We only have one."

"For now, but there might be another after yesterday in the woods," she said rubbing her stomach.

They sat talking for a long time about him leaving the family to be back in the Bahamas to carry-out his job. Dready gave Christiana some special advice for staying alive in Jamaica.

"I don't want you wandering off to anywhere without telling mother or father where you are going. Never go anywhere without either Graves, Venrece or Ackeeface," he said.

"I promise I won't do any of those things," she said. "But from what Graves told me, it seems that I will be busy doing research on the people in Venny's book, I won't have the time."

"Good," he said. "Please forward the findings to me; but only when I ask."

They kissed again only this time it was a rather lengthy one.

The days of the week flew by quickly, because everybody was having fun. Dready found that the bothersome thoughts of the case were subdued somewhat because of the festive distractions. He had many long conversations with Graves, Christiana and Venrece about the people mentioned in the book, and concluded that there were still someone above them.

It was the morning of New Year eve. Dready was up early to watch the sun ascend from the East. He plunked himself on the bench under the mango tree to watch this event and at the same time to give thought to the case. Although he had some suspects in mind, there seemed to be an elusive person still in existence somewhere.

"It's the Octopus," he thought, "and they are in the Bahamas."

He was summoned to breakfast by Pamela. He enjoyed it. But

his mind was still on the case in Nassau. This went on all day, even though he went to assist his father at the farm for a while.

After breakfast, he once again sought the solitude under the mango tree in order to think more. This time he took Venrece's book, the notes he received from Graves and three beers with him. An hour of perusing those documents, passed.

Then Christiana came out to join him.

"What's the matter darling?" she asked.

"I'm seeking a way to net an Octopus," he answered.

"Good," she said, "but be very careful."

Once again she reminded him of the care necessary in dealing with the people involved.

They became so engrossed in their conversation, that they were totally unaware of the time. It was Ackeeface who came to remind them about the New year eve's Party at the Grand Lido in Negril. They rushed into the house, showered and quickly changed, and were on their way to Negril.

After the excellent three hour show, which lived up to it's billings, Ackeeface introduced Dready to his friend Lawrence Chung, and left them to talk.

"Where in England did you live?" asked Dready.

"Wandsworth Road, London," replied Lawrence.

"Did you know what your brother, Orville's, business was in Jamaica?" asked Dready.

There was a lengthy pause as Lawrence gave thought to his brother's activities.

"No, not really," answered Lawrence. "We wrote letters to each other and spoke on the telephone a couple of times, but he never once told me. Well, not in so many words, what he was doing. In one letter," continued Lawrence, "he said he was on to something that was going to allow him to build a new house for his wife and children, but he didn't say what."

"Did you know any of your brother's friends here in Jamaica

or in England?" asked Dready.

"Not really," said Lawrence. "Once a white man named something or another Phillips, came to see me. He told me that Orville asked him to contact me."

"What did he want?" asked Dready.

"He wanted me to accompany him to Buckley, Slough, to meet somebody who Orville asked to bring a package from Jamaica, but I told him to screw off."

"Did you ever see him again?" asked Dready.

"He called me up about a month before Orville died and asked me to meet him," answered Lawrence.

"Did you? Where did you meet him?" asked Dready.

"Yes I did. He came to my place in London with a woman and invited me to dinner with them," said Lawrence. "We went to a posh restaurant in Welwyn Garden City in his Jag. He told me that a man named Bass sent him to see me, and that Orville had sent me something and he wanted them. But I didn't know anyone named Bass or what thing Orville was supposed to have sent me, and told him so."

"Then what happened?" asked Dready.

Lawrence let out a roaring laugh as he replied,

"He told me that my brother had stolen some things from Bass and thought he might have sent them to me for safekeeping. Then the arse hole wanted me to deliver a package of unknown quantity to someone in Devon, but I refused."

"What does this man look like, can you describe him?" asked Dready.

"Well, he's tall, well dressed, balding man of about six foot, and is fat. He's a Brummy, you know, from Birmingham."

Dready realized that the person described by Lawrence Chung as Phillips, was in fact the man he had met in the Bahamas named Smithers.

Have you ever met a woman named Rona Samuels?" asked Dready.

"Yes," answered Lawrence. "She was with that Phillips man

and told me that she was his wife," again Lawrence laughed. "Here's something funny, when we got back to my place in London, she told him to leave because she wanted to go to bed with me that night in my apartment. Can you imagine that?"

"Some people do behave like that," said Dready. "Can you describe her?"

"She's about five foot three, with dark hair and big knockers," said Lawrence.

"Anything else? What about her eyes?" asked Dready.

"She had green eyes man," said Lawrence. "It's the first time I had ever seen someone with dark green eyes like hers, and I thought it was weird. I thought she might be one of those witches you read about."

Rona Samuels description was the same woman he met in Nassau. He thanked Lawrence for his very valuable information and stood there talking about the burial of Orville and the assurance of his wife getting the house.

"I'll help her with my bother's children as much as I can," said Lawrence. "If you ever want to talk to me again, just ask Ackee-face to bring you to my place in Lucie."

They shook hands and parted company.

When the Perkins team met in the parking lot for the drive back to the house, Dready took Christiana aside and told her the entire conversation he had with Lawrence Chung.

"Tell Graves to keep him on ice," said Dready, "he might know more than he told me. But remember not to approach anyone without the presence of Bernard or Carlton, these people could be vicious if they believe you're getting too nosey."

Christiana agreed and they got into the car and headed home.

"Ackeeface," said Dready, "I want you to keep a close eye on Christiana while I'm away. Don't let her meet or speak with any of those people alone. I want you to take her wherever she wants to go, but make sure she is never alone, okay?"

"Right," answered Ackeeface.

The partying was too much for Christiana and she fell asleep in the car leaving Winston and Ackeeface to talk, which they did all the way home. Ackeeface and Evelyn slept at the Perkins home that night and left the next morning for their home in Ocho Rios.

About noon Bernard Graves came to the Perkins house, and asked Christiana and Dready to accompany him to the office in Mandeville to check out the names on the list for any possible connections between the old boys of the Bridge Club and those in Nassau.

While the two cops talked in his office, Christiana asked and Graves got another officer to take her into the evidence room to search through the belongings of Karlheinz Bass and that of Captain Smith, for any information regarding people of the old Bridge Club with new identities and faces.

Dready told Bernard Graves all that was happening in the Bahamas, including his suspicion of Donald Daniels. Graves assured him that the Chief of police in Bahamas was an up-standing person.

"Someone is still doing business out of Guyana," said Dready, "and I will have to go there to find out."

"Fine, I'll give Captain Maraj a call," said Graves.

Graves dialled the Guyana number and switched the phone to intercom.

"Hello Elton," said Graves into the phone, "how are the wife and children?"

"Hello Bernard," answered Captain Maraj, "nice to hear from you old boy. The wife and children are doing fine, it's me who needs the sympathy. What's happening in Jammy town?"

"Lots," said Graves, "everybody here loves diamonds, especially for Christmas gifts and we can't afford it. So Winston will be coming there in a few days time to do some business with some of your people. Maybe you'll have to alert your men of his presence so that he doesn't get killed accidentally."

"Not a problem," replied Captain Maraj. "I will personally get him from the airport. Just tell him to call me from Nassau before getting on the flight."

"Do you have any shoppers in your town?" asked Dready.

"Yes we do," said Maraj, "some we know about and some are very illusive."

"Can you keep them on ice?" asked Dready.

"Maybe and maybe not," replied Maraj, "but if you have a plan we could seek them out, and you know what."

"Okay," said Dready, "I could show you a very economical way to do it."

"Fine," said Maraj, "call me."

"Will do Elton," replied Dready .

For the next two hours Dready, Christiana and Bernard talked about the case and the things they are expecting to find. Then it was back to the house. Dready bid his family and his son good-bye, and collected his luggage for his trip back to Nassau.

Graves took Dready to Montego Bay Airport. Christiana was granted permission to follow her husband all the way to the plane. She kissed him before he boarded.

"One other thing Bernard, make a thorough check on Garfield Smith and call me with the information," he told Graves, " and please keep her out of harms way."

"Sure will friend," said Graves.

"See you darling," she said, "and call me every night please, if you can."

He promised. He felt very sad leaving her there. After all it was New Year's day and he should be with his wife and son; instead of leaving them to go on a risky trip.

Chapter Seven

The Blackjack Dealer.

"*I*t's New Year's Day," mused Dready, as he stood at the corner of Bay and Market streets watching the Jankunoo parade go rushing along the street. The beer he was drinking had gone flat because he had not drank much of it since he purchased it. He thought about going into the corner bar to replenish it but felt he might loose sight of the person he was watching.

He looked at the slimly- built but shapely, dark-haired woman of about 40 and five feet seven, dancing to the beat of the soca music, like at a party, having fun with her two friends. She looked much better than when he saw her in Jamaica at the police station; although that was only for a brief moment when she came to sign her statement about her father's involvement in the smuggling affair. Graves had taken her to the airport, put her on the next flight back to Nassau to prevent her from staying in Jamaica. He hadn't seen her until today.

Earl had pointed her out to him the night before he left for Jamaica, at the casino and warned him about her jealous boyfriend, a fellow named Clinton Reeves. Because he didn't want anyone getting suspicious of him or connecting him to Earl, he was very cautious in approaching her. He wandered about the street thinking about the warning and weigh the consequences of being caught talking to her. He was getting anxious, wanting to approach her before it was too late. He threw caution to the wind and decided to approach and introduce himself to her.

"Nice music isn't it?" he shouted into her ear over the din of the music.

"Yes," she replied, "do you like it?"

"Yes, I can't get enough of it," he said.

There wasn't any more said for a long while until the last of the rushing bands went by.

"That was great," she said. "The next side will be coming by in about an hour and twenty minutes time; want to go for a drink in the meanwhile?"

"Yes, why not," he responded. "There is a good place across the street. Shall we go in there?"

"No," she said, "I never go into that place. There's a nice quiet place down the road called the Pirate, let's go there. You can always find a cozy seat there."

They walked through the crowd in silence along Shirley Street to the basement restaurant which he knew so well, and sure enough they found a cozy seat at a secluded corner table.

"Are you hungry?" she asked him and directed his attention to the menu on the wall.

"Not really, but I could eat something," he replied.

The waiter came and they ordered some drinks.

"You know what I'd like?" she said. "Johnnie cake and stew fish, but it has to be grouper. I just adore the taste of grouper. What kind of fish do you like Rasta man?"

Dready laughed, remembering his last visit to Nassau. It was then he was introduced to the so called poor man's dish, and liked it.

"Sure, why not," he said, "it will keep me until supper time; but make mine snapper," he said turning to the waiter.

"Fine," replied the waiter as he took the orders and left.

"Okay," she said, propping her head in the palm of her hands as she leaned across the table, "what's your pitch?"

"Pitch?" he asked, "what pitch?"

"You know, your pick up line?" she said with a wide smile.

172

"I'm sorry but I don't have one," he replied.

"That's strange," she said, "usually when I am approached by a handsome tourist man as you, they always have a line and a story of their wealth back in the United States. Telling me lies about their miserable lives or how badly they are misunderstood by their wives, and all the time their only objective is to get me into bed. Then later on I would hear about their five kids or find out that they really liked young boys."

"Well, I'm sorry to disappoint you but I don't have any such lines," he replied smiling, "but I do have a lovely wife and a two month old son."

"Then why did you come to me?" she asked, looking sideways at him.

"I just happened to be standing near and thought you were a nice looking woman and wanted to talk, that's all."

She sat in puzzlement for a while.

"Where are you from?" she asked.

"Jamaica," he replied, looking at the picture on the place mat.

"Ah! ah!" she said in a surprised voice, "just as I thought, a smooth talking Jammy dreadlocks here hustling my arse. Why didn't you tell me before that you just wanted to have sex with me?"

"I didn't, because I don't want to," he replied, "I just wanted to.....".

"Okay," she said, "so what the hell do you want?"

"You're one very suspicious bitch, aren't you?" said Dready. "I've already told you, I saw you and just wanted to talk to you, but if you're going to be awkward about it, let's just enjoy the food and part company."

They sat in silence for a long while eating the food.

"My name is Tanya," she said suddenly. "Tanya McKenzie, eh no, I'm Tanya Bachstrum, I use to be McKenzie but I divorced the bastard after.....oh forget that, just call me Tanya."

"I'm Dready Winston," he replied and stretched his hand to

173

her. He could feel the softness of it and knew that she didn't do any hard work.

"Pleased to meet you Dready Winston," she replied smiling.

"So what do you do for a living Tanya?" he asked.

"Nosy bastard aren't you? I'm not a hooker, if that's what you think" she replied harshly.

"I didn't think you were," he responded. "You look more like a secretary or a manager of some establishment."

"No, I'm neither of those, I'm a blackjack dealer in the casino over there," she said, pointing in the direction of Paradise Island with her fork.

"Good!" he said. "Maybe when I come to your table you'll let me win a couple of times."

"Sure, come over anytime in the evenings," she said, "except Mondays, I don't work Mondays. That's when I get my hair done and my occasional......eh, sex."

"I thought you said......" he began but quickly changed his mind. "You have a man then?"

"Not really," she replied smiling, "he just thinks he owns me and I use him to satisfy my crotch whenever I need to."

"Is he a very jealous man? What if he comes in here and sees us together?" asked Dready.

Tanya laughed as she stuffed the last of her Johnnie cake and fish in her mouth.

"He would beat you to death," she answered. "He's a very jealous man, and behaves like an idiot; but don't worry about him, right now he's in Florida."

"Good," said Dready, "I'm allergic to cuts and bruises."

"But that won't last too long," she said smiling, "I intend on kissing him off when he comes back."

He knew that he was beginning to appeal to her.

"So tell me Tanya," he said, "after today, can we meet again to talk?"

"Sure Rasta," she said, "but we haven't talked about anything as yet."

"Absolutely right," he said. "What can we talk about that wouldn't be offensive to you?"

"Anything except money," she said. "I have to look at it every night in the casino and need a freeking break from it. Tell me; what are you doing in Nassau and how long are you staying?"

"Firstly, I am here to purchase some land to build a house, because I would like to live here permanently, and secondly I will be here for two more weeks for that purpose."

"Good," she said, "then it's okay to come and see me at the casino."

They completed the meal and began walking back up the road to watch the rest of the bands coming through.

"Ever been in Nassau before Dready?" she asked.

"Yes," he answered, "but never on New Years Day."

"When will you be coming to see me?" she asked.

"Maybe tonight after dinner," he said, "but I won't be staying long because I have to meet a friend also."

"Oh, a lover eh!" she said sarcastically, "your very reason for not wanting to.....to make love to me today."

"Not really, but I cannot tell you about it right now," he said as the music became too loud to hear her talk, "tell you later," he shouted.

Dready stood there watching Tanya dancing in the street wondering if she was the same person who had been shot a year ago.

When the last of the bands passed their spot, they parted company with him promising to visit the casino that evening. He stood there admiring her arse as she walked down the road away from him. He had now met and spoken with Tanya McKenzie, the daughter of Karlheinz Bass, the same girl who was arrested in Jamaica when she came for his funeral, and realized that she didn't recognized him. It seemed that she had recovered from the trauma of the shooting in

Miami and the charges in Jamaica.

He smiled to know that Tanya really wanted to have sex with him, but all he wanted was some information from her. Yet, he was not sure how he would get it without having sex with her. There were many questions he wanted to ask her but they will have to wait for the appropriate time.

"She had introduced herself as a Bachstrum and not a Bass, why?" Dready reflected.

He walked mindlessly along the road, oblivious to the crowd of people milling about, towards the market.

"Ah," he said aloud, "I must see Earl."

Then he remembered that Earl had gone back to the far-out island to be with Judith Wakefield, so he walked casually until he reached the bus stop. He climbed aboard the almost empty Carmichael bus, and sat as the driver directed his carriage towards it's destination. It hadn't gone any more than a mile when he saw Cynthia walking in the opposite direction on Bay Street.

"Let me off here please," he shouted at the bus driver. "Let me off please."

When the bus came to a stop at the corner of Nassau Street, he ran back to the corner of Cumberland where he had seen Cynthia and looked around but couldn't find her.

"Damn, she must have gone into one of these buildings," he thought and waited.

About fifteen minutes later she emerged from the office in which she had entered.

"Hello Mr. Dreadlocks Rastaman," she said as though she was expecting him to be there at that time, "I saw you from the window and came out."

"Hello Cynthia," he replied. "I saw you walking along here and rushed to catch up with you, but you disappeared and....., how are you doing?"

"Fine," she answered, "now that I see you. I want to remind

you of our date. Remember you promised me before leaving for Jamaica? Can we have it today?"

"Maybe, but first I must talk to you about the phone calls and secondly I have to meet a friend to talk about some land in Eleuthra," he said trying to divert her mind from his promised interlude of sex.

"Oh!" she responded. "Thinking of purchasing Bahamian land, eh?"

"Maybe," he said. "I'm thinking about it because I might want to stay here for the rest of my life."

"With or without your wife and or lover?" she asked.

"With the wife's money and a lover," he said smiling, "and that could be you if you behave like I'm expecting you to."

Cynthia didn't reply, but within her mind she felt it might not be a bad idea to keep close to him for personal reasons.

"Just tell me when you're ready and I will be available to you," she said. "But you can meet me tonight after work and I will tell you all about the phone calls. And if you need to meet a really good real estate person, I could introduce you to one."

"I've already met one," he said. "Where should we meet?" he asked.

"Outside the Palace at twelve-thirty sharp," she said.

"Fine," he replied, "see you."

He stood there watching as Cynthia re-entered the office. He then took a quick glance at the names on the plaque on the wall.

He decided to go into The Colonial Bar to have a beer, and to see his friend Lincoln. He was told that Lincoln had just left and maybe was across the street with another fellow.

Dready left the bar and hustled across to the pizza place to see Linc sitting in the company of two nice looking women.

"Hello Mr. Grey," he said as he sat beside him. "Just got back to town and wondered if you have the time to talk."

"For you my friend, any time," replied Linc. "Ladies, we will have to resume our conversation at another time, okay?"

The two women left without a flinch and the two men decided to walk outside to do their talking.

"Let's go to the park," said Dready. "It's more comfortable and private there."

Linc agreed and they left the pizza parlour and walked along the road to a little park near the hotel.

"Now," said Linc, "I'm going to tell you about my time on the police force and some of the people I had dealings with and why I was removed from duty."

Linc took a long drag on his cigarette and began his story.

"I was born on the island of Andros and attended school there, like many poor people's children do. My parents had to work hard to send me to that prestigious high school here in Nassau, where they thought I would get a good education and the opportunity for a good job on completion. In that school, I met and befriended Earl Monroe and a few more boys like myself. I also met people such as Hubert, Ralph and Bernice Bachstrum, Tanya and Rosita Bass, whom at the time I thought were Bachstrum's, and a fellow named Rupert Reynolds. I met Cynthia and her sister Francis Mason and their half brother Tullis Burke; there was also another fellow named Abbot, Rupert Abbot.

The Bachstrum boys were always snobbish towards Earl and me, and never wanted us to be friends with their sisters. Well, at the end of high school, many were going on to universities and to jobs in their parent's businesses. I realized that my parents couldn't afford to send me to a university, so when the police offered a job, I joined like many of the children in that school did. They made the offer and many of the young men like myself took it."

"That's good," said Dready. "You should be proud of serving your country."

"Yes I was," said Linc. "But during training, things began to change and people began to associate themselves with each other. Firstly, Earl was dismissed for selling Rupert Abbot the answers to a

178

test."

"Was he?" asked Dready.

"No," replied Linc, "he was assisting the dumb ass with his test paper and was caught by one of the officers."

"So didn't you all protest the fact?" he asked.

"Yes, but Abbot told the commander that Earl asked him for money and they believed him and Earl was ousted."

Dready reflected on the words of Linc and realized that there was more to come.

"Go on," he told Linc.

"Well, I was on the force about a year and was stationed on Crooked Island. As time passed I got to meet some of the residents of that island. One day, I got a tip from Rupert Reynolds that some people were moving drugs through his property to Nassau. I, like a fool, went there alone to apprehend the criminals single handedly and found them to be boys I knew from school days. They were the Bachstrum boys, so I arrested and took them into custody. To my surprise, the Commander came to me and asked for the case to be squashed, because there wasn't enough evidence to convict them. I argued the issue and was told that my father, who used to work for the Bachstrum family, was paid off with monies from that deal."

"Was he?" asked Dready.

"No, but he did work for the Bachstrum family at that time and I couldn't prove it," said Linc. "My father died because of that."

"How?" asked Dready.

"Heart failure," replied Linc.

"Okay, go on," he requested.

"I never stopped watching that family," said Linc. "I found out many unscrupulous things about Zenon's business and some of the people he dealt with in Trinidad and Jamaica. I found out about Karl-heinz Bass, Arthur Collins, Rosita and Harvey Ambross, Peter McKenzie, Lilly and Patricia Green and many more. But I couldn't take it to the Commander or any of the top brasses because I was afraid of losing my job. So one day, in desperation, I stupidly told Rupert Abbot about my suspicions and we planned to stake out Zenon's house. We did, and we were caught by Donald Daniels and a team of men, which I learned later, was sent by the Commander. You see, my dear friend Rupert had told it to the Commander, who sent Daniels to arrest us."

"So you were caught, so what?" said Dready.

"So what, is right," said Linc. "Only one problem; Mr. Abbot had brought along a Kilo of cocaine and it was found in my car."

"Oh shit!" said Dready.

"Oh shit is right," said Linc. "The Commander called me into his office the following Monday morning and dealt with me."

"So what happened that morning?" asked Dready.

"I was charged for false accusations, and planting of illegal evidence," said Linc, "and with a plea of guilty, there weren't any trial and I was dismissed from the force."

"Could this be the doings of the Bachstrums?" asked Dready.

"It sure was," said Linc. "Then to make matters worst; about a week later, the US cost guards arrested a launch with four men on board that had approached a ship they were watching, after chasing them almost into the harbour."

"So what's so different with that?" asked Dready.

"One of those men was the Commander of our police force," said Linc.

"Was he charged?" asked Dready.

"Yes," replied Linc.

"Where is the Commander now? I would like to speak to him," said Dready.

"Go to hell," said Linc.

"What?" asked Dready. "What was that for?"

Linc let out a chuckle.

"You would have to go to hell to meet him; he committed suicide the following day in his office. A week later Donald Daniels was appointed Chief.."

"What happened to the three men who were with him?" asked Dready.

"Case dismissed for lack of evidence," said Linc.

"What? How did that happen?" asked Dready.

"They told the court that they were on a fun ride with the Commander and didn't know what he was up to, and since he was already dead, there wasn't any evidence to contradict them," said Linc. "The jury bought their story."

"Man! That must have hurt your new Commanding officer," said Dready.

"It did," said Linc, "and ever since, he has been trying to get the goods on them, but every time he tried, something goes wrong and they eluded him."

Linc began to laugh softly and Dready became curious.

"What's the joke?" he asked.

"You never asked who the three men were," said Linc.

"Okay, who are they?"

"Zenon, Hubert and Ralph Bachstrum." said Linc.

If he wasn't at first, Dready was really in a state of shock now. Lincoln Grey had laid a bummer on him and was laughing about it.

"I see," he said. "Is Donald Daniels being paid by the Bachstrums?"

"Don't know," said Linc, "but in my opinion, he's too much a cop to jeopardise his position for a few extra bucks. He's too smart to allow them to buy him."

Dready sat with Linc for another hour, listening to the different stories about his many encounters with the family and their dealings in their country. He told Dready about the sinking of their ship near the coast of Florida, and the death of Zenon, the two South Americans, Elta and the disappearance of Ralph.

"What about Sanderson?" asked Dready.

"Pirate," said Linc. "In the smuggling community here, he is known as the Admiral or the Commodore. He is usually on his boat

181

out in neutral waters with his South American and Caribbean friends, from where he transmits instructions to his employees over radio and telephone."

Lincoln told Dready about Sanderson and his South American connections, who he believed got him to walk the plank.

"Now that he is dead, who is in charge?" asked Dready.

"Don't rightly know, but rumours have it that an Englishman is the new commander in chief," said Linc.,"and no, I haven't seen him as yet."

"Have you ever heard of a Garfield Smith?" asked Dready.

"No," replied Linc. "Is he in The Bahamas?"

"Maybe," said Dready, "what about Ralston Weekes?"

"Not in the Bahamas," said Linc., "but if he is, then Donald Daniels would know. He keeps a track on every shady character that comes in here."

"Good," said Dready.

When he was tired of hearing the story, he told Linc to save some for another time, but in his mind he meant an inquest.

"This is going to be one hell of a story," he told Linc, "and I hope you'll repeat the same words at that time."

"Brother, I will never forget how those bastards ruin my life and that of my children."

They shook hands and Linc went back to his lady friends, while Dready got on the next bus to Cable Beach. He took the elevator to his room, had a quick shower, then lay down on the bed for a short rest before leaving for the casino to meet Tanya.

He woke up and looked at the clock and saw that the it was almost ten thirty in the night. He got dressed quickly and descended to the lobby. He stopped at the front desk long enough to speak to Cynthia and gave her a line for not being able to see her that evening and didn't wait for her to become angry. He just dashed out the door to the parking lot and into his rented car and headed straight for the Paradise Island Casino.

182

Slowly, he walked into the casino and looked around to see if there was anyone there who might recognize him. He walked over to the cashier, bought some chips, then looked across the room until he saw the table where Tanya was busy dealing cards. He walked over to her, sat on a stool and placed his chips in front of him.

"Deal me a jack and an ace please," he said.

She smiled at him.

"You'll have to take your chances like everybody else sir," she replied.

"Okay," he said, "deal me in."

He lost the first five deals and was getting ready to leave her table when she dealt him a king and a ace.

"Now, that's better," he said, "keep them coming."

For the next six deals all the cards were winning hands. He looked around the table and saw he was one of two people sitting there; everybody had left and the other fellow seemed too intoxicated to care.

"Maybe you should double your bet sir," she suggested in a casual tone.

"Maybe I should," he replied, "but......"

"Be brave man, take the chance and you might succeed," she said, "and maybe, just maybe, you might discover more than you expected to."

He could see a sinister glitter in her pale-blue eyes as a wide sardonic grin caressed her lips, and wondered what was her mind set. Nevertheless, he slowly pushed all his chips towards her.

There was a long pause. Finally, she dealt him a five and a ten then dealt herself two queens.

"Hit me," he said.

She dropped another five in front of him. He hesitated; but before he could say stop, she dropped an ace in front of him.

"Twenty one, sir," she said smiling. "This seemed to be your lucky night."

"So it seems," he replied, "thank you. Maybe I should quit

while I'm ahead."

"Suit yourself sir, but sometimes a little danger can spice-up ones life," she stated.

Dready realized that Tanya was indicating spending the night with her, and somehow thought he really wanted the information to patch his case together; so he decided to sit where he was. For almost two hours, Tanya dealt him more winning hands than losing ones, and by the time she took her break, he was four thousand dollars in the black. She waited until some more bodies came to the table before announcing the new dealer.

"Meet Charles Shirley of New Jersey," she announced as the skinny fellow that resembles a mole, moved into position behind the table. "He's the best blackjack dealer in all Nassau. I have to hit the washroom."

Dready, being the none gambling man he was, slowly got up from the table, cashed in his chips and head for the bar. He signalled the waiter and ordered a beer. He drank four, before he realized that Tanya had not returned from the washroom.

"Shit," he whispered to himself, "she dumped me."

He was furious for Tanya's disappearance and was about to leave when he spotted Cindy Heron walking towards the washroom.

"Hi good-looking," he said as he caught up with her.

"Hello handsome!" she replied, surprised to see him. "What are you doing in here?"

"Looking for some action," he replied.

"How could you?" said Cindy. "Rona said she was spending the night with you in her room. She said she was having dinner, gambling and some....you know, screwing, with you all this evening."

Dready realized that he was discussed without his knowledge and wanted to know what went down behind his back.

"Holly hell!" he said slapping his forehead with the palm of his hand, "I totally forgot that I had promised her dinner, sex and gambling this evening."

He lied because there weren't any such agreement.

"Well my friend, you've missed a good screw," Cindy said smiling.

"Are you here alone?" he asked.

"No, I'm with Austin," she proudly answered. "He's over there gambling."

"Okay," said Dready, "better luck next time."

"Maybe," Cindy replied, "but I'll be alone tomorrow; because Austin and Rona will be going fishing and I will have all day alone to do whatever. You can find me on the beach in the morning."

Dready smiled to think what this flat chested woman would look like in a bikini bathing suit.

"That might be a good idea," he said, "maybe I will meet you there."

"Good," she said, "see you."

Dready left the casino and entered the parking lot with the intention of driving back to Cable Beach to find Rona. But when he got to his car, there sitting on the hood of someone's car, was Tanya waiting for him.

"What took you so long?" she asked.

"I was busy looking for you," he said.

"You should have followed me when I left the table," she said, sliding off the car.

"Then why didn't you say so?" he asked. He held her by the elbow directing her towards his car.

"Because we are not allowed to make dates with patrons in the casino," she stated, "but is free to do so outside."

"Okay," he said smiling. "What are we going to do about us now?"

"First," said Tanya, "I would like a couple of drinks, a dance, a little talk and a nice screw; are you capable?"

"I could try," he answered.

"Then let's go," she said and danced her way around the car

to the passenger's door.

They drove to the Jankunoo Club and parked the car.

"Hi Ralphie, hi Earnest," she said greeting the two bouncers at the door of the Jankunoo club.

"Hi Tanya," the boys replied while eyeing Dready.

"Friend," said Tanya pointing her head at him.

They found a table away from the music speakers and sat. Within a minute the waiter came and they ordered drinks.

"Dance?" asked Tanya.

"Sure do," he replied.

Dready discovered that the woman was really a great dancer and enjoyed doing so with her, although he thought she was a little crazy. This went on for most of the night and Tanya began to get intoxicated.

"Take me home now please," she requested.

Dready had no objection, and it was off to her house. The place was located in a very exclusive part of the city where most of the wealthy Bahamians lived. He entered the house behind her. Within minutes of getting in, Tanya flopped herself on the bed and fell asleep.

He laughed at the entire scenario, secured the door after making sure she was comfortable in bed, and left without getting the information he wanted.

"Three-thirty," he said looking at the radio clock in the car, "too late to see Cynthia Mason."

He directed the car back across town towards the hotel, but changed his mind and drove to Village Road, found St Andrews Drive that lead to Manchester Street, where Cynthia lived, and turned in. He sat for about ten minutes contemplating his next move. Finally he opened the door, entered the gate to her house, tapped on her window and within a minute she opened it to him.

"You came back!" she said jovially. "Just a minute, I'll open the door."

She ran to the door to let him in.

"Thank you," he said, "I couldn't sleep so I decided to take you up on your offer."

There wasn't any more to be said. Cynthia was already ripping off his shirt and pants.

"No more excuses," she said, "this morning is ours."

Dready laid in bed looking out the window, that had the curtains open, at the blue sky of a lovely Bahamian morning. It was the first time he had ever made love to another woman since he got married, but considered it as being in the line of duty. His thoughts momentarily flashed to Tanya, and wondered what she would be thinking of him leaving her alone. He could hear the clunking in the kitchen and knew that Cynthia had not gone to work.

"What time is it?" he asked.

"Twelve-fifteen," she hollered back.

"No work today?" he asked as if he didn't know.

"No sir," she happily replied, "and neither will you. We are going to spend the entire day in this house, just you and me."

"Okay," he said, "but you will have to tell me about the phone calls and what really is your relationship to Paul Mason."

"Come for breakfast," she said.

He got out of bed and into the bathroom, where he got washed and joined her at the table.

"Tell me about the phone calls," he said as he began to eat.

"There was a call from a woman named Amanda Bachstrum to Rona Samuels, the same woman whom you were with in the casino and in whose room the meeting was held that night."

"What did they talk about?" asked Dready.

"Well, the Bachstrum woman did most of the talking, which was about moving some products from her store. She wanted to know if Rona's man was still interested in making the deal because she wanted, whatever it was, out of her place immediately."

"Did Rona give her a definite answer?" asked Dready.

"No," answered Cynthia, "but she told her that a Mr Smithers would call her the next morning."

"Is that all?" asked Dready.

"Except for the call from Hubert Bachstrum to your room," she replied.

"And?" he said.

"And nothing," said Cynthia. "I asked him if he wanted to leave a message, but he hung up without saying anything else."

They were both quiet for a long while before talking again.

"Do you know who Hubert Bachstrum is?" he asked.

"Yes," she answered, "I worked for his family some years ago."

"Where is Ralph Bachstrum today?" he asked.

"Couldn't tell you," she answered. "I heard he drowned near Florida with his father."

"Who is Paul Mason to you?" he asked.

Cynthia gave a long thought to his question before answering.

'He's my brother," she answered.

Dready knew she was lying but didn't contradict her.

"How long had you worked for the Bachstrum family?"

"Six years," she answered.

Who told you to inform me about the meeting in Rona's room that night?" he asked.

"Tullis," she replied.

"Why?" asked Dready.

"I don't know," she replied. "He told me that if I saw you, I should tell you that I heard it on the line."

"Why?" he asked.

"Because he wanted Hubert to meet you privately, I suppose," she said.

"Mmmmm,"said Dready. "We're all in the same business yet he chose to be deceptive to me."

Dready was bubbling with ideas and wanted to call Graves to bounce some of his findings off his head.

"Are you going into work today?" he asked.

"No," she answered.

"I'm going to see a man in Abaco," he said. "The rest of our programme will have to wait until tonight."

"Why?" she asked in a sorrowful tone. "I took the day off to spend it with you and now you're leaving me alone?"

"Business my dear, I have to find a horse," he replied. "I will see you this evening at work."

"I won't be going in this evening, so meet me here," she said as he walked out the door.

He got into his car and raced to the hotel, as he kept thinking of all the changes that the investigation was taking. He gave thought about the murdered students in Canada, the five bodies in Nassau and the many dealers he had met so far. He felt assured that he knew who the imposters and dealers were and their connections to those in his Jamaican case. His only task now was to gather enough evidence to prove it to his boss, who will have to convince the authorities to make the arrests.

He turned the car into the parking lot and walked briskly into the lobby, looking to see if any unscrupulous person was waiting for him. He took the elevator up to his room, secured the place and quickly checked for the money he had stashed in the corner of the closet amongst his dirty clothes.

When he was satisfied that nobody had invaded his domain he turned on the T.V. to watch some garbage. Just then the phone rang.

"Hello," he said into the receiver, hoping it was Christiana.

It was Cindy Heron.

"Remember I told you that I would be on the beach today? Well I am," she said. "Care to join me?"

Dready thought about her invitation and concluded that it wouldn't hurt to speak to her, and probably learn something about the English operation from her.

"I'll be there in a minute," he said and hung up the phone.

He put on his swimming trunks and rushed down to the beach to find Cindy laying on a towel at the very edge of the crystal clear water. He was amazed that a woman with such great shape had no breasts.

"Flat as a pancake," he mused smiling. "Not even enough for a mouthful," he thought. "Hello," he said, standing over her.

"Hello Mr. Winston," she said, "I'm delighted that you came. What can we do together today?"

"I don't have a clue, maybe you should tell me so that I don't step over the boundaries," he said although he already knew what her motives were.

"Well, the day is available to you and whatever you desire is yours," she said getting to her feet. "I think we should have a little splash-about in the sea first, a few drinks and then the rest of the afternoon in my room."

"That sounds delicious," he said. "Shall we begin?"

He took a running start and dove into the water and swam out to a distance. When he stopped and looked back, he noticed that Cindy was still where he had left her.

"Come on in," he shouted. "The water is fine."

"No," she replied, "I'm not a swimmer, you'll have to come and get me."

He did and they both entered the water with her hanging around his neck. They splashed around with her body clinging tightly to his, and at every moment she would kiss him. Finally, she reached down to grab hold of his penis.

"Not here," he said as he removed her hand slowly. "The room is better."

"Okay," she said, "but I would like a couple of drinks first. It will help me to get started. But when I do, I'm hard to handle. I hope you are in shape to handle me."

"Fine," he said, "let's go back on the beach to drink and talk."

They emerged from the water and quickly ordered the drinks.

"Tell me about your job with Mr. Smithers," he asked to open the conversation after getting the drinks.

"Well, I met him and Rona in a London night club about three years ago and talked about life," she said as she sipped her Daquarri. "He invited me to have a drink, and we ended up spending the night together. The next morning he asked me to accompany him here for a holiday and we've been together ever since."

"Did you find it strange that a perfect stranger would invite you for a holiday trip to Nassau on such short notice?" Dready asked.

"Yes, but I wanted to get away from what I was doing also, and his invitation came at a very opportune time," she replied.

"And did you find it exciting?" asked Dready.

"Yes, being Mr. Smithers escort is fun," she answered.

"Oh?" he replied. "You're only his escort. I thought you were in the diamond business also. I mean one of the persons who are well paid for dealing it "

Cindy looked at him questioningly.

"Yes I am well paid," she said, and asked. "Aren't you one of the dealers?"

"Yes I am, only that I employ the mules...I mean ladies, to carry my stuff to Canada and I assume the roll as escort," he said.

Cindy was quiet for a long moment. Then as if something hit her mind, she said,

"Is that what I am, a mule? I will have to discuss it with him later. I would like more money and more time to......"

Dready realized that she had become angry, so he asked,

"Are you acquainted with any of his friends here, or those in London?"

Yes," she answered. "Last time we spent the entire week on his Trinidadian friends yacht with a man named Bachstrum, and had to have sex with all four of them."

"Is that bad or good?" he asked.

"Bad, because I didn't like any of them," she replied. "But I like you and want us to go into the room to prove it."

Before he could reply a waiter came.

"Mr. Dready sir," said the waiter, "there's a phone call for you. You can take it over there at the towel shack."

Dready excused himself from Cindy and rushed over to the shack. He dialled the operator and gave his name and she switched the call.

"Hello Rasta man, what are you doing today?" said Tanya's voice.

"Nothing, just hanging out on the beach," he replied, not telling her that he was with Cindy Heron.

"Why didn't you have sex with me last night?" she asked in a semi-angry tone.

"I told you that I wasn't interested in making love," he said, "I just wanted to talk to you and........"

"You're the first man to ever have me in this state and didn't rape me," she said. "Am I not desirable enough?"

"Yes you are," he said. "But as I told you, I don't want to; my only interest was talking to you. But if I did, I would rather make love to you when you're awake."

"Then come to visit with me today, please," she begged.

"Okay," he said into the phone, realizing that he would be giving up Cindy's offer. "See you in an hour."

He shuffled back to Cindy still sitting in the deck chair waiting for some kind of explanation.

"Sorry lady, but I have to leave," he said apologetically. "The person I have been negotiating with just decided to conclude the deal today; and since I don't want to lose the shipment, I must forfeit everything else to do so."

Although Cindy was furious at him for leaving her in the state she was, she also understood enough of the business to know that one has to strike while the iron is hot.

"Okay," she said, "go ahead. But I know we'll never get an opportunity like this again tonight, because Rona will be back and will be holding on to you."

"Maybe," he replied. "Remember now, she's a heavy drinker and could go to bed early, leaving us alone."

"True," she said, "only we'll have to get rid of Austin also."

"That will be your job," he said, "see you later."

Dready went to his room, got dressed and drove leisurely to Tanya's house. He didn't have to knock because she was already standing at the verandah waiting for him. She wore a skin-tight track suit pants with her brassier representing the top.

"Good to see you sir," she said, "come in and kick your shoes off."

"Is this how you greet all your men friends?" he asked.

"Not all of them," she replied, "some don't get this far and some who are allowed in don't get to take their shoes off. So consider yourself privileged."

He followed her orders.

"What would you like to drink Rasta man?" she asked in a Jamaican patois tone.

"How about a beer?" he asked.

"Canadian, American or English?" she offered.

"Canadian please," he accepted.

Tanya disappeared into the kitchen and returned with the two bottles and handed them to him. He opened them.

"Cheers," he said.

"Yes, here's to us," she replied, "and I'm not going to get drunk this evening, I want to be awake to enjoy it also."

Quickly, she again disappeared into the kitchen leaving him alone. A few moments later she shouted that supper was ready. He joined her and they began to eat. He hoped that she wasn't the person who had poisoned Wakefield.

"What do you think of me now?" she asked.

"Well, I really don't know," he replied. "At first you seemed so arrogant and suspicious of all men, then you invited me to have

193

supper and sex with you."

Tanya laughed loudly.

"As I told you Rasta man, only the special ones gets it," she said.

"But I'm happily married and have a child and......" he began.

"That's alright," she said. "It's I who is doing the stalking at this time, so don't feel guilty. Furthermore, you had the opportunity to screw me and you didn't."

Dready smiled as he said,

"So what if I rejected your offer now?"

"I certainly would feel dejected, but wouldn't be overly upset. But I want to, because I feel like doing it with you," she stated.

"You had been married, so you do understand my reason, don't you?" asked Dready.

"Yes, and have three children," she answered, "but let's not talk about them right now. Firstly, I would like to get into bed and exercise my, my..... you know what, then talk later."

She got up from the table and literally dragged him to the bedroom and within a minute she was standing in front of him totally naked. She had a beautifully shaped body for a woman in her forties. One who had experienced a traumatic near death attempt on her life only a year ago. Yet, she showed no sign of depression.

"Come on then, clothes off," she said and began to loosen his buttons. "Take everything off. We must do it naked."

Dready was a little apprehensive about having sex with a strange woman without a condom and said so.

"Okay," she said, "if you're so afraid, then use one. I don't like them but....."

She seemed anxious to begin the intercourse. But as he was about to get in the bed, the back door opened and someone shouted.

"Tanya, where are you? It's Marge. I am here to pick up the clothes you promised for the Bazaar."

Quickly they jumped out of bed. Tanya grabbed a dressing gown and rushed to meet her friend while Dready put his clothes on, opened the extra beer he had taken into the bedroom and sat in a chair by the window.

After getting rid of Marge, Tanya returned to the bedroom to see Dready dressed, sitting at the window.

"That bitch is a nuisance," she said angrily. "She always come barging in without knocking. Can we resume now?"

Dready didn't respond. He walked to the kitchen to get himself another beer, feeling relieved for not having sex with her.

"So tell me Tanya," he shouted from the kitchen. "Where are your husband and children now?"

"As I told you earlier," she said, "I am divorced."

"Bad marriage?" asked Dready.

"In a way, yes," she answered. "He wanted to force me to do things I didn't want to, so I took my leave of him. Imagine he wanted me to courier drugs to England and the USA."

"Why?" he asked as he re entered the bedroom.

"Because he and his gang have been doing it for years and I would have been just another one of their mules," she said.

"What gang is this?" he asked.

"Well, there was a gang operating in the Kingston, Jamaica Bridge Club for years, ran by my father Karlheinz Bass and some other English army officers and some politicians, which included my husband and many friends. They had many of the younger women carrying the stuff to Europe and everywhere from there," she said without reservation. "I was told by my cousin Hubert that Barbara Smith, Lilly and Patricia Green were the recruiters who directed the transportation to England."

"Did you ever meet them?" asked Dready.

"Many times, in Jamaica," she replied. "They were bitches just like Althea and Amanda here. I refused to do it. I separated and moved myself to Miami for safety."

Dready sat quietly listening to Tanya telling all she knew about the old gang of the Bridge Club. She told him everything she saw and heard from Peter, Rosita and Jack Walter. He knew she wasn't lying and didn't interrupt, because he wanted to hear more about the connection between those in Jamaica and these in the Bahamas. Tanya talked about how her children were taken away from her and of being shot in Miami.

"That was the last straw," she said. "Some arse hole sent a hitman to kill me, but luckily the bullet only grazed my head. Look, see for yourself."

She moved her hair back so Dready could see the bullet mark along her scalp.

"That's a damn shame," he said sympathetically.

"Yes sir, they tried to kill me," she said angrily. "Then to make matters worst they tried again while I was in the hospital. Luckily a friend came to smuggle me out and brought me back to Nassau. When I got to Nassau, I told the chief of police my story and he spoke to the Jamaican police and they agreed not to charge me. I was summoned to Jamaica, and had to meet them at the Montego Bay airport to sign a statement and was released from suspicion. Imagine I couldn't even go to my father's funeral."

"Why not?" asked Dready.

"Because I was in the hospital. He was killed just about the same time that I was shot. And when I went there, if I had gone to his grave site, I could have been arrested like my sister Rosita was, and put in jail."

"I see," said Dready, "then what about your children? Why are they not living with you"

"My dear," she said, "they were taken away from me after the divorce. One boy died recently in Canada, something about a suicide; one is at a school somewhere in Sweden and the girl is somewhere on planet earth, I don't know where," she answered. "Someone told me she was in England.

"Are you sad to loose your children that way?" he asked.

"Damn right," she answered. "He was a good boy, but his father decided for him to be in the smuggling business as he was, and that is the end result. He often came to Miami to visit me, they must have followed him to my apartment to do the job."

"How old was he," asked Dready.

"Colin was twenty-five when he died and Cindy will be twenty-three next month."

"Do you believe he did himself in?" asked Dready.

"No," she answered, "he wouldn't do it. Colin loved life and wouldn't commit suicide. Somebody murdered him."

Dready felt sorry for her and decided to change the subject.

"How was your childhood, was it a happy one?" he asked.

"Well, yes and no," she replied dejectedly. "You see, my father Karlheinz had sent us, my sister Rosita and I, to Nassau to live with his brother Zenon Bachstrum. I found out later that my mother was having an affair with his other brother and accidentally died in a restaurant in Kingston. But we lived here with my uncle until we were sent to college in America."

"I bet you were a looker when you were young and had all the boys on a string?" asked Dready.

"Yes, I was a looker," she answered happily. "But I didn't have any string. I wasn't allowed to have one."

Did you ever fall in love with any other man when you were young?" he asked.

Yes," she answered smiling. "He was a wonderful but shy black man, who was afraid to approach and talk to me throughout our years of school. But one rainy day we did talk and agreed to find a secluded place away from my guardian's eyes. It was the most beautiful thing to happen to me."

Dready could see the glitter in Tanya's eyes as she spoke.

"What's his name?" he asked.

"Earl," she said, "Earl Monroe, and I loved him. But the family wouldn't allow us to be together and threatened to send him to prison if he persisted in his pursuit of me."

"Is he still alive?" asked Dready.

"Very much so," she said, "but we still cannot be together because my cousin Hubert would kill him. Let me tell you something. When I was shot in Miami, it was Earl who smuggled me out of the hospital before the killers could finish the job, and brought me to safety."

"Then what happened after your return to Nassau?" asked Dready.

"Since my cousin was so adamant against my desire to marry Earl, and I wanted to spend time with him, I bought him a boat and sent tourists to him for trips to the islands. Apart from this he did odd jobs for others."

"Like picking up crates of fish?" he asked.

"I presume so," she said. "Sometimes I would even charter his boat so that the two of us could be alone together," she answered.

"Is he the father of your children?" asked Dready.

This time Tanya looked at him in a questioning tone.

"Yes they are, but he doesn't know it,"she said.

"Why didn't you tell him?" he asked.

"He would want to see them and cousin Hubert would kill him instantly," she answered.

The phone rang and she answered it.

"Hello," she said into the mouth piece. There was silence.

"What? Who did it? Where? Okay I'll come right away," she said and hung up the phone.

"That was Earl,"she said anxiously. "Someone came aboard his boat while he was away and shot a woman who was asleep on it, and he wants me to come quickly before the police. He's afraid."

They quickly got dressed and soon were speeding to the yacht club. He parked the car and they hurriedly walked to Earl's boat, to see him sitting on deck with his head in the palm of his hands. Tanya rushed to him and they began to hug and talk. Dready waved to him for silence allowing Tanya to make the introduction.

"This is Dready Winston," she said, "Earl Monroe."

The two men shook hands as though they were meeting for the first time.

"What happened?" asked Dready.

"Somebody shot a woman who was sleeping on my boat," said Earl.

"When did it happen?"

"Just this afternoon, and her body is still down there," said Earl.

Dready told them to leave the boat and go to Tanya's house.

"And when the police ask you, you were there together all day, okay?" he said.

He slowly descended the stairs to find the red haired woman he saw in Abaco, dead. He inspected the cabin and the body to find three bullet holes in her chest, one had entered directly through the left nipple of her breast.

Dready went into the yacht club and waited until he was sure that Tanya and Earl were comfortable in her house, then he got up from the stool to call Daniels.

"Chief," he said, "I have another dilemma for you. I came to Earl Monroe's boat a few minutes ago to find he was not there. Instead I found a naked woman's body in the boat."

"Dead?" asked Daniels.

"Sure is," said Dready.

"I'll be there in a few minutes," said Daniels, and hung up the phone.

It didn't take long for Daniels and Abbot to reach the marina and raced down the steps to the boat.

"Okay, where's the body?" asked Daniels.

"Down here," said Dready.

They looked around for awhile then the coroner and company came in to begin their search and to do whatever they do.

"Where is that Monroe fellow," asked Daniels.

"Couldn't tell you," said Dready, "but if you find Tanya McKenzie, I mean Bachstrum, you might find him."

Daniels signalled Abbot and gave him some instructions. Abbot rushed off, presumably to find them.

"Now tell me the entire story again," said Daniels.

"As I told you before, I came to Earl's boat for him to take me to the far-out island to see Mrs. Wakefield," said Dready. "I hollered for him but there weren't any answer; then I remembered that he sometimes sleeps on board. I called out again without response, so I went down there and saw her lying there. I called you immediately."

"Have you ever seen her before?" asked Daniels.

"Yes, she was that horny woman I told you about on Abaco; the one who invited me to have sex with her, allowing me to escape when she fell asleep."

"When was the last time you saw her alive?" asked Daniels.

"Mmmm," said Dready. "Two nights ago at the casino."

"Alone?" asked Daniels.

"No; I saw her with Hubert and Amanda Bachstrum, Althea Bass, Tullis Burke and Austin J. Smithers. What's her name?"

"Darlene DeLeon," replied Daniels. "She is some kind of a fashion designer from somewhere in Europe; she hung around with those people whenever she come here."

"Good, then you don't have far to look for her murderer," said Dready.

"Maybe so, but I will still have to talk to Mr. Monroe first," said Daniels.

Everything was done and the body removed to the morgue by the proper authorities, leaving Dready and Daniels standing on the deck talking. Dready told him the story about Abaco and the boat incident for the umpteenth time.

"...and as I said," began Dready as Abbot drove up with Earl and Tanya.

"Aaah!" said Daniels. "Are you people ready to make a statement?"

"Yes sir," replied Tanya. "I will tell you everything from start

200

to finish."

"Okay, let's go to the station to do that," he said. Then he turned to Abbot, "pick-up Hubert and Amanda Bachstrum, Austin Smithers, Judith Wakefield, Tullis Burke Althea Bass and Clinton Reeves. I want them all at the station by six o'clock this evening."

"Right sir," said Abbot and dashed off.

"Coming to the station?" asked Daniels.

Dready thought about it.

"No, I don't think I will need to," he said, "you are capable of making them talk without my presence. Furthermore, if I need any information for the story, I can always come to visit you."

He turned, winked at Earl and parted company.

He walked to the parking lot where he had left his rented car, got in and began his drive to the hotel when something hit his mind. He turned into the office of the telephone company instead.

"I would like to speak to the president please," he requested of the receptionist.

"No you can't sir," she replied in a stern tone of voice, "but the manager is over there."

Dready followed her finger to the fellow standing at an office door.

"I would like to speak to the president please," he said.

"Not today sir," said the manager, "he is very busy today."

"That's all right," said Dready, "maybe you can help me then. You see sir," he said, flashing his police credentials, "I cannot trust the phones at the hotel because people are always listening and I have to make a very important call to Jamaica."

The manager guided him into his office and Dready explained what he wanted done. The manager didn't object.

The call to Graves office was placed immediately.

"Talk as long as you want, it's toll-free," said the manager as he left him alone.

Dready and Graves talked for almost an hour in private. Graves told him about the development in Jamaica and how well Christiana was doing with the documents from the case.

"My friend," said Graves, "Christiana found the picture of Mr. Phillips and matched it to the man you met in Nassau. It's apparent that he switched identity with the real Austin J. Smithers in London, after murdering him. The Bobbies found the body in Wolverhampton about a year ago with the ID of Phillips, but had no suspicion of a switch. We also found out that Mr. Ralston Weekes have moved to the Bahamas some years ago, but Chief Daniels is still unable to locate him. Maybe you could check to be sure."

"I will," replied Dready. "What else?"

"Remember that ship?" asked Graves.

"Yes," said Dready, wanting to know what happened to it.

"My friend, it was laden with cocaine, guns and illegal people," said Graves, "all seemed to be destined for Jamaica. Some had American passports and addresses in the USA. We've arrested everybody and have contacted their countries of birth to see what was required of them. We have also contacted the USA."

"Now comes the wait," said Dready. "What else?"

"We found out that Zenon Bachstrum is the brother of Karlheinz Bass," said Graves. "Surprise you?"

"Not really," said Dready. "I found out that Karlheinz had sent Rosita and Tanya to someone in Bahamas to take care of them, and realized that it had to be a relative of some kind. Thus the reason I sent you the photograph."

"His face was done over by Bass, and with a new identity he was deposited in the Bahamas," said Graves.

"Yes, but we still have to know why," said Dready.

"Diamonds, maybe," said Graves.

"You could be right," said Dready, "but I will find out when I get to Georgetown, Guyana."

"Good," said Graves.

"What about Garfield Smith?" asked Dready.

"Scotland yard is checking," said Graves.

"Good. Please tell Christiana I will call her tonight at home," said Dready.

"I will," replied Graves. "See you."

Dready sat in thoughts for about ten minutes, then he dialled Commissioner Dillon's number.

"Hello, Dillon here," said the Commissioner into the phone.

"Hello sir," he said, "I'm very close to completion, but I need to know something more."

"What's that?" asked Dillon.

"Check if detectives Jack Colly and Avery Mathews ever visited Nassau and when was the last trip," Dready said.

"Hold a minute," said Dillon.

The wait seemed longer than the three minutes it took for Dillon to make the check.

"They first visited Nassau three years ago with their wives, then two years ago they went again," said Dillon. "It was when I installed Charles Chrittendon as my ears there."

"Did their wives accompany them?" asked Dready.

"No, they were alone," said Dillon. "But five months ago they returned there while on their Florida vacation."

"How did you know that, sir?" asked Dready.

"About three months ago a phone call came in for Mathews," said Dillon, "which Captain Morrow took because it was Mathews' day-off. It was from a Rupert Abbot in Nassau; and when questioned, he told Morrow that he had met them on their vacation and wanted to speak to them. Well, Morrow thought nothing of it and forgot to give him the message until later. Is there a problem?"

"Yes sir," replied Dready. "I believe those two are the ones using the codes, but I will have to be absolutely sure of my suspicions first before making an accusation."

"Okay," said Dillon, "I will ensure they are kept under tight surveillance."

"Right sir," said Dready, "we'll talk later."

He wanted to go to the hotel for a little sleep but his curiosity caused his adrenalin to begin pumping, so he decided to walk over to the police station to see what was going on.

"Chief Daniels please," he asked the desk Sergeant.

"Go right in," said the Sergeant, "he is waiting for you."

Dready walked in to see Earl and Tanya were still giving their testimonies, which was being recorded by a tape as well as a stenographer. He sat to listen as Earl told Daniels all about his and Tanya's love affair from childhood days to the present, his dealings with Hubert, and the tourists and fish he was asked to carry to different islands. He heard about Earl's thoughts of the Bachstrum's family involvement in the smuggling over the years, intermingled with statements by Tanya about her father and uncle.

He was well aware of most of the happenings in Jamaica, during the Arlene Felscher investigation, and knew that Tanya was very perturbed by the fact that they wanted to kill her. She told Daniels all about that; well as much as she knew. He was thankful that Earl didn't divulge his identity and felt assured that he would not do so.

When the interview was over, Daniels told Earl and Tanya to leave.

"But don't leave the island," said Daniels, "I might want to talk to you two again."

"We'll be around," said Earl as they walked hand-in-hand through the station doors.

Dready invited Daniels to go for dinner before his interview with Hubert Bachstrum.

"That's a fine idea," said Daniels. "I want to be comfortable when I speak to that man."

They walked to a small restaurant near the station and ordered the food. It seemed that the place was a regular hangout for the men on the force, because there were many in there.

"Have you ever spoken to a man called Arthur Collins?" asked Dready.

"Sure have," said Daniels. "He was a fine officer until he got involved in that gang in Jamaica. I was surprised to know of his part in it."

Dready, knew that he would somehow have to tell Donald Daniels of his knowledge of what was going on in his force, but then was not the right time.

"Tell me about your association with the two Canadian police officers, Jack Colly and Avery Mathews, who came to Nassau for a visit two years ago," said Dready.

"Those two came to my office, introduced themselves and wanted to know about our operations," said Daniels. "I introduced them to Abbot to be their liaison guide and they hit it off well. They sometimes called to talk, but it was usually with Abbot, and the time when they came with Chrittendon, although I was notified by Commissioner Dillon that he would be coming, I didn't see him. I haven't seen them since that first time."

"What about the Chrittendon fellow, how did he presented himself with the job he was assigned to?" asked Dready.

"Why your question on Chrittendon; are you a police officer?" asked Daniels.

"No," said Dready, "I'm a crime reporter who wants all the facts; that's all."

"Then how did you come up with Jack Colly, Mathews and Chrittendon?" asked Daniels.

"I've been on to them for almost two years and their trail leads here," he replied.

Dready was surprised when Daniels told him all about the people he enquired about, and also about finding Chrittendon's body on the beach.

"Who killed him?" asked Dready.

"I believe it was Hubert Bachstrum and I intend to prove it this evening when I interview him."

Dready wasn't sure how, but he intended to listen.

"How come you have never arrested him before now?" asked Dready.

"Simple," answered Daniels. "We never could pin anything on him because no witnesses would come forward. Now, we have Earl Monroe and Tanya McKenzie as well as some circumstantial evidence."

"Did you know that Sanderson was a pirate?" asked Dready.

"Yes, but couldn't arrest him either," said Daniels.

"Why not?"

"He always stayed outside of my jurisdiction," said Daniels. "International waters; and those who got caught wouldn't talk."

"Ever encounter a Garfield Smith?" asked Dready.

"No. Is he in the Bahamas?" asked Daniels. "If so, then I want him."

"What about Ralston Weekes?" asked Dready.

"No. He doesn't reside in Bahamas," said Daniels.

"Good," said Dready, "shall we go?"

They left the restaurant and slowly walked back to Daniels office. Daniels directed him to an observation room with a two way mirror and speakers, off his office. He entered and sat in a comfortable chair to observe the action.

"Are they here yet?" asked Daniels of the desk sergeant.

"Yes sir, they are in the back room," the sergeant replied.

Daniels directed himself to the room and opened the door.

"Good evening folks," he said, "sorry to detain you this long, but I have a dead woman named Darlene DeLeon on my hands and I would like to ask you all some routine questions."

"Why?" asked Hubert.

"Because she was seen in your company in the casino last evening, that's why," replied Daniels. "Hello Mrs. Bachstrum, please follow me; we can talk first so that you can get home for your late evening tea."

"Good," she said, "let's go."

"This won't take long," he said as he signalled for the steno.

He got settled in his office, asked the Sergeant to switch on the tape recorder and nodded to the stenographer to begin.

"Please state your full name and nationality," he said.

"My name is Amanda Torino Bachstrum," she said. "I'm Dutch, but I've lived in the Caribbean for most of my life."

"Bachstrum is your married name, isn't it?" he asked.

"Yes, my maiden name was Wakefield," she answered.

That brought a slight stir from Dready.

"Now tell me Amanda, how long have you known Darlene DeLeon?"

"About a year," she said.

"Where did you meet her?" he asked.

"At the casino," she answered.

"Did someone introduce you to her?" asked Daniels.

"Yes, Hubert did," she answered.

"Did you both become friends instantly?" he asked.

Amanda paused for a moment, wondering why he was asking so many questions about Darlene DeLeon, after telling her that it was routine.

"Yes," she said. "We had so many things to talk about seeing that she was from Belgium and I had spent some of the war years there."

"Did you admire her for her fashions or because she was a business woman?" he asked.

"Both," replied Amanda. "I envied her flair for travelling, and the places she had been, so we......."

".......became friends so that she could deliver goods in Europe for you," he said in an abrasive tone.

"No, nothing like that," said Amanda. "We only talked about the people and places she had been and......."

"Do you want me to play the tape of the bug on your phone? To prove that you two have been conducting business for some time now?" said Daniels. "I could tell you the date of your first shipment, and even the night she and Hubert slept together at your house."

At this point Amanda became distraught and haggard-looking. Her seventy-year old face was drawn because she realized that she was caught.

"I think you'd better tell us the story, rather than make me pull it out of you," he advised her.

Within minutes, Amanda told him her entire life story and the times of her activities, which included her times with the Jamaican contingent of Karlheinz and her husband Zenon.

"We were required to transport the commodities to England and other parts of Europe," she said, "and couldn't object."

"So what's been going on here?" he asked.

"That I couldn't tell you," she replied in a depressed tone. "You will have to speak to my son about that. I'm too old now to worry."

Dready could see that Amanda was being evasive but couldn't ask any question without compromising his anonymity. He looked at Daniels conducting the interrogation and saw that the police man now realized that he had made the point with the old woman.

"Thank you Amanda, you were of great help; and I hope you understand that you cannot leave the island or speak to anyone about this case," he said, and watched as she left his office nodding her head.

He signalled the police woman to escort Amanda outside.

"Put her in a cab for home," he advised, "and have Constable Reed watch her place. And hey!" he continued. "Have someone cut her phone line. Send in Hubert Bachstrum."

He waited for about five minutes, then Hubert walked in.

"What the fuck do you have me in here for?" asked Hubert.

Daniels sat in his plush office chair swinging from left to right with a pencil in his mouth just staring at Hubert.

"Folks, meet Mr. Hubert Bachstrum, a man whose family

208

came to the Bahamas many years ago under false pretences," he said as though unaware of Hubert's burst of anger, "and has been perpetrating criminal activities throughout that time without penalties. Tell me Mr. Bachstrum, where were you today?"

"At my home alone, relaxing in my pool," replied Hubert.

"Good," said Daniels. "You'd better have a hundred witnesses because I have ten that can place you at the Bahamian Yacht Club at noon."

"No you can't," said Hubert, "I wasn't anywhere near the place."

Daniels smiled.

"Did you hear what I said? I said I have ten witnesses that can prove you were at the Yacht Club at noon," said Daniels, "and I'm sure the jury will believe them more than you and your friends."

"Well, I wasn't," said Hubert, "and that's my word."

"Which is no good anywhere in the Bahamas," said Daniels. "Do you know Darlene DeLeon?"

"Yes, she's a high-class hooker who partied on my boat a few times," he replied. "She is not my friend. She was hired by me to entertain some of my clients from South America and England."

"Well, she's dead and I suspect that you did it," said Daniels. "I think she refused to carry out your request, so you killed her to demonstrate your might."

"That you'll have to prove," said Hubert.

"I intend to," said Daniels.

There was a long pause before Daniels signalled to the mirror.

"Do you know a man named Karlheinz Bass?" asked Dready over the speaker.

Hubert looked around the room trying to locate where the voice came from.

"Who the fuck are you?" asked Hubert.

"I'm a reporter," answered Dready. "I wrote the story on him in the Jamaican case last year and hope to write this one also."

"Yes I do," said Hubert.

"What's his relationship to you?" asked Dready.

"An associate, that's all."

"What about Peter McKenzie?" asked Dready.

"Yes, he was a friend of mine, but...." said Hubert.

"Then you must be acquainted with Lyle Alexander, Arthur Collins, Lilly and Patricia Green, Barbara Smith and....." said Dready, before he was interrupted.

"Yes, yes, I know them all," shouted Hubert. "But what the fuck do they have to do with me and Miss. Darlene DeLeon?"

"Nothing," said Dready, "I just wanted to attach your name to the list of characters for my story."

Dready could see a deep concerning look in Hubert's eyes and realized that he had made the point to him without alerting Daniels to his identity. Just then Daniels decided to play a trump card.

"Hubert Bachstrum, you are under arrest for the murder of Miss. Darlene DeLeon, Bartholomew and Judith Wakefield, Charles Chrittendon and......,"

"Let me call my lawyer," said Hubert.

"Sorry," replied Daniels, "I can hold you for a long time without allowing you the privilege of a phone call - unless you're willing to cooperate and sign a confession."

"Kiss my arse," said Hubert angrily.

"I won't, but there are some real nice fellows in prison who would be willing," replied Daniels.

There was a long moment of silence, then Dready said,

"The Jamaican story I did last year included a man called Ivan Burkowitz, who is currently serving a life sentence in Guyana. We could contact him to find out if you know each other."

This time Hubert didn't wait for another statement, as he said.

"I didn't kill either Wakefield or Chrittendon, it was Clinton Reeves."

"He works for you, doesn't he?" asked Dready.

"Yes but....." said Hubert.

"You gave him the orders," said Daniels, "which makes you an accessory to the fact, thus the gallows. Charge all of them with murder. Amanda Bachstrum, Austin J Smithers, the young Judith Wakefield, Tullis Burke, Althea Bass and Clinton Reeves, and get a signed confession from each of them," said Daniels to Abbot.

Dready realized that Daniels was already in possession of all the facts he needed, thus the reason he was confident in his action. He waited until everybody was locked up before telling Daniels that he was tired and needed some rest also.

"I'll be at the hotel," said Dready. "If you need me please call me there."

"Yes," said Daniels, "only if I need you."

"Good," said Dready, "and while you're at it, look for a man named Garfield Smith."

"Who is he?" asked Daniels.

"He is the grandson of British army Captain Smith, a former chief- of- police in Jamaica," said Dready.

Donald Daniels stood there watching Dready as he walked away from him.

"Now, how the hell did he know that man?" he questioned himself.

Chapter Eight

So they Live; So they Die.

$\mathcal{T}$he plane touched down at the Freeport, Grand Bahama airport at 9:45 in the morning. Christiana got off as all the touristy-looking people did and followed the signs to the immigration. She was still wondering why Winston asked her to meet him there rather than in Nassau, and why he had her leave Montego bay the night before to stay in Miami. But within her mind she knew he had a good reason and trusted his judgement. She also understood that he was concerned for her safety, just in case someone in that town should ever see them together and blow the case-hence the reason she had her hair dyed, wore dark glasses and clothes that gave her the appearance of a regular tourist. Her small shoulder strap purse gave the impression of not having enough money to attract any thief.

In her mind, she was certain that he wanted to talk about the case face-to-face and not on the phone, and the fact that he wanted to make love to her like they did in Jamaica a year ago; and doing it in the Bahamas, seemed like a wonderful idea.

She found her over-night bag and quickly entered the gate to the customs-officer's table.

"What have you to declare?" asked the officer.

"Absolutely nothing," she answered.

"How long are you planning on staying in Freeport?" he asked.

"Four days," she replied.

"What is your business in the Bahamas?" he asked.

"I'm here to seduce a very handsome man and hopefully to have his child," she said. "I hope that's not a crime in your country. Is it?"

"No, it's not," said the officer smiling. "I see you've removed your marriage band. Any reason why?"

"Don't want him to know that I'm cheating on my husband with him," she said.

The officer smiled.

"You've come to the right place for that Miss," he said. "Most people come here for a vacation, and get involved with others; but good luck and enjoy your seductive four days of sexual interaction."

She took her passport from his hand, winked at him and slowly walked outside. She stopped to take a deep breath of the fresh salty air, viewed the surrounding scene and silently observed that it looked just like Jamaica.

Dready approached and kissed his wife almost immediately. He stepped back to admire her jeans, running shoes and tee shirt and wondered why she did not dress up for the occasion.

"Hello darling," he whispered, "is everything all right?"

"It is now," she answered. "Nice to see you too."

"What do you want to do first?" he asked.

"Take me to the nearest hotel and ravish me," she said.

"Which hotel?" he asked.

"Any one," she replied, "because we cannot make love in the airport parking lot and there are no bushes around here."

"Good," he said, "but there are a lot of places on these islands that we must visit and we only have four days to do so."

"That's fine with me," she replied, "just as long as we can

214

have sex during all of this island-hopping you've planned."

There wasn't anything else he could add, so he signalled Earl to come.

"Earl, this is Christiana Perkins," he said. "We are having a love affair behind her husband's back, and whatever we do in the next four days should not be mentioned to anyone, living or dead. Got it?"

"That's fine with me," said Earl. "Where do you want to go first?"

"Take us to the Princess in the West End so that we can spend a couple of hours together, then we will decide where, after."

"Good," said Earl. "But if I were you, I would go to that nice quaint little place up on Water Cay, rather than spend the money at the posh expensive place in the West end."

Dready took Earls suggestion.

"Let's go to Water Cay," he said and signalled for him to lead the way to the boat.

Earl docked the boat at the appropriate place and led them to the little motel he suggested.

"How do you know about these little places?" asked Dready.

"Remember this is my home?" said Earl. "Well, I do have to take tourists to many parts of it in the quest of making my living; and for me to stay in business, I have to know these little romantic places to bring them to."

"That's nice," said Christiana, "because I would like to see some of the houses on the other islands also, and some of the hide-away's where we can make love freely."

"Just leave that to me," said Earl. "Go and have some fun now and I'll be back in two hours for you."

They stood and watched as Earl got back into his boat and headed out to sea in the direction of Abaco. When the boat was almost out of sight, Dready picked up Christiana and carried her over the threshold like newly weds do.

At the desk sat a ghastly obese, elderly, half black woman

with a pipe in her mouth.

"A room please," he said to her.

"North or East?" she asked.

Dready looked at Christiana and she replied,

"East please."

"How long?" the woman asked.

"How long what?" asked Christiana.

"How long are you staying?" asked the woman.

"About a couple of hours," replied Christiana.

"Why only two hours?"

"Because we want to make love in many parts of the islands before the four days are up," explained Christiana. "If it were you, would you spend it all in one place?"

The woman didn't answer, just gave them a scornful look.

"Well, it's thirty American dollars a day," said the woman, "and I don't care how long you stay. Just pay me up front and leave whenever you want to."

The woman took the money and stuffed it into her bosom then lead them to a room over-looking the sea.

"This is it," she said, "and don't make too much noise because there is an elderly couple sleeping in the room next to you."

"Thank you," said Dready.

They waited until the woman left before entering the room. Inside, they looked around and noticed that every wall had a mirror and a painting hanging on it. This intrigued Dready somewhat because immediately he suspected that the woman was running a scam of either taping the visitors or watching them through the mirrors.

Quickly he turned and left the room then signalled Christiana with his finger to follow him. He lead her out the back to the beach area before talking.

"This woman is a voyeur," he said, "and we cannot take the chance of her listening to our conversation or seeing what we are doing."

Christiana gave thoughts about what Winston had suggested.

"Well, darling," she said, "we don't have to talk about anything important; we could talk about us cheating on our respective spouses and make it exotic for the old bitch. Give her something to masturbate on."

Dready thought about the suggestion and smiled.

"Very good," he replied. "And it might be a very good cover for us later."

They re-entered the room and began removing each other's clothing.

"Darling, I missed you," said Christiana. "This is the most wonderful idea for us to get away from my husband and you from your wife."

"Absolutely," said Dready. "They will be in Freeport waiting for us while we are here enjoying ourselves."

They dove into the bed and began kissing and doing sexual things to each other.

"Oh darling, I love you," Christiana cried. "you are the best. My husband could never do this for me."

"I love you too sweetheart," he said as they got locked into a steamy, sexual interlude.

Afterwards, they lay in bed talking about their spouses and generally putting on a good show for the woman; by walking around naked and making love in different position and places. This went on for the entire time. Finally Dready looked at his watch, and they got showered and dressed quickly. They deliberately walked to the front desk to look at the woman and noticed that her face was flushed.

"That was wonderful," she said to the woman. "It's always nicer when it's stolen with someone who is desirable."

The woman didn't answer. Just sat there with that look of satisfaction on her flushed face.

"See you," said Dready, handing her an extra twenty. "Maybe we'll come back again if we can get away from our spouses. But if anyone asks you about us, we never stayed here, okay?"

They walked out with arms wrapped around each other in the direction of the dock area where Earl was supposed to meet them.

His boat wasn't there, so they hung around kissing and cuddling because they could feel the woman's eyes were still upon them, and they wanted to continue the show for her.

Fifteen minutes passed before he noticed the boat coming towards them. It was Earl speeding into the dock.

"Sorry I'm late," said Earl as he stopped the boat at the dock, "but I got caught up with a girl over there and....."

"That's okay," said Dready, "no need to apologise. Everything went well for us and the landlady."

Earl didn't understand what he meant, but assisted them to board his craft and sit before he reversed the boat back out into the sea and headed towards Abaco.

Within minutes he docked the boat again in a little cove on the south end of the island.

"Where is this?" asked Christiana.

"This is Abaco," said Earl. "This is the place where we found the bodies in the house, the money and drugs."

"Oh!" said Christiana. "What bodies and what drugs?"

"Dready told her about the find he and Earl had made, also about how he got the police to come there and what was said between Abbot and Daniels.

"Well, let's go see it," said Christiana.

Earl started up the incline towards the dirt road. Christiana smiled and thanked God that she had worn her running-shoes instead of the regular ones, because now she had to climb this hill to get were ever they were going.

At the top of the little hill and the beginning of the dirt road, stood a small car with a man inside.

"Who is that?" asked Dready.

"A friend of mine," said Earl.

Earl had gotten one of his friends to meet them for the drive to the place on the north side of the island near Marsh Harbour, where they had been to the house with the bodies.

On reaching the town, Christiana looked at her watch.

"Hey!" she shouted. "It's past two o'clock, can we have lunch before going on to wherever we are going?"

"Sure can," said Dready. "Where is a good place Earl?"

Earl looked at his friend and the man drove to a little restaurant not far from where they stood. They entered and found seats.

"What would you recommend Earl?" she asked.

"Try the conch chowder," he replied, "they make a good one here."

Christiana was willing to try anything. She was famished from not having her breakfast. They ordered the food and a couple of beers and waited.

"You know most of these islands don't you Earl?" she asked.

"Damn right," he replied smiling. "In my business of taking tourists fishing and sight-seeing, I have to know where to take them for fun and recreation."

"And the people who don't?" she asked.

"They are hungry and broke," said Earl.

The conversation stayed on the trivial side until after lunch. They left to continue their adventure to the place of interest.

"This is it," said Dready as Earl's friend stopped near the gate of the house.

"From this angle, it sure looks different," said Dready. "Different than when we last saw it."

"Sure does," said Earl. "The last time we came up from the beach side over there, remember?"

"I do," said Dready as they walked towards the house.

219

They quietly entered the empty house and began looking around. It appeared the same as he had left it that day. He led her through the house to the huge master bedroom and to the door in the closest. The place didn't smell stink as it did that day, because the bodies and fish had all been removed.

"I brought Daniels here to show him where everything was," said Dready. "The drugs were in crates and boxes over there and the money was in suitcases like that one in the corner."

Christiana opened the suitcase to look inside but it was empty.

"Did the police take the money?" she asked.

"I presume they did," Dready replied.

"Did you find out who the people were?" she asked.

"Yes," replied Dready, "and the police are the only ones who can give us a motive. Although I'm positive what it was and who killed them."

They looked through the entire house.

"Who owns it?" asked Christiana.

"This house was built by a man called Sanderson," said Dready, "but he died and left it to his daughter Elaine. It was sold to some Arabs by Wakefield and used by someone else to store the goods."

"How did Sanderson die?" asked Christiana.

"Drowned," said Dready and began to tell her about the misadventure of the Olympic gold medallist swimmer.

"What shit luck," she said. "Here's a man, who could out swim Johnnie Weismuller, and *he* accidentally drowned. I don't think it was an accident."

Dready laughed.

"Maybe they were working for the Americans against the Arabs and the Eastern boys had them killed," said Earl.

"Could be right Earl," said Christiana, "but if it was done by the Arabs, they would've told the world it was in the name of allah; so that rules them out. I think it was done by someone who wanted to blame the Arabs. Someone who lived in this house."

Dready, in the meantime, was looking around the walls for breaks or patches. He asked,

"Hey Earl, you worked for Hubert Bachstrum, didn't you?"

"Yes," replied Earl, "I occasionally picked up crates of fish for them."

"Did you ever bring those crates of fish to this location?" asked Dready.

"No," said Earl. "It was always to Andros, Berry islands or to New Providence, never here."

"Then someone else was delivering to this location," said Christiana.

"I guess so," said Earl, "but who?"

Their search took almost all afternoon and part of the night but nothing, beyond what Dready already knew, was found.

"I wonder if anybody in the neighbourhood knew who was living here and about the Sanderson man?" said Christiana.

"Don't know," said Earl, "but my half brother Sonny lives about three miles from here, maybe he could tell us something."

"Let's go find your brother," said Dready.

The driver took them to Sonny's four bedroom house, which stood on a little hill in the middle of his farm.

He parked the car and they got out.

"Where's Sonny?" asked Earl of the teenage boy who was busy chopping coconuts in the dark.

"Hello uncle Earl," said the boy. "He is inside the house."

They entered the verandah and Earl shouted,

"Sonny, get your arse out here! I have some people who want to talk to you."

Within a minute the man came out wearing only his pajama-pants, followed closely by his wife.

"What's all the noise?" he asked. "I was having a nice sleep."

"Well not anymore," said Earl. "First, these people want to ask you some questions about Mr. Sanderson who lived down the road there."

"Who are these people?" asked Sonny.

"They are friends of mine from Nassau," said Earl. "Dready Winston is a journalist and his...eh, wife Christiana; meet my brother Sonny and his wife Gertrude. They want to know about Sanderson for a magazine article they are doing."

"Good; are you going to mention my name?" asked Sonny.

"I might," replied Dready. "Only if your story is good."

"Fine," said Sonny and began the tale.

"Sanderson came to the Bahamas from America, with two large boats and set up his food-import business here. He sometimes hired people, as myself and my boy, to pilot them from Miami, although at times we would have to off-load the stuff from ships out at sea. He became known as the Admiral or the Commodore because he was an excellent captain and gave numerous Bahamians work; especially those with their own boats."

"Was he a pirate?" asked Dready.

"He sure was," replied Sonny.

"Did he ever kill anyone?" asked Christiana.

"Not to my knowledge," said Sonny, "but I wouldn't put it past him."

They all sat in silence for awhile.

"Was he a friend of Hubert Bachstrum?" asked Dready.

"He sure was," said Sonny. "Look, every Friday evening or some times on Saturday mornings, they all would meet on his cruiser for a day time party. There would always be two Columbians and two Trinidadians. Those men were regulars there. Most of the others were English and American. The Dutchman and some others were monthly visitors."

"How many Bahamians and other Caribbean people were there?" asked Dready.

"Not many," said Sonny. "Although there would be many prostitutes like Fran Mason there. She brought the black ones."

"Who brought the white ones?" asked Christiana.

222

"Darlene did," said Sonny. "Elaine also supplied some; mostly the Americans."

"Have you ever seen a man by the name of Garfield Smith?" asked Dready.

"No, the name doesn't ring a bell," replied Sonny.

"Okay," said Dready. "So Sanderson had these wild parties at sea for his friends and associates; where were you when all this was going on?"

"Remember I told you that I was the pilot of his boat?" said Sonny. "Well, figure it out."

"So," said Christiana, "Sanderson treated you well."

"Yes, he did. Look, Sanderson was okay," said Sonny, "it was his daughter who was the bitch."

"Why do you say that?" asked Christiana.

"That man would give you anything he had," said Gertrude, "but the daughter would let you pay it back double."

"Look," said Sonny, "it's late and I need some sleep. Why don't you all stay tonight and we can talk about it in the morning?"

Dready looked at Christiana and vice versa.

"Agreed," said Dready.

Quickly Gertrude took them to the rooms.

"The older children are gone and don't come home as they use to," she said, "so these rooms are vacant more than I would like to see them."

They stayed overnight at Sonny's place.

Next morning, Christiana got up early to admire the beautiful rising sun. She left the house and walked down the roadway towards the beach. About fifteen minutes later she saw Dready, Sonny and Earl come out of the house and take some chairs to sit on the verandah, with mugs of coffee in hand. She decided to walk back up the path to join them. Quickly they got involved in a conversation about the Sanderson man, which was a continuation from the night before. She looked in the window and decided to join Gertrude, who was busy in the kitchen making breakfast.

"Good morning Gertrude dear," she said to the woman of the house.

"Good morning Chrissy," answered Gertrude. "Sleep well last night?"

"Sure did," said Christiana. "Although the thoughts of Sanderson's daughter was stuck in my mind. What do you mean she was a bitch?"

"She used to bring groceries from the States with her father's boat and have Sonny sell them for her. He also did odd jobs for her," said the jealous sounding wife.

"Did she ever pay him?" asked Christiana.

"Yes," said Gertrude, "with her pussy; and he did it every time she asked."

"What happened to her?" enquired Christiana.

"After her father died, she went to Florida to live with her two bastard children," said Gertrude. "One of the children belongs to my husband."

"How do you know that?" asked Christiana.

"She told me so, and I saw the child with my two eyes," said Gertrude. "Furthermore, he admitted it."

"And the other child?" asked Christiana.

"That one is for Garth, my brother in law," she answered.

"Where is Garth now?" asked Christiana.

"Don't know. He could be anywhere," said Gertrude. "Maybe in Florida."

Somehow the name Garth got to the ears of Earl.

"Where's that son of a bitch," he shouted. "I would like to lay my hands on him."

"Why?" asked Sonny.

"It was he and his pirate friend Man-Man who were shooting at the people on my boat, and I want to choke the bastard," said Earl.

"He didn't kill anybody, did he?" asked Sonny.

"No, but he almost shot me," said Earl in a furious tone.

"We don't know where he is, but I think they are still using Sanderson's boat to bring groceries from Florida," said Gertrude.

Gertrude called the three men and the two younger children into the kitchen for the provided breakfast.

There was silence during the meal.

"Who sold the house?" asked Dready, breaking that period of silence.

"It was sold by a man named Wakefield to some Arabs," said Sonny.

"Did the Arabs live there?" he asked.

"No," said Sonny, "it was always Wakefield and some of his friends who used it occasionally."

"Did Elaine ever return there at any time?" asked Dready.

"Not to my knowledge," said Sonny.

"Never mind him," said the angry Gertrude, "he would lie for the little floozie. You'd have to find Garth. He could tell you if she did or not."

"Fine," said Dready, "we'll have to do that."

After a short thank you and goodbye, they rode to the far-out island of Long island to look at Wakefield's house. This time he wasn't as afraid of the water or the speed of Earl's boat as he was on the previous trip, because Christiana was beside him. Earl's path was in the Atlantic coast over Eleuthra and Cat Island, and then down to their destination on Long Island. Along the way they passed three anchored ships.

"Pirates," said Dready to Christiana.

She didn't respond.

Earl docked his craft. They walked up the path to the house and knocked on the door. It was empty. They entered the large living-room area and looked around for any signs of life. There were none.

Dready and Christiana took one direction and Earl took another in search of anything. Unlike the last time when they found Judith masturbating in the bed room, this time the room was empty.

He showed Christiana where he had found the book he gave to her and the money in the safe. They talked about the things Judith told Earl when he returned there to make love to her. When they were satisfied they left, and since it was getting late Dready was anxious to get away quickly.

"Where to now Earl?" she asked.

"We're going to Crooked Island to see the other house that Dready believe is owned by Robert Reynolds father," said Earl.

"Good," said Christiana, "he was one of the dead students in Toronto."

"What students?" asked Earl.

Christiana realized that Dready had not told Earl about the dead students in Toronto so she quickly changed her words.

"There was a young man in school in Toronto," she said, "who got himself into some trouble and I have to talk to his father about it."

Earl didn't question any more, as he directed the boat to the appropriate place and docked it.

"Where does he live?" asked Earl.

"Don't know," she said, "but we could ask someone in town."

Although Earl didn't mind doing things for Dready, he felt angry to be traipsing around in the dark looking for someone without proper directions.

"Let's try the police station," said Christiana.

"Not me," said Earl, "we don't seem to see things in the same light."

He walked them to the station door and left.

"I'll be in that bar over there," he said. "When you're finished with the police, find me there."

Christiana and Dready went into the station and approached the desk officer.

"Good evening Sergeant," she said. "We are looking for a friend named Reynolds, I was told that he has an orange farm near

226

here."

The Sergeant looked at the both of them.

"The Reynolds' farm is about seven miles out of town on the way to Pompey bay. Why do you want him?"

"We are Canadians and friends of their son Robert," said Christiana. "He told us that whenever we come down here we must see his father."

The police officer didn't ask any more questions.

"If you're driving," he said, "take the road out there going in that direction and you'll come to the farm house on the right side of the road."

"Thank you sir," said Dready.

They quickly crossed the street to find Earl in the Bar where he said he would be.

"Food and a place to sleep for the night," said Dready to Earl.

"Right here," said Earl.

They left the bar and entered the little motel and restaurant beside it, spoke to the man in charge and after eating, paid the night's rent.

When they awoke the next morning, they found Earl waiting for them in the little restaurant with a coffee in front of him.

"Didn't sleep last night?" he asked his taxi driving friend.

"Yes," answered Earl, "but I got up early to find a friend to take us where we have to go today."

The introduction and drive into the country side didn't take long, mainly because the fellow was a maniac. When he got there Dready paid him forty dollars for the stressful trip.

"Wait for us," instructed Dready, "we won't be here long."

Dready and Christiana approached the house with caution because there were two vicious looking dogs lying in the yard.

"Hello! anybody home?" he shouted from the gate.

A few minutes passed before a man's head appeared at the door.

"Who do you want?" he asked.

"Mr. Reynolds please," said Dready.

"Just a minute," said the man.

He came to the door dressed only in coveralls without shirt underneath..

"Come in," he said, " and don't worry about the dogs."

Dready was happy to have made it to the verandah where he sat down. The man went inside and returned with some beers for everybody.

"Now, what can I do for you?" asked the man.

"Well sir," said Christiana, "I have to tell you that your son Robert in Toronto, is dead."

Reynolds didn't seem surprised.

"That is stale news," he said, "I thought you were here to tell me about the insurance money. They have been stalling to pay it, saying that it was suicide and not a murder."

"We are here to clarify that same thing sir," said Christiana. "But first we must know who his friends were, and if there was anyone in particular he used to visit regularly."

"Oh, that's easy," said Reynolds. "Robert left our house and moved in over there to that Wakefield man's house with that horny little wife of his. I told him that some day something would happen to him but he didn't care. Maybe it was her husband that killed him."

"We don't know that sir," said Dready, "but whenever Chief Daniels finds out, he will certainly tell us and we will process your claim and send your money to you."

Do you know what Mr. Wakefield's business was?" asked Christiana.

"No," said Reynolds. "He very seldom talked to me. It was either to my wife or my son; never to me."

"When did Robert meet this man?" asked Christiana.

"Don't know," said Reynolds. "You see, he grew up with his mother in Abaco, and wasn't directly under my supervision until about two years ago when he came asking to stay with me. Well, since then, there has always been a constant battle with her and him about behaviour. Then Mrs. Wakefield began coming around and he finally left our house for theirs."

"Was he screwing Mrs. Wakefield?" asked Christiana.

"He must have been," said Reynolds, "she was always kissing and fussing over him, and from what I was told, Mr. Wakefield was always away somewhere, leaving them alone in that big house."

"Does his death mean anything to you?" asked Dready.

"Not really," replied Reynolds, "only the promised insurance money."

"Okay sir," said Christiana, "we'll contact you when it's all cleared up and the cheque has been posted to you."

"Good," said Reynolds, "that will be good to pay back all that he cost me during his stay here."

"Thank you sir," she said shaking his hand, "maybe we will meet again."

"Maybe," he said. "But please bring my money soon."

Christiana led the posse of two outside.

"I would like to see the Wakefield's house again," she said. "Today!"

"Not in the daytime love," said Dready. "We can only go there after dark to evade any prying eyes."

Christiana understood his reason, but Earl didn't appreciate having to wait.

"Tonight?" asked Earl.

"Yes, if you don't mind," she said.

"Okay by me," said Earl, "but I won't be going back to Freeport tonight."

"Fine," said Dready, "we could sleep in that house."

Earl's friend drove them back to the boat and received another twenty from Dready for his effort.

"We'll have to spend the rest of the day on the beach," said Christiana.

"Okay," said Dready. "We could always get food at the

229

restaurant over there and leave at the appropriate time."

"Well," said Earl, "I will see you later."

"And where are you going?" asked Dready.

"To a friend's place," said Earl as he left them and walked towards a house close by.

The duo sat around talking most of the time; occasionally walking to the road to get a coconut or some other fruits. Finally, Dready found a shady tree, constructed a bed from the coconut bows and lay down.

"Wake me when it's time to leave," he said.

Although Christiana felt romantic, she quietly lay beside him and they both fell asleep.

She woke to see Dready swimming in the sea. She took a check on her timepiece and realized it was almost six-thirty.

"What time are we leaving?" she shouted at Dready.

"Whenever Earl gets here," he shouted back.

Within a couple of minutes she saw Earl, with grocery bags in hand, and a young woman coming in their direction.

"She'll be coming with us," he said. "I'm not sleeping in that house without a woman beside me."

Neither Dready nor Christiana made any comments. They loaded themselves into the boat and Earl started up, put the lights on and comfortably drove to the next island.

They entered the house, got showered and relaxed with a couple of the owner's drinks.

While Earl was busy showing his woman around the house and kitchen, Christiana, on the prompting of Dready, called Althea in Nassau.

"Hello," said Althea into the phone.

"It's Christiana Felscher here," she said, "remember me? We met in Tullis Burke's apartment in the Colonial."

"Hi dearie," said Althea in a joyous tone, "are you back in Nassau?"

"Yes and no," said Christiana, "I'm at......just say I'm hiding out."

"Why?" asked Althea.

"Well, both Paul and I were arrested in Toronto on the last trip," she said winking at Dready, "I got bailed out by some unknown person and thought it was you, so I came down here for help."

There was a long pause and Christiana recognized that Althea wasn't aware of the arrest in Toronto.

"No, it wasn't me," said Althea, "but I could certainly assist you to hide."

"Well, whoever it was, I'm thankful," said Christiana. "You see, I skipped bail and grabbed the first flight here."

"Where are you now?" asked Althea.

"I'm in the Bahamas and desperately in need of protection," she told Althea, "and I know that you would protect me with everything you have."

"Yes, I would darling," said Althea, "Come to me; better yet meet me in Nassau and I will get a boat to take you to my hide away on another island where we can be lovers and where they cannot find you."

"I cannot take that chance," said Christiana, "Hubert might get to the island to kill me."

"I wouldn't let that happen to you darling," said Althea, " I wouldn't let that prick find you. I would love to have you with me here and could get you some protection; if I know where you are," said the anxious Althea.

"I cannot tell you now," she said, "but stick by your phone and I will call you back in the morning; good night."

She quickly hung up.

"She bit the bait," said Christiana.

"And what will you tell her tomorrow?" asked Dready.

"I will tell her that I'm here at this house and see who comes to meet me," she said.

"Then call her back now and give her the information," said

Dready, "then we'll see who she sends in the morning."

"What if the people come tonight?" she asked.

"Earl," said Dready, "would anyone leave Nassau in the night to come out here?"

"Not really, unless they were expert sailors like I am," he answered.

Quickly Christiana picked up the phone again and dialled Althea's number.

"Hello Althea," said Christiana, "I'm calling back because they are all in bed now. I'm at the Wakefield's house on Long island. Do you know where it is?"

"No," said Althea, "but I have a friend with a boat who knows the islands well. I will ask him in the morning to bring me there."

"Good," said Christiana. "See you then."

They all ate the chicken and bread provided by Earl, drank some beers and went to bed.

The night in the Wakefield's house and bed was very relaxing for Dready and Christiana. They made love in the same bed where he and Earl saw Judith masturbating on his first visit. He told the story to his wife and slept.

The still of the morning was broken when there was a heavy clunking noise in the kitchen area. Dready ran out to see what was the problem and saw Earl's girlfriend trying to make coffee. He concluded that she didn't have a clue how the electric appliances worked and accidentally dropped the pot on the floor.

Christiana made the coffee, comforted the crying woman and promised to send her one for her house after things were completed.

"Do you think they left Nassau yet?" she asked Earl.

"Maybe, but they wouldn't arrive here until about noon," he said.

Christiana returned to the kitchen with Florence, Earl's woman, to make breakfast and to teach her how to use of the appliances. Breakfast ran into lunch and after that meal was consumed,

232

Earl advised that they should leave to hide the boat and wait to see who came with Althea.

The wait wasn't very long, because right after Earl returned from hiding the boat, they watched from their hiding place as a boat came into the dock. There were two men and a woman. Christiana identified Althea, but the men were new faces to them. One was a tall blond haired fellow in his thirties with buck teeth and the other was a short fat fellow with a large moustache.

The three people slowly walked to the door. The two men quickly entered in a crouched position with guns in hand. A few minutes later they returned to the woman standing outside, apparently after searching the house.

"It's empty," said the tall blond-haired fellow with the buck-teeth. "I think they have left."

"Shit!" said Althea. "That little bitch is somewhere on this island and we must find her, and quick."

"Maybe the people took her to another island," said the short, fat guy.

"Maybe they did, but where?" she asked.

"You should have made sure before getting us out here on this wild-goose chase," said the fat man. "Hubert won't like this, not after Reynolds told you that they were there asking questions."

Althea stayed quiet.

"Nothing to do now but go back to Nassau and wait for her to call again," said the blond fellow, "and next time please make sure that she is where she is supposed to be."

With that they got back into the boat and left.

Earl took them to Freeport and saw them checked into the hotel before leaving.

"I'll be back for you tomorrow," he told Dready.

The two lovers stayed in bed for that night and part of the next day making love and discussing the case - plotting out what they intended on doing when they meet in Guyana. Dready gave her many instructions, because he knew that he couldn't risk making the necessary phone calls to her in Jamaica, knowing that Cynthia could be listening and could easily tell it to someone whom she might be working for.

"Get Graves to accompany you to see Jeremiah Bailey," said Dready. "I really would like to know what he knows about Barbara Smith's son."

"We sure will," she promised. "As a matter of fact, we will be going to put a head stone on my mother's grave next week."

"Whose idea was that?" he asked.

"Venny's," she replied. "And I loved it. But I will tell you all about it later."

"Give her my love," he said.

"I will."

Christiana left the following morning for Jamaica, delighted to have had the four days of seeing the islands, and making love to her husband in some of the most romantic spots in the Bahamas.

Chapter Nine

The Pork Knocker's Story.

*D*ready sat in bed contemplating his day's duties.

He was delighted to have had a lovely undisturbed sleep the previous night, after his three-hour phone conversation with Christiana. He was happy that she got back to Jamaica without any incidents and that both she and Venrece-Thomas were in good health and comfortably-relaxed in his mother's home. On her trip to Nassau, she was able to give him a host of information about the Bass-Bachstrum family and their affiliation to others.

With the help of Bernard Graves, she was able to talk with Lyle Alexander, aka Arthur Collins and Peter McKenzie in prison, and found that they were living a very comfortable life there. She told Dready about her meeting with Peter.

"He appeared strange when I told him about his son's death in Canada," she said, "and wasn't really surprised to hear, but did not comment."

"What about his connections to the outside world?" asked Dready.

"Well, his reaction to Bernard's promises for early parole in return for his testimony against his Bahamian friends was totally negative. He seemed disengaged from any such happening."

"What about Arthur Collins....I mean Lyle?" asked Dready.

"Same," she answered. "He too seemed relaxed and contented in his prison environment, and refused to talk."

She told him all that she was able to extract from her father in conversation and from his book; also the things she concluded from searching through Karlheinz's junk.

"There are some details of their operation and the track they used to ship the stuff around the world," she said, "and I'm sure there still remains someone at the top."

"What about Garfield Smith, anything?" he asked.

"Nothing yet," she replied. "Graves called Scotland Yard but there's no reply as yet."

They discussed this and realized that someone was still leading the gang, despite having those who were in prison. The question was, who could that person be? But the problem of where to find them, still remained a mystery in their minds.

He decided that a shower was the first order of business, followed by some breakfast and a few phone calls. He got out of the shower and was arranging his locks under his tam when the phone rang.

"Hello," he answered.

"Hi handsome," said Cynthia's voice, "are you busy today?"

'Not really," he replied. "Is it very important?"

"Might be," she said. "Come to meet me at the Carmichael restaurant, I have something for you."

"Okay," he responded, "see you in half an hour."

He hung up the phone, dressed quickly and was on his way to Carmichael to meet Cynthia.

He got into his rental car and slowly drove along Gladstone Road then to the dirt road to the restaurant; wondering all the way what could Cynthia have found-out that was so important. He carefully parked and got out, at the same time peeking to see who was present in the restaurant.

He saw her down at the water's edge playing in the sand, and decided to walk along the side of the building to approach her.

"Hello good-looking," he said as he got close to her, "what have you got for me?"

She planted a hot, wet kiss on his lips. Then, because he didn't respond as she wanted, she pulled away and produced a sheet of paper.

"This is a log sheet," she said. "The supervisors keep these to remind them of phone messages to the rooms. This one gives you a detailed account of some calls into the rooms in recent days."

Dready took the paper and read. There were six calls in from Rupert Abbot to different people there. Three to Rona Samuels, two to a Mr. Phillips or Smithers and one to his room.

"So tell me about the conversations," he said.

"The first call was to a Rona Samuels. He asked her what was happening with the deal and she told him that there was a dealer who will be purchasing three hundred thousand dollars worth by this weekend, and that it was agreed with Hubert to complete it. That was the end of that conversation."

"Did they talk again?" he asked.

"Yes, he called her later in the afternoon and told her that some dead bodies were found in a house in Abaco and he wasn't sure if Hubert had anything to do with it. She in turn told him to keep his eyes open for any danger to themselves."

"Okay, that's two calls to Rona, when did he call this Phillips man?" asked Dready.

"Well, he called this person, whom he referred to as Phillips, after the first call to Rona and they talked about a shipment of stuff coming from South America. Phillips told him that there was a dealer here who might purchase the entire lot for three hundred thousand dollars and that a meeting would be set up for that purpose some time this week."

"Good, what else?" asked Dready.

"On the second call, which was made after his second call to Rona, he told Phillips about the dead people and that the deal was too hot for him, and for Phillips to get the hell out before the shit began to fly," said Cynthia.

"Yeah! and what did Phillips say?" asked Dready.

"Nothing much," said Cynthia, "all he said was 'thank you,' and hung up."

There was a long pause before Cynthia continued.

"Then he called Rona Samuels again and had a quarrel with her over the shipment that he refused to handle. She called him an idiot and threatened to do it by herself."

"But why?" asked Dready.

"Well, according to Abbot, it seemed that she is hell bent on dealing with a new person she met, and he didn't like the idea," said Cynthia.

"Did any of them mention who this mysterious person was?" asked Dready.

"No, except that he was a Canadian," she replied.

"Mmmmm," he said and remained silent.

"Then he called your room at 10:46 p.m," she said.

"I wonder what he wanted?" he said nonchalantly.

"Maybe he believed you are the dealer she wanted to do business with," she answered.

"Mmmmm," he said again, "that makes me very curious. Did Rona call any one?" he asked"

"Yes," she said opening the paper again. "See this number? It belongs to a woman named Amanda Bachstrum. That is who she called."

"What did they talk about?" he asked.

"Nothing," replied Cynthia. "There was only silence."

Dready didn't acknowledge her statement. They left the beach and as Cynthia spoke, Dready slowly directed her into the restaurant and sat in the corner reserved for Earl.

"Want to eat?" he asked.

"No, but I would like a drink," she said.

He signalled the waitress and ordered lunch for himself and a couple of drinks.

"Have you seen Earl today?" he asked the waitress.

"No sir," she said angrily, "I haven't seen the bastard for two days."

"Are you in love with him?" he asked.

"Yes, for many years now," she replied, "and he won't even notice me."

"Did you know that he is your cousin?" said Dready.

"No!" she said, surprised to hear the announcement. "How could he...."

"He loves you also but couldn't bring himself to tell you," said Dready. "But in due time he will."

The waitress didn't stay around to hear any more, she just whirled and disappeared into the kitchen. He and Cynthia talked about many things relating to the phone calls and their morning together in her house. She wanted more, and slyly suggested that he leave his wife and lover for her.

"And how do you suggest I live?" he asked, "Without her money, I couldn't last a week in this place."

"We could do some of the business these people are doing and....." she said.

"We wouldn't last a week without money," he assured her.

"I thought you were a dealer?" she stated.

"Yes I am," he replied, "but if I could find the money, I would purchase the three hundred thousand dollars worth of diamonds and then sell them in Canada for a profit of maybe seven hundred thousand, but I cannot do it without her money."

Cynthia sat there looking into space knowing that she couldn't match that kind of requirement. Finally she got up.

"Do you want to make love or not?" she asked.

"Not really," he replied, "I'm still recovering from our last bit."

"You promised me that if I got you the information you would make lo ...." she began.

"Okay, okay," he said trying to prevent her from creating a scene in the restaurant. He handed the waitress three American twenty dollar bills.

"Have a dinner on me," he said as they left the restaurant.

Dready walked into the casino, and sure enough, there she was sitting on her favourite high chair in front of the blackjack dealer.

"Hello Rona," he said as he sat beside her.

"Hello Dready Winston," she replied, "where have you been all day?"

"Around town," he said with a wide grin. "I went to meet some people on Abaco about the purchase, and found out that they are mixed up in some killings. I decided to lie low for the day so as not to attract attention to myself. I don't want to be mixed up in anything like that."

"Pity," she said. "Smithers and Hubert are still hoping you will do business with them."

"How can we, when there are so many things....murders going on?" he asked.

"Simple," she answered. "We, you and I, could go to get the merchandise directly from the source and take it directly to Canada and not have to come back here to Nassau to share it."

"Oh great!" he said. "Where is the merchandise located?"

"Have you ever been to Guyana?" she asked.

"No," he replied. "Is that where they are?"

"Yes," she said smiling, "and I have many friends there, so there won't be any problems to get them."

"What about the money?" he asked.

"You can pay it to me," she said.

"In Canada?" he asked.

"Yes, either there or in the Caymans," said Rona.

Dready gave thought to her suggestion and agreed to carry out the deal with her.

"But, how do you suggest I get the money into Guyana?" he asked.

"You will find a way," she said. "Necessity is the mother of invention, isn't it?"

"Right," he agreed. "Just tell me when and where, and I'll be ready."

Rona turned to face him. She took his hand and slid it under her dress to her crotch.

"Don't disappear on me again tonight," she said. "I must have it tonight."

"You certainly will," he replied and retrieved his hand from between her legs.

Rona smiled as she got off the chair and kissed him lightly on the lips.

"I'm going to get a shower and change my clothes first," she said. "I will meet you back down here at seven o'clock for dinner and a little gambling."

"That's fine by me," he said and watched her disappear into the elevator.

He quickly ran to his room to make a phone call to Jamaica.

"Commissioner Graves please," he said to the receptionist.

In a few seconds Graves answered the phone.

"I'm going to Guyana with Rona Samuels to collect the goods and she will be the courier to Canada," he said.

"Is she the English woman?" asked Graves.

"Yes, and a good friend of Smithers, Bass, Lyle Alexander and Burkowitz," he told his friend.

"Okay, I will make a phone call to Guyana in the meantime," said Graves.

"Good," said Dready, "and please tell Captain Maraj that I will be carrying three hundred thousand American dollars in cash and

241

must be cleared at the airport."

"Will be done," said Graves.

"Get Christiana to come along also," said Dready, "she might be of help. No, wait a minute. Ask Christiana to call Althea in Nassau and tell her that she will be coming to town and would like to see her."

"Good," said Graves. "Will Christiana know the reason for the phone call to Althea?"

"Yes she will," said Dready.

"Fine, see you," said Graves.

"By the way Bernard," said Dready. "Did you find out about Garfield Smith?"

"Yes, he grew up and was schooled in England," said Graves. "He had a good job with the Home Office until five years ago."

"What happened?" asked Dready.

"He disappeared," said Graves, "and nobody knows where he is now."

"Did he resign?" asked Dready.

"Apparently not," said Graves. "They said he disappeared."

He hung up the phone, had a quick wash and change, ready to meet Rona Samuels for dinner and gambling. As he passed the desk he signalled for Cynthia to meet him at the desk.

"Check on a call from room 937," he said, "I would like to know who she spoke to and what was said."

"I can tell you that now," said Cynthia. "She called for Hubert Bachstrum but the maid said he was away. Then she called a woman named Judith Wakefield and there was no answer."

"That's all?" he asked.

"She also called the airport for Tullis Burke, and he also was away," said Cynthia.

"Didn't she speak to anyone?" he asked.

"Yes, a woman named Cindy Heron in room 977. She told the Heron woman that they will be going to Trinidad tomorrow morning on the 9:30 flight."

Dready thought about Cynthia's report.

"Thank you my dear," he said smiling, "I can't explain right now but I will have to make it up to you when I return."

"When will that be?" she asked.

"In about three days," he said and dashed off to meet Rona.

Dready realized that time was of the essence, because he wasn't totally prepared for the hurried entry into Guyana. He needed to stall them. He hurried to the hotel casino to find her, but she found him first.

"Hello handsome," said Rona as she approached him, "I've been looking for you; where have you been?"

"I was out looking for a dealer," he said.

"Then look no further my darling man," she said. "I am going to take you to a place where you can purchase directly from the people in the fields."

"In the Bahamas?" he asked.

"No stupid, we are going to Trinidad first then on to Guyana for that purpose," she said. "Remember I told you that I have some friends there?"

"And how will we get there?" he asked.

"I have secured three tickets for us, you, Cindy and myself," she said showing him the tickets. "I didn't know your real name so I had them leave it blank."

"How could you do that?" he asked.

"I have friends in high places," she said handing his ticket to him.

"What if I get arrested for having a bogus ticket?" he asked.

"That, my dear man, is your problem," she said as she started for the restaurant. "If you really want the product, you'll find a way there."

They found seats at a table and ordered some drinks. Within a few minutes they were joined by Cindy Harron.

"I thought I would find you here," she said to Rona as she sat. "I've been looking all over for you."

"Well, you've found me," replied Rona. "What's the fucking problem?"

"Nothing, just wanted to know when we were leaving for Trinidad," said Cindy.

"Tomorrow morning," replied Rona, "and if you miss the flight there won't be another until late Tuesday night. Which means we won't get to Guyana until Wednesday morning."

Cindy looked at the tickets.

"Well," she said, "we'd better get to sleep early so as not to miss that flight."

They ate the dinner and had desert. On the suggestion of Rona they rushed off to her room for a drink. Dready made a quick stop in the pharmacy before joining them.

The fifty-five minutes flight from Port-of-Spain into the Cheddi Jagan airport at Timeri, was somewhat pleasant. The BWIA McDonald-Douglas 84 plane rocked from side to side as the pilot guided it through the thick heavy black rain-clouds that loitered over Guyana. He felt assured that the pilot would do his utmost to avoid any kind of emergency, but still felt a tense moment of uncertainty until he landed the bird and parked it just like he would a Cadillac.

Dready stood on the tarmac observing the newly renovated building and sucking in some of the mid-morning air of the country. In conjunction with the well deserved airport's name-change, Dready observed that many changes had been made in the lounge area since he was there a year ago. It was when Ivan Burkowitz was arrested and charged for smuggling diamonds, and subsequently sentenced to life in a Georgetown prison.

He smiled to think he had deceived Rona and Cindy last night by slipping some sleeping compound into their drinks, thus giving himself some time to contact and enlighten certain people he wanted, before they came.

"They will miss the flight and be late by at least a day or two," he thought, "which will give me that much time to talk with Captain Elton Maraj. I hope both Bernard Graves and Christiana got here safely."

The female customs officer, who seemed happy to have a Jamaican in her country, welcomed him.

".....and how long will you be staying sir?" she asked.

"I'm not sure as yet," he said, "but I must visit a few friends and places, like......"

"That's fine sir," she said, "I'll give you four weeks."

"Good," he said. "Thank you."

As instructed, Maraj came directly to the airport customs office to meet him personally. He quickly got his only bag and the briefcase of money checked and was on his way.

"Meet Khan," said Maraj, "he's a trusted taxi driver who will take you to the place where you'll be staying, and wherever else you need to go. I will meet you at the Pegasus hotel for a lunch and some talk after," said Elton.

He shook hands with the young man and they were off. He sat quietly listening to Khan as he pointed out some of the places along the 26 miles coastal highway going into Georgetown. First, he took him to the Tower hotel for a late breakfast, where he had salt fish and bakes, then to the Cara Suites.

"If you need me, just call this number," said Khan handing him a business card.

"I will," he replied.

He got checked in, had a shower to wash off the stickiness of the humid day from his body and got dressed in shorts and tee shirt for the hot afternoon.

He stood looking out the window of the Cara Suites, which stood proudly at the corner of Middle and Waterloo streets. He could see the plants in the Promenade Gardens and remembered walking through it before. He smiled recalling the soccer match that was played on the ground across from the park the last time, and the now blooming poinciana tree which he had sat against while watching that game, as it waved in the gentle breeze that blew from the south-east.

He also recalled seeing the work that was being done on the doctors residence behind that field last time also, which is now completed. He was happy to be in Guyana again.

He left the hotel after asking Alphonso, the security guard, about a jewellery shop on Quamina street, because he wanted to browse for a ring for his wife and had already been to the King store next to the Suites. He slowly walked along Waterloo Street to get there.

"Hi good-looking," he said to the attendant on entering the shop, "how come you get the easy job?"

Without smiling she replied,

"It only looks easy because I make it that way."

"Then why can't you smile?" he asked.

"I am smiling on the inside," she said. "This is my work day face."

Within a few minutes they were chatting like old friends. She showed him many pieces; rings, bracelets and chains that she thought his wife would like.

"I would like one with a nice diamond in the settings," he said. "Do you have any diamonds?"

"We sure do," she said.

She went to the back room and returned with a large tray of sparklers. He browsed and found one he liked.

"How much to put this stone into a ring this size?" he asked.

Quickly she weighed the ring, then the stone. She took her calculator and added some numbers together.

"Fifty-nine thousand Guyana dollars," she said.

"Fifty-nine hundred Canadian?" he asked.

"Right," she said.

"Damn, that's too much money," he said. "I think I'll wait

until I speak to my friend Ken, before making the purchase."

"You do that," she said, "then come back to me and I will give you a generous discount."

"Is that all I will get?" he asked.

"I could give you up to thirty percent off," she said hoping to make the sale, "anything more will depend on my feelings for the day."

"No," he said. "My friend knows a wholesaler, and I am sure we can get it cheaper from him. Furthermore, I want to buy many pieces to take to the Bahamas."

She looked at him with a questioning gaze.

"Are you a dealer?" she asked.

"In a way, yes," he responded, "and I have three hundred thousand dollars to spend."

"Then you will have to purchase from someone like David DeFreitas," she said. "He's the only one I know who would carry that amount of diamonds at any given time."

"Where can I find him?" asked Dready.

"He's on Regent street, but I would have to take you there," she said, "he doesn't let any strangers in."

"Good," said Dready. "I will come back to see you and we could go there together."

"No," she said. "I will meet you on Wednesday afternoon at the Guyana Store and we could go from there."

"About one thirty?" he asked.

"Make it two thirty," she said.

He nodded in agreement and left the shop without asking for her name. He returned to the Suites.

After a little rest, he got showered and dressed in a pair of pants and long-sleeved shirt and descended the stairs to the hotel door. He observed that it had begin to drizzle again. He walked to the corner of the street and waited, then jumped into the first taxi that stopped in front of him.

"The Pegasus please," he said.

"Yes Sir," said the young Indian driver as he looked up at the tall Rastafarian.

"How much for a short drop?" asked Dready.

"Two hundred Sir," said the driver.

Good," he replied and eased back into the seat.

He took out the money and paid the fare, walked up the steps to the lobby and found a seat in the restaurant. He ordered a regular coffee because they did not have decaffeinated. Within five minutes Elton Maraj entered the restaurant and joined him.

"It's nice to see you again Winston," said Maraj as they shook hands, "I hope we'll be able to put a stop to these bastards this time."

"Maybe," replied Dready. "I do have a couple of people coming in on Wednesday morning from Nassau, and would like for you to put a good man on them, but not too close, allowing some latitude for contacts. I want them to feel free."

"That will be done," said Elton. "Bernard and Christiana are already here and is staying in this same hotel. Do you want them down for lunch?"

"No," said Dready, "I don't want any kind of public contact with them at this time. Which rooms are they in? I will go up to see them after we finish talking here."

"Christiana is in 634 and Bernard is in 633," said Elton.

"Good, I will go to see them after," he said.

Dready and Maraj ate and talked for almost an hour, in which he outlined his ideas to capture the people he had in mind. When the lunch was over and they separated, he directed himself to Christiana's room and knocked on the door.

"Who is it?" she asked.

"A dreadlocks Rasta," he replied.

She opened it and he quickly ducked in unnoticed by anyone. She closed the door behind him. She was as happy to see him as he was to see her and they began ripping-off each others clothes in silence.

"I missed you," she whispered," as she pulled him into her.

"Ditto," he replied.

They became so lost in their hour-long love making that neither of them heard the phone ringing, or cared to.

Finally, there was a knock on the door. Christiana got up and slowly opened it to Bernard Graves and Elton Maraj.

"Sorry to disturb you," said Graves, "but I couldn't wait to talk to you two together. I've set up an interview for yourself and Mr. Burkowitz for Thursday morning at nine," he told Dready. "He has been made to believe that you are a journalist doing a story on him, as was done on his friends in Jamaica last year."

"How did you get him to agree to it?" asked Dready.

"Elton was able to get a guard to slip one of your magazine with the story of Karlheinz to him and he requested to talk to you directly," said Graves.

"Good," said Dready, "I can always bring a message from Rona to him and see what he sends back. Where are you keeping him?"

"In our most prestigious prison, in Mazaruni," said Elton with a smile.

"Where the hell is that?" asked Dready.

"On an island near the mouth of the Mazaruni river," said Elton. " It's hard to escape from, and many have died trying."

"How do I get there?" asked Christiana.

"We could drive to Parika then take a ferry-boat to Charity then on to Bartica," said Elton. "Then we would have to take another boat to Mazarumi."

"That sounds like a long ride," said Christiana.

"Yes it is," said Elton, "but we are going to fly you to Bartica then you can go by boat separately to the prison. Or we could fly you into the prison directly."

Nobody questioned his suggestion.

"Now hear this," said Graves. "Elton has arranged for you all to attend the President's dance on Saturday night, Christiana will be my escort and you will bring along the two women. We will then introduce her to them and she will let on that she was a 'mule' to win their confidence, and with her name being Felscher, it will be easy."

"Then," said Maraj, "she will mention her connection to Karlheinz Bass and Burkowitz, and how she has an appointment to see him. We hope Mrs. Samuels will want to see him also or ask her to deliver a message to him."

"Yes," said Graves, "it would be very interesting to see her reaction."

"Fine,"said Dready, "then Rona will not suspect me and probably will want Christiana on our expedition to Rupanuni to meet her contact."

"Right," said Maraj. "She will want to meet whomever Ivan Burkowitz suggests meeting or whomever he is already dealing with up there."

"Fine," said Dready. "Now, if you two don't mind, I would like to spend some time with my wife, please."

The two policemen looked at each other, smiled and left the room.

The rest of the afternoon and evening was a thrill for the two lovers. They were able to catch up on many things in their lives. She spent an enormous amount of time telling him about Venrece-Thomas and his grandparents.

"He's going to be spoilt," she said. "Mother is allowing him to rule her and he is smart enough to know of his new-found freedom."

"Let him enjoy it now," said Dready, "because you are going to have him and his brother to deal with when we return to Canada."

Christiana produced her book with everything laid out. She had graphics and diagrams to show the flow of the gang's movements throughout the years.

"They have been a well-oiled machine for a long time," she

said, "until the Jamaica affair. Now, everybody is running to and fro trying to piece things together to maintain the protocol of their business."

"Helter Skelter," said Dready nonchalantly.

"Who the hell is Helter Skelter?" Christiana asked.

"It's nothing darling," he replied. "It's a song done by the Beatles some years ago; which was said that Charles Manson and his girls played as background to murder Sharon Tate. Never mind that now, it's not important."

The conversation continued throughout the night in between their love making, until the sleep overtook them.

Tuesday morning they were up early with the Guyanese sun. Dready told her about his little delaying, deceptive-tactics and of going to the airport Wednesday to fetch Rona and Cindy.

"Remember now," he said, "we are strangers whenever they are introduced to you at the party."

I will remember, darling," she said kissing him, "but if any of them believe they can hold on to you, I will scratch their eyes out."

They both laughed at that as he called Khan, his official taxi escort.

"I'm at the Pegasus, can you get me?" he asked.

"No I can't," said Khan, "but I've arranged for a friend of mine to do the job for the rest of the week. His name is Harold and is a very good man."

That's fine by me," said Dready. "Send him over."

Almost twenty minutes went by before Harold came.

"Hello Mr. Winston," said Harold, "I'm here to pick you up, and will be at your service for the rest of the week."

"Good," said Dready, "but you must call me Dready from now on."

"Right sir, Dready," replied Harold. "Where to?"

"Anywhere," said Dready. "What I would like is to find someone who could tell me about the pork knockers. Do you know of any such person?"

"Yes! I know all about them," said Harold, "I use to be a manager for some of them."

"Great!" exclaimed Dready. "Find a nice restaurant where we can talk. I would like to hear all about the pork knockers and their diamond-mining business. Is there anything you can tell me about them?"

"Sure," said Harold, "I could take you to the library where there are books about them, then to the museum to see a statue of a pork knocker and some history of them; and then you can formulate your own opinion. But I could tell you of my experiences with them."

"Tell me your experiences," said Dready.

Harold found a Chinese restaurant on Regent Street. They sat and he began to tell Dready how in the old days some fellows would form teams of 4-5 or 6 men, then they would travel the forty-five minutes to Parika, get on a speed boat for the hour's drive to Bartica, set up supplies and credit with one of the shops there, then move on to set up their base camp, somewhere in the interior on the Rupanuni river. He heard how most of their excavation was done on land, except for the rare occasions in the rivers.

"At times," said Harold, "these fellows had to travel miles up the river in a boat, and whenever they came to a waterfall they had to unload the boat and carry everything manually, including the boat, past the falls; which was hard work."

"But that could take hours!" said Dready.

"Precisely," replied Harold, "Their period in the interior lasted between four weeks and six months, and they could dig for all that time without finding anything, and end up broke with a large debt at the store; you know, in the red."

"So what happens if they found some gold or diamonds?" asked Dready.

"They were compelled to sell to the shop-owners or to the manager who financed their expeditions or to a dealer," said Harold.

"Which means some of them got ripped-off. You see, some of them just loved to party, and at the end of every work week they would even walk three to four hours in the forest to find the party places. These were usually set up by the dealers who would watch as they spend out the money on rum, women and food. Then when the pork knockers were intoxicated they would steel or purchase the diamonds very cheaply from them.

Many of them left their wives and children in Georgetown, or wherever they originated from, and got hooked up with some of those shops and camp women; some of whom moved there in the first place for that very purpose. Some of the men took it in forgetting about their families wherever they were. Those women turned their heads with the help of the rum and love talk. Some of the pork knockers, after finding some diamonds, usually come to the shops to show-off."

Dready listened to everything Harold had to say about the pork knockers. He learned that the term, "Sucking blows," meant hard times and "Close the shop," was the time when the pork knockers intend on paying for everything purchased and ever end up in the red. "Warishis," is a back pack. "Want a clean eye," meant to see the diamonds close-up and the "Hot Spot," was usually where the camp toilet is erected.

"Unfortunately, some didn't anticipate the abbreviated life they would encounter and died penniless," said Harold. "Many of them died from malaria, animal bites, mainly snakes, and fights over the women and the product."

"Why was that so?" asked Dready.

"Because people are people and some just like to steal," he said. "And when they get caught, the fights usually break out and then somebody gets hurt. This usually happens between the team members during "jigging," a term used for sifting or sorting the diamonds, when one of the fellows decide to hide some of the good ones for themselves."

"How did they do that?" asked Dready.

253

"They could flip them into their mouth, or drop them into their pant cuffs," said Harold.

"Then what about the diamonds?" asked Dready. "Where did they go?"

"They were bought by the shop owners, the managers or a dealer," replied Harold.

"Now! How do the new pork knockers operate today?" asked Dready.

"Today, some of them are building nice homes, purchasing vehicles and saving some of their labourious worth, just in case." said Harold, "but the majority still pisses it away."

"Are any of them assisting relatives or friends with their money?" asked Dready.

"Yes, some are being realistic in that respect," Harold replied. "Look man, pork knocking is a very important-but diminishing-art, which is good for the economy of our country. Unfortunately it's a very demanding business and the young men of today are afraid of the challenge, not wanting to get their fingers dirty."

"How so?" asked Dready.

"Well, these men worked hard to find the goods, sell it to a dealer or shop owner, be it legal or illegal. They spend the money within the community and at least some of that money somehow find it's way to the government, the banks and eventually to some of the ordinary people in Georgetown."

"What about the white ones?" asked Dready. "How many of these pork knockers are white?"

"White!?" shouted Harold. "I've never heard of any pork knockers being white men. The only white men are those with the dredges and the chemicals which are poisoning off all the rivers and streams of our country; which infuriates me."

"Tell me Harold," said Dready, "who are the main buyers or distributors in Guyana today?"

"I don't know who the main ones are," said Harold, "because there are many in and around town. Some of them should be at four corners, you know, the house on Durban street."

Dready snickered when he realized that Harold was referring to the prison.

"Ever heard of a Ralph Bachstrum?" asked Dready.

"No," replied Harold.

"What about Ivan Burkowitz?"

"Never heard of him either," replied Harold. "Who are they?"

"Some men who use to work for a Canadian mining company here," said Dready.

"There are many of those operating in Guyana today," said Harold.

"I get to understand that," said Dready. "I heard that there are many of these people flying in and out of here to and from the many private airstrips in this country; I don't think the government even knows about them."

"The white pork knockers?" asked Harold.

"Damn right," replied Dready.

While Harold sat dumbfounded, Dready requested to return to the suites to make some phone calls.

"I will call you later if I'm gonna go out," he told his new taxi driving friend.

"Okay," said Harold and drove to the Cara Suites.

Dready lay on the bed contemplating going back to the Pegasus to spend time with his wife, but the chance of someone seeing them together crossed his mind. Phoning was out of the question, because he also realise that people do listen in on other people's calls; even in Guyana.

He lay there looking at the winking lights across the street announcing the "Caribbean Rose," restaurant, and instantly felt like eating something. He dashed out of bed and rushed down the stairs to the front door.

"How's the food over there?" he asked Alphonso, the security man.

"Excellent sir," said Alphonso, "they have great food, you'll enjoy it. Tell them Alphonso sent you."

"Okay," replied Dready, "I'll remember that."

Quickly he rushed across the street towards the sign. The restaurant was at the very top of the building without an elevator, so he negotiated the forty-three steps to his destination, which seemed like half-way to heaven. At the top, he was greeted by two nice young ladies who escorted him to a table.

"Welcome to the Caribbean Rose, sir," said one. "My name is Marcella Chappell and this is Trisha Wilson; we'll be serving you this evening."

"Thank you ladies," he said. "Can I have a coffee please?"

"Certainly sir," Marcella said leaving the menu with him while Trisha disappeared into the kitchen for his coffee.

The restaurant was an oblong, pale-blue and white neatly-decorated place with the roof raised to allow air to flow through the entire space. He scrutinized the menu, and when he felt he selected out something, he signalled and Marcella came.

"What's good?" he asked.

"Everything sir," she replied.

"Well, I would like the Caribbean fish with rice and fried plantain please," he said.

"Okay sir," she said and rushed off to the kitchen.

Although there weren't many patrons there, he didn't get the opportunity to strike up any conversation with anyone, except the two courteous waitresses. After desert he decided to take a stroll along Middle Street past the Promenade Garden to the corner of Main Street. He looked left then right and decided that left it was. He passed the Tower Hotel on the left and the Guyana stores on the right. Another left brought him in front of St. Georges Cathedral at North Road and Church Street. Somehow he walked an hour too long and too many turns to remember his route back, so he signalled a taxi.

"The Cara Suites please," he said to the driver.

"Yes sir," said the driver.

Within two minutes he was deposited in front of the Suites. He silently laughed to himself to think how close he was to the place. It wasn't as far as first thought. He watched a little television then went to bed.

"Wednesday morning," he whispered as he bounced out of bed. It was the morning when he had to go to the airport to meet Rona and Cindy on the flight from Trinidad. The airlines told him that the plane would not arrive until 10:30, so he had time. He left the hotel and stood outside for almost half-an-hour, eyeing the light rain which had been falling since he got to Guyana, and sucking in some of the morning's atmosphere. Slowly he walked towards the coconut-man who had stopped his cart across from him.

"Chop me a jelly," he said.

He watched in amazement as how the man whirled the machete without doing any damage to his hand. He drank two small ones then walked back to the Cara Suites front door and stood talking to a couple of the security men, whom he had befriended since arriving, not completely sure what he wanted to do next.

Finally one of the taxi drivers approached him.

"My name is Edgar sir," said the taxi driver. "Is there somewhere you wanted to go?"

"Yes, but I would like another water coconut before going to the airport.," he replied.

"Jamaican?" asked Edgar.

"Yes sir, all the way, except I am beginning to like Guyana," he said. "My name is Dready Winston, a journalist from Canada."

"First time here?" asked Edgar as he stuck out his hand for a shake.

"No, been here four or five times on business," said Dready.

He got into Edgar's car and the man began the drive to the airport. As they proceeded along the familiar coastal highway, he reminded the man about the coconut. Edgar stopped at the market and quickly purchased two large ones. They sat on the bench to drink them and ate the jelly before proceeding.

"Then maybe I could show it to you and your company," said Edgar as they got back into the car for the journey to the airport. "I know almost every part of this country, including the interior."

"Oh yeah?" exclaimed Dready. "What do you know about the diamond business?"

"Man, you come to the right person," Edgar enthusiastically answered. "I have some cousins who are pork-knockers, they are in that business and I could take you to them."

"How far away are they?" asked Dready.

"Not far, just up Bartica and some in the Rupanuni river area," said Edgar. "You will love places like Esequibo. The people there are nice."

"Good," said Dready. "I will call you when I'm ready."

He noticed that Edgar used the same route to the airport as Kazan took coming. The driver turned into the parking lot and waited for him to get his people.

He stood by the rails watching Rona and Cindy walking towards him. He noticed that they were dressed for the hot Guyana atmosphere.

"What happened to you two Monday morning? " he asked quizzingly.

"Couldn't wake up, and was late for the flight," said Rona. "I don't know what happened, I've never been that drunk before."

"I told her that she was drinking too much," said Cindy, "but she didn't pay shit attention to me. I got up, but couldn't awaken her; so we were late and couldn't get another flight until last night."

"I waited for you but the plane was boarding, so I got on without you two," he lied.

Edgar took their luggage and placed them in the trunk as they entered the cab.

"Take us to the Pegasus Hotel please," said Dready.

"Where are we sleeping?" asked Rona.

"You're booked in at the Pegasus," he said. "It's the best hotel in GT."

All the way there the conversation ranged from the beauty and heat of Guyana to the parties in Nassau.

"Do they have a casino in that hotel?" asked Rona.

"Don't know," said Dready, "but you can always ask."

"...and where are you staying?" asked Rona.

"Same place," he replied nonchalantly.

Dready slipped Edgar three American twenties; much more than the fare to the airport and back.

"I would like you to standby for a trip tomorrow morning," said Dready. "Is that possible?"

"Fine sir," replied Edgar. "Everything is possible in GT."

"Wait here for me," he said, "I want to go some place else."

They entered the doors to the hotel and quickly got Rona and Cindy booked in. He told them about the dance on Saturday night and advised them to be ready to attend by 7:30 sharp.

"...and where will you be staying?" asked Rona.

"With a girlfriend I met on the plane yesterday," he replied grinning, "but I will see you later this evening."

He left then in the lobby for his unknown destination.

Edgar let him out in front of the Cara Suites. He quickly ran upstairs and phoned Harold.

"Are you busy?" he asked Harold.

"No, where would you like to go?" asked Harold.

"Come and I will tell you," he said.

He asked Harold to take him to the Guyana Stores to meet the girl from the jeweller shop. He found her standing at the back doors; and with a short greeting they left to find her contact on Regent street.

"Now," she said, "don't come out and tell this man how much money you're carrying. Remember this is Guyana and there are many 'choke and rob' men around; so be coy and we will make the deal."

"....and you will get your cut, right?" he stated.

"Right," she replied. "Everybody in this country expects to get a cut of anything they are involved with."

When they reached in front of the shop she signalled for him to stop.

"Wait here for me," she said, "it's better if I speak to him alone first."

Dready stood by the door and waited until she beckoned for him. A chubby, mixed Portugese man of about medium-height got up from his chair to shake his hand.

"Welcome to my store," said the man, "we are in the business of pleasing our customers in everyway."

"I'm delighted to hear that," replied Dready, "I'm tired of meeting people whose intention is to rip me off."

"So you're looking for a diamond for your wife and a few extra to take back with you," said the man as he reached into a safe. "Take a look at these and see if the quality matches your needs."

Dready took the magnifying glass to scrutinize the products. Although he wasn't sure of what he was looking at, he chose to say,

"This is pure junk; why don't you bring out the good stuff?"

The man glanced at the girl and she returned his glance.

"If you're not going to show my friend the real thing I will take him to another place," she said and angrily left the shop.

Quickly, the man reached in and brought out another bag; this time he spread them on a black piece of velvet cloth on the counter.

"Maybe these will tickle your fancy," said the man.

Without looking at them he picked out a large one.

"This might be what I want," he said. "My wife would just love this one set in a eighteen carat gold ring."

"Excellent choice," replied the man. "When do you want it?"

"Right now," he replied.

"Sorry, I cannot do that job in an hour," said the man. "It will take at least four days and..."

"...and it's cash American money," said Dready.

"Okay," said the man. "I might be able to do it but I will require a fifty percent deposit and a name; strictly for the government."

"Oh!" said Dready. "You do pay the tax then?"

"Yes sir, I'm an honest businessman. Everything is above board," said the fat man taking the money from Dready's hand.

"By the way," said Dready, "do you know a man named Ivan Burkowitz?"

The question seemed to catch the man off guard and Dready noticed the shocked look in his eyes.

"No, not personally, but I've heard about him," said the man.

"What did you hear?" asked Dready.

"I heard he was a high-class mover; you know, the ones that deals in the millions," said the man.

"Oh!" snickered Dready, "and what do you deal in?"

"I'm small fry compared to that man," he answered.

"What about the white bushman?" asked Dready, "I've heard he is the man to see. I've heard he does the purchasing of diamonds in Rupinuni; do you know him?"

"No, but I've heard of him also," said the man as he nervously looked around the room.

"She's gone," said Dready realizing that the man was looking for prying ears. "You've hurt my friend's feelings, so she left."

"She'll be back," he said smiling, "she always come back for the money."

Dready bade the man goodbye and left the shop.

He slowly walked back to the Guyana stores to find his taxi friend. Along the way he looked for the girl but she had already gone.

"Where to?" asked Harold.

"Let's go to the Austin's book store," he said, "I have to meet someone there. We might go for dinner from there."

He wanted to kill some time and to agitate his mind about the new developments in Guyana. He persuaded Harold to leave him there and when he thought the coast was clear, he began his walk back to the Cara Suites. He dined alone at the Caribbean rose then back to the Suites to make a couple of phone calls, watched some local television and sleep.

The next morning he was up early. He stood at the window overlooking the park and wondered if he had everything in place for the events to follow. He got dressed in shorts and a tee shirt, called Christiana to tell her where he was going and to ask her to tell Graves and Maraj of his intentions, then went for a walk. He walked around the park for thirty minutes then along Waterloo Street back to the hotel. There he found Edgar waiting for him at the corner of the street.

"Hey Bro," said Edgar greeting him, "where are we going this early?"

"Remember you said you know some pork knockers? Well, I would like to meet one of them," said Dready.

"This early?" asked his new friend. "Them boys don't get up this early in the morning."

"Well, somebody must be up," said Dready smiling, "because I have three hundred thousand American dollars to do some business, and if anybody wants some of it, they must be ready to do business with me this early."

Edgar laughed loudly.

"Brother Dready you sure do things differently," said Edgar. "Some men would be afraid to tell me what they wanted and how much money they have. Ever heard of choke-and-rob?"

"Yes I have my friend," said Dready, "but they would have to get through me first. There is a large fee in it for you, if you can find me a good diamond man. I don't want any bullshit ripoff just a plain old fashioned ordinary deal, okay?"

Edgar understood quite well and began to drive.

"Breakfast?" asked Edgar.

"Yes, let's get a snack on the way, but have lunch after you find me the person I man seek," said Dready.

They talked about many things during the forty-five minute drive, on the rough road to Parika, the place where they had to take a boat.

"Want breakfast now?" asked Edgar.

"Definitely," said Dready.

Edgar led him into a small cook-shop nearby and they ordered food. In the meanwhile, Edgar quietly spoke to the river man who agreed to take them; for a fee of course. After breakfast they boarded the boat where some others were also waiting, and although Dready was afraid of travelling on the small boat without a life preserver, he was happy that none of the seven other people noticed his fears.

The one hour boat ride on the river was enjoyable and scenic, and left him smiling internally for having been there to see it again. Edgar kept a running conversation about the animals and birds in the area, and Dready listened.

They landed and Edgar directed him to a house about a half mile from the river. As they approached the house, Dready could see a half-naked, mixed breed, medium built man coming towards them, with a machete in his hand.

"Hello cousin Edgar," said the man while keeping a permanent stare on Dready, "what brings you here this morning?"

"I brought you a customer," said Edgar. "Dready meet Packus; he is the only man who can sell you what you want."

"Hail Packus," said Dready in his pronounced Jamaican, "I man come to see you because I have a market in Jamaica and need some real stuff. I don't want to deal with the city people, because last time a man sold me some bad things, and I want good things this time."

"How much?" asked Packus, looking at Edgar.

"Three hundred thousand American," said Edgar.

"Boy you mad?" said Packus. "I don't handle anything that big. Up to five thousand I can supply, but for them big money like that, you'll have to see the bushman."

"Who is the bushman?" asked Dready.

"He's a Whiteman from Venezuela, who most of the pork

knockers sell to," said Packus. "He comes in here once a month with cash to purchase the diamonds, and everybody usually gets here early to sell to him."

"When will he be coming back?" asked Dready.

"Next week Thursday," replied Packus.

Dready thought about it.

"Can't wait for him," he said to Edgar. "I will have to find somebody else to do the business, because Packus don't want my money. Come on Edgar, let's go back to GT. There must be someone there."

"No!" said Packus. "Give me a couple of days to contact him. I will try to convince him to come across."

"How will we know he is here?" asked Dready.

"Ever heard about a phone?" said Packus. "Here is a number to call me; I'll be there tomorrow evening."

"Does he ever go into Georgetown?" Dready asked.

"No," replied Packus. "I am his GT man. I do all his deals in town."

"I see!" said Dready. "Then you must know Ivan. How many times have you spoken to Ivan?"

"Ivan who?" asked Packus.

"Why, Ivan Burkowitz of course!" said Dready.

"Never heard of him," said Packus. "Who is he? Is he a dealer also?"

"I believe so. He's a good friend of David DeFreitas," said Dready.

"Never heard the name, but he might be the man I saw with Mr DeFreitas up in Baramita a couple of years ago," said Packus.

There was total silence. Dready realized that there was some-one else making contact and moving the product across to Suriname and that Packus might know who, but wouldn't say.

"Dready smiled and signalled for Edgar to come along.

The ride back wasn't as bad as coming because the boat

264

wasn't as crowded; there were only four of them this time. Edgar kept a running conversation about their expedition until they got back to Georgetown.

"Dready my boy, I do believe we are in business," said Edgar. "Packus don't like to lose money and he will make every effort to get the man there."

"Do you think so?" asked Dready.

"You bet," replied Edgar, "it's not every day American dollars drop in Guyana, and Packus won't let it pass his eyes."

"What about you Bro, can you let it pass your eyes?" Dready asked.

"Look man," said Edgar, "this land is hard and everybody needs money to survive. I'm no different, but I will not commit a serious crime to get it. Well, not a big one anyway."

Dready thanked him for the effort and handed him four American twenties.

"See you when I make the phone call," he said as he shook hands with him.

Dready left Edgar at the door of the Cara Suites and went up to call his official driver Harold. He came in just a few minutes.

"Police headquarters," he said to Harold.

Without question, Harold took him to the police headquarters. He slowly walked along a pathway and entered the doors to the reception desk, where sat the duty sergeant.

"Hi Mike," he said.

The Sergeant looked up and recognized him from his visit the previous year.

"Hey, Lieutenant Perkins!" said the Sergeant, jumping from behind his desk to shake his hand. "Nice to see you again; how are you and what are you doing in Guyana again?"

"Just a little vacation and to visit Captain Maraj," he replied. "Nice to see you again Mike."

"Good to see you too Dready," said the Sergeant. "The

Captain is in his office over there."

Dready knocked on the door, opened it and peaked in.

"Can I come in?" he asked.

"Sure Winston, enter," said Maraj. "Where are you coming from this late evening? Graves told me you weren't in the hotel."

"I went to Bartica today to see a pork knocker named Packus something or other," said Dready. "He is going to introduce me to a white diamond dealer."

"The Venezuelan bushman?" asked Maraj.

"The same," replied Dready. "Do you know him?"

"Never met him personally," said Maraj, "but I heard he is doing a very thriving illegal business out there. I would like to lay my hands on him, but he has been very elusive."

"Maybe he's being protected by the other pork knockers," offered Dready.

"Absolutely right," said Maraj, "and I would like to know where he's getting the money from to pay them off."

"Planes fly over Guyana every day and Americans posing as geologists, herbal doctors and even religious people come in here and disappear into the interior and are never heard from; so I'm not surprised," said Dready.

"...and there are many airstrips for them to fly to and from," said Elton. "I've heard that the white bush-man goes to places like Baramita, Kurupung, Apoteri, Lethem and as far away as Grin's Strip, but every time we thought we could anticipate where he would be, he dodged us."

"Maybe this time we can corner him," said Dready.

The two men talked about the pork knockers, smugglers, pirates and visitors to Guyana for some time.

"I would like to take you to Esequibo, so that you can meet a very important pork knocker to us," said Maraj. "He has been giving us the info about the many travellers in that part of the country and who have been selling diamonds to a white bush man from Venezuela. Maybe he could help us with this operation."

"Maybe we could contact him next week," said Dready, "but we must be very careful not to alert them. Everything I do must appear like what a Dreadlocks criminal would do and not look like a police operation."

"This man is fine," said Maraj, "we can trust him."

"Then maybe you could send up some police to stake out the place before we go there," said Dready.

"That will be done; I will have some men posing as pork knockers. Your bag of money is in my safe," said Maraj, "just tell me when you will need it."

"Will do," said Dready. "Not ready for it as yet."

Chapter Ten

The G.T. Party.

*T*hey were dressed for the party when Dready got to their room. He rushed off to his room to shower and change into a suit and tie to appear respectable for the party. Both Rona and Cindy had brought along proper dresses fit for the occasion. He looked across the room at Christiana in the company of Graves and one of the President's representatives, and noticed that she was also properly dressed for the occasion. He smiled to know she was his wife.

Captain Maraj began introducing the people that he felt needed to know each other.

"This is Christiana Felscher," he said to Rona, "she's visiting our country with a Jamaican diplomat friend." and pointed to Graves.

"Nice to meet you Christiana," said Rona smiling. "Are you the daughter of Ludwig Felscher?" she asked.

"Yes," said Christiana. "Do you know my father?"

"Well, yes," said Rona, "we met in Jamaica some years ago at a party in honour of a friend called Ralston Weekes. That party was held at Karlheinz Bass' house and I'm also a good friend of Arthur Collins."

"Oh good," replied Christiana directing Rona away from the listening ears of Captain Maraj. "Please don't blow my cover, I don't want them to know that I'm here to do some business."

"Diamond business?" asked Rona.

"Definitely," said Christiana. "You see, I'm here posing as a journalist who wants to interview Ivan Burkowitz for a magazine, and in turn he will tell me who to contact for the goods that I will take back to Jamaica with me."

"Great!" said Rona. "And while you're at it, I would like you to give Ivan a message for me."

"Okay," said Christiana, "not a problem."

"If we could meet tomorrow, I would tell you what I want him to know," said Rona.

"Be willing to assist a friend," said Christiana.

She left Rona and Cindy talking, and rejoined Bernard with the government man.

They all danced and drank for most of the night, and although he spoke to Christiana and Bernard, he kept it to a basic conversation so as not to attract any attention. On one occasion while dancing with Cindy, she whispered in his ears,

"Remember we have some unfinished business to conduct."

"What business?" he asked.

"Remember the day on the beach?" she said. "I would like to accomplish that fete tonight."

"Are you sure we should do that?" he asked.

"Yes we should," answered Cindy.

"Then what about Rona?"

"Leave her to me," she said. "I will take care of her."

He agreed and took her back to the table. As he passed the table where Christiana and Graves sat, he signalled them for help.

For the rest of the evening he noticed that Cindy kept feeding Harvey Wallbangers to Rona, knowing that she would be drunk soon and she would have free access to him for the night. When the time was right, she came to inform him that Rona was slushed and must be taken to the room. Without hesitation Dready took Rona, closely followed by Cindy, to the room. He placed her in the bed and watched as Cindy removed her clothes and covered her with the top sheet.

"Now it's my turn," said Cindy and she began to remove her clothing also.

"Has it got to be right now?" he asked.

"Yes sir," she replied, "because we are alone together and there isn't anyone else down stairs for you tonight."

He was cornered and knew it. He sat on the sofa chair with a scotch in his hand hoping that Cindy would also fall asleep and he would avoid having sex with her, but the woman was determined. She went to the bathroom, returned in a short while and flopped herself into his lap.

"I don't have a condom," he whispered hoping to avert her advances.

"Don't worry, I have some in my purse; although I hate the feel of them," she said as she began removing his pants.

Suddenly, there was a knock on the door. Cindy tried to prevent him from opening it, but he did. It was Bernard Graves.

"Sorry to bother you sir," said Graves, "but as we were talking earlier about Jamaica's exports, I wondered if I could have a word with you."

"Sure, come on in," said Dready. "Can I get you a drink?"

"No, I am fine," said Graves.

The two men sat and talked for almost an hour. Cindy in the mean time, angrily got up and went into the bedroom, leaving Dready and Graves to talk. Dready softly opened the bedroom door to see Cindy curled up on one bed while Rona was paralytically asleep in the other. He slowly closed the door, assured that they were soundly asleep. They left the room. He silently thanked Graves for rescuing him and went to his room.

When the morning light blazed into the room, Dready awoke

to hear the voice of a crowing cock. He entered the washroom to do his constitutional thing, then flopped back on the bed.

"It's too early to have breakfast and too late to go back to sleep," he thought.

He sat in the window chair admiring the stillness of the Guyana morning and the emptiness of the usually busy sea wall. He gave thought to the development of the case and wondered what Rona wanted to say to Burkowitz. But he would hear that from Christiana whenever she got it from Rona.

Seeing as it was Sunday morning, he decided to leave the hotel for a walk along the sea wall to cogitate his case, with a thought that he should have gone to Christiana's room. Suddenly he got the notion of going to see her and began his walk back, only to see her coming towards him.

"What happened?" she said on passing him. "Couldn't sleep?"

"No darling," he replied, and joined her. "I had you on my mind all night."

"Good," she replied. "Sneak into my room in a few minutes and we'll lock the door. We can always order in our food."

"Fine," he said, "see you in a few minutes."

Spending the entire Sunday afternoon and night with his wife was delightful for Dready, although he was afraid of anyone seeing them together and making the connection which would blow the entire case. All their conversation was conducted in a whisper. They talked about the case whenever they were awake during the day and night. The phone rang many times but neither of them answered.

The next morning, being Monday, he waited until there were no sound outside their door before leaving his wife's room. Just as he was about to open the door to his room, Cindy came out of hers across from him.

"Going or coming?" she asked.

"Coming," he said. "I went for a walk."

"What is this place?" she asked. "Yesterday I went to find a

272

beach because this one is so dirty, but the taxi driver told me that the others were far away. I had to stay indoors all day listening to Rona bitch about you deserting her Saturday night, and her talking on the phone to some idiot in Nassau. I wanted to tell her that we slept together in the bed next to her the night before, but didn't have the heart to disrupt her mind."

"But that would be untrue," said Dready.

"Well, I wanted to tell her that just to screw up her mind, "she said.

"Well don't say anything," he suggested. "She might take it to heart and do something drastic to herself."

"Can I come in with you now?" she asked.

"No!" he whispered angrily. "What if she came knocking?"

"She is asleep!" said Cindy.

"Maybe, but she could wake up just as we got started."

Okay," she said, "I will wait until we get back to Nassau. See you at breakfast."

They all met in the restaurant for breakfast. Dready sat with Cindy and Rona at a table situated almost in the centre of the room. He noticed that Rona kept a constant stare on Christiana who was alone at a corner table.

"Why don't you go talk to her?" he suggested. "Ask her to join us."

It seemed that was what Rona wanted to hear. Without hesitation she waved to Christiana and quickly rushed over to her, and in a short time, returned with the lovely Mrs. Perkins to their table.

"Remember Christiana Felscher from the party?" she asked.

Both Dready and Cindy acknowledged her.

"Hello Christiana," said Dready, "nice to see you again after the party."

"Yes," she answered, "that party was nice although there weren't many people present."

"Sometimes those kind of parties are the best," said Cindy,

273

"not too many people to cramp your space."

The breakfast was consumed in almost silence, except for the occasional comments about the food and the country. Finally Rona made her move.

"Come Christiana dear, let's go powder our noses," she said. "Cindy, you stay to keep Mr Winston's company. We'll be back soon."

The two women left the table to go to the bathroom. As they entered, Rona took the note from her bag and handed it to Christiana.

"Please give this to Ivan for me," she said.

"Will he give me a return note for you?" asked Christiana.

"Maybe and maybe not," said Rona. "He might only give you a verbal message."

"Okay," said Christiana. "I would like the job of carrying the stuff to wherever you want it delivered."

How good a courier are you?" asked Rona.

"I've made many excursions for Althea in the Bahamas and a couple for Ralston Weekes in Jamaica," she said to booster her confidence.

"Good," said Rona, "I think you'll be just fine for this job."

Within fifteen minutes they returned to the table.

"Thanks for the hospitality," said Christiana without sitting, "but I must run."

"That's fine," said Rona, "we have to make tracks also."

They all left the restaurant for their individual rooms.

Dready entered his room and made a fast change into a pair of shorts and a tee shirt and quickly rushed out of the hotel. When he got outside he saw her leaning against the building, like a hooker waiting for a bus. She wore a tightly fitted navy-blue shorts with a white stripe on each side and a frilly top to match. He noticed that her running shoes and white socks were new, and realized that she was ready for a walk. He winked at her as he passed and continued his walk towards the taxi.

"The Stabroek Market please," he told the driver.

He could see Christiana getting into the other taxi behind him. He entered the Stabroek Market and walked slowly, hoping she would do the same. She followed him into the market. In her mind she wasn't sure if her plan would work, but was willing to try. She waited until he had perused some of the stalls and was walking towards her before making her move. She deliberately bumped into him.

"Oh, hello sir," she said excitedly as though their meeting was accidental. "Remember we met last night at the party?"

"Yes," he replied, "nice to see you again."

They shook hands.

"Nice talking to you," she shouted as she walked away.

He left her in the market and went to find his taxi-friend, but he wasn't there. He promptly walked up the road until he found one and got in heading back to the hotel. He waited until he got into his room before removing the piece of paper Christiana had stuck into his shirt pocket.

"She would make a good pick-pocket," he thought as he read the brief note. It said: "Hello Ivan, could you tell me who would know where to find Karlheinz? Send a return message with my friend Ludwig. Thanks, Rona."

Dready carefully refolded the note and placed it in his breast pocket. He decided to walk along the road to find Edgar again and this time he was in luck.

"Hey Edgar!" he said on approaching him, "ever hear about a dealer named David DeFreitas?"

"Yes, but how did you know about him?" asked Edgar.

"I met him at a party last night and he said if I needed some things I should see him," said Dready.

"His office is just down the road there," said Edgar, "want to go there?"

"Yes," said Dready and got into the car.

The drive was only a couple hundred yards but Edgar was

eager to please.

Edgar led Dready along the side of the house, past the guard with a sawed-off shot gun, to a door. He looked at the sign on the door that read:- "David DeFreitas Company of Georgetown."

He knocked on the door although it was open, and could see the man sitting behind the desk.

"Hi David," he said, "remember me? We met the other day."

"Sure do Winston my boy, come in and sit," said DeFreitas.

"Well, we were talking last time about Mr Burkowitz and the white bush-man from Venezuela," said Dready, "I would really like to know more about them because I do have the market up there for the diamonds."

David began to talk, telling all about his acquaintance with the two men with whom he had dealings with over the years. He talked about the many times they crossed paths in Bartica, when he, DeFreitas, went there to make purchases from the pork knockers. He talked about the many times Ivan Burkowitz tried to implicate his good name in the smuggling business and the many times he rejected his offer.

".....then he got caught," said DeFreitas. "Something to do with a ring out of Jamaica, Trinidad and the Bahamas."

"A diamond ring?" asked Dready.

"You might say so," replied David.

"Did you say that the goods go to Jamaica, then Trinidad and then to the Bahamas?" asked Dready.

"That's right," said DeFreitas, "after first going through Suriname Man, I didn't want anything to do with those people. He got a life sentence here in GT."

"How were they getting it to Suriname?" asked Dready.

"I don't know!" said David. "Maybe they had people in GT or Berbice taking it there for them or...." he paused, ".....you know what I think? I think they must have gone to Rose Hall, or better yet, Corriverton. That's a good crossing point into Suriname."

276

"Can you show it to me on the map?" asked Dready.

Quickly DeFreitas got out of his chair and pointed to a map on the wall.

"Look! Here it is," he said. "This might be a good place to carry it across."

Dready didn't acknowledge his suggestion.

"Then what about the bushman, where is he now?" asked Dready.

"Don't know," said DeFreitas. "He is too elusive for the law or anyone else, and is still around out there. He flies in and out like Santa Claus."

"Who does his business in GT now that Burkowitz is out of commission?" asked Dready.

"Don't know and don't care to," said DeFreitas.

"Well, as I've told you, I must make a purchase to take home and somebody will have to sell me," he said. "Can you assist me in finding a pork knocker?"

"Sure can friend," said David, "but everything must be above board."

"How does three hundred thousand sounds to you?" asked Dready.

"Three hundred thousand American?" DeFreitas asked, his eyes popping.

"Exactly," said Dready, "and paid in Grand Caymans."

DeFreitas smiled, and Dready could envision his thoughts.

"No sir, I would prefer to be paid right here in GT," said DeFreitas.

"Can be arranged," said Dready. "Just say when."

DeFreitas smiled as he handed Dready the ring he had made with the diamond.

"Your wife is going to love you for this," he said, "and I will tell you when."

He questioned the man some more about his involvement with Burkowitz and was told about the smuggling ring again.

"......and that is to the best of my knowledge," said David.

"Thanks David old boy, we might be able to do business together after all," he said. "Find me the man who will deliver the stuff and the cash is yours."

Dready left David DeFreitas' establishment without telling him that he knew about his own crooked dealings with the pork knockers during his trips to the interior, and how he supplied the women and booze to intoxicate them. He realized that David DeFratus wasn't as honest a man as he hoped he would have him believe, pretending to be loyal to his country. Finally Dready thanked him and left his office.

"See you around," he told DeFreitas.

He got outside to the street to see Edgar waiting for him.

"Where to?" Edgar asked.

"Somewhere where I can call your man Packus in private," said Dready.

"Call him from the hotel phone," suggested Edgar.

"Then drop me off and I will do the honours," said Dready.

He got into the hotel and asked the receptionist to place the call. She did so and handed him the phone.

"Hello Packus," he said, "this is Dready. Find your man?"

"Yes," said the pork knocker, "he'll be in Essequibo on Friday afternoon. Get cousin Edgar to bring you up, okay? and don't forget the money."

"That's fine," said Dready, "see you."

He returned to Edgar to tell him of the deal with Packus.

"We'll have to leave early on Friday morning," he said. "Will half past eight be good for you?"

"No man, we'll have to leave about half past five to get there by twelve," said Edgar.

"Okay, see you then," said Dready.

He walked into his room and closed the door behind him. Quickly he picked up the phone and called Captain Maraj and told him what was planned for Friday afternoon.

"I'm gonna need that money and you'll have to place a couple of your boys along the road for security," said Dready.

"Better yet," said Maraj, "I'm going to leave Thursday night so as to have my men in place when Mr. Bushman comes to town on Friday."

"Please take Graves and Christiana along for the ride," said Dready, "they might want to see this."

"Excellent idea," replied Maraj.

"Okay," said Dready, "you two can iron out the wrinkles. I'll be going to see Burkowitz tomorrow morning and hopefully he can give us some more information on the bushman."

"We will have it on tape," said Maraj.

"Good, see you," said Dready.

After talking to Elton Maraj, he decided that it was time to see Rona and Cindy, and since he had been away all day, he felt it would be nice to have dinner with them and to implement their phase of the deal.

"Hi girls," he said when she opened the door, "sorry to leave you all day, but I had to make contact with a man."

"That's fine darling," said Rona, "I'm sure it was worth it."

'Are you ready for dinner?" he asked.

"Certainly," answered Cindy, "let's go, I'm starving."

They descended to the restaurant and sat at a table close to Graves and Christiana.

"Hello there Christiana," said Rona, "nice to see you again. May we join you?"

"Yes you may," replied Christiana, "nice to see you also."

The waiter found them a larger table and they all ate dinner in silence, except for the occasional comments about clothes. Nothing was said until the floor show began.

Rona leaned over to Christiana and whispered,

"Let's go to the washroom," she said, "I would like to talk to you."

Christiana didn't hesitate, and the two women left the table.

"It was a nice day wasn't it?" asked Christiana.

"It sure was, but it will be better tomorrow if you can tell me something nice from a dear friend."

Christiana realized that Rona was talking about her visit with Ivan so she answered,

"I'm sure he will tell me something favourable; I too would like to know where to find Karlheinz, and would also like to talk to Harvey Ambross," she said randomly hoping that it might impress Rona.

"You're so right darling," said Rona smiling, "we are going to be rich after this is done. Would you like to live permanently in Nassau?"

"No," replied Christiana, "I will be getting married and most likely live in Toronto somewhere, and will need this money to begin that life."

Rona didn't reply immediately.

She reached into her bag and handed Christiana another note.

"Give this to Ivan for me," she said, "I want to be absolutely sure that my friends are still my friends."

"Good," replied Christiana.

Rona finished touching up her lipstick and they both returned to the table.

Dready in the meantime was racking his brains for a solution. He thought about Rona's mention of both Ludwig and Karlheinz' name in her note to Ivan and wondered if it was some kind of code.

"Maybe it was a code to identify Christiana as the person to carry the note," he concluded in his mind.

Just then he got an idea. He secretly winked at Graves then got up from the chair.

"Excuse me ladies, my bladder calls," he said and directed his body towards the gents' washroom.

Within a minute Graves was standing beside him at the urinals.

"Change of plans," he whispered. "Send Christiana with the note to see Burkowitz in the morning and I will visit him an hour later."

"Why?" asked Graves.

"I think that note is a code and if anybody else took it to him, we will never get the answer," said Dready.

He handed the note to Graves, left the washroom and went back to the table.

The show was a local comedian, who played the steel pan and made jokes about the government and the six different nationalities in their country. None of the women understood the dialect so Dready had to explain the meaning to them. When the show was over, Rona suggested they go to relax in her room with a bottle of rum.

"Good idea," said Cindy, looking at Dready.

They quickly said their good night to Graves and Christiana, got the rum, glasses and ice, and rushed to the room to begin the planned drinking. This time Rona wasn't falling for Cindy's tricks to get her drunk, so at about one thirty Dready got up and went to his room leaving the two women to watch each other. During the night he decided to sneak over to Christiana's room, but on peaking out, he saw Cindy sitting on the floor in the corridor.

"Maybe she's watching me," he thought, "and if I let her into my room I won't get any sleep."

He gave up his thought and went directly to bed alone.

He had a decent sleep and felt refreshed when he awakened the next morning. He looked out the window towards the sea-wall wondering if Graves was able to tell Christiana of the new plan. Then he looked down and saw her taking the taxi. Slowly he got dressed, allowing enough time for Christiana to do what she was asked to. He then walked down the six floors of stairs to the lobby and out the door. He glanced down the road to see Edgar walking towards him.

"Where to boss?" asked his taxi driving friend.

"The prison," he said.

"The prison?" asked Edgar.

"That's what I said, the prison where they keep prisoners," said Dready.

"Why?" asked Edgar.

"There's a friend of mine serving time there and I want to see him," replied Dready.

The puzzled Edgar escorted him back to the car, and without any further question drove to the prison on Durban street.

"Stalag 13," said Edgar.

"Wait here for me," said Dready without comment regarding his statement.

He showed his pass to the guard, and waited for them to open the gates. He was escorted into another building and he again showed his pass to another guard. He was allowed to enter and was taken to a waiting room.

He looked through the window into the recreational area to see Christiana talking to Ivan Burkowitz at a table. He saw when she gave him the note and he read it. In a short moment he was telling Christiana something in a whisper, then just as quicky she got up, shook hands with him and was on her way out. He waited for approximately ten minutes before signalling the guard to let him in.

"Ivan Burkowitz please," he shouted.

"Over here," said the balding man. "Are you the journalist?"

"Yes sir, Dready Winston is my name. I wrote the article about Karlheinz Bass and Arthur Collins," he said.

"Very nice article," said Ivan.

"Thank you," said Dready, "I tried to be objective in all my stories, even about people in prison."

"Ah! Ah!" said Ivan smiling. "So what are your plans for mine?"

"I don't know as yet, I have to hear it first, then I can formulate a scenario," he replied.

"Good," said Burkowitz. "Make it a good story and have it translated into different languages to let the world read about me. I want every man jack to know what happened to me and where it landed me."

"I shall do my best to publish your story throughout the entire world," said Dready, "and in the mean time put myself in position to win the big prize."

"Great," said Burkowitz, "shall we begin?"

They talked for over an hour and he was even given a bottle of pop to quench his thirst. His note book was almost full by the time he was through. Finally a guard came in.

"Time's up gentlemen, if you want to prolong this conversation you'll have to get another pass," said the guard.

"Thank you Mr Burkowitz, you'll read about yourself in my magazine next month." said Dready.

"No my good man," replied Ivan. "It is I who is grateful. Thanks for coming and allowing me this one day visit to civilization."

"What?" asked a shocked Dready. "I thought this is where you are residing."

"No sir, I am at the 'Hotel Messaruni,' and it's not quite as nice as this," said Burkowitz. "But I'm still working on the appeal."

"Good," said Dready, "keep fighting."

All the way back to the hotel he could see the question in Edgar's eyes and a change of demeanor. His eyes seemed to be wondering about the man he had befriended a few days ago, but was afraid to ask.

When he got to the hotel he found Rona waiting for him. She had a broad grin on her face and he realized that she already got the message from Burkowitz through Christiana, and wanted to tell him where they were going to meet the person who would take them to purchase the diamonds.

He grinned.

What Rona didn't know was that Dready had already spoken to Christiana, Elton Maraj and Commissioner Bernard Graves about the return message to her from Burkowitz, and had already set thing in place for whenever they made contact with the person she was supposed to meet.

He smiled even more, because Ivan Burkowitz himself had told him some cock-and-bull story about their long ago gang, led by Karlheinz Bass and some of his old cronies. He realized why Burkowitz was so willing to tell the story, and was pleased that the man hadn't a clue who he was; the Dreadlocks cop.

Chapter Eleven

Agents, Dealers and Couriers.

*D*ready walked into the hotel with Rona at his side. She had been waiting at the door for him all afternoon. The broad smile on his face was indicative as his thoughts, knowing that she had received her message. He could see the happiness in her as she was busting to tell him the news of the person they were supposed to get the diamonds from. He had spent almost all day talking with Christiana, Graves and Maraj, planning out the strategy for their meeting with the great pork knocker after reading the message. He was somewhat happy that Burkowitz had been taken in by Christiana's charming presence and had given her the passwords to his friends and where to find them; unaware of her police status.

Rona opened the door and they entered.

"Come in darling," she said. "Come in quickly."

He went directly to the sofa and sat beside Cindy, patiently awaiting the happy news from Rona.

"We will have to move fast," she said, "because the man we have to meet is only going to be at the designated place for a few hours on Friday."

"....and where is that?" he asked.

"I don't know as yet," she answered, "but someone will be coming with that information and maybe to take us to him."

"Who?" he asked.

"Don't know that either," she replied. "He will be making contact with me this evening at the sea wall, and there he will tell us where, when and how we will go to the designated place."

"What time?" he asked.

"What time what?" she asked.

"What time do we meet your contact?" he asked.

"Tonight at eight o'clock sharp," she said.

"Good," he said looking at his watch, "we have thirty-five minutes to get there."

They walked out the door and along the road towards the band-shell, which was only about 300 yards from the Pegasus. Edgar saw and quickly approached them.

"Where are you going?" he asked.

"For a walk on the sea wall," replied Rona.

"Down this side or Kitty side," he asked.

"Kitty side," said Dready.

"Is it far?" asked Rona.

Edgar, although curious, was happy to oblige his friend and company, but thought better of his ripoff scam.

"It's right up there," he said pointing to the area, "but be very careful. The choke and rob boys are always on the look-out for a target."

Rona looked at Dready then said,

"With him beside me, I'm sure we can walk there safely."

Rona told Cindy to stay with Edgar at the band-shell among the crowd.

"Listen to the music and catch some sea air," she said. "We'll be back soon."

Rona and Dready walked along the sea wall, all the way to the designated spot. Within minutes they were confronted by a sinister looking person in a long shirt, which extended almost to his knees covering his jeans, and a hat pulled down over most of his face.

"Karlheinz Bass is a friend of mine," said the voice in a Guyanese accent.

"Mine also," replied Rona, "but he's on a permanent vacation somewhere in Jamaica."

"So is Harvey Ambross," said the voice. "Rona Samuels?" asked the man.

"Yes," she answered, "and you?"

"Doesn't matter," he answered. "I will meet you at five o'clock on Friday morning in front of the hotel and don't be late."

"We'll be there," said Rona. "Where are we going?"

"Up the Essequibo river," said the man.

The person turned and literally disappeared amongst the crowd on the sea wall, without another word.

"Is that all?" asked Dready.

"That's all," she replied.

"Was that the password?" he asked.

Rona paused to look at him.

"Yes it was," she answered abrasively, "Karlheinz Bass."

Dready shrugged his shoulders and began their walk back to his taxi driving friend and Cindy.

After telling him he would not be requiring his services for the rest of the night, Dready reminded him of the early morning trip on Friday.

"Remember now," said Dready, "five o'clock in the morning. But I will see you tomorrow, right?"

Edgar nodded his head, left them as they stood in front of the Pegasus; quickly disappearing into the night.

"It's Wednesday night in Georgetown, what is there to do?" asked Cindy.

"How the fuck should I know?" shouted Rona. "Maybe we should have asked the taxi driver to take us somewhere."

"Maybe we should have," said Dready, "but I heard that there is going to be some entertainment in the hotel later tonight."

287

"No," said Rona, "I don't want to do that; why don't we get a bottle of rum and go to the room instead?"

"I'm not interested," said Cindy. "I'm going into the bar, maybe I will find a man there, and get screwed tonight."

"Well girls, that is your prerogative," said Dready, "I'm going to lie down for a little while, then later I will come down to hear the music."

Dready excused himself from them and went up to his room. As he reached Christiana's door he knocked. Within a few seconds she opened it and he slipped inside and she locked it behind him.

"What happened to your two women?" she asked.

"I ditched them," he answered. "They are planning to curl up with a bottle of rum and I needed to spend some time with my wife."

"Good," said Christiana, "I was beginning to wonder if you find them sexier than I; are they?"

"Not at all darling," he replied smiling, as he began to remove his clothing, "but we must remain quiet and anonymous to each other until this is all over."

They showered together in silence, and seeing as that the bathroom was against Rona and Cindy's room, and any kind of noise could be heard, they did it quietly.

The bed was as inviting as that of his wife's body. They made love and slept late.

The morning sun awakened them and without much effort, they quietly got up and showered.

"We cannot talk here," she whispered, "maybe we could meet in a park somewhere."

"Make that the Promenade Gardens on Middle Street at noon," he suggested. "Have a taxi take you there and I will meet you."

"No," she said, "meet me at the Guyana stores; I want to get some cosmetics and some....., mine is getting low."

With a nod of his head, it was agreed.

Just then the phone rang and Christiana answered it.

"Hello!" she said into the receiver.

"Hi Christiana, it's Elton. Please get Dready and come to meet me at the station," he said. "I have someone who would like to talk to him. But be careful of being seen together."

"Okay," she said and hung up.

After dressing, Christiana kissed him, opened the door and peeked out to ensure that nobody was there. Dready then sneaked off to his room. He locked his door and flopped himself on the bed and immediately began to think out his action for when they met with the man. He wondered if it was the person he had in mind and whether he would be able to get the man to incriminate himself.

Christiana went to the front door to get a taxi while Dready called his friend Harold for his ride to the station. She got there a few minutes ahead of him and was already sitting in Elton's office when he walked in. Bernard Graves had been picked up earlier by one of the official police escorts and was also there. Everybody greeted one another and sat. Elton asked a police woman to bring in the man.

"I hope he is the one; the one I have in mind," whispered Dready.

"Hello everybody," said the man. 'My name is.......just call me Dante. I'm the man who met you and Rona Samuels on the sea wall," he said directly to Dready. "I'm a pork knocker, and I can answer all your questions."

Christiana took out her notebook and pen.

"What's the name of the white pork knocker?" asked Dready.

"Don't know," said the man called Dante. "Everybody calls him the man from Venezuela or the Bush-man."

"How often do you meet him," asked Dready.

"Once per month," said Dante.

".....and he never tells you his name?" asked Christiana.

"No, we do business and leave it at that," said Dante.

"I heard that he flies into many private airstrips within the interior, true?" asked Dready.

"Absolutely," said Dante.

"How long have you been a pork knocker?" asked Dready.

"Too long," said Dante and began telling them about the life of a pork knocker.

To Dready the story was similar to that told to him by Harold.

"....and the commodity is sold to a dealer, shop owner or a sponsor," said Dante.

"Does the white pork knocker ever do business in Georgetown? Graves asked.

"No sir, he has someone here do things for him," said Dante.

"Whom could that be?" asked Maraj.

"As I've already told you Elton," said Dante, "I'm not too sure, but you should check out David DeFreitas or a fellow they call Packus."

Nobody questioned the names. But within Dready's mind he was now sure of the persons doing business for both the white pork knocker and Burkowitz.

"Do you know a man named Ivan Burkowitz?" asked Dready.

"Heard of him but never met him," said Dante. "Some time ago I met a fellow in New Amsterdam who wanted me to meet him but that meeting never came about."

"Why not?" asked Graves.

"He was arrested and eventually got tried and imprisoned," said Dante, looking at Elton Maraj.

"I've heard that the diamonds are travelling to Trinidad via Suriname, true or false?" asked Dready.

"True," said Dante, "and many more places like that."

"I think the place they are using to cross into that country is Corriverton, am I right?" asked Dready.

"Right," said Dante. "But you might have to talk to the Ali brothers about that," said Dante.

"Are you friendly enough with them to get me introduced?"

"No," said Dante. "But if I ever introduce you and they get arrested later, someone would definitely find me and rip my balls out. But I could tell you where to find them. It's bad enough I'm here talking to the police much-less to take you into their camps."

"What about your man DeFreitas, can you introduce Christiana and Graves to him?" asked Dready.

"Yes," replied Dante, "but what about yourself?"

"I've already met him," said Dready. "We already know each other."

"I see," said Dante. "Double checking, eh?"

"Thanks Dante," said Dready. "By the way; are you being paid for this information?"

"No, but Captain Maraj and I have an understanding," replied Dante.

"Thanks again," said Dready.

After the informant left the room the four police officers sat discussing the case and the strategy necessary to entrap the perpetrators.

"Fellows," said Captain Maraj, "you have a lot more to do in Trinidad and other parts of the Caribbean than I. My job is right here in Guyana and it will be an ongoing process to find and resolve some of the illegal operators here."

"There's something bothering me," said Graves. "Dante said he never met Burkowitz personally yet he was the one who brought the message from him to Rona."

"That's easy," said Maraj. "There is a prison guard working for DeFreitas; he brought the message from Burkowitz. DeFreitas then ask Dante to carry out the function on the sea-wall with Dready and Rona; which he did under my instructions."

"Good," said Graves, "I'm satisfied."

"What will you do with David DeFreitas now?" asked Christiana.

"I will be able to use him to find many others," said Maraj.

"He doesn't know it as yet but his arse is mine from here on."

Bernard Graves got up from his chair, took Elton's hand and shook it.

"I don't envy you my boy, your work here is just beginning."

"I know," replied Elton, "but we still have some to catch in this phase."

They left the police station separately. Christiana and Graves took taxis back to the Pegasus and Dready took his to the Cara Suites to collect some clothing before going to the Pegasus.

He lay on the bed giving consideration to the vast complexity of the case. He realized that he now had a complete understanding of the movement of diamonds from Guyana; be it the large companies or the private cartel like that of Burkowitz and the Bachstrums in the Bahamas. He thought about their ruthlessness in dealing with their people, and realized that they had no respect for anyone, much-less the young students in Toronto.

It didn't take long for him to doze off. When he was awakened by the knock on the door, he looked at his watch and realized that he had slept for two hours. He opened the door to see Rona standing there.

"What's the matter lover?" she asked. "Why are you asleep on a nice day like this?"

He didn't have an excuse to offer, but caught himself telling her about going to a meeting with a politician friend.

"We agreed to have lunch and a conversation whenever I get to Georgetown," he said. "We met in university in Canada, so this meeting is very important to us."

"Well then, go on to your meeting," she said angrily, "Cindy and I will get a taxi to somewhere for the day."

He didn't answer. She spun and disappeared down the hall to the elevator.

In a way he was happy to be rid of her for the day. Although

Maraj had told him that he would have a police officer follow her everywhere, he would rather be able to keep an eye on her himself; but that was a chance he had to take. He looked out the window and saw when the two women got into the cab; only then he decided to leave the room for his down-town adventure.

He got one of the hotel taxis to drop him at the Guyana store. He slowly walked along Main Street to the department store for a browse. Christiana was standing at the cosmetic counter talking to a clerk about facials and other beauty paraphernalia.

"You look beautiful without those things," he remarked as he approached her.

"You might be right, because my husband doesn't like them either," she replied.

"Could I interest you in having lunch with me?" he asked.

"Certainly," she said accepting his invitation.

"Where is a nice local restaurant?" he asked the clerk.

"Try Kisskadee on Regent street," said the clerk. "Ask any of the taxi drivers to take you there."

Christiana quickly selected some products and paid the bill, then they were off to the road. They crossed over to the taxi stand in front of the Tower Hotel, asked for his friend Edgar and was told that he would be back in a minute. Within twenty minutes Edgar came.

"Hey man!" said Edgar, "been waiting long?"

"No," replied Dready, "just a few minutes. Can you take us to a nice secluded, restaurant where we could sit and talk in private?"

"Sure can," said Edgar, "get in."

"Where are we going?" asked Christiana.

"Berbice," replied Edgar. "McKenzie is a nice place to visit. Sit back, relax and enjoy the scenery."

The scenery was relaxing for the two lovers, including the ferry ride across the river.

A couple of hours later they were in New Amsterdam at a very nice place enjoying a beer, some curried fish and ground provision.

The restaurant had a covered out-door area with tables, allowing the patrons the sights of the surroundings. As in Jamaica, Christiana felt relaxed and comfortable with the provided food. She ate well.

Edgar left them to see one of his friends in town.

"Okay now, talk," she said.

"It is my belief that Rona is a manager of some sort, and she came down here to carry back some kind of instructions from Burkowitz," he said. "That's the reason he gave you that coded message."

"Yes," replied Christiana, "the very reason; and only their people will be able to understand it."

"Rightly so," he said, "but I think it can be broken."

"How?" she asked.

"By following their trail or by getting one of them to talk," he answered. "I'm sure that he also gave me some coded messages in the interview, hoping that I will publish them so that his friends will get them."

Christian gave it some thoughts before replying.

"If we take your written notes," she said, "we could compare what he told me to see if the same phrases were given to you, then it would be obvious what they were and then work..........."

"That will take too long," said Dready. "I would have to use one of the police computers to do it, and we would never know who might see it," he said.

"Then we must make Rona believe that we know more than we actually do," she said, "and the way to do it is by letting her think that someone else did the talking."

"Good idea," he said, "but if the man we are going to meet is the person I believe he is, then the project will be wrapped up at that time. Only two things are still bothering my mind."

"And what's that?" she asked.

"I would like to know why Rona kept Cindy from finding out that she is Tanya's daughter and why Hubert is willing to go to prison without naming the head man," he said.

"Maybe he's afraid of getting killed," she said. "I'm sure the head man is right under our noses and we are unable to pin-point him."

"If my suspicion is correct," said Dready smiling, "I will be able to touch him within the next week. But we will have to know who the pork knocker is; and if he is who I think he is, then we have them all."

Christiana smile and Dready noticed it.

"Okay, he said, "what is it?"

"When Rona and I were in the washroom, I casually mention-ed that I would like to talk to Harvey Ambross and just the look on her face told me that his name was an active code for them," said Christiana.

"Mmmmm," said Dready. "Harvey Ambross eh?"

"Yes sir," she replied. "That name really meant something to her."

"I think I know what it means but I cannot say right now," he responded.

"Maybe they are using his name as a contact," said Christiana.

"Maybe," replied Dready.

In his mind, Dready was certain that he knew what the code meant and who was involved. He was sure that he had broken their code and could begin his summation of the crime.

Christiana told him how Rona insisted on her coming on the expedition to Essequibo with them.

"What did you tell her?" asked Dready.

"I told her I would only be there if my friend Bernard Graves could come along also," said Christiana.

"What did she say?" asked Dready.

"She said it was fine," replied Christiana.

They exchanged thoughts on the subject for almost two hours, then Edgar returned and they requested to be taken back to GT.

"Did you enjoy your day?" asked Edgar.

"Sure did," said Christiana, "But don't tell his wife."

"Not me," said Edgar, "people's affairs are not my business. Taxi driving is my business, and my duty is to ensure that my customers have a good time by showing them everything about Guyana; nothing else."

On reaching the hotel, Dready slipped Edgar five American twenties.

"That's too much for the trip," said Edgar.

"That is also hush money," said Dready winking.

They all laughed and parted company.

That evening was a laid-back, uneventful space for everybody. Dready went to see Rona and Cindy, and for most of the time they were involved in unsubstantial, meaningless conversation, just biding their time. He sat looking at the two women knowing that they were not aware of his knowledge and the fact that he had solved the code. They were not aware that he had spoken to Burkowitz, the only white man in the Georgetown prison, and that he knew about the operation of the pork - knockers and their bosses, as well as how the diamonds were getting out of Guyana to Nassau.

Finally, at about eleven o'clock he decided to go to his room and told them so.

"I think I will need some energy to ride those rough roads tomorrow," he said.

"Me too," said Cindy. "I can't visualise why we have to go there. Why can't those people come here? Those roads are literally a pain in the arse."

Both Dready and Rona looked at each other.

"Cindy my girl," said Rona, "in this business people have to go where the deals are made, and some people have to do the leg-work in order to get paid. You are one of the leg-work people, so shut your fucking mouth and be glad to get the money at the end of it all."

Poor Cindy didn't have a rebuttal, so she remained silent.

"I'm going to bed," said Dready smiling as he got up from the chair.

"See you in the morning love," said Rona.

For Dready, the bed was the most welcomed place to be that night. It gave him the latitude to think out the things that were to happen in a short time from then. He was certain that Captain Maraj will meet them and would arrange to have the person present when they got there, also the rest of his force, just in case they became violent. He lay there in thought about how the mining companies were moving out the diamonds with their planes from the private air-strips. But that wasn't his job. His job was to find those in the Nassau gang. He gave thoughts to the line used by Earl Monroe about the Octopus.

"The Octopus is the person I seek," he thought. "The person who is in control of the entire operation and who is somewhere in the Caribbean."

He realized that someone was in direct contact with Burk-owitz and doing the business in Georgetown on behalf of the white pork knocker.

"David DeFreitas!" he thought. "That's my man in GT."

He was concerned that Christiana will be there among the possible gun fire, jeopardizing herself and the possible baby in her stomach. He wasn't sure at what time he fell asleep.

He was up like a shot, got dressed and quickly rushed down to see Edgar standing at the door. His van was parked across the way.

"Good morning," said Edgar, "looks like you are up before bird's wife."

"Eh?" he asked. "What the hell was that?"

"It means getting up early," said Edgar. "In Guyana we say Mr Bird is always up early to begin chirping, but his wife is always up earlier to make his breakfast."

'Oh," said Dready. "Are the others down yet?"

"No," said Edgar.

Dready quickly ran back inside and knocked on Rona's door.

"Time to go," he shouted as she opened the door.

"Go ahead," she said, "I have something to do first."

He grabbed Cindy's hand, took the elevator down and stood beside the van. About ten minutes went by then he saw Rona coming out with everybody else marching behind her.

"These people are coming with us," said Rona.

"Why?" asked Dready.

"Because they are friends of mine," she answered.

"You should have told me this before," said Dready angrily. "I am carrying three hundred thousand American dollars and don't fancy too many people, I'm not familiar with, being in on the deal."

Quickly Rona re-introduced him to Christiana and Bernard Graves.

"She is a friend of a friend of mine, and he is her friend," said Rona angrily. "Stop worrying about them, everything will go down perfectly."

Cindy and Dready sat in the same seat while Bernard and Christiana occupied the seat behind them. Dante sat in the seat to his right while Rona was up front with Edgar.

"Let's move out," said Rona, winding down the window and putting her feet on the dash.

The drive to Parika was uneventful and mostly in silence. At Parika they got into the speed boat for the trip up the Esequibo river. Everyone was silent, only the sounds of the motor, the birds and the rustling river against the boat could be heard. They made a stop at Charity. Dready realized that Elton had provided a launch full with police, dressed as pork knockers, to escort them for the long ride up the river. He noticed that Rona was very relaxed and contented to absorb the scenery along the river way.

They landed at the designated area in Esequibo and were immediately greeted by Packus. The smell of burning wood was in the air.

"Bring the money?" asked the pork knocker.

"Sure," replied Dready patting the small suitcase, and at the same time allowing the butt-end of his gun to show. "Ready whenever you are."

Packus lead the team to the house on a small hill and directed them to a rear patio like deck. Dready could see the carcass of an animal on a skewer over a fire.

"Sit," said Packus. "Relax and have a drink, the bushman will come when he feel it is right."

Dready noticed that Packus sat close to the man known as Dante and presumed it was to prevent him from doing anything surprising. Christiana, Graves, Rona and Cindy sat together, while Edgar sat on the other side of his cousin Packus. He glanced around to see if he could see any of Maraj's men, but saw nothing. All of Packus' men, some armed with sub machine guns, sat singularly in a semi-circle on the perimeter of the deck.

After a long forty-five minute wait and two beers, there was the rumbling sound of an engine coming in their direction. It was that of a Land Rover. Within a minute a white man, dressed in khaki shorts and shirt with a bowler hat, stepped out and approached them. He was a slenderly built man in his late forties with scruffy long, darkish blond hair and a moustache to match. His blue eyes, set in a crimson red face, were surrounded with crow's-feet wrinkles, while his obvious false teeth kept chewing on a piece of stick.

"This is the Bushman," whispered Packus. "Be ready to make your deal because he doesn't like to stay around in one place too long."

"Greetings Bushman," said Packus excitedly jumping up from the seat.

They shook hands and Packus began to introduce everybody. The man looked at the eight people sitting, and said in a scornful tone.

"Who are all these people and why are they here?" he asked. Without warning Rona rushed up to him.

"I've always wanted to meet you," she said. "Mr Smithers often talked about you and the excellent product you supply. I am Rona Samuels and I'm...."

But as she did, and before she could complete her statement, she was grabbed by two of the bush-man's bodyguards. In a minute she was searched for weapons and slammed back into her seat. Dready, seeing what was taking place with Rona, decided to remain calm, and watched as Cindy was also searched by the bushman's friends. He waited to see if they would also search Christiana, but the bushman waved them to sit.

"Hello, I'm Rona Samuels," she said again, "and this is Dready Winston the buyer........."

" I know who you are bitch," he said. "Don't waste my time with trivial discussions. How much diamonds do you want?" he asked turning to Dready.

"As much as three hundred thousand American dollars will buy," said Dready as he retrieved his briefcase of money, "but I must first see and inspect them. I want a clean eye."

"Certainly," said the man.

He snapped his fingers and one of his henchmen brought a bag from the vehicle, spread a piece of cloth, emptied it the contents of the bag on the table and retreated to his position.

Dready began his inspection as though he knew what he was looking for.

"Mmmmm, good," he said.

"Where is the money?" asked the man.

"Right here," said Dready, reaching for the briefcase.

He handed it to the man who made the count to assure that it was correct.

"And where are you going to sell these diamonds?" asked the man.

"Well, it was supposed to go to Canada, but now I see that I could make more by taking it into Nassau first, allowing the price to double, then sell it on the German market," said Dready.

"But why?" asked the man. "We have a very good system up there?"

"Had my boy," said Dready. "Times are changing and I think it's time to bypass the cartel and establish some independent dealers. Your Old Boys Club and ideas are antiquated. They have been in business for a long time and now we want that action. Furthermore, most of them are either dead or in prison."

"Like whom?" asked the bushman.

"Karlheinz Bass, Ivan Burkowitz, Arthur Collins, Peter McKenzie, Lilly and Patricia Green and Harvey Ambross. Then there is Smithers, Wakefield, Hubert Bachstrum and....." said Dready.

"Okay, okay," said the man, "let's get this over with."

Everybody stayed quiet watching the process as Dready played for time, by looking at almost all the diamonds that were in front of him. When he was satisfied, he scooped the stones into the bag and got up from his seat.

"Good," he said, "I wish Peter and Olivia Bass were here, we could kill them and stuff their bodies with the goods and ship them to Germany."

"Are you a........?" the bushman began, but stopped himself. He looked at Rona and back to Dready.

"You are the police, aren't you?" he asked.

"Not really," replied Dready. "I'm a journalist, but I know all about your people in the Bahamas, Jamaica, Canada, Germany, England and America. Some of them are already dead, some will be shortly, and the rest are heading for a prison just like Burkowitz."

There was a long period of silence as the bushman contemplated his next move. He turned, looked at the strange man that sat beside Packus then at Packus himself.

"You fuckers sold me out, and that carries a penalty. Why the fuck did you bring me this police man?" he asked angrily. "Now I will have to eliminate them all."

"No! No! No!" shouted Rona, jumping from her seat again. "It was Smithers who put him up to it. I had nothing to do with it. It was Smithers and Hubert who brought him on board."

"Shut the fuck up, bitch," shouted Packus. "Now Edgar, who is this man and why did you bring him to me?"

"I didn't know he was a......." said Edgar, "and furthermore he took my taxi and asked me about the diamonds and I thought......."

"You don't think, arse hole," shouted Packus. "You were supposed to make sure of anybody you bring to me. Now you will have to suffer the same fate as they."

Dready looked across at Graves and Christiana, and realized that they were ready for action. He decided it was time to play his cards.

"I don't think that would be a wise move Ralph," said Dready. He paused to allow the bushman to digest this new wrinkle. "Mr Ralph Bachstrum, I presume? Everybody in Nassau thinks you are dead and yet here you are alive and well. Ladies and gentlemen, meet the famous Mr Ralph Bachstrum; the geologist who conveniently disappeared in Venezuela after his father's death in Florida. His brother, Hubert, control the distribution up there and is the murderer of some very important people. You were supposed to have died in the boat accident that killed your father, weren't you? Or maybe it was you who set it up?"

Dready could see that Ralph was becoming agitated and wanted to turn the dagger in some more. But before he could say another word, Ralph pulled his gun and pointed it at him.

"I could kill you right here and now, but I will leave that in the capable hands of my dear friend Packus and his men," he said.

Dready could hear the noises, as the police who were hiding in the bushes sprung to engage the bushmen's bodyguards. Everybody's heads turned to see the commotion. Dante, Edgar, Christiana, Cindy and Rona fell flat on the ground as the bullets from the police and the pork knockers came a blazing.

Dready leapt forward and latched on to Ralph, just as Bernard pulled and pointed his gun at Packus. Dready struggled for awhile but finally knocked out Ralph and slowly dragged him behind some bushes. Graves called for Christiana, Rona and Cindy to follow him to the front of the house. The shooting lasted for almost twenty minutes, because the bodyguards were quick to answer but the police were much faster and better.

A few minutes later it was all over. The Sergeant came around leading the ones that were wounded but alive, handcuffed.

"Five dead sir," he said, "and we have four in custody. One officer is wounded but will be okay. "

"Well done Sergeant," said Maraj. "Place them under arrest for questioning, some of them will tell us what's going on out here in the bushes."

By the time the police brought their vehicles into view, Dready had tied Ralph Bachstrum's hands behind his back.

"You'll be coming back to Nassau with me," he said, "I think Chief Daniels might want a word with you about the murder of your father Zenon. He might also want to hear about Mr Smithers and Wakefield. So ell me Mr Bachstrum, where are these diamonds destined for, and how do you get them out of this country?"

"Fuck you," said Ralph, and stayed quiet thereafter.

As they walked back to the river Dready laughed.

"Okay Winston," said Graves, "what's on your mind?"

"This bullshit," he replied. "All of this is part and parcel of the old colonialist implementation of their criminal activities throughout the Caribbean. The pirates of old operating with new technology and perpetrating the same old crimes. The Jamaican bridge club gang, once ruled by doctor Karlheinz Bass, has spread its tentacles into all the islands; and like an octopus it can move the tentacles in any direction, independent of any one else, and is willing to recruit the young ones to maintain it's involvement. But the head is stationary somewhere in the Caribbean and I have a damned good idea whose it is and where to find it."

303

Graves realized that Dready wasn't about to say any more until he completed his interrogation of Ralph Bachstrum, so he decided to wait for the explanation.

The trip back to Georgetown was long and boring. The silence was almost deafening for those who were eager to talk. Christiana sitting beside her husband in the van, cuddled up in his arms and fell asleep. Rona and Cindy rode in the other van with Maraj and his other police officers.

At the station, Dready watched as Captain Maraj secured Ralph Bachstrum and the others in separate cells. He knew that Maraj would release Dante and Edgar after it was assured that their reputation was still intact. He decided to get some sleep.

It was noon when his eyes opened. He felt relaxed after that lovely four hour sleep in the arms of his wife. He got showered and dressed before Christiana stir.

"Where are you going sweetheart?" she asked in a sleepy tone.

"Have to talk to a horse," he said. "You can stay in bed for a while longer if you like."

"Going to interrogate Ralph Bachstrum?" she asked.

"Yes," he answered. "Have a little work to clean up."

"Wait for me," she said and quickly jumped out of bed, "I don't want to miss this."

Dready sat in the chair at the window overlooking the sea-wall in thought while Christiana got showered and dressed. He reflected on the development since his wife spotted the newspaper article on Colin McKenzie, to now.

"Who is the octopus?" he asked himself. But before an answer could be obtained, Christiana awakened him.

"Ready," she shouted.

"Good," he replied and they walked out of the hotel into the streets.

An officer was standing outside waiting for them.

"Good morning sir," said the officer, "the Captain is waiting for you."

"Thank you," replied Dready.

Dready asked the officer to stop so that they could get a couple of coconuts; which they downed in a couple of gulps. They walked into the police station to see Elton Maraj and Bernard Graves standing in the foyer waiting.

"Good morning Elton, hi Bernard, lovely morning isn't it?" said Dready."

"Absolutely," replied Maraj. "Who do you wish to interrogate first, Ralph or Rona?"

Dready waited until he was served a mug of coffee before answering.

"Rona Samuels please," he said.

Maraj lead them to a room next to his office and they all sat.

"Bring in Mrs. Rona Samuels," said Elton Maraj to the orderly officer.

Within minutes the officer escorted her in.

"Hello Rona," said Dready, "I think your story will be a hit with the Canadian readers and I intend to make it an interesting one."

She looked at him in a sidelong glance.

"Maybe so," she said, "but after today I might not be alive to read it."

"Oh?" said Dready. "Afraid of your friends, eh? I presume you will be telling all then?"

"Yes," she answered. "I hope the courts will be lenient when it comes to my trial."

Dready looked at Maraj.

"I think something could be agreed on," said Elton.

They all watched as Maraj switched on the tape recorder.

"It's January 10th. 1997 and we are in my office talking with Ms Rona Samuels of Liverpool, England. Ms Samuels was charged with accessory-to-the fact after being in the company of Mr Ralph Bachstrum and Packus Bellows, two known diamond smugglers in Guyana. Present are Commissioner Bernard Graves of Jamaica,

Dready Winston, a journalist from Canada, and Christiana Felscher, RCMP. Now Ms Samuels, can you tell us what you know about the business and your connection to the arrested people."

"Well, to begin with," she said in a stern tone of voice, "I have been a courier for a lot of years, ever since I was introduced to Karlheinz Bass in Jamaica. My trips take me from England to Europe, to the Bahamas and occasionally to other parts of the Caribbean."

"How did you get involved?" asked Maraj.

"Some years ago....." Rona paused. "Can I get some rum and ginger?"

"You sure can," replied Maraj. He signalled for the orderly officer to accomplish the request.

"Go on," said Maraj, returning to Rona.

"I met Captain Smith in England and he invited me to have a holiday in Jamaica," she began. "At a party thrown by Karlheinz Bass, I met a man named Samuels whom I later married. But before leaving Jamaica, I was again invited to a meeting at Karlheinz's house and there I was propositioned to carry a parcel to England."

"And did you carry it?" asked Maraj.

"Yes I did," she answered, "and was paid handsomely for it."

"Did you know what it was?" asked Maraj.

"Yes, marijuana," replied Rona.

"Okay, go on," said Maraj.

"Well, I did the trip many times that year and half of the next but was given some time off. A few months later I was contacted by a Mr. Green," she said.

"What did he want?" asked Graves.

"He wanted me to accompany a man named Sanderson to the Bahamas to bring back some diamonds," she said.

"Did you?" asked Maraj.

"Yes I did," she replied, "only I had to return alone to England without escort."

"Why?" asked Dready.

"Don't know," she said. "Mr Sanderson told me that he want-

306

-ed to stay in the Bahamas to make a land purchase deal and that I should travel alone. He promised to contact me for the next trip. But when I got angry and insisted on an explanation, he told me that his daughter would be joining him in Nassau the following week and wanted to spend some time with her."

"What does he looks like?" asked Dready.

"He's a tall, skinny man with an handlebar moustache. He was an Olympic swimming champion; gold medalist I believe," replied Rona.

"Did you make other trips to Nassau?" asked Graves.

"Not for about a year," she answered, "but I was kept busy in London directing the younger women who came in from Jamaica."

"I see," said Maraj.

There was a long pause for everyone to refill their coffee mugs and Rona to fill her glass with rum.

"Then how did you know who the new couriers were? How did they identify themselves to you?" asked Dready.

"By codes," answered Rona.

"What kind of codes?" asked Dready.

"Simple ones that wouldn't attract attention," said Rona.

"Such as?" asked Graves.

"Well firstly, I would get a phone call from someone in London to inform me that a person was arriving at either Heathrow or Gatwick. I would go there with a sign that says, "Looking for the Mitchell, Bass or Green party," and the person would come to us."

"Wouldn't they have to use a password to identify you?" asked Graves.

"Certainly," said Rona. "The person would then say, 'I'm a sick jewel from the Bahamas and need to see a doctor immediately,' and I would say; 'Dr Bass is a friend of mine,' and directed them to whomever was the designated person in London."

"Then what would happen?" asked Dready.

"They would take a cab to the address I gave them and they would take care of things from there," she answered.

"Okay, now tell us about the diamond movement from the time it leaves Guyana," said Maraj. "We want to know where it comes from and where it goes to, and to whom."

Rona paused for a moment to gulp down some more rum.

"The diamonds are shipped from Guyana through Suriname to Trinidad or Jamaica then to Bahamas for shipment to Europe and North America."

"No, not that," said Maraj, "I want to know who, when and where."

Rona began to smile.

"For instance," she said, "Packus would get the message to Ivan, via the person we met on the sea-wall, as to when Ralph would be coming to deliver the goods. Ivan would send his purchaser up the river to make the deal. Packus would meet the person with the money, which would represent a months payment to them, and give him the diamonds. That person, along with their entourage, would take it to Aran Ali, known as the coolie man in Suriname, where it would be repackaged and shipped to his cousin Gasgaralli Ali in Trinidad. Gassy, as he's known, would then pack them in the belly of fishes, crate and ship them to the Bahamas."

"Do you know the name of the purchaser?" asked Maraj.

"No," answered Rona.

"Does it always work like this?" asked Dready.

"No," she replied. "Some times they would bring the goods directly to him here in Georgetown unannounced or to the Bahamas."

"Who would?" asked Maraj.

"Mainly Packus or whoever Ivan chose to do it," she replied.

"Where in the Bahamas?" asked Dready.

"Don't know, it could be anywhere," she answered. "All I know is they would leave in a boat and return later with the goods."

"But how?" he insisted.

"Packed in fishes, I've heard," she answered.

"What kind of fish?" asked Dready.

"How the hell should I know?" she said angrily. "A fish is a

308

fish."

She turned to face Dready.

"Remember the night Smithers invited you to come fishing with him?" she asked.

"Yes," responded Dready.

"Well, the next morning they were going out to retrieve some," she said, "and he only invited you to come along because he thought you were a dealer."

"And why did he think I was?" he asked.

"Because I said so," she answered.

"Thank you for attesting to my credentials," he replied, "but why did you do it?" he asked.

"Because I liked you and wanted to......." she said, paused and looked at Christiana, "....to screw with you, but you were too much of a gentleman to take advantage of me in my drunken state."

"I see," said Dready.

"That's when I suspected that you were a cop," she said.

"Then if you thought I was the police, why did you continue with it?" he asked.

"I wanted to end my relationship with them and didn't care what happened after all of it," she said.

"Well, to disappoint you, I'm not really the police just an investigative reporter," he said.

"I know that now, but at that time, all I wanted was a screw, but........" she said.

"How often did you go to Canada?" asked Dready.

"Only once," said Rona. "I have only been to Canada once, and that was to see Ludwig Felscher about a shipment that a young woman took there."

"When was that?" he asked.

"About four years ago," said Rona.

"What happened to the girl?" asked Dready.

"Don't know," she replied. "But I suspect that Harvey, who takes care of things up there, might have killed her."

"How?" asked Graves.

"He usually sends them on a vacation to the Caribbean and have someone kill them. It would be viewed as them wanting drugs and thus the end result," said Rona.

"Now," said Dready, "how deep is Cindy's involvement in the affairs?"

"Aaah Cindy," replied Rona. "Cindy is just a young girl seeking some thrills. We found her hanging out in London, after her car accident and hospitalization and decided to use her to carry the stuff. All she can remember is being born in the Bahamas but cannot remember anything about her parents. Her face was changed so that nobody there could easily recognize her."

"Do you know who her parents are?" asked Dready.

"No," said Rona, "and don't care either; but Smithers does."

Dready realized that there were no loyalty among criminals

"Okay," said Dready. "Tell me some more about the phone calls."

"A string of phone calls would be made by people who had never seen each other. First to Florida, then the person there would call someone in Jamaica. The person in Jamaica would call Toronto, and the message would be relayed to Nassau and wherever else they wanted the product to get to," said Rona.

"How?" asked Graves.

"It's like this," she answered. "When someone like Ivan passed the word, he would send the message out to the person we met on the sea-wall and code it like this, "It is the love of money that killed Karlheinz, but if you know Harvey Ambross call him.""

"Okay," said Dready, "so where is the code?"

"It's the name Harvey Ambross," she replied. "On the dial pad of the phone the numbers to the name Ambross, is 262-7677. All that is necessary after that is the area code to the places of the country you must call."

"So, Ambross is in every phone book in the western world."

"Damn right," she answered.

"So all the agents are given that number and a area code to call, and anyone who hears it will make the initial call and the chain reaction begins, right?" he said.

"Right," answered Rona.

"Everybody has a specific area code along with that number to call," he said.

"You got it," she said, "only you'll have to find out who and where they have to call."

"So who determines the area codes?" asked Dready.

"Don't rightly know," Rona replied. "All I know is that somebody decides the route and call the person in that loop, and the chain begins," she answered.

Dready got up and walked out of the room leaving Rona to complete her statement to Captain Maraj and Bernard Graves in the presence of Christiana. He wanted to look at the notes he had made while interviewing Ivan Burkowitz and to give some thought to what Rona told them. He was positive that the code was in there somewhere and he was intended to finding it before he spoke to Ralph. He also knew that there would be someone in Canada who would read his magazine and start the phone calling chain mentioned by Rona. He was also positive that someone in Guyana was a link to the North American gang. He was not sure what was the procedure to finding out who. When he got back to the room, he could hear Ralph shouting about his rights and refusing to talk to anyone.

"Fuck all of you," shouted Ralph, "I'm not telling you anything. If you want to make a case you'll have to do it on your own."

"Hello Ralph," said Dready as he entered the room.

"Who the fuck are you?" asked Ralph. "If you're the police, don't bother to ask."

"No, I'm not the police," said Dready. "As I have already told you I am an investigative reporter and I have just completed an interview with Mr. Burkowitz and wondered if I might speak to you in private."

The word private seemed to trigger Ralph's mind and he became willing to do so. Elton, Bernard and Christiana looked at each other in a knowing manner. They got up and left the room for the one with the two way mirrors.

"You see," continued Dready, "last year after I had written the piece on Karlheinz Bass, Arthur Collins and Peter McKenzie, my readers flooded the office with letters and phone calls asking for more. My editor, being the curious person he is, asked me to follow-up on the story and I was sent to the Bahamas to interview two men named Smithers and Wakefield. During one of those interviews, your brother Hubert's name came into the picture, and I went to speak to him; only to find that he was charged with multiple murder of two men and his father. Then someone, maybe Hubert, mentioned your name as one of the people who died on the boat that day, only your body was never found.

In the meantime the police had been investigating the diamond thing that included Ivan Burkowitz, and he mentioned your name to me in an interview a couple of days ago. Since I was there in Nassau and heard your name being included in the conversations, and believing that you were still alive in Guyana, I mentioned it to Captain Maraj when I got here, and here you are."

Ralph didn't know how to counteract Dready's statement and wasn't sure how much he knew, so he kept quiet.

"Then," said Dready, "Burkowitz kept telling me about a man named Harvey Ambross and insisted I print the name in the story as many times as possible. It was Captain Maraj who deciphered that it was a code to alert the gang members in America, Canada and other parts of the Caribbean. The name Ambross is the numbers, and the area codes are the places they have to call, am I right?"

Ralph sat there for along time with his mouth open.

"You've broken the code but word is already out about my arrest," he said, "and things will shut down."

"Not really," said Dready. "You see dear Ralph, all of your friends are in jail and the only news about you are in the hands of the police and mine; and I will not go to prison for your cause."

Dready could clearly see that he had Ralph flabbergasted and wanted to poke some more coal in the fire.

"Think about yourself first Ralph," said Dready. "You, being the boss, will be doing time either here in Guyana or in the Bahamas and they will be having a good time moving the diamonds to where ever, and collecting the money for themselves."

"I'm not the boss," said Ralph in a dejected tone.

"Then who is?" asked Dready.

"Don't know," said Ralph.

"Well," said Dready, "I think you are and I will tell the readers just that. Let them decide. It's either you or Ralston Weekes who ordered the killing of the students in Toronto."

Just then Elton Maraj and Bernard Graves came into the room.

"Mr Ralph Bachstrum," said Maraj, "you're under arrest for murder and will be taken back to Nassau to face those charges on Monday morning."

After Ralph was taken to the lock up leaving Dready, Captain Maraj, Graves and Christiana in the room, they talked about the plans to entrap the messengers in Canada, America and the Caribbean.

"We know the numbers and we have a damn good idea where the calls will be going," said Elton Maraj. "All we need now is the definite knowledge of whom and when."

"Yes," said Graves. "Why don't we ask the phone companies to tap into the lines of our calls to whomever, and then hear who they call?"

"Excellent idea," said Dready. "Let's begin with the call to Toronto. But first I must call Commissioner Dillon so that he can clear things up there."

"Good," said Graves.

Dready called Dillon and told him everything that was

313

planned and he agreed to make the arrangements in Toronto. Then Graves called Jamaica to do the same while Maraj called Trinidad for the same purpose. Dready asked Maraj to dial the number in Toronto knowing that the phone company would trace the call. Maraj dialled the Toronto number.

"Hello," said the female voice on the phone.

"It is the love of money that killed Karlheinz, but if you know Harvey Ambross call him," said Maraj.

"Okay, thank you," said the voice and hung up.

"Now comes the wait," said Christiana, "and I have a good idea that it will be concluded in Nassau."

"Maybe and maybe not," said Dready, "but let's wait and see."

It was, indeed, a long wait for the first call back from Toronto. After two hours they got the first return call assuring them that their plans were implemented and ready.

"Your call was answered by a Jean Malotello and her call went to a house on Old Hope Road in Kingston, and was answered by a man named Rodcliffe Tullouch," said Dillon. "Let's hope the people in Jamaica can get on his trail."

"Thanks," said Graves, "I will call to have him picked up immediately."

Within minutes the phone rang again, this time it was Graves people in Jamaica.

"Commissioner Graves please," said the voice.

"Speaking," answered Graves.

"Sir, this is Sergeant Mallet. A man named Rodcliffe Tullouch made a call to a Miss Sanderson in Tellahassee Florida," said the voice. "Do you want him picked up?"

"Yes, thank you, Sergeant Mallet," said Graves, "and keep him isolated."

"Right-o sir, consider it done," said Mallet and hung up.

The next call was from Chief Daniels in Nassau.

"Hi Bernard," he said, "we have been watching the house that owns the number you sent me and were present when the call came. It was to a fellow named Tullis Burke. He received a call from Miss Elaine Sanderson in Tallahassee Florida about twenty minutes ago; but since we already have him under wraps, I gently persuaded him to make his call, and he called the Wakefield's house in St Lucia. Want him kept in custody?"

"I thought you already had him in jail?" asked Dready.

"Yes I did," said Daniels. "But the judge didn't think we had enough to keep him and Amanda in jail, so I released them, but under surveillance."

"Please do," said Graves, "and call Florida to have them arrest Elaine also. Get her to Nassau for Monday morning, because we will be bringing you Ralph Bachstrum, Cindy Heron and Rona Samuels on Monday morning also."

"Good," said Daniels, "I need to see that man's face again."

"Better yet," said Dready, "why don't you meet us in Port of Spain on Sunday evening? We have a meeting set up with Kwami Singh of the fraud squad there and...."

"Good," said Daniels, "he might want to hear how the diamonds are moved through his country, but I cannot be there. I have some unfinished business to attend to here. Pirates."

"A round up?" asked Graves.

"That's right," replied Daniels, "and I want everybody."

"Right," said Graves, "see you in Nassau on Monday afternoon."

"Will Dready be coming also?" asked Daniels.

"No, he will be going on to Barbados for a few days," said Graves.

The phone was hung up after some goodbyes.

The flight into Port of Spain Trinidad, took thirty-five minutes from Georgetown and everybody felt happy to meet Kwami Singh. They greeted one another and loaded their belongings into the cars provided, while Ralph, Rona and Cindy were loaded into the prison-

315

er's vehicles separately and carted off to a jail cell.

"Welcome to my country," said Singh. "We all have something in common and that is a reason for us to better cooperate in the duties to bring about a decent life in our countries. Now tell me all about this business; I want to know how the diamonds and drugs are moved from country to country and the roll mine plays in it."

Dready sat quietly as Bernard Graves brought Singh up to date with the operation and the people involved. Including the pirates.

"The people in Suriname and Trinidad were bypassed this time because it seemed that there is a separate code for them, but we could create a back pressure if we make the call from here and have them believe that something is wrong and bring them out of their hiding," said Graves.

"I know about this Gasgaralli fellow and his brother Aran," said Singh, "but couldn't touch them all these years because of lack of evidence, until now. How are we going to do this?"

"Dial the number," said Dready, "and I will do the talking. But let's do it from a public box, I don't want any slip ups."

Kwami Singh had no problem leading them to the phone box outside the station. Dready got in and dialled the number.

"Hello," said the female voice on the other end.

"I would like to speak to Mr Gasgaralli Ali please," said Dready.

"Who should I say is calling?" the person asked.

"I'm a friend of Karlheinz Bass," said Dready.

"Just a minute," said the person as the phone was placed on a table.

"Hello, this is Gasgaralli," said the male voice.

"Hi Gassy," said Dready. "It is the love of money that killed Karlheinz, but if you know Harvey Ambross call him."

There was a long pause and Dready feared that he had blown it. But the individual answered.

"Yes I know," said Gassy, "he's a friend of mine also. But

what the hell are you doing in Trinidad?"

"Problems in GT," said Dready. " Ivan wanted a direct contact to bypass Aran in Suriname, so here I am."

"With the stuff?" asked Gasgaralli.

"Three hundred thousand American worth," said Dready.

Long pause again.

"Where are you staying? Give me the number and I will call you tomorrow to arrange a place to meet," said Gassy.

"Don't have a place and I want to be out of here by morning," said Dready, "so whatever you have in mind, you'd better do it early or I'll be leaving for Nassau with it."

"Okay, okay," said Gassy, "call me back in an hour and I'll have a solution to the matter."

"Good," said Dready and hung up.

They all looked at each other.

"He's going to call Suriname now to verify something and I hope he will ask Aran to come to Trinidad," said Singh, "I need him here."

The police officers sat in a restaurant over coffee, to await the expiration of the hour. But since it was almost dinner time they decided to eat as they wait. They spent the entire time planning out where, and how to react to the proposed meeting. Finally the time was up and Dready returned to the phone box to make the call.

"Hello," said Gasgaralli, "I will meet you at Macqueripe beach, do you know where that is?"

"No, but I will find it," replied Dready.

"I will meet you there at about ten tonight. Be there with the stuff," said Gassy.

"Right," said Dready.

He went back to the table and told them where and when the meeting would take place.

"Here's how it will go," said Singh. "You and I will travel together while my men will already be there in hiding. Graves, Maraj and Christiana can follow my men."

"Sounds good to me," said Dready, "but I would rather drive alone, because they will be watching to see who is in the car."

Singh agreed and disappeared into the station. In a little while he returned to tell them that five other officers would also be coming along.

"You've got to keep them out of the way," said Dready, "I must appear as normal to them."

"Will do," replied Singh, "you'll never know that they are there."

The three hour wait was spent between the restaurant and the station, and the conversation ranged from the diamonds, the people moving them, to police cooperation within the Caribbean. It wasn't until Dready mentioned the possible gun fire that Singh gave them arms.

They got into the cars and sped off to the designated area. Dready was the last to leave. He slowly drove to the place and parked as casually as possible, so as not to cause any suspicion. He lit a cigarette and waited. Finally, a car drove up. He could see the two men sitting in it. After a short wait, the two men came walking towards him. He got out of the car and began walking towards them with the briefcase in hand.

"Hello friends," said Dready, "I'm a sick jewel from the Bahamas and is in need of a doctor."

"You're in luck sir," said the tall African one, "I have a friend named Karlheinz Bass, maybe he could help you."

"Maybe he could," said Dready, " but I hear he's on a long vacation in Jamaica."

"I'm Gasgaralli and this is Castle," said the short Indian man. "Have you got the stuff?"

"Sure do," said Dready.

"Let's see it," said Gassy.

"In the dark?" asked Dready.

"I have good eye sight," replied Gassy.

"Good," said Dready, "Ivan told me that you do have great sight. Maybe that's the reason he wants to bypass Aran."

"He wants to bypass Aran? Why?" asked Gassy.

"I Don't know. Mr Burkowitz works mysteriously," said Dready. "Maybe he felt he was getting ripped off."

Just then a third man emerged from the car and came in their direction.

"This is my brother Aran," said Gassy. "Aran, I think Ivan is trying to cut us out of the business."

Dready recognized them as the two men he saw going into the house on Abaco.

"Why?" asked Aran of Dready.

"Well, from what he told me, he believed you two are working with Ralph and Hubert to take over the empire, thus the reason Wakefield and his wife, Smithers and Chrittendon was murdered. He believed that the Toronto man is also part of the takeover as well as Packus. But what he doesn't know is that I want a piece of the action also, and if things go right between us tonight we can have that deal in place."

Somehow, whatever he said seemed to spark the interest of the company and they appeared relaxed. He opened the briefcase and told them to turn on the car's headlights to see the diamonds.

"Yes," said Aran, "this could be a great amalgamation."

"And this, gentlemen, could be a long-lasting relationship that could take years to break," he said as the policemen appeared from their hiding places.

"You are all under arrest," said Singh. "I have been waiting for this day for a long time. Nice to meet you Mr Ali."

There wasn't any resistance, as they were handcuffed and led to the waiting cars.

"You will be joining the rest of your colleagues in prison," said Maraj, "and they have a damn good one in Guyana also."

When everything was concluded, Dready signalled Christiana to come. They both got into his car and left the others standing there, with the diamonds and cash.

"We can get a hotel in Port-of-Spain for the night," he said.

"Sounds good to me," she replied smiling. "We have to get working on the second child."

"As you say dear," he replied and stuffed her into the car.

The next morning Dready watched as the plane took off heading to Nassau with Bernard Graves, Christiana, Captain Maraj, Kwami Singh, Rona Samuels, Cindy Heron, Ralph Bachstrum, Gasgaralli and Aran Ali. He felt sad that his wife was leaving him again but knew that she and Graves could better enjoy themselves among the police in Nassau, than with him. He knew that they would wait until he got there before talking. He had some loose ends to tie up in Barbados and St Lucia and didn't want them there.

He got on the L 1011 Tri-star airbus for his 35 minute flight to Barbados. He sat in thought, anxiously awaiting his meeting with Mr. Wakefield in St Lucia; but first he must talk personally to a man in Barbados.

The plane landed. He slowly walked to the customs counter and was greeted by a short slightly-balding man. The customs officer checked his passport and allowed him a one week stay. He took his small overnight bag and walked out to the exit, amazed at the changes made to the Grantly Adams airport since his last visit five years ago. He signalled and a taxi pulled up in front of him.

"Where to sir?" asked the driver.

"To the Divi resort in St. James," he answered.

"That's a long way away," said the driver looking sheepishly at him..

Dready enquired of the man the about a clean hotel that was closer.

"Nothing is wrong with the Divi," said the man, hoping not to lose the fare.

Without hesitation the driver began a story about his country's history in Cricket, pointing out the names on each round-about as they passed them. The man's talk kept Dready's interest throughout the long journey across the country to their destination.

"The Divi sir," said the driver as he pulled up in front of the resort hotel.

Dready thanked him and quickly got checked in. It was nice of Bernard to use a friend's name to get him set-up there.

"Where can I find a phone?" he asked the desk clerk.

"Over there sir," she said pointing to the table in the foyer.

He checked the phone book and made the call. In a minute he was back outside asking the taxi driver to take him to an address in Christ Church.

"We just came from Christ Church," said the taxi man. "Why didn't you make your call from out there?"

"That's my business," said Dready. "Do you want the money or not?"

With that the driver kept quiet and drove back across the country to the address.

Dready knocked on the door and his friend emerged.

"Hey! Dready my boy! What's going on? Come in and tell me what you are doing in Barbados," said Egbert.

"I've come to seek your assistance, dear friend," said Dready. "I need the advice of a wise man in a case I'm involved with."

They were happy to see each other after all those years in the university in Canada. The two men hugged, talked and sized up each other. Finally Egbert introduced him to his wife and gave her a rough story of their friendship in school. It was agreed to go for dinner at St. Lawrence gap, so off they went in his friends car. They entered the Witch Doctor restaurant and ordered the drinks and food.

They talked about many things of their past and present involvement, while Egbert's wife, Joanne, talked about her teaching

321

job and the new attitude of the young children in her school. Finally, Dready began to talk about the case involving the diamonds and drugs smuggling throughout the Caribbean and about the prestigious cartel operating there.

"I am in search of the headmaster," he said.

"...and you think he is in Barbados?" asked Egbert.

"No, he's not here," replied Dready. "I know where he is but I would like to find out his background before confronting him."

"Then how can I help you?" asked his friend.

"I know that you have done some research on the old colonial families in the Caribbean," he said. "I mean, of the old plantation and slave owners. What I would like to know is how many of them are still in existence today and where are they living."

"Oh, that's easy," said Egbert. "Which one of the families do you want to know about."

"Let's start with the Wakefields," said Dready.

Without much thought Egbert was able to tell him about the plantation and slave-owner, Wakefield.

"Don't know how he came to Barbados," said Egbert, "but he did. He brought along his wife and two sons with him from England, claimed some land and began working our ancestors. His other two children were born here."

He talked about the father's friendship to Queen Victoria and to the eventual King George VI, and the many times he was house-guest at the palace.

"He became very influential with the British politicians after emancipation and had many of them stayed at his house here. He had three sons and a daughter," continued Egbert. "One of the boys died during a riot with the maroons in Jamaica in the 1890's, one got killed in WW I, the girl married a Lord and went back to England to live; leaving the youngest boy here. There are only two members of that family still living in Barbados. Most of the old ones have died and the young half-breeds are in England. The last son of the original Wakefield family is now 96 years old and lives in St Lucia; his name is Bartholomew Wakefield. He was once a world renowned geologist. His work in Brasil, Guyana and Venezuela is known the world over."

"Oh?" said Dready in a surprised tone. "Tell me about him."

Egbert gave thought to the question before continuing.

"Back in 1948 or '49, after the old man died, King George wanted to give Bartholomew a Knighthood," said Egbert, "but when he went to England for the ceremony he took along his German friend and somehow the King cancelled the event, citing that he Bartholomew was a Nazi sympathiser."

"Was he?" asked Dready.

"Don't know," replied Egbert. "All I know is that he took a man named Karlheinz Bass with him to England and it caused an uproar with the politicians there."

"So where did he meet this Karlheinz Bass fellow?" asked Dready.

"Don't know exactly," replied Egbert. "All I know is, he returned to Barbados for a while after the incident in England, and began exploring South America right after that."

"Maybe they met in Argentina," said Dready nonchalantly.

"Don't know," replied Egbert.

"Did Bartholomew have any children?" asked Dready.

"Many," replied Egbert. "His wife had three. One boy and two girls, but the house maids and other European women had children for him."

"Where are they now?" asked Dready.

"Don't rightly know," he answered. "I presume they are all around the Caribbean somewhere."

"Then what about the Weekes?" he asked.

"There are many of them here, which one specifically?" asked Egbert.

"I'm looking for one named Ralston; Ralston Weekes. Know him?"

"Certainly, he was one of the Jamaican Weekes." said Egbert.

"He was a big-shot representing Jamaica in England back in the sixties."

"Has he been back to Barbados lately?" asked Dready.

"Many times," said Egbert. "I've seen him many times at the government functions here. Is he one of your suspects?"

"No," said Dready, "but his brother is."

They left the restaurant and Egbert took Dready to the villa where they talked some more. After a couple of rums they decided to leave. As he walked them to the parking lot Egbert stopped.

"Did you know that Ralston Weekes was one of the bastard sons of Bartholomew Wakefield?" asked Egbert. "Yes sir, his mother was a Weekes from here. They went to Jamaica when he was a small boy, and that's where he grew up."

That piece of information seemed to surprise Dready and caused him to lose some sleep during that night.

He was up early in the morning, due to his restlessness that night, and decided to go for a walk along the beach to clear his mind. He was so engrossed in his thoughts that he didn't see the naked black woman lying on the deck chair, at the rear of one of the villas, until he was almost passed her. He said good morning to her but she pretended not to notice him, so he walked on. Finally, he got to a comfortable looking part of the beach, dropped his towel on the sand, ran to the water and plunged in. He swam out for a while then just as quickly swam back to shore, grabbed his towel and began drying himself. He pulled up a beach chair, opened it flat and lay on his stomach to relax.

It was the sweet, sexy voice of a female that startled him.

"Want me to dry your back?" she asked.

He looked up to see a topless, long-legged, black woman standing over him.

"Please," he said handing her the towel, unable to take his eyes off her breasts. "Were you the person......."

"...lying in the back yard? Yes." she answered beating him to

324

the question.

"What are you doing on the beach this early in the morning?" he asked.

"Waiting for a bus," she replied as she knelt beside him to begin wiping his back. "I was up early so I decided to come out to get some fresh air and to allow myself the privilege of walking naked along the beach. My name is Laska, what's yours?"

"Dready Winston and I'm a....." he began.

".......journalist," she completed for him. "I'm quite aware of who you are; a mutual friend already alerted me to your presence in Barbados. They sent me a copy of your magazine with your picture on it. So I waited here hoping that I would get to meet you."

"Why?" he asked.

"Well," she said, "I am a model, and hoped that you might be able to help me to expand my aspirations in America."

"I hate to disappoint you miss, but that is not my forte," he said. "I write crime stories about real criminals and their activities."

"I know that," she said grinning, "I've read your stories."

He was confused, and so there was a very lengthy pause.

"What do we do now?" he asked.

"Maybe you could take me to breakfast, then some shopping downtown and.....we'll see what life offers after," she suggested.

He looked at her firm breasts and the skimpy bikini.

"Fine," he said. "But I have to return to my room to get some clothes - as you will also have to do. Where will I meet you?"

"My car is parked across the road, meet you there in fifteen," she said.

Dready was surprised at the lovely woman's offer, which he was unable to refuse, and was anxious to hear more of how she knew he would be staying at the Divi.

The fifteen minutes expired. They got into the car.

"We are going to eat at the St Lawrence Gap," she said. "Ever been there?"

"No," he replied, not wanting to let on the number of times he had been there. They drove in almost silence.

About twenty-five minutes later she parked the car in the lot across the street.

"This is the Pieces Restaurant," she said, "and they have really great food."

They walked into the foyer of the all-wooden structure built on the beach, with one part hanging directly over the water, and was escorted up the spiral staircase to the dining area. He was impressed with the decor which he had seem every time he comes to Barbados.

"Why Laska?" he asked after ordering the drinks.

"Because my father couldn't spell Alaska," she explained.

They both laughed at her mis-adventure.

"So tell me Alaska, why were you waiting for me? Who sent you?" he asked.

"Please call me Laska," she said. "My brother called from Nassau asking me to escort you around Bridgetown to find a real pork knocker."

"Is your brother Lincoln Grey?" he asked.

"Yes," she replied.

He wondered how Lincoln Grey knew when he would be in Barbados, but decided to question that when he returned to Nassau.

"Pork knockers; are there such people in Barbados?" he asked. I thought they are found only in Guyana?"

"Yes they are," she replied. "But in Barbados you have to search for them."

The breakfast was consumed in a delightful light-hearted fashion and the bill was paid. The two new friends jovially left the Gap to explore the downtown shops. She parked the car and began the tour of the city on foot. After stopping at many different jewellery stores, including the Cave Sheppard, she directed him into a small shop in a side street. The place seemed empty.

"Can I be of help to you?" asked the voice from below the

counter.

They looked around wondering where the voice came from; then the man stood up. He was a short, bald-headed man in his mid sixties, with thick horned-rimmed glasses which sat at the very end of his nose; his clothes were thirty years out of date.

"I'm the proprietor," he said. "My name is Ovid Telfer. What can I offer you?"

"I'm looking for a pork knocker, do you know one?" asked Dready.

"Yes," replied Ovid, stretching out his hand for a shake. "I am the pork knocker you seek - retired of course."

"Good," said Dready. "Can I have a few words with you?"

"Certainly," said Ovid. "We can go up to the Nelson's Arms for a drink and a talk."

The man quickly closed the shop and they began their walk along Strand Street to the suggested place.

The waiter brought the beers and the trio toasted each other. Telfer quickly got into his story and held nothing back in describing the movement of illegal diamonds that come through his shop, by a white man from England with his two female mules.

"What do they look like?" asked Dready.

Ovid described Rona and Cindy. At this point Laska told of her experience of carrying the stuff to Trinidad and once to Jamaica.

"....then it happened," she said. "One day Mr Ali called for me to take a hot shipment to England that weekend. He told me to get caught and do a short prison term there to relieve the tension of the police surveillance, but I flatly refused to do it."

"Why?" asked Dready.

"I didn't want to go to prison," she said. "Furthermore I called Lincoln in Nassau and he advised against it. A short time later I was put out to pasture along with Ovid here, and now we're only used in emergencies like now."

"What happened this time?" asked Dready.

327

"Well," said Ovid, "about a week ago I got a call from Hubert in Nassau, asking me to get Laska to carry the stuff to them. I asked Laska to call her brother there to find out if there were any danger. He said 'yes,' and that's when he told us about you coming to Bridgetown."

"Is Lincoln one of them?" Dready asked.

"No sir, he an undercover cop in Nassau," said Laska. "The only people who know about him are Chief Donald Daniels and Mr Chrittendon."

"Where's Chrittendon now?" he asked.

"Dead," replied Ovid. "Somebody told me that he was killed and his body was buried in a house on Abaco island."

"Okay," said Dready. "So what is supposed to happen this time?"

"The meeting and exchange is slated to take place tomorrow evening at 9:30 at my shop," said Ovid. "Laska is to pick up the person from Guyana this evening and take him to a hotel in Christ Church, then tomorrow she will fetch the Trinidadian with the money and bring them both to the shop in the evening."

"How much do you get paid for this service?" asked Dready; wondering why these people were so willing to have their friends apprehended.

"Twenty-five thousand American cash," replied Ovid.

"Then why are you willing to give that up?" asked Dready.

"Because I want to see them bastards in prison," said Ovid.

"Why?" prompted Dready. "Care to tell me about it?"

Ovid looked at Laska then directly at Dready.

"Because they killed my wife, three children and my crippled father in a mid-night house fire," said Ovid.

There was silence, then when Ovid realized that Dready was waiting for some more details he said,

"About five years ago a man named Ralston Weekes offered to purchase my shop; when I refused, he threatened to kill all my children. I never thought he meant it and ignored his threat. A year later I was in Miami on business when I got the call telling me about the late-night fire which killed my entire family."

"Didn't you tell the police of Ralston's threat?" asked Dready.

"Yes, but they said I was mad to imply that a respectable person such as he could do such a thing," said Ovid. "Nevertheless, three young Rastafarians were tried and convicted for the crime."

"And what about you Laska? What's your reason?" he asked.

"I'm a cop," she said, "and have been working on this thing for two years. I couldn't get an angle until now. Thanks to you."

Dready saw no reason to question their loyalty anymore. The trio sat in silence for a long time; which was only broken when Laska said,

"I would like to take you for dinner at Blakey's tonight after I've done my chore. You deserve it."

"Where is Blakey's and what kind of food they serve?" he asked.

"Don't worry," she replied, "the food is excellent."

He had no reason to doubt her and silently agreed. They parted company with thought of capturing the two culprits who were coming tomorrow evening to do business with Ovid. She took him back to the resort where he excused himself for some rest, until she came back for him at 8:30 that evening.

She was dressed in a very short skirt and a tight low-cut top, which allowed her firm breasts to be exposed more than they should. Her hair was done and he realized that she had spent some time at the hairdressers that afternoon.

They got into the car and she sped along the coastal highway to St. Lawrence Gap, then followed the winding road, passing many restaurants along the way, to Blakey's. He had not been there before and found it to be a lovely, locally owned, comfortable and relaxing place. They had dinner outside under the umbrellas while the soft romantic music soothed their souls.

He sat across from Laska wishing that she was Christiana but felt very comfortable in her company.

"Tell me Laska," he said, "what made a pretty woman like you get into the police business? It's not customary for beautiful girls to do this sort of thing."

She chuckled, took a bite of her fish then said,

"It was a matter of conviction - a sort of loyalty to my country. You might say I'm a patriot who despises any kind of criminals doing illegal business in my country."

"Oh," he said, "I thought you might have had a bad experience as a child and wanted to get revenge by doing this."

Not really," she answered. "But I've seen and heard enough to understand that there is a need to put some of these people out of business."

After dinner, Laska strongly suggested they spend the night together, and he didn't have the heart to refuse her.

When the morning sun blazed into his eyes, he got up and awakened her.

"Come on my dear," he said, "you do have some business to conduct at the airport this morning."

Quickly she got up, showered and hurriedly dressed to carry-out her chores. She kissed him goodbye and rushed off.

He stood at the plate-glass window looking out to sea thinking of the enjoyable night he had spent with Laska, and wishing it had been Christiana. He wanted to tell her last night of his wife and child but doing so might have jeopardized his cover, which was skilfully provided by Graves. As far as Laska and Ovid knew, he was a journalist/diamond dealer from Nassau working for the police; and it seemed to be working.

He checked the time, quickly grabbed his towel and rushed down to the beach for a dip. The deck chair, placed under a tree in the shade, provided a relaxing bed for a snooze which lasted two and a half hours. When he woke, he realized that he had not had breakfast as yet and ran back to the villa to shower. He got dressed in shorts and tee shirt then rushed down to the gates for a taxi.

"Where's a good place to eat?" he asked the man.

"The Coach House is just down the road sir," said the driver. "They have good food there."

"Fine, it's the Coach House then," he said.

The Coach House was a very comfortable, outdoor patio type restaurant, with a couple of gazebos for eating. The bar occupied the entire back-wall of the building and was attractively displayed. The waiter came and took his order of rice and peas, flying fish and fried plantains. He noticed that some of the helpers kept looking out at him without saying anything.

"Good afternoon sir, my name is Elaina, the assistant manager here," she said. "It's so nice to have a known writer like you dining in our humble restaurant. If there's anything you need, please call on me I would be delighted to get it for you."

He wondered how the woman knew who he was, but didn't ask.

"Thank you Elaina, I'll defiantly remember that." he replied and continued to eat.

She was back about fifteen minutes later.

"Anything else sir?" she asked.

"I would like some corn pone please, if you have it," he said.

The assistant manager rushed off and brought it to him personally. After his very enjoyable brunch, and some prompting from her, he promised to be back later that evening for dinner.

He left the Coach House and began his walk towards the Divi. He needed to walk to have some solitude for his thoughts. It wasn't until he reached the Chefette that he realized that he had passed the Divi and the distance he walked to where he was.

He saw a Dreadlocks Rastaman selling coconuts in a parking lot across the street.

"Hail Dready," he said as he approached the cart.

"Hail high Far I ja," replied the man. "Jamaican?"

"Yes High, but this is yard also," he said. "Gimme a good jelly; I man is thirsty."

The man chopped the fruit. They talked for a long time about the ridiculous persecution of the law for doing what he considered as making an honest living, and the teachings of the bible in which the Babylonians were not living up to. He was so engrossed in his conversation, he didn't realize the time had passed so quickly. It was now 6:45 p.m. He excused himself from his brother's presence and hurriedly walked back to the resort.

The phone rang as he entered the room.

"Hello," he answered into the mouth piece.

"Where have you been?" she asked. "I have been calling since 2:30."

"Why?" he asked to be facetious.

"Because I wanted to come back to you and resume........" she began but cut short her statement. "I will be there in about twenty-five minutes."

He hung up the phone and lay on the bed to meditate.

Laska knocked on the door precisely at 7:10. He realized that she was a very punctual woman.

"Are you ready?" she asked.

"We only have a few minutes to eat before going to the shop to meet those fellows," she said. "Furthermore, I would like to tell you their names and their business prior to getting in there."

"Fine," he replied. "Maybe we could eat at the Coach House down the road then leave from there."

"Fine with me," she said as they entered the car.

The drive to the restaurant took five minutes. He noticed that Elaina wasn't as pleasant now as when he was first there, and treated Laska with contempt.

"Is she your friend?" he asked.

"Sister," replied Laska.

"Did you tell her about me?" he asked.

"Yes," she replied.

"Why?" asked Dready.

"Just to make the bitch jealous," she answered with a grin.

Dready was astonished, but decided to conclude the discussion on the pretext that he never understood women.

"Now," said Laska, ignoring Elaina's attitude, "we have to be prepared for anything with these boys, so I have a gun in the car for you."

"What's their names?" he asked.

"The one from Trinidad is Walborough (Wally) Costas and the fellow from Guyana is David DeFreitas," she answered.

Dready smiled to know that his man David, who wanted him to believe he was totally innocent, was there to conduct some illegal business.

"What time are you bringing them to the shop?" he asked.

"At nine-thirty," she replied.

"Good, you can drop me off downtown before fetching them," he requested.

Laska sped to the downtown area, let Dready out and took off to complete her task.

He stood across from Ovid Telfer's jewellery shop, watching. He saw when Laska drove up and parked in the space where Ovid had placed the no parking sign earlier. David was the first to emerge from the vehicle as though he was in a hurry; then came Wally. Laska and the two men, with their briefcases in hand, entered the shop without looking in any other direction than ahead. In his mind, Dready knew they felt confident by Laska's assurance that all was clear. He waited another ten minutes to ensure that everything was laid out before crossing the street.

"Good evening gentlemen," he said, on entering the shop.

The look on David's face was as though he had been hit by a

hammer or seen a ghost.

"What are you doing here?" asked David.

"Well, I told you I had to make a deal somewhere; and this is it," said Dready.

He could see that Ovid and Laska was just as surprised. There was total silence.

"This is Wally Costas," said DeFreitas in a dejected tone.

"Well, it's nice to meet you Wally," said Dready, "I didn't know about you until now. But David," he said turning to the man from Guyana, "you assured me that you had no knowledge of Ivan Burkowitz or Ralph Bachstrum, yet here you are making their deal. You will have to come to Nassau to testify or else face charges here."

DeFreitas gave it some thought.

"Okay, I will," he said in a nervous tone.

"What about you Wally?" asked Dready.

"Whatever David says, goes for me," said Wally. "Although I would really like to know what's going on."

"I'll tell you later," said David.

"Okay Laska, you can arrest them now and escort them to Nassau tonight," he instructed. "The flight leaves at 12:45 a.m. Don't miss it."

Just then Laska produced two sets of handcuffs and placed them on their wrists. She checked her watch and saw that it was 10:20 She called her boss and then the airport to arrange for the seats.

"Gentlemen, it's eleven thirty. I would advise you to have a piss now because when we get to the airport, nobody will be allowed to do so."

Ovid quickly locked and secured everything about his shop then joined the others in the car for the ride to the airport.

"Are you not coming?" asked Laska of Dready.

"No," he replied, "I have some business in St Lucia. But I will meet you in Nassau in two days time."

He stood at the corner of Strand and Leslie Streets to watch as the car slowly disappeared down the roadway. He was happy for the arrest in Barbados. He knew that Laska and Ovid would secure the prisoners on the flight to Nassau. Quickly he took a cab to the Divi to make his calls to Commissioner Dillon in Canada and Commissioner Graves in Nassau. He told them all that went down and whom to expect in Nassau.

"And where are you going next?" asked Graves.

"I'm leaving for St Lucia in the morning and will be in Nassau the day after, in the afternoon."

"Good," said Graves, "see you."

The early morning St Lucian air was refreshing to Dready as he left the Vigie airport in Castries. He signalled the taxi driver from across the street.

"Where to sir?" asked the man.

"I have to see someone in the hills," he said, "but first take me to a hotel downtown."

Without hesitation the man sped to a clean looking hotel and waited until Dready checked in.

"To the hills please," said Dready, "I must see a man."

"Whom might that be sir?" asked the driver.

"I have to see a Bartholomew Wakefield," said Dready. "Do you know him?"

"Certainly sir," said the taxi driver, "everybody in St Lucia knows that family."

The man began telling about the respectable family.

"... except for some of the younger ones," he said. "They have become a thorn in that old man's side."

Dready listened to everything the man had to say about the Wakefields as they drove up the winding road to an area designed especially for the rich. Finally he stopped in front of a large house, which was set back deep in the extra large and beautifully manicured gardens.

He paid the driver and entered the yard hoping that there weren't any mad dogs lying in the bushes. He rang the bell and within a minute a woman opened it to him. She was a mixed black woman in her mid to late sixties, who seemed to have control of the entire household.

"I am Dready Winston, the journalist," he said. "Mrs Ursella Billings I presume? Mr Bartholomew Wakefield please," he asked.

The woman stretched her hand to him.

"Come on in Mr. Winston," she said opening the door wider. "It's nice to see the face after talking to the person on the phone. I am the curator of this castle, manager and nurse maid to this king."

He entered the large livingroom where the walls were adorned with paintings of family members and royalty.

She led him to a patio at the rear of the house where an old man was sitting.

"Hello sir," he said taking the boney, wrinkled hand of the ninety six year old man. "Sorry to be a nuisance, but I had to come to meet you personally. I've heard so many good things about you and your work, I would hate to be in St Lucia and did not meet a man of your stature."

The old man wasn't even conscious of his being there.

"He cannot hear a word you say," said the woman, "and I told you so a week ago when you phoned. Remember I told you that I don't know any of the people you mentioned?"

"Yes you did," said Dready, "but please understand my desire to meet the man I believe to be the world's greatest geologist. It's a pleasure to shake his hand, and to let him know that his work is still being carried on in Guyana, Venezuela and Brasil."

The aged nurse was very grateful and happy that someone had come to the house to talk.

"Would you stay for lunch Mr Winston?" she asked. "It would be a pleasure to make lunch for you."

"Thanks, but no," he said, "I have another appointment in town this afternoon and promised to have lunch with that person."

"That is a shame," she said. "We don't get many visitors to

the house anymore. None of his old friends come around much, except Mr Weekes, who comes here once a week to answer the telephone."

"Good, at least one person does," he said grinning. "Where does Mr Weekes live?"

"About a mile down the road there," she said pointing in a general direction.

"Is there any way you could call him for me?" he asked.

"No, he doesn't have a phone at his house; thus the very reason he comes here to use ours," she answered.

"When will he be coming back here?" asked Dready.

"Maybe this evening or tomorrow," she replied.

"Good," he said, "I will call him this evening or tomorrow then. Thank you for the hospitality."

He rushed out of the house and got into the taxi and within a few minutes he was back in front of the hotel. Dready went to his room, showered and lay on the bed for what seemed like an hour, but which turned out to be six. It was the best sleep he had, had for the last three weeks. He got dressed and went outside to find a restaurant and found the taxi man waiting.

"I would like some good home-cooked food," he told the driver.

"Not a problem sir," said the driver, "I know a great place."

"Lead on my friend," said Dready.

The man pulled up in front of the small restaurant and directed Dready in.

"I can't stay with you, I have a fare waiting," said the man.

He sat alone in the restaurant and had a wonderful dinner. His solitude was enough to allow him time to think about the entire case scenario and the approach he intended on taking to prove his case to the rest. He was now sure who the head of the octopus was and knew exactly where to put his finger on the person.

He got back to the hotel and made the call to Wakefield's house.

"Hello," said the male voice.

"Hello sir," he said, "I have a message for you from a friend in Guyana."

"And what message is that?" the voice asked.

"It is the love of money that killed Karlheinz, but if you know Harvey Ambross call him."

There was a lengthy pause, then the voice answered.

"I heard he is on a long vacation in Jamaica," said the man.

"Ralston Weekes, I presume?" asked Dready.

"Precisely," said the man, "and what commands this call?"

"You're summoned to a meeting in Nassau," said Dready, "but if you want more details meet me in town at King Ralphie's Restaurant and I will up-date you."

"I'll be there in fifteen minutes," said the man.

Dready hurried across the street and along the road to the restaurant, and waited. He counted the minutes since the call, to the time of the man's arrival, and it was exactly seventeen minutes.

Ralston Weekes was a fat, clean-shaven, slightly balding man of medium height with a large paunch. His obviously capped teeth seemed too large for his mouth, and his ears moved whenever he spoke. Dready smiled because he had 'conned' the man into meeting him.

"Okay, here I am, start talking," said the man.

"Are you Ralston Weekes?" asked Dready.

"Sure am," Weekes answered.

"Well, I must be certain, so I will ask you a few questions to be sure," said Dready.

"Ask away," said Weekes.

"Who was Peter McKenzie?" asked Dready.

"He was the president of the Bridge Club in Jamaica," Ralston answered.

"Good,"he said. "Now, what was the real name of Arthur Collins?"

"Lyle Alexander," he said angrily. "Let's stop this foolish charade and get on with the task at hand. They wouldn't send you directly to me unless there was something important going on."

"Ivan Burkowitz told me to call you personally, and to thoroughly check the codes to be assured that you were authentic," said Dready. "You see, there seems to be a hole in the foundation and things are beginning to get wayward. He believes that some people; some pirates, have penetrated our system and are deliberately diverting our goods for their benefit."

"Where is the hole and who does he suspect?" he asked.

"Don't know, but Rona Samuels and Hubert Bachstrum are getting nervous, and demanded an emergency meeting in Nassau tomorrow evening. They have eliminated a few people but it didn't stop the flow, so this meeting is to think out a new direction."

'I thought something was wrong!" said Ralston. "When I didn't get the usual call from Amanda I realized that something has gone wrong," he stated. "Last time when she did, she told me some cock-and-bull story about being arrested along with Hubert; although she was only questioned and released."

"Maybe that was to divert your mind," said Dready. "Maybe she is the one taking over. I heard that Ralph is back in Nassau also, is that true?"

Ralston gave thought to the question and quickly decided to go to Nassau with him.

"Nobody told me," whispered Ralston. "There's something going on, which I really don't understand. I want to be there to hear from the horses mouths directly; and you beside me just in case you are lying," he said.

"Not a problem sir," said Dready. "I would prefer to work for you rather than any of those women. We could leave on the first flight tomorrow morning."

"Good," said Ralston Weekes, "I will meet you at the airport at nine o'clock in the morning."

Dready sat there watching as the overweight man lumbered

out the door to the streets, and smiled to know that Mr Weekes had not connected him to the case in Jamaica, which saw the down-fall of his age old Bridge Club gang and his two sons.

"Got you, you bastard," he whispered as he dug the spoon into his bowl of cherry flavoured ice cream.

Chapter Twelve

The Octopus:-
"One Brain and Eight Tentacles."

*T*he flight from St Lucia to Nassau was only about
an hour long, so Dready took a window seat to look at the islands
below; and all the way there Ralston kept quiet. He never spoke a
word to the man who was his escort and had introduced himself as a
friend. In his mind, he was sure that there was something sinister
about Dready but didn't know what. He was angry to know that
someone somewhere was up to no good and wondered if Dready was
the one. Nevertheless, he did use the proper codes to get him to come
with him.

They landed at the Nassau Airport and Dready insisted they
had breakfast before going to the meeting, which was slated to be
held in the conference room at the Crystal Palace Hotel. Earl picked
them up on time, drove to the British Colonial Hotel at Dready's
suggestion and escorted them into the restaurant area.

"This is a fine place and the food is good," said Earl.

They sat, and in a few minutes, ordered the breakfast. During
all that silence, Dready noticed that Ralston kept a sidelong distrust-
ful stare on him.

"What's happening Ralston, don't you think I'm genuine?" he
asked.

341

"I'm not sure what's going on fellow, but........" he paused, "I presume I will find out soon."

"You sure will," said Dready nodding his head in acknowledgement and they completed the breakfast in total silence.

"Come on Earl, take us to the Palace," said Dready. "I think Mr Weekes is anxious to see his friends."

As they walked through the bar area, Dready stopped to greet Lincoln Grey, the bartender and undercover-police friend.

"What's the word?" asked Linc.

"Good. You might get some satisfaction from it, but I can't tell you now. Let's hook up later," he replied.

"Fine, where?" asked Linc.

"Meet you in Carmichael this evening,"said Dready. "Can you make it?"

"Definitely will," replied Linc. "See you later."

They shook hands and quickly entered Earl's taxi, who wasted little time getting to the Crystal Palace.

Dready opened the door to look in at the crowd. They all sat in a theatre style setting in the conference room awaiting his arrival. He thought it was a nice setting, because it allowed him to see everybody's face wherever they sat. They all had concerned expressions on their faces; yet seemed cool and collected. They were curious about the empty chair immediately to the right of Daniels, but didn't ask any question.

At the centre of the large table sat Chief Daniels. Beside him to his left sat Commissioners Dillon and Graves. Christiana sat beside Graves. In the audience, the chair directly across from Daniels was occupied by Althea Bass, nee Wakefield. To her right were detective Jack Colly, Hubert, Ralph and Amanda Bachstrum. There was an empty chair beside Amanda Bachstrum. In the row behind them sat Gasgaralli and Aran Ali with Frazier Hendicott, his wife Sasha, Robert Reynolds, Clinton Reeves, Rupert Abbot, Rona Samuels, Cindy Heron and Mr. Phillips. In the back row directly behind them were David DeFreitas, Walborough Costas and the three white men he saw at the house on Abaco. Captains Maraj and Singh sat in the very back row with Ovid Telfer, Laska, Dante and Edgar. Off to one side of the room sat Tanya McKenzie, Cynthia Mason, Elaine Sanderson, Edith Muir, the voodoo woman, and Tullis Burke. Behind them sat Sonny and two others. He smiled to know that the phone calls brought out all the interested ones. Earl Monroe joined Tanya and the rest in the corner.

He was happy that Daniels had rounded up the people he had been investigating all these years. He was already told that most of the underlings of the Nassau gangs were already charged and in a jail.

Just then Graves handed him two letters. He opened the first one which was from Jeremiah Bailey, read and refolded it then placed it in his pocket. He read the contents of the next one.

Interpol, London. Subject:- Garfield Smith, some times uses his father's name, Captain Byron Smith, when travelling. Not found in England. It is believed that he is either in Canada or the Caribbean, mainly Bahamas.

Features:- 5 foot 9, bald with bark brown eyes and handlebar mustache. Excellent angler.

Subject:- Smithers; Devon farmer. Missing since 1990. Wife believes he has run away to Germany with a younger woman.

Features:- 5 foot 9, dark-brown to black hair, white streak in the middle, handlebar moustache and smoke a pipe.

Sorry no more info.

Dready smiled.

"Did you check with Commissioner Dillon?" asked Dready.

"Yes," replied Graves. "He is waiting to tell you."

He allowed Ralston Weekes to walk in ahead of him, Weekes stopped in his tracks, surprised to see the number of people in the room, some of whom he recognized.

"What the hell is all this?" asked Weekes when he entered the room.

"A wake my friend," said Dready. "Your wake. Good after-noon ladies and gentlemen. We are gathered here to pay homage to Mr Weekes here and to congratulate some of you for the fine efforts you've made in your lives."

Nobody answered so he directed Ralston to the vacant chair beside Amanda and indicated for him to sit.

"Firstly, I must introduce myself; I'm Dready Winston, the crime investigator who wrote the story about some of your colleagues in Jamaica last year. I know you're all wondering why you are called to this meeting at such short notice; so I won't waste too much of your valuable time. The story I'm going to tell you is about some modern day pirates and an Octopus. It won't take long to describe, but the suspense I hope, will thrill you to death," he stated.

Nobody answered, so he continued.

"It really began right after Columbus came to the Caribbean in 1492. His brother, Bartholomew, returned later bringing some cut throat criminals to inhabit these islands, as well as some African slaves to do their work. Meanwhile, the British and Dutch had also got involved in the slave trade, transporting these innocent Africans through the middle passages to a degrading life in America and the Caribbean. In the process of transporting the slaves, some of these swashbuckling men became Buccaneers and began hijacking one another ships for the wealth they possessed. Those criminal activities manifested themselves in these islands, and in later years included some of the African offsprings.

I would like to take your minds back to the 1950's. It's a time when a group of friends in a bridge club in Jamaica, felt their hold on that country would wane if it were to become independent from England. They decided to formulate a cartel for the purpose of smuggling marijuana and diamonds to Europe. It was head by Dr. Karlheinz Bass, Captains Smith and Green, Colonel McKenzie and Mr Ralston Weekes here, who was then aide to Lord and Lady

Brimley.

     Karlheinz Bass, a German who went to South America from his birth country, met and befriended a man named Bartholomew Wakefield of Barbados, who was in South America doing some geological explorations. Somehow he got Wakefield to invite him and his family to Barbados, where he met Wakefield's family and somehow convinced them to assist him in getting around the Caribbean. Their friendship grew strong and Wakefield told Karlheinz all about the diamonds and gold he had discovered in Guyana. But that friendship eventually cost Wakefield a chance for knighthood, when someone in the British government accused him of being a Nazi sympathizer. He became despondent with the government and settled into his exploration business.

     When the Caribbean confederation talks began, the British government asked Bartholomew to take part in it, but he cared less for the potential financial loss he might suffer and assisted Karlheinz to go to Jamaica to set up his practice.

     A few months later, Karlheinz moved to Jamaica from somewhere in South America and took with him the plastic surgery skills he had perfected some time before and brought along with him from Germany, a list of dead people's names and their identifications. He became Wakefield's mentor, and was able to dictate what the very respectable Englishman's life was to become.

     When the suggestion of forming the cartel was brought to his attention, Karlheinz wanted to pattern it off the system applied by the pirates of old, who used to roam the Caribbean sea. So when they began operating, Karlheinz went to see his friend Bartholomew, who had already moved to St.Lucia from Barbados, and told him about the planting of people throughout the Caribbean for that very purpose. Bartholomew got upset and wanted to scrap the idea, but Karl was able to convince him to form an import and export company to move the goods out of Guyana to St Lucia and on to the Bahamas.

     Bartholomew did, and placed his eldest daughter in charge of the new company. Karl was delighted and very instrumental in setting up the company. He also convinced Amanda to move to the Bahamas to open a subsidiary of the Wakefield company to carry out the business there. In the mean time he began bringing many of his criminal friends from Europe to Jamaica. He changed their faces and gave them new identifications and dispatched them throughout the Caribbean; thus a very strong gang came to fruition. The beauty of it all was that, nobody knew about each other and their only connection was by telephone codes, which were conducted through Bass only. He also brought his two brothers, Hoss and Peter, from Germany. Hoss face was changed and he was renamed Zenon Bachstrum, and was planted in Nassau. Karl also arranged for Zenon to meet and marry Amanda Wakefield and Peter got married to Althea.

Amanda and Zenon had three children, namely, Hubert, Ralph and Bernice to begin the Bachstrum family in these islands. Zenon began moving the diamonds, which were coming in via Burkowitz, through his father-in-law's company, to his brother in Jamaica. He formed a security wall around himself by befriending some politicians and the chief of police to redirect any suspicion from himself."

At this point people began to shuffle in their seats and looking at each other. Dready could see a questioning look in the eyes of Mr. Hubert Bachstrum when he mentioned the dead Chief.

"Yes sir," he said looking directly at Hubert, "I know all about your relationship with the Chief and how he killed himself after being caught by the US coast guards. I heard all about how you, your father and your brother got off, claiming that you had been with him for a pleasure cruise. It's a very frustrating thing for a jury not to hear the facts from the man in charge, and had to let you off. The question is; was the Chief forced to do it or was he paid for it?"

Nobody answered.

"When Captain Green went back to England he convinced an old army friend to join him. The flamboyant Mr Mitchell became the leg-man in Europe, while McKenzie and Green controlled England. Mitchell eventually murdered McKenzie and had his boys killed Mr. Green so that he could take over the entire operation there. The North American market was then controlled by Karlheinz Bass and Captain Smith along with his new man, Lyle Alexander, aka Arthur Collins.

During the next year, there were many problems within the cartel and some were even murdered for challenging the leadership of Karlheinz Bass. He decided to change things around so he brought Mitchell to Jamaica and transformed him into Ivan Burkowitz.

Burkowitz was then placed in charge of the diamond smuggling business in the Caribbean, doing the purchasing and distributing and worked between Guyana, Trinidad, Bahamas and Jamaica. He was one of the few people to know who was who in the business.

Things went well until one very sad night when an eight-month pregnant woman named Arlene Felscher, was murdered in Jamaica. This was on the orders of Bass and was implemented by Arthur Collins. And the reason to kill her? Simply because she refused to carry the shipments to Canada. Also, because they thought she wrote things in a diary about them and threatened to published it. I'm sure Mr Weekes could tell us more about this. The murder of Arlene Felscher, began a series of changes within the cartel. Green and McKenzie was murdered in England because of that diary. Smith was killed in Jamaica for the same reason. With the support of Lilly and Patricia Green, Barbara Smith, Harvey Ambross and Peter McKenzie, Collins was able to wrestle the leadership from the aging Karlheinz Bass and he began searching for that same book; which became his down fall."

Everybody sat quietly listening to the story as though they were hearing it for the first time.

"Last year," said Dready, "the daughter of that dead woman went to Jamaica and demanded the case of her mother's murder be reopened; and in so doing, the police stumbled upon the cartel and it's international implications. They found out about the murders of

Smith, Green and McKenzie. In order to cover up the fact, Collins ordered the killings of Karlheinz Bass, Lilly and Patricia Green, Orville Chung, Sargent Malcolm Richards, Venrece Alexander, Tanya McKenzie, Rosita Ambross, Christiana and myself. He employed Sultan and Ralph Weekes, the two sons of Ralston Weekes, to do the job, but had two others doing the actual murders; namely the Lenois cousins, Peter and Jaques; who became Langley Peters and Juiles Thasault. They were all caught.

That brought about the downfall of that empire where Collins were sentenced to five life terms, Burkowitz was given a twenty-five years stretch in Guyana, Patricia Green and Barbara Smith got life while many residing in Europe were arrested, tried and sentenced to different terms of imprisonment in their respective countries. They also lost their number one killer in Harvey Ambross, who is now in a Canadian prison serving a double life sentence."

"So what the fuck has that got to do with us?" asked Hubert, getting to his feet.

"I'm getting to that, my dear boy," answered Dready.

"Just shut up Hubert and listen," said Ralph, "because after this, I intend to sue the entire police force and the government of the Bahamas."

Dready nodded his head.

"Firstly, the deaths of Colin McKenzie, Salina Mason, Celia Bachstrum, Zena Hendicott and Robert Reynolds, the five students who were murdered in Toronto, caught the attention of Christiana and sparked our interest and as to why they were classified as suicides when they were clearly murder.

Commissioner Dillon had the investigation turned over to us. Christiana noticed that there was nothing mentioned in the autopsy reports about the position of the murder weapon; but when she asked the landlords, they were able to tell her where the knives were in each case. That might seem like an oversight to some, but to me it was in fact a fatal mistake, that was deliberately done to confuse the issue.

A mistake like that might happen in one case perhaps, but not in five deliberate murders. We were also able to connect Colin McKenzie to Peter and Tanya of the Jamaica incident.

A curious search of the students homes and their belongings turned up the fact that they were all residents of the Bahamas studying in Canada. We found a list of many friends from other parts of the Caribbean and Europe; also some diamonds in Robert Reynolds and Celia Bachstrum's apartment. After questioning their landlords, we discovered that they were berley able to pay their rent, yet they were quite able to travel to Nassau regularly. Those young people were the real jewels of the Bahamas.

Again the question of why the police didn't do a thorough search of the student's residence, came to mind. At first, we thought it was someone in the Toronto area who was the real culprit and who was murdering these youths as a cover. But a letter found in one of the students possession, was signed by a TB in Nassau, indicated that there were some connections to this city and the diamonds.

In consultation with Commissioner Dillon, it was agreed to set up a shipment from Nassau by using Christiana as the mule and to watch who got involved. He made a phone call to Chrittendon here, which was taken by another person. He told the person that she was Ludwig Felscher's daughter and wanted to make contact with the TB in Nassau. The person assured him that it would be done and that the contact would meet her at the airport. It turned out to be Mr Tullis Burke over there.

Upon her arrival in Nassau, Christiana was contacted by Tullis Burke at the airport and was told that he would meet her at a later date; because he thought she was Christiana Felscher the daughter of Ludwig Felscher of the old bridge club gang in Jamaica. We didn't know at that time that the use of the name Felscher was indeed a password. That same evening, my friend Earl informed me that a Mr Wakefield had been murdered and he Earl was a suspect for that murder. When I asked Chief Daniels about it, he told me that the man

Bartholomew Wakefield, had died from poisoning and not the blow on his head as first thought. The question of who did the job, puzzled me for a while, until I remembered that Karlheinz Bass had killed his wife Olivia, and his brother Peter, in the same way some years ago."

He took a sip of his water, lit a cigarette and scrutinised the faces around the room. Everybody stayed quiet.

"To quote Arthur Collins in Jamaica; 'poison is such a hard weapon to use as proof against a suspect.' Somebody here wanted to emulate that procedure as a diversion to their deed, and it had to be somebody who knew what the result of the Jamaican findings in that case were.

One evening, while Earl and I were having dinner in the Carmichael Restaurant, I met Rona Samuels, Cindy Heron and a man who was introduced as Austin J Smithers. Rona made the effort in making our acquaintance, and invited me to an evening of drinking and gambling at the casino. Although Rona wanted to have sex, her main interest was to persuade me into doing business with them. In her drunken state, Rona, who thought I was a dealer, told me many things about herself and the diamond business in the Caribbean and the process of shipping it to other parts of the world.

That evening, Commissioner Graves told me that Captain Maraj in Guyana was having a problem with illegal diamonds leaving his country, and although he had arrested some suspects he couldn't pin-point who was responsible, and how they were able to elude his traps. I noticed that during my conversation with Chief Daniels he never once mentioned any diamond problem in Nassau. I realized later that he was mainly concerned with the drugs that was coming through and left the diamond problem to another officer, named Rupert Abbot.

A couple of days later, Christiana was contacted by Hubert Bachstrum and Tullis Burke to courier the shipment to Canada, with Paul Mason as her escort. They were arrested at the Pearson airport, and Paul agreed to assist in setting up a sting to catch the Toronto group, who are all in jail there now."

350

There was a surprised groan from the gathering.
"So where is Paul now?" asked Tullis Burke.
"In jail awaiting trial," said Dillon.

Dready thought it was amazing how everyone remained composed and focus throughout his speech. He continued.

"Commissioner Graves and Christiana dug up a lot of information about the gang in Jamaica. While they were searching through Karlheinz possessions, they uncovered the fact that Zenon was the brother of Karlheinz Bass, and confirmed that Hoss Bass, whose face and name had been changed, was planted in the Bahamas. Thanks to the picture found in Karlheinz Bass house and the one stolen from Zenon's house, they were able to make the match.

When Karlheinz had the problem with his wife and brother Peter, whom he poisoned in a restaurant in Kingston, he asked Zenon to take care of his daughters Tanya and Rosita, and raised them as his own while the older twins Hansel and Gretel, returned to Germany to set up their end of the network.

The girls grew up under tight scrutiny in Nassau amongst their cousins and close family friends; and although they went to school with the local students, they weren't allowed to befriend any black ones. At the tender age of seven she fell in love with one, and was caught with him on a beach by her cousin Hubert. He and his family was thoroughly warned to keep away from her, and she was sent to school in America. By the time they returned to Nassau they were grown women. Rosita got involved in the business by marrying Harvey Ambross, the family hit man, and moved to New York City to become the money courier. Tanya, who never wanted to be involved with the business, reluctantly got married to Peter McKenzie on her father and uncle's insistence. She hated being told to marry someone she never loved and blatantly argued his request for her to courier drugs to England. After their separation and ultimately divorce, she returned to Nassau to Earl, the man in her life and the father of her three children. But the fear of her uncle's threat to kill any man she befriended, drove her to move alone to Miami, Florida, leaving her children to the family. That's where she was shot."

Nobody responded. Only a daring look from Hubert. Dready continued.

"But Zenon liked to entertain his friends lavishly and to talk about the business with them; and seeing that Amanda was allowing herself to become fat and tastelessly dressed, he bought a boat so he could party off-shore with some younger more appealing women and ended up in a long term love affair with Darlene DeLeon, the fashion designer. This infuriated Amanda and she took exceptions to his attitude. She talked to her two sons about their father's attitude and his lack of concerns for the business. They concluded that Zenon wasn't planning on becoming big as they wanted. Amanda wanted him dead while Hubert and Ralph wanted control of the diamond and drug operations in the Bahamas, so an accident was arranged for that very purpose.

When I began asking about the boat accident everybody clammed up; including the police. But I met a man in town who told me about who was on the boat when it happened; and I came to the conclusion that it was deliberately done. In my opinion, Hubert found out that his father was cheating with his money-hungry wife Elta, and decided to kill him, while Ralph wanted to kill him for blocking him from doing what he wanted to do. Amanda didn't object because she also wanted him dead for the insurance money, which she used to purchase the properties and opened the gift shop on Market street. So a conspiracy to murder was manifested between mother and sons, and orchestrated by Hubert. I noticed that all the autopsy reports on those bodies read: misadventure. Somebody must have gotten to the doctor.

Right after that accident, Ralph made himself disappear in the interiors of Guyana and Venezuela and began feeding the diamonds to Ivan Burkowitz, who had his network of people moving them through Suriname, to Trinidad then to Jamaica, Bahamas, England and Canada. Hubert handled the international deals, Tullis was in charge of personnel selection, Amanda was responsible for the shipping, and Althea was in charge of the mules. With Ralph, the geologist, safely planted in Guyana and Ivan Burkowitz the exporter, Hubert decided to secure himself by surrounding his family with people such as Clinton Reeves; whom I will talk about later. Being friendly with members of the police and some government officials, he felt untouchable, and at times by-passed Karlheinz, the real boss, in Jamaica.

Hubert became a powerful man in Nassau, alienating some of the upper brasses, such as Bass, Collins and even Burkowitz himself. Many feared him, while others, including his old school mate Donald Daniels here, loathe him. Over the years, Daniels have suppressed evidence and sometimes passed on information to Hubert, in hope of trapping him. In his heart, he really wanted to find some kind of evidence with which to prosecute Hubert, but all his efforts were being scuttled; and the reason he couldn't find the evidence was because others, including Abbot, were deliberately misleading him and re-directing the information before he could carry them out. All his efforts were being undermined and he just couldn't find out by whom. But an old friend, who shall remain nameless, assisted him to bring about today.

When the bust happened in Jamaica last year and Karlheinz was killed, Burkowitz and Collins were imprisoned, the gang lost a lot of money and credibility with their usual customers. The pipeline was broken. That was when a new Octopus came to the head. The Octopus called a meeting to repair the damage and to reimplement the codes and the lines of passwords, because lack of code usage allowed everybody to know who was who and posed a risk to the Octopus and the organization. Thus the move of Ralston Weekes from England to St Lucia. But Hubert wanted to rebuild the pipeline faster. He wanted to animate and spruce-up the organization. He quickly setup Frazier Hendicott in Toronto, who didn't know that his wife Sasha was really Bernice the daughter of Zenon, and began using the young students

353

of family members to carry the stuff there. Which the students did without protest because they wanted the money. It was only then that Hendicott understood why Sasha was always going off to England and other parts of Europe, but since the money was coming in and he was getting his 'bit' from Rosita and Elta he didn't mind.

When it was realized that too many people had knowledge of the bosses, Hubert decided to eliminate many of them, including his niece Celia; the daughter of Ralph, to maintain his anonymity."

Dready watched as Ralph gave a questioning look at his brother Hubert.

"Then came detective Charles Chrittendon to Nassau. His presence caused a further eruption within the cartel. But luck was on Hubert's side, because shortly thereafter two detectives from Toronto, came to Nassau on a vacation, took a tour of the police headquarters and luckily met-up with one of his people, namely Rupert Abbot, and they became friends.

You see, Chrittendon, was sent to Nassau by Commissioner Dillon to work undercover. His job was to investigate to find-out about some resident Canadians, who Dillon believed were purchasers and couriers working out of this city; and for Charles to send the information to him personally. In the beginning, he Charles, was preforming his job perfectly, but he got greedy. He phoned Jack Colly in Toronto, his old friend of many years, and informed him about his new job in Nassau. Colly instructed him on how to benefit from it and suggested for Charles to send him a copy of the same information he was sending to Dillon with the coded instructions; Chrittendon did.

Allow me to tell you about Mr Jack Colly. He and his brother grew up in Toronto, and were friends with a pear of criminal cousins named Jaques and Peter Lenois. After he was accepted in the police force, he made a deal with his two friends to protect their activities; and was successful for years. But when the news got out that the two cousins were caught and imprisoned in Jamaica last year, he was devastated and had no recourse to free them. So he decided to find other business partners in the lucrative Caribbean islands, and set his sights on the Bahamas. That opportunity only presented itself when his friend Charles Chrittendon contacted him.

Finally, Chrittendon developed the courage to demand from Hubert, a cut of the inside pie, and Hubert told him where to get off. He told Jack Colly about Hubert's refusal and Colly came to Nassau, using Avery Mathews as a decoy; toured the police headquarters and somehow met up with Abbot. He told Abbot about Chrittendon and his undercover work for the RCMP in his city and asked Abbot to keep an eye on him. He also promised Abbot that when he returned to Canada he would find out the communications lines of Chrittendon and seek a way to convince him to join their business."

Dready watched as people began looking at one another.

"Colly found out the codes and called Abbot. He also called Chrittendon and told him what he had in mind, but was rejected. But that, however, did not prevent him from getting into the business. First he made a phone call to Chief Daniel's office and spoke to Rupert Abbot. Then he took a vacation to Miami, crossed into Nassau and quickly talked Rupert into joining forces with him to make some money. He told Abbot that they would have to first persuade Chrittendon to join. They went to see Chrittendon together, but was confronted with strong objections for their efforts. So he and Abbot conspired to have Chrittendon killed. Abbot introduced Colly to Hubert, and in a few days Charles Chrittendon was killed by Clifton Reeves - sitting over there - on the orders of Hubert. His body was found on a south-side beach on this island.

I believe Reeves is also responsible for the bodies found in a basement-closet of a house on Abaco island. They were those of Mr. Phillips, the real Mrs. Judith Wakefield and a prostitute named Fran Mason, the sister of Cynthia Mason. Ladies and gentlemen please meet Clinton Reeves, whose real name is Samuel Colly, the brother of detective Jack Colly of Toronto."

355

Nobody reacted, so Dready continued.

"They planted Samuel Colly in Chrittendon's place and with the help of Jack and the codes, it was an easy job for him. I found out that the real Clinton Reeves was a blackjack dealer from New Jersey, who came to Nassau by answering an ad in the local newspaper in his hometown. He met and fell in love with Tanya, not knowing that her cousin objected to any man who became attached to her, and was killed for that reason. Samuel Colly did the honours and assumed his identity. Samuel Cully, or should I say, Clinton Reeves immediately became Hubert's special contractor just as Harvey Ambross was to Karlheinz and the Jamaican crew.

On occasion, Jack would send Rupert the daily codes and Rupert would send back the names of the people bringing the stuff, to him. Dillon would get the communication a day later. He would then have his custom-officer friends clear the person and take them to the drop area to picked up the money and everything would be clean. He didn't know that Hubert Bachstrum sent someone to kill the students right under his nose in Toronto; so in his nervous state of mind and to prevent Dillon from discovering his pipeline, he asked Avery Mathews to put him on the case. He was then able to get the coroner to rule them as suicides.

In the meantime he continued to send the codes hoping to get things repaired in Nassau. He was shocked when Christiana asked for the files on the students in Toronto and reluctantly handed them over to her. He didn't want to alert anyone here about it because he wasn't sure what her findings would be.

Then Paul Mason was arrested in Toronto and quietly told the police about the people in the drop zone. Colly was really surprised when he discovered they had arrested his older brother John, along with the others in his Toronto connections. Christiana, do you recall what Cecil Wright and Maggy Walker told us in describing the man who visited the students?" he asked.

"Yes," she replied. "Maggy Walker said the man who visited

the girls was black with dark eyes, almost to black, and had a white streak in the middle of his hair like a skunk."

"Correct," said Dready. "Then Cecil Wright described him as coloured with the same eyes and hair. The fake Judith Wakefield told me that the white Mr. Smithers had a white streak in his hair. That also puzzled me for a long time, until I figured out that the person had to be an actor who wore a wig to visit these people; and the only actor that came to mind was Frazier Hendicott, who had told Christiana that he was an unemployed actor. He was also an old school friend of Tanya and Rosita Bass when they were in the USA. Someone told me he was caught in bed with Elta Bachstrum, is that right Tanya?"

"Yes," she answered, "and Hubert swore to kill him for it."

"That's right," said Dready. "He and Hubert's wife had a long affair, even while he was having one with Rosita Ambross in New York. But Hubert just couldn't kill him like he would others; Frazier was his sister's husband, and she was classified as a schizophrenic. It was Hubert who asked Frazier to do the job on the students to prevent Harvey from killing him. But neither Frazier nor Hubert knew that Harvey was already serving time in Kingston prison in Canada."

Dready could see the nervousness in the eyes of the concerned ones as their demeanor changed.

"But Frazier is black through and through and couldn't change pigmentation from time to time; so I concluded that the actor had to be a white man using make-up to make those changes," said Dready.

"What about his eyes?" asked Althea.

"Contacts," replied Dready. "The killer wore contact lenses."

"And who would that be?" asked Ralph.

"Don't be in a hurry Ralphy boy," said Dready, "I'll get to it in time. Those five young people murdered in Toronto were the real jewels of the Bahamas and deserved some respect. Those murdered were, Colin McKenzie, Celia Bachstrum, Farn and Salina Mason, the younger sisters of Cynthia. By the way Cynthia, I know that you are the mother of Paul Mason and not his sister. Also murdered were

Zena Hendicott, the niece of Frazier, and Robert Reynolds, the son of a friend of the Bachstrum family from school days. The real Phillips who was posing as Austin J Smithers. Gerald Wakefield - who was using his father's name - was poisoned and banged on the head. I would like to inform you that Bartholomew Wakefield is a ninety-six year old man, who is still alive in St Lucia. Zenon was killed in that boating accident along with Elta, and two Columbian gentlemen, whose names are still in question. Darlene DeLeon was killed on Earl's boat and Mr Sanderson 'accidentally' fell overboard while fishing."

He could see questioning looks in some eyes and decided to enlighten them.

"Bartholomew Wakefield is the father of Gerald, Althea and Amanda Wakefield. Gerald came from St Lucia using his father's name to deceive the authorities and stayed to extend his sister's export business. Whenever the police made a check on him, they found him living a comfortable retired life in that country and wouldn't search any further. He got deeply involved with his sister's business and became acquainted with people such as Burkowitz, Bass and Collins, and finally moved to Bahamas after marrying Judith. When she was murdered for talking to Donald Daniels, he found a drifter who was in the Bahamas looking for an easy meal, marry her and had her assume Judith's name

He was murdered because he refused to cut Elaine Sanderson from the business after her father's death. Although Althea never expressed her displeasure, she was angry with Hubert for doing it and testified to that fact when she was asked. I would like to tell you that Elaine Sanderson is Althea's daughter who changed her name from Bass after her mother married Mr Sanderson and moved to Florida; leaving everyone here thinking that she was in Germany. Elaine's two children belong to Sonny and Garth Monroe, the brothers of Earl, who used to bring the boat-loads of goods from the States here, for her."

Dready paused awaiting some kind of response, but nothing came.

"You see," he continued, "when the trouble came down in Jamaica last year, it ripped the gang's continuity apart. Collins had ordered the killings of many, including Tanya McKenzie, also known as Bass and sometimes used the name Bachstrum whenever it was advantageous to her. Lucky for her the shooter missed and the bullet only grazed her head. She was furious about it and told me her entire story. Earl and Tanya had been in love from the third grade, but were never allowed to manifest that affection when they grew up; mainly because he was a poor boy. When Earl found out that she was hurt and was in the Miami hospital, he risked being caught to get her out and back to Nassau. She was happy that he had taken the initiative to assist her, but knew what her cousin Hubert would do to him if he was told.

When Hubert found out, he felt the family owed Earl, so he paid him what it cost for his efforts in cash. But Tanya was in love with Earl, and as her pay back to him, she offered him a new boat which he could have for his own business. She made that offer privately and filtered the money to him through the blackjack table in the casino, a few thousand dollars at a time so as not to attract attention. Earl purchased the boat without letting the family know about his involvement with Tanya. He then advertised that he was now a boat owner, and quickly Hubert decided that he could use Earl to pick up the crates of fish whenever they were delivered at sea. Earl was delighted to get the jobs and the money and jumped at the offer. You see, Earl use to operate Hubert's or his associates boats to do the job prior to getting his own."

He paused again to light a cigarette.
"The Sanderson drowning bothered me for a while. Here is a man, an Olympic gold medalist in swimming and a certified diver, accidentally drowned. He, being a lover of the sea and his quest for adventure, decided to bring his boat load of goods to Nassau from the

USA. He was widely known in the community as the 'Admiral or the 'Commodore'. He hired many local sailors and began transporting goods regularly from the USA. He was either talked into it or was the one who instigated the hijacking of ships to steal their cargo, but that became his business. I wasn't sure about his death until my friend told me about the many pirates docking in the Bahamas, and of the fellows working for Elaine. That's when I realized that she was the person directing the team of pirates left by her father, and that she was the person who set his demise in motion. She obtained his duties and became the Admiral herself. He was made to 'walk the plank' just like the pirates of old did. Am I right Elaine?"

She did not answer.

"The crated fish was their way of getting the diamonds and drugs ashore, knowing that the police, through Abbot, wouldn't search the craft of respectable persons as Earl, Sonny or Garth. But they tried to frame Earl for the murder of Wakefield so he refused to show himself to the police until I was able to straighten it out with Chief Daniels. Then they tried to kill someone on his boat without success, but succeed with killing Darlene DeLeon, leaving her body on his boat. It was Earl who told me about the "Octopus," with the one brain and the independent tentacles, which caused me to think of your operation in the same light. I realized that there was only one brain controlling the entire gang, like those in Jamaica last year; thus began my process of elimination of the people involved.

Christiana and Commissioner Graves checked with Interpol and informed me that a Mr Phillips had taken over from Mitchell aka Burkowitz in the gang and was doing the route from England to Bahamas with his mule Rona Samuels. But Mr. Phillips wanted to be clever, so when he met a man named Smithers in a pub somewhere in Buckley Slough, he switched identifications with him. He then recruited Cindy Heron, who was wandering around London after her motor vehicle accident, for the purpose of carrying the diamonds.

Incidentally, Cindy is Tanya's missing daughter, but with the plastic surgery on her face, Tanya couldn't recognize her, and Cindy didn't want her to know that she was in the Bahamas."

Tanya began to get out of her seat, but Dready waved her to silence.

"Phillips was reported killed in England, but in fact he was very much alive and well in London; because he personally went to visit Lawrence Chung using his real name, which he also did on his last trips here.

His problems began in England when he met a man called Smithers in a Slough pub, not knowing that the man had killed a farmer and assumed his identity. They talked about their respective criminal activities and agreed to exchange names for the purpose of travelling and confusing the police. He began coming to the Bahamas as Smithers and taking the diamonds back to England. In the mean time the man caught on to his game and wanted in, so he came to Nassau and found himself in the midst of these well-organized criminals, and liked it.

When Phillips came to Nassau this last time, he stupidly switched names again with Smithers and was killed by Clinton Reeves on the order of Hubert Bachstrum, who thought Smithers was here for another purpose. So the real Phillips was dead and buried in the Abaco house along with the rest."

He paused for a long moment.

"Mr Garfield Smith, I presume?" he asked the man posing as Phillips. "Or better yet, Kent, the son of Barbara Smith?"

"How did you know it was me?" Smith asked.

"Cynthia listened in on your phone calls," said Dready, "she heard all your local calls of you being referred to you as Mr Smithers, but whenever you called London you used the name Phillips. After I spoke to Lawrence Chung in Jamaica and got the description of Phillips, I knew a switch had been made. The British police told Commissioner Graves that your body was found in a remote beach area in England. I do believe you must have killed some poor bastard and left your ID with his body to be found. Also a photo of you on the stage in London was found in Karlheinz possession. I also suspected that you were the killer of the people in Toronto plus you became Bucky when you, along with Althea, came looking for Christiana that night on Long Island. You are one great actor sir, using make up to look black, coloured and white. But why the wig with a streak of grey down the middle?"

Smith didn't answer.

"A favourite play of yours, I presume," said Dready.

"But how did you know that I was Barbara Smith's son?" asked Garfield in a soft voice. "I was never mentioned in the records in Jamaica."

"True," answered Dready. "Graves and Christiana searched Karlheinz's place. They found a letter which indicated that Barbara Smith had two sons, not one as first believed. We knew that Denrick Miller, who was killed in Jamaica last year, was her first child; but the possibility of another child was eminent."

Dready pulled the letter from his pocket.

"But there is a retired Jamaican police officer called Jeremiah Bailey, an old bull dog of a cop. He told me that Barbara Smith gave birth to another child privately in her home, and that her father, Captain Smith, had taken the baby to England five days after he was born. Only Karlheinz Bass and the mid-wife knew about him. Graves asked Scotland yard to search England for him and found out that the boy grew up in London to become a great stage actor, but disappeared a few years ago in New York or somewhere in the Bahamas. So with that evidence I realized that it had to be you posing as Smithers or Phillips."

"But how did they know my name?" asked Garfield.

"You see," said Dready, "that mid wife was once married to Jeremiah Bailey, and was a dear friend of your mother; she was the one to named you Garfield.."

He smiled because now there were some uneasy grumbling

amongst the ranks.

"It was you who persuaded Sanderson to revamp Karlheinz's theory of piracy in the Caribbean, wasn't it?"

"Yes," replied Smith in a distraught tone.

"Sanderson wasn't the Admiral, was he?" asked Dready.

"No," said Smith.

"Was it Elaine?" asked Dready.

"No," replied Smith.

"You are the Admiral, right?" asked Dready.

"Yes," answered Smith.

More silence.

"That would have worked well, but you made the mistake of telling Rona about your deed in England and your plans of staying permanently in the Bahamas. She also decided to come here to be near John Belamy, her late husband half-brother and her lover, leaving the England end of the business open to intruders, which infuriated the Octopus.

Then things began to happen. Rona was able to check on the property you bought in Freeport and on Crooked island and felt that something more was happening behind her back. In the process she found out that it was you who killed John Belamy, then you shipped the body to Abaco to hide it among the others; which made her more angry and wanted out of the organization. The police were unable to identify him until she told me his name and I asked Commissioner Graves to check, and he sent the information to Scotland yard. Ironically, that is the same house the Bachstrum's used to conduct their corrupt deals and storage of drugs and diamonds. Yet another peeve for the Octopus. The network was falling apart just like it did in Jamaica; even though that didn't directly affect some of the people here.

Nice work Rona dear, you had me fooled for a while. When we met at the Carmichael Restaurant, you already knew, through Colly, that I was here investigating for a magazine and you checked with the Jamaican connections to confirm that fact. What you didn't know was that the guard who took the message to Arthur Collins was also feeding the information to Commissioner Graves, thus the false info back to you from Collins. You were the person who recruited and presented me to Smithers and Hubert as a dealer, pretending that you weren't aware of my business. But in Guyana, you loose your cool at the meeting with Ralph Bachstrum and admitted to knowing that I was a police officer and demanded that Packus kill me. That wasn't an accident, it was really meant to be, to prevent me from sending the messages to the others.

You see dear Rona, in Guyana you asked Christiana to take a message to Ivan Burkowitz in prison, which he would answer with a set of codes he used to contact the rest of your people, not knowing that I would be visiting with him that same afternoon. When I did meet with Burkowitz, he gave me a statement and some quotations for my magazine article, which I discovered were codes to be sent to all involved. When we compared his instructions to Christiana with my notes, the wording was the same except for the change from Karlheinz to Collins. He told her, Quote: "It is the love of money that killed Karlheinz, but if you know Harvey Ambross call him." But he told me; "Collins is enjoying life in a resort like mine. Don't bother to call Harvey Ambross just send him a card."

I instructed Christiana to change the instructions and password that Ivan sent to you, and had Captain Maraj's informant impersonate your contact that evening on the sea-wall. We have locked him up after he made the phone call to assure the parties that we were legit. The message to you was changed to say:- Karlheinz Bass is a friend of mine," and you were to reply that he was also yours and that the contact would identify you by name.

You see, Burkowitz sent out a message which he hoped would be done through my magazine, and somebody, somewhere would start making the pre-arranged phone call to an unknown person, who in turn would make the call to the person in charge. Something you chose to tell me to distract attention from yourself and onto others.

I realized that these people were not familiar with one another, their only connection was through Ivan, who gets his directions from the Octopus. I asked Commissioner Graves and Captain Maraj to watch you and to trace the phone calls you made. They had the police in Chicago trace the person who received it and found-out they called a number in St Lucia. I called that number and found Bartholomew Wakefield and Ralston Weekes.

When I called Cynthia Mason to ask about the phone calls to your room, she told me that Rupert Abbot called four times without success; that's because he didn't know you were in Guyana and the call he had received did not make any sense. I realized that there were different area codes for the different numbers with other people get called. I called the coded number that Ivan gave and it ended up being a number in Nassau, which belongs to Rupert Abbot. You, on the other hand couldn't call to warn him of the development there in Guyana without attracting attention to yourself, so you wanted Christiana to get the message to Ivan who would give it to me and I would publicize it to inform the rest. But unfortunately for you, I was able to decipher it's meaning before we left that country and made the calls to began the string. I realized that although Smithers behaved as if he was the boss, you were the real boss in the dark."

"No, I'm not!" Rona protested, jumping to her feet. "That is preposterous; it's ridiculous."

"Maybe you're not the Octopus," said Dready, "but most definitely a leader. When I called Toronto and gave the password to call Harvey Ambross, it caught everybody off guard and a confusion to the bosses; because it wasn't time for that call to be made. But everyone had to carry out the routine and the calls were traced to Jamaica, New York, Chicago, Tallahassee, Nassau and to St Lucia."

"Then why didn't someone call England?" asked Rona.

"Simple," said Dready, "you were here in Nassau thus the call to the hotel from Abbot."

365

Again there was that profound space of silence.

"Ladies and gentlemen, meet the bosses of the world-class gang of pirates. Rona Samuels is the real boss in England, Ralston Weekes is the boss who direct traffic in the Caribbean, Jack Colly takes care of things in Canada while his brother does the killings in the Bahamas, Rupert Abbot is the coordinator of operations in the Bahamas along with Hubert Bachstrum doing the deals with America and local. Ralph Bachstrum is the field buyer, David DeFreitas is the shipper in Guyana, his boss is Ivan Burkowitz. The Ali brothers in Suriname and Trinidad does the repackaging and shipping. Poor old Wally here is the money transfer man and will be doing time in Barbados for his part in the business. Elaine Sanderson is second in command to Garfield Smith, and is in charge of piracy. Her local men flourish well in these islands."

"Arrest them all," said Daniels. "Take them away. Charge all of them with murder, conspiracy to commit murder, trafficking of drugs, guns, money and diamonds. Charge them with embezzlement, fraud, illegal conducts and........."

"That's fine," said Dready interrupting Daniels, "but we still have to know who the head of the Octopus is."

He smiled again.

"The day the bodies were found on Abaco, Chief Daniels had Hubert and Amanda Bachstrum along with Tullis Burke brought in. I sat in on the questioning and listened to him talk to Amanda, the quiet old lady of the group. She made the police feel sympathetic towards her, and released her from custody. At first I wondered why they would insult her dignity by bringing her in for questioning, and felt relieved when she answered their questions in the manner she did."

"What did she say?" asked Ralph.

"Firstly, she answered that she met Darlene a year ago at the casino through her son Hubert, and they became friends instantly. Then she said it was because Darlene made so many trips to Europe with her designing business and because she was a Belgian; a place she had spent time during the war, they found much to talk about. But to ice the cake, she told Daniels a long story about her involvement with Karlheinz in Jamaica and how she was forced to carry the drugs to England as a young girl. He sympathised with her and released her.

I thought about what she told him, then I remembered what Venrece Alexander told me about her coming to Jamaica to make a purchase from Peter McKenzie on behalf of Smithers and Wakefield. It also dawned on me that she should be aware that Darlene DeLeon was really Althea's other daughter with her first husband, Peter Bass; and who married a Belgian man - the one to whom she delivered the diamonds.

To back track When Christiana came and was being prepared to carry the merchandise to Canada, Althea did that preparation in Tullis Burke's apartment in the hotel. She wasn't pleased about something and Christiana observed this. But as an old lesbian, she couldn't pass up the opportunity to invite Christiana to have sex with her when she returned to Nassau. That night when Christiana called her from the Wakefield's house on Long island, she quickly made arrangements to come for her. The next morning she came with two killers, and I wondered why she would want to kill the girl who promised to sleep with her and realized that she was ordered to kill Ludwig Felscher's daughter. That order was given by someone who knew Christiana or got the word from Arthur Collins in Jamaica

. It wasn't until I met Ralston Weekes in St Lucia that I realized that there was someone else at the top. He told me that he had made a call to Amanda the week before, and heard that she, along with Hubert, was arrested. He was angry that he had not received his usual phone call from the appropriate person and wanted to know why. By the way Ralston, I'm aware of you being a Wakefield. Was it you who took the diamonds from Ludwig's trunk in Toronto?" asked Dready.

"No," replied Ralston. "I asked John Belamy to go to Canada to retrieve them without telling Ludwig. He did while the family was away on vacation."

    "When was that?" asked Dready.

    "That was in the middle eighties," replied Ralston.

    "Why was he killed?"

    "Because; because he stole some," said Ralston.

    "So you ordered his execution, right?"

    "No!!" shouted Ralston

    "Then who did?" shouted Dready

    "I.....I don't know," he replied angrily.

    "Was it Garfield Smith?"

    "Yes," said Ralston.

    "On whose orders?"

    "I don't know," shouted Ralston. "Please ask somebody else, I'm tired and I don't have the answers."

    "Who ordered the killing of the students?"

    "Hubert did," said Ralston. "And Garfield carried it out."

    "Who killed Gerald Wakefield?"

    Ralston turned to look directly at Amanda.

    "She did," said Ralston. "She poisoned her own brother."

    Dready paused.

    "Ralston, when I asked you to come to Nassau for a meeting because of the problems with someone wanting to take over the operations, you quickly accepted; even-though you found my request very strange. When I left you that day, you dashed back to the Wakefield's house to make a call to your half sister-Amanda's house in Nassau, didn't you?"

    "Yes but........"

    "......but got no answer and your curiosity rose even more so, right?"

    Ralston nodded his head.

    "Indeed. Something Rona also did while in Guyana with the same result. I knew then that you would be angry with someone specifically, and all during the meeting today you kept a constant stare on Amanda while she kept her eyes on the ceiling in deep thoughts; because she knew that the empire was crumbling before her eyes.

Yes, ladies and gentlemen, the real boss is none other than Amanda Bachstrum. She is the Octopus who sends the messages to kill, whenever it pleases her. She could handle everything else except a change of code and organizational directions."

Just then Amanda's body fell from the chair to the floor and everybody rushed to gather around her. Christiana applied CPR but it was too late. Amanda Bachstrum was already dead. For Dready, it was a pleasure to watch the friends and relatives shedding tears for the woman who was king of the cartel lying on the floor. He knew that Daniels was happy to have wrapped up his case and his lifelong pursuit of the family, that had been perpetrating these criminalities in his country for all these years and to know that he had found the man who had hampered his efforts.

Dready looked at Christiana and they both quietly left the room, signalling Earl and Tanya to follow them outside. He kissed Tanya and shook hands with his friend Earl.

"I wish you both the very best for the future," he whispered. "I have to meet Lincoln at the Carmichael Restaurant; want to eat with us?"

"Wouldn't miss the opportunity," said Earl. "Come on."

"Just a minute," said Dready, as he rushed back inside to fetch Laska so that she may have a meal with her brother.

"This has got to be goodbye," he said to her.

"I do realize that," she replied wrapping her arms around his neck. "When I came to Nassau and met Christiana, I realized that my hopes of us getting together was not to be; but I must say that our encounter in Barbados was exciting and enjoyable. I sincerely hope we can remain friends."

"We sure could," he said. "Just keep in touch."

"I will," she replied.

They walked out to join Christiana, Earl and Tanya in the car.

Earl drove to the restaurant and directed them to his special corner, where Lincoln already sat. After the greeting and introductions the six people sat enjoying their conch chowder, stewed grouper and corn bread while Dready told the entire story to a very pleased Lincoln.

"......and that's the end," said Dready.

Lincoln wrinkled his nose as he replied,

"I hope so friend; but as life goes, I'm not too sure of the future."

"C'est la vie," said Dready. shaking his head and shoulders.

He kissed Laska and shook Lincoln's hand.

"Goodbye Laska," he said. "See you Linc; Earl, please take Christiana and I to Freeport's West End. We want to spend a few days making love everywhere in that resort."

"Why?" asked Tanya. "There are many more exciting places here in Nassau, and you could come to visit with me at the casino."

"No thank you," said Christiana. "We have to work on the second child and we can only do that without interruptions - which this city has too much of.."

Dready and Christiana got on the boat. Laying on the bench seat, they watched Earl directing the boat out to sea with Tanya at his side.

"Now, that's love," he whispered to Christiana, who was now lying on his stomach.

"Yes, and so is this," she replied.

He patted her arse.

"Yeah," he answered, "and so is this is right."

The End.
Is it Really?

Other Books by
W.L.(Stan) Martin.

"Loyalty and Integrity." ISBN 0-9682546-0-3

Autobiography of Stan Martin. It is the account of his military experiences as he served in a company of British commandos in the far and middle east.

"Murder in Jamaica." ISBN 0-9682646-1-1

Is the first adventure of Christiana and the Dreadlocks Cop. A fictional mystery set in Jamaica, about their investigation of the brutal murder of Christiana's mother.

Watch for......

"The Secret Passages."

The life and death of a dear friend, Catharine Harrison.

"War: Life After."

The second part of Loyalty and Integrity. Which is about his life on returning to England after service. He talked about the racism he faced in the country that sent him to war; where he couldn't find an apartment to billet his young family.